Y0-ABV-160

Her Two Men *In Sonoma*

What Readers Are Saying

Praise for Her Two Men in London

"This book… this book was everything I wanted it to be and more. It was hot, it was sexy, it was knock your socks off great. I'm ashamed to say I have never read any books by these authors until now, but you can bet that will change. … This book was far more emotional than I was expecting, but aren't all the great ones that way. I sincerely hope you will all check this book out. You will not be disappointed."—Jodi, *Ruby Red Romance Review*

"I have never been so envious and turned on while reading a book in my entire reading existence. …when they came together as a duo or triad it was freaking panty wetting or wet spot worthy. I squirmed, cried, made the dreadful mistake of reading this in public, and so many other TMI moments. To say I am a fan and true promoter of this series of Dana and Kristine duo would be an understatement. The scenes varied, the storyline flowed, and the conflict was there. … This MMF is a downright MUST READ for the summer but be sure to have a man or two on standby."—*Reading By the Book Blog*

"What an amazing new novel that I came across by Dana Delamar and Kristine Cayne! Two new authors that will be on my radar from this fantastic MMF novel that I consumed in a matter of hours! *Her Two Men in London* is scorching, emotional and a breathtaking unputdownable novel that will be on your mind long after you are finished!"—*Up All Night with Books*

"You will definitely need a couple pairs of panties and a new supply of batteries!!! This book should come with a public health warning and its own fire extinguisher. This book is the hottest book I have read in a really long time. … This book set my Kindle on fire and my sheets. This book should NOT BE READ IN PUBLIC or you will drown before you can relieve the burn. I gave this book 5 stars but I'd give it more if I could. If this book was a curry it would have 7 chili peppers!!!"—leopardwolf, Goodreads reviewer

"Wonderful start to the Total Indulgence series by new-to-me authors Dana Delamar and Kristine Cayne that kept me captivated from beginning to end with unforgettable characters and a well-crafted MMF bisexual ménage romance. I loved the instant attraction and skin scorching intimacy… Fans of this genre will love *Her Two Men in London* and I look forward to book two in this hot, sexy series."—Pamela R. Mitchell, Amazon reviewer

"This is my 2nd MMF book. And by God its was freaking AMAZING. Riley and Carter will have you panting with their intense sex scenes. Their love triangle with Paige was so emotional, especially when Riley poured his heart out to Carter. I have cried so many tears with this spectacular book that I want all of my FB family and friends to read what I did with this book. … Kristine Cayne, boo, thanks for this spectacular wonderful story."—Jackie Marbury, Amazon reviewer

"Ménage fans will just LOVE *Her Two Men in London*. It's a smoking hot and sexy ménage a trois story with as much heart as heat, and a touch of snark as well. Believable characterization tops the list of good things in this smoothly written MMF bisexual romance."—Melanie S, Amazon reviewer

Praise for Her Two Men in Tahiti

"I am at a loss for words to describe just how much I love this story. I am an emotional reader and I fell in love with every character in this story. Even Damon, Nigel, and Vanessa. While reading this story, I felt everything these characters feel: their joy, their fears, their hope, their heartbreaks. I felt everything. I enjoyed every single second of it. I could not put it down, absolutely addictive. I am truly sad that the story is over and I cannot wait for the next one!"—Gigi, Amazon reviewer

"It only gets better in Book 2, *Her Two Men In Tahiti*! It drew me in from the beginning! I felt so bad for Dev and his family. Then Sky feeling like she might be the third wheel. Then Rod trying to keep his friendship with Dev even though he was in love with him. My heart was breaking for all of them! There were so many emotions in this book. They all had such a great relationship together that I was cheering them on. Thank you for such a great read and I can't wait until Book 3!!"—Donna T, Amazon reviewer

"I loved it. I have always wanted to go to Tahiti and in a sense this read makes you feel as though you are there plus the instant connection with the three characters. The push and pull as well as the electrifying connection between them will leave you not just hot & swooning but begging for more."—Ryan Grey, Amazon reviewer

"After reading Cayne and Delamar's first book, *Her Two Men in London*, I knew I wanted to read this next book. I've been intrigued with the MMF romance trope. Honestly, in my mind, I'm never sure if it will work, and there are plenty of books who do not do it justice. That is not the case with this second offering from these two authors. In fact, I liked this book better than their first book."—Amy D, Amazon reviewer

The Total Indulgence Series

Her Two Men in London (Book One)

Her Two Men in Tahiti (Book Two)

Her Two Men in Sonoma (Book Three)

Her Two Men in St. Moritz (Book Four) – coming 2019

HER TWO MEN

In Sonoma

TOTAL INDULGENCE, BOOK 3

DANA DELAMAR
KRISTINE CAYNE

THREE ORCAS PRESS

Copyright © 2018 Three Orcas Press LLC

All rights reserved.

ISBN (print): 1-949071-05-7
ISBN-13 (print): 978-1-949071-05-4
ISBN (ebook): 1-949071-04-9
ISBN-13 (ebook): 978-1-949071-04-7

Publisher's Note: This is a work of fiction. Names, characters, places, and incidents either are the product of the author's imagination or are used fictitiously, and any resemblance to actual persons, living or dead, business establishments, events, or locales is entirely coincidental.

Cover artwork & series logo design
© 2018 L.J. Anderson of Mayhem Cover Creations
mayhemcovercreations.com

Cover photo: © Kim Killion

Dana Delamar author image courtesy of LGImages

Editing, proofreading, and print formatting:
By Your Side Self-Publishing
www.ByYourSideSelfPub.com

Without limiting the rights under copyright reserved above, no part of this publication may be reproduced, stored in or introduced into a retrieval system, or transmitted, in any form or by any means (electronic mechanical, photocopying, recording or otherwise), without the prior written permission of the copyright owner.

The scanning, uploading, and distribution of this book via the Internet or via any other means without the permission of the copyright owner is illegal and punishable by law. Please purchase only authorized electronic editions. Your support of the author's rights is appreciated.

ACKNOWLEDGMENTS

Many thanks (once again) to our husbands for putting up with our marathon phone calls, silliness, and shenanigans. We love you!

And many thanks to our readers for your enthusiastic reviews and heartfelt support. You mean the world to us!

Prologue

JAVIER

Surrounded by gyrating girls in skimpy wet bikinis and shirtless guys humping the girls' asses, booze flowing profusely in the all-inclusive resort, I was having the time of my life. It didn't hurt that my freshman-year college roommate, Daniel King, was grinding right alongside me. Daniel was hot as fuck, long, lean, with a taut, sculpted chest and stomach, muscular arms, and hard thighs. I wanted to run my tongue over each inch of him. Lick him. Love him. Make him mine.

But that wasn't going to happen. Despite the looks I sometimes got from him, looks I was obviously misreading, Daniel was straight as a pin. At least we were friends. Best friends even. I'd lucked out when the dorm gods had assigned us both to the same room in Panther Hall at Florida International University in Miami. Daniel wanted to study business, and I was aiming for a degree in accounting. And then we'd ended up in the same marketing class, where we drew up an elaborate plan for a business that would provide high-end trips. We got an A, and that gave us the idea to organize this spring-break trip to Cancun for our entire dorm. It wasn't exactly high-end, but it was a million times better than what the northerners got in Daytona or Fort Lauderdale for their spring-break vacations.

Even better, the trip had given me the perfect excuse to spend more time with my roommate. And now here we were on the beach, dancing away under a dark Cancun sky littered with bright stars.

Two girls from our dorm, Erica and Shauna, shouldered their way through the crowd of dancers, somehow managing not to spill their green drinks on everyone. Probably Electric Hurricanes. The girls were pretty and athletic, and I suspected, quite possibly bisexual. I'd caught more than one heated glance between them. Erica threw her arm around Daniel's waist, hip-checking his dance partner out of the day while Shauna slid in between me and mine. I barely had time to move my hand out of the way before she spilled my Mai Tai, which would have been a terrible shame. I hadn't even eaten the wedge of pineapple stuck to the rim yet.

She rose up on her tiptoes and shouted next to my ear, "Want to get out of here?" adding a tiny suck on the lobe before pulling back and grinning.

I glanced at Daniel and saw Erica nuzzling him.

"Just me… or both of us?" I asked, forgetting all about my stupid Mai Tai and the pineapple wedge. Since the girls did everything together, I was quite certain of her answer, but I wasn't one to assume anything.

Her hand trailed down my chest to my stomach. My muscles quivered under her touch. I was suddenly grateful to Daniel for all the times he'd thrown my chip bag into the trash and dragged me down to the gym or the swimming pool. I'd been an overweight math nerd all through middle school and high school, ostracized by pretty much everyone except my best friend Arianna. I'd almost stopped caring what anyone thought of me. Until I walked into my newly assigned dorm room and saw Daniel sprawled on his narrow bed.

"Both of you, of course." Shauna kissed the corner of my mouth, and I caught the orangy tang of the curaçao in her drink.

Damn. If this went the way I hoped it would, maybe I'd get to see Daniel in action. I'd heard him masturbating when he thought I was asleep, and his soft moans undid me every time. Christ, I was a fucking mess. In love with my straight roommate.

Over the girls' heads, Daniel's gaze met mine. I raised my brows in question. He waggled his in suggestion. I laughed out loud. I was excited by the idea, as could be attested to by the hard cock in my shorts. I was also really fucking nervous. Seeing Daniel in action meant he'd also see me. Christ, I hoped he didn't laugh.

Daniel and Erica came over to me and Shauna. "Your room or ours?" I asked.

"Yours," the girls said in unison, having clearly thought this all through before approaching us.

"Ours it is then." Daniel threw his arm around Erica's shoulders and, surely if a little unsteadily, led the way through the dancers toward the swanky hotel. One night in this gorgeously decorated marble and granite paradise cost less than one night at Motel 6 in Miami.

Daniel swiped the lock with his room card and we tumbled inside.

Since we were the trip's organizers, the resort had comped us a large room with two queen beds and a sitting area that opened up onto a huge balcony facing the ocean. I loved Miami and its views of the Atlantic, but the Caribbean was something else entirely.

For fuck's sake, Cordero, focus! You're about to get a much better view than the Caribbean.

The girls giggled and Daniel cleared his throat. Startled, I looked up. They were all staring at me. "Everything okay, buddy?" Daniel asked. He was draped around Erica's smaller body, his hand down the back of her tight shorts.

I plastered on a smile. "Uh… sure. Why wouldn't it be?"

"You looked like you were lost in thought there for a minute."

Lost in thought? Try scared shitless. Being the resident fat boy in high school, not to mention the fact that Ari and I had been basically glued together at the hip, meant that I'd seen very little action, okay, none, until I got to college. This last fall, with Daniel's help, I'd lost some weight and gained a bit of confidence. Enough to finally lose my virginity. It hadn't been with Ari, as I'd always dreamed it would be, but even though she was only two years younger than me, she still seemed so innocent and pure. Besides, how could I tell her that I had feelings for her, when I so clearly had feelings for guys too? If I was going to be with Ari, I wanted it to be forever, and I wanted to be sure I could commit to her. Right now, I didn't know what to make of my attraction to girls… and guys. Was I gay? I certainly wasn't straight.

I downed the rest of my Mai Tai and set the empty glass on the television stand. "What this party needs is some music!" I exclaimed with more enthusiasm than I was feeling. I grabbed the remote and turned the television on, setting it to a radio station that played popular music.

The girls hooted and started dancing together. Daniel and I joined them, one on either end of the girls who faced each other. Both of us ground our hips into our partner's ass. Daniel's handsome face with his sexy smirk was right in front of me. Jesus. He finished off his beer and set the bottle on the television stand. Then his hands went to Erica's hips. I mirrored his actions. Watching him with her was so fucking sexy. I hoped I didn't come in my pants and look like a total loser.

His hands went under Erica's shirt and skimmed up her stomach to cup her tits. I did the same to Shauna. She moaned and pressed against me. I lowered my lips to her neck, kissing and nibbling her smooth skin, then blew on it. She shivered in my arms, and I felt like a king. A rustling sound caught my attention. I looked up and Daniel's eyes were on me. Hot and hungry. He'd removed Erica's T-shirt, and his mouth was on her shoulder, his hands undoing the button of her shorts.

I grabbed the hem of Shauna's shirt and tugged it over her head. The warm skin of her back melded to my chest, and I groaned at the sensation of all that heat. I slid my arms around her waist and slipped one hand down the front of her shorts into her panties. She was wet, dripping wet. I had to taste her. Pulling my hand out, I brought my fingers to my mouth and sucked.

A deep groan tore from Daniel's chest. "Fuck, that's hot." His voice was low and raw.

My cock, already hard, turned to granite. I'd never been so turned on in my life. If I couldn't have him, I was sure as fuck having Shauna. I sat on the edge of the bed, undid her bra and spun her around. Now her firm tits were at the perfect height. I cupped one breast and closed my lips around the nipple. She whimpered and squirmed. Her fingers dug into my hair, holding me firmly in place.

She straddled one of my legs, rubbing her pussy on my thigh while I moved to her other tit. I had to get her out of those shorts.

I quickly undid her button and zipper. Catching on, she rose up, and I slid them down her long, tanned legs. She really was pretty, and she seemed very much into me. To say it was an ego boost would be a huge understatement.

Shauna grabbed my hands and pulled me to my feet. "I want to see you too," she said.

When I nodded, she fished out the tie to my board shorts, loosened it and tugged my shorts down my legs. I could feel Daniel's eyes on me, maybe Erica's too. Would he think I looked fat? Too pudgy? Too soft? I know I wasn't over my eating issues, but I had made a lot of progress.

Something warm and wet surrounded my cock. I gasped and almost shot my load. "Fuck!"

Shauna giggled and the vibrations traveled up my cock to my spine. Her tongue flicked the length of my shaft and rounded the edge of my head. Jesus, she was good at this.

"Javi," Daniel said. "Suit up."

I barely had time to look up and catch what he'd tossed to me. A condom. My eyes sought out my roommate. Erica was on the bed on all fours, beautifully naked, her red hair flowing down the porcelain skin of her back. Daniel stood behind her. Naked. Hard. Beautiful.

I swallowed.

Shauna took the condom wrapper and seconds later, she rolled the latex down over my cock. My eyes shot back to Daniel. Were we really going to do this? Fuck girls in front of each other?

He made an impatient get-on-with-it motion that had me grinning. Yep, we were really going to do this.

I took Shauna's hand and helped her onto the bed, positioning her so she faced Erica while I stood behind her. My hand went to her pussy, where I rubbed her wetness around her entrance and up to her clit. She moaned and pressed against my hand. Accepting her invitation, I slid two fingers down and into her opening. My eyes on Daniel, I pumped my fingers in and out, curling the pads so they rubbed downward. It was a tip Daniel had given me one night when we were watching porn. And fuck if he wasn't right.

Shauna arched her back. "Oh God. Fuck me already, Javi."

I leaned down and pressed little kisses along her spine. "Of course." Spreading her ass cheeks for a better view, I pushed the head of my cock into her pussy. Once the head was inside, I thrust my hips and bottomed out.

"Oh shit!" she cried.

I stilled for a moment. When she squirmed, I gripped her hips and started moving. My thrusts were slow and shallow, gradually building up and going deeper.

On the other bed, Daniel had his hand between Erica's legs, but he hadn't penetrated her yet. I arched a brow. He smirked. "Ready, darling?" he asked as he patted one round ass cheek.

Erica swallowed, her round eyes cemented to her friend's face. "Yeah, I'm ready."

Daniel bit his lip, an adorable action he did whenever he was concentrating hard. He pressed on Erica's back until she lowered her chest to the bed.

At first, I didn't know why he'd done that, then I didn't care, because I could see his cock. Long, hard, thick. Fuck, it was perfect. He positioned himself, then kept his eyes on my face as he slowly sank into her. His gaze softened and the muscles around his mouth tightened.

He pulled back, and I almost died at the beauty of his cock slicked in pussy juice. Beneath me, Shauna wiggled her ass, and I realized I'd stopped moving. "Hold on, girl. Things are about to get serious," I teased.

Her fingers clamped onto the bedspread. "Give me all you've got, big boy," she said.

Now there was a challenge.

My eyes on Daniel, I gave it my all, pounding her sweet pussy until even Daniel seemed impressed. Or maybe he was just enjoying Erica's pussy and the drilling he was giving it. It was certainly working for me. I couldn't help imagining what it would be like to have his cock working my ass that way. I wanted that so fucking bad.

But this would have to do.

Shauna gave a swirl to her hips and reached between our legs to clamp her fingers around my balls, tugging lightly. "Oh fuck. Jesus. I'm going to come," I cried.

"Shit, me too," Daniel said.

"Yes, yes!" Shauna moaned.

I watched Daniel. I couldn't help it. I wasn't embarrassed because the girls couldn't keep their eyes off each other either. But Daniel? He lowered his eyes, shielding them from my view. It didn't matter. I was so close, even a nuclear explosion couldn't have stopped me.

Daniel bucked his hips, bit his lip, and then his head fell back onto his shoulders. His mouth opened, and he let out a rumbling moan as he found his release.

Seeing him like that, undone, didn't just push me over the edge, it catapulted me into the stratosphere. I came with an embarrassing shout and fell over Shauna's back. I reached between her legs and rubbed her clit, continuing to rock into her until she came too.

We fell into a heap on the bed, too boneless to even cover up. My chest sawed with the effort to catch my breath. This had been good. Much better than the last few times I'd had sex. Shauna was sweet, but the truth was, I barely knew her.

No, the real difference had been Daniel.

Watching him. Hearing him.

Experiencing this with him. The connection we seemed to have. It had been more intense than usual, hadn't it? Had Daniel felt it too?

But that wasn't possible. My roommate was straight. Right?

After a few minutes, the girls stirred and put their clothes back on. I wrapped a sheet around my waist and walked them to the door. I kissed Shauna lightly. "Thank you. I hope you had fun."

She touched my chest. "How could I not? You're one hot lay, Javier Cordero."

With a last wave, the girls disappeared down the hallway toward the elevators. I stepped back into the room. Still naked, Daniel had moved over to the sitting area and was sucking on a fresh beer. "Join me?" He held up a Corona.

"Thanks, man." I approached him cautiously and sat beside him on the couch. What was going on? The girls were gone. I'd more than expected him to be dressed by the time I got back from seeing the girls out.

Daniel crossed one arm over his well-developed chest and his bicep bulged. He'd told me he'd played at the national level in high school, and given his body, it wasn't hard to believe he'd probably been one of the best. He drank from his bottle and looked over at me. "Have fun?"

"Yeah." I tucked the sheet more tightly around myself. "I've never done anything like that before."

"Fucking with other people around?"

"Yeah. What about you?"

His eyes darkened. He took another sip. "I've done it before. Just not…"

"Not what?"

"Not with anyone I liked."

"Oh…" I frowned. Did he mean like in a club or something? No, we were too young for that. Maybe with teammates? "Did you like it?"

He nodded. "More than I thought I would."

His posture and the fact that he kept this gaze averted had nervous pins going into my spine. "What do you mean?"

Daniel shifted and my attention was drawn to his crotch where his cock no longer lay flaccid against his thigh. Instead, it was slowly filling as I watched.

"Daniel?"

When he remained silent, I touched his jaw with a finger and slowly turned his head to face me. "It's okay." I pulled the sheet away from my lap, exposing my own hardening cock. "Are you interested in doing more? I mean…" I swallowed the knot in my throat. "With me?"

The tip of Daniel's pink tongue poked out between his lips. He wet them with a quick lick. Then he nodded.

Jesus. Oh fuck. I hadn't really expected him to agree. "What do you want?"

He shrugged, leaving the decision up to me.

Did he even know what he was doing to me? How much I wanted this? I nodded. "Okay." I shifted on the couch, turning to face him, my bent leg between us. Leaning in close, I lightly touched my lips to his. They were firm and tasted of Corona. My mind spun. I was actually doing this. Kissing Daniel. My best friend. My crush.

I placed one hand on the back of the couch and the other on his shoulder. I tilted my head and deepened the kiss. He opened his mouth for me and I slipped my tongue inside, tasting him fully for the first time. It was everything I'd ever imagined and more. I pushed against him gently until he lay down on the couch, me on top of him.

He was unresisting. Pliant.

I frowned.

His cock still pressed hard against my leg, but the rest of him? Completely soft. Submissive. And his eyes? Closed.

"Daniel," I said.

He was unresponsive.

"Daniel," I said more sharply.

He opened his eyes, but it was like no one was there.

A chill swept through my body. What the fuck was going on?

Then, as though a switch had been flipped, Daniel shoved me off him. I fell to the floor as he scrambled over me. Without looking back, he tugged on his shorts and grabbed a shirt off the floor before racing out the door barefoot.

Shocked to the core, I stayed on the floor, the clanging of the door echoing in my mind. What in the hell had happened? Why had he freaked out like that? Even if he'd just been experimenting, it was no big deal. Just a kiss. But that dead look in his eyes…

My gut churned. I'd never seen anything like it before.

I'd really thought he'd wanted this. He'd fucking been hard. Just like me. The taste of him, the feel of that beautiful body against mine. God, it had meant everything to me. I loved him. I knew it now. This wasn't just a crush. It was love. I was in love. And the love of my life had just gone barreling out of our hotel room after a kiss.

Had I lost Daniel forever? Was this the end of our friendship? My dreams of a future with him? A business with him?

Goddamn. I could feel it in my bones. I'd let my cock lead and I'd fucking ruined everything.

Chapter 1

ARIANNA

Twenty-nine years old, divorced, and childless. Not exactly my happiest birthday ever. But I pasted on a wide smile for both sets of grandparents, for Mamá and Papá, and for my sisters, Mariposa, Isabel, and Seleste, as I hugged and kissed them and everyone else in the Rodriguez clan goodbye. They'd thrown me a lovely party, and I'd even forgotten about my troubles for a while.

But now it was time to go home, eat a pint of ice cream, drink a bottle of wine, and cry my eyes out. Alone.

As I walked down the driveway of my parents' home, a light breeze cut through Miami's humid air and cooled my face. Night had fallen a couple hours ago, and the sound of laughter behind me was cut off as someone shut the front door. I'd just reached my pearl-white Lexus parked in the drive when I heard a light step behind me. "Arianna."

I closed my eyes. Only Javier Cordero, the man I'd loved all through my teenage years, could make my name sound like a caress. His rich, velvety voice curled around me, leaving me both warm and bereft at the same time. I'd grown up believing that Javi and I would marry one day. And then he'd crushed my dreams by telling me he was gay.

Pasting on another smile, I turned to him. "What is it, Javi?"

He leaned against my car, his broad frame partially blocking the glow from the motion-activated light mounted above my parents' garage door.

"You managed to give me the slip." He reached out and touched my elbow. "That's not like you, *corazón*."

Corazón. He'd always called me that, and I'd never told him how much it hurt to hear it. *Sweetheart*. Like we were lovers.

"I'm just really… tired." My voice shook a little, and I looked away.

He frowned. "You look like you're going to cry."

Fuck. He read me so well. I sucked in a breath, unable to look at him. "It's been a long day, Javi."

"A long year, you mean. Well, almost a year."

He was alluding to my divorce from Daniel King, Javi's best friend and our partner in Total Indulgence, the high-end travel company the three of us ran together.

"I *really* don't want to talk about this. I just want to go home and wallow in my misery and not have to smile for anyone."

"*Corazón*—"

"Don't." I raised a hand, fighting for control. "Javi, just don't. I'm not your *corazón*. I'm not anything to you, other than a friend." The words came out sharper than I'd intended, and he looked like I'd slapped him.

He held out his hand. "Give me your keys."

"What?"

"Arianna Rodriguez, you are in no condition to drive."

How dare he tell me I was drunk? "I'm perfectly fine." I'd only had a few drinks, and that had been a while ago. Well, except for that last one I'd downed right before leaving.

"You had at least three mojitos that I saw, and you haven't snapped at me like that in ages. And the last time you did, you were furious. So even if you're not drunk, you're too upset to drive."

Heat flashed up my neck and over my face. Javi hadn't pissed me off this badly since he'd told me about his sexual orientation. And yeah, I had been furious that time. This time, I was just… imploding. "Don't treat me like a child."

Javi leaned closer, his delicious spicy scent washing over me. "I'm not. I'm treating you like someone precious to me. I'd be gutted if anything happened to you." He held out his hand again. "Let me drive you home."

He was killing me with this kindness, and he didn't even know it. "I just really, really need to be alone right now, Javi." I couldn't keep my voice steady any longer.

Reaching out, he smoothed my long black hair out of my face and cupped my cheek in his warm palm. "What you need is a friend. Your best friend in the whole world. And that's me." He pulled me into his arms, and a sob rose up in my chest. "Let me take you home, put you in a warm bath, and listen to how much you hate life right now."

He hugged me tight, and I burst into tears. After I sobbed all over his white silk guayabera, I finally wiped my eyes and stepped back. "O-okay," I hiccupped and handed him my keys.

I was done putting up a front; if Javi wanted to deal with me in this state, who was I to say no?

When we pulled up to my house in Coconut Grove—the house I'd shared with Daniel during the five years we'd been married—Javi shut off the car and hurried around to my side, opening the door and giving me a hand out. "*Mi reina*," he murmured. *My queen.*

I smiled up at him and shook my head. "Damn it, Javi, why do you have to be so wonderful?"

He grinned at me. "Ruining you for other men?"

"Yeah." It was the truth. "And it's really not fair, because I can't have you, can I?"

He offered me his elbow and I took it. That last mojito was starting to hit me, and I was wobbling a bit in my stilettos. No sense breaking an ankle on the flagstone path that led to the house.

Ignoring my question, he unlocked the front door, but before I could step inside, he scooped me off my feet and carried me over the threshold like I was his blushing bride. The way Daniel had when we'd bought this place. My heart started pounding, and I stared up at Javier. "What are you doing, Javi?"

"Turn on the lights," he said, carrying me over to the switch plate on the wall.

I did as asked, then he carried me through the dimly lit living room and down the shadowy hall to the master suite. "Javi?"

"Lights," he said, motioning with his head to the switch inside the bedroom door. I complied.

"What's going on?" I asked again.

He carried me into the spacious master bath and paused by the doorway, waiting for me to turn on the lights again. Once they were on, revealing the gorgeous white bathroom that Daniel and I had designed together, Javi took me over to the plush white vanity bench in front of my sink and set me down. "Stay there," he said, the commanding tone in his voice warning me not to argue—and turning me on at the same time. Damn him. Why did he have to be everything I wanted in a man?

Outside of Daniel, that is.

Grabbing a tea rose bath bomb from the canister on the edge of the huge tub, Javier turned on the water. He really was drawing me that bath. Steam swirled up from the tub, the rushing of the water echoing off the tiles.

I looked around, taking in the travertine marble Daniel and I had chosen for the shower, the granite we'd chosen for the countertops, the chrome fixtures we'd argued over before settling things with a sloppy kiss in the middle of the showroom floor, a kiss that had led to us barely making it home before we'd had wild sex just inside—and against—the front door, and then again on the kitchen table, and then on our brand-new sleigh bed, and then on the old black and white bathroom tile floor that we'd hated...

My bottom lip started to tremble. I missed him so much.

But it was his fault we'd divorced. He'd lied to me. We never should have married in the first place. He could have saved us so much heartache, if only he'd been honest with me.

"Hey." Javier crouched down in front of me, placing his hands on my knees. The heat of his palms seared through the fuchsia linen sundress I was wearing.

I looked into his handsome face, with its high cheekbones, my gaze traveling over those dark eyes framed in thick black lashes, down to his perfectly straight nose and full lips. Sometimes I thought *Dios* had peered into my dreams and fashioned a man just for me.

But in the ultimate cruel joke, *Dios* had also made him gay.

Tears formed in the corners of my eyes. "Why is life so fucking unfair?" I asked.

"If we got everything we wanted, our lives would be downright boring." He used his thumbs to wipe away the tears sliding down my cheeks.

"I was supposed to have a baby by now," I said, the ache in my chest threatening to turn into a wail. I swallowed it down and tried to smile. "Remember when you promised me that if I was thirty and single you'd marry me? And we'd have babies?"

"I remember."

"Why? Why did you say that, when you knew it wasn't going to ever happen?"

His gaze dropped to my lips for a moment, then his eyes locked on mine. "I said it because I wanted to make you happy." His gaze dipped to my mouth again, and a tingle of electricity ran through my body. "I wanted to make us *both* happy."

"But... but you're—"

He leaned in, his forehead touching mine, his warm breath washing over my lips. "About that. I might have left something out."

"You're gay. What exactly did you leave out?"

He cupped my jaw in his hands, angling it just so, as if he were going to kiss me. "It's a little more complicated than that."

"Complicated how?"

He touched his lips to mine, the kiss so gentle, so tender, I had to pull away, shaking my head. "Javi, you can't do that. You can't kiss me like that. I can't take it."

He reached back behind him and shut off the tub's faucet before it overflowed. The sudden quiet revealed the harshness of my breathing. The harshness of his as well. Was he... was he turned on? I looked down between his legs to see a sizable bulge tenting his slacks. I gestured to it. "Care to explain that?"

"I was trying to." He slid a hand down to cup the nape of my neck. "When I told you I was gay back in high school, I thought it was true. But I've come to realize it's not the full story."

I narrowed my eyes at him. "Is this some kind of riddle?"

One corner of his mouth lifted up into that lazy half-smile I knew so well. "I'm bisexual, Ari. It took me a long time to sort out who I am, and by the time I realized it, you were already dating Daniel."

"So, you're saying those women you brought as your dates to family parties weren't just cover? They really were dates?" He nodded. "Does Daniel know?"

"Yeah."

I frowned. "Another thing he never told me. No wonder our marriage was doomed. So why didn't *you* tell me sooner?"

"There really wasn't a point, once I'd figured it out. You and Daniel were getting serious. High school and college were a confusing time for me. I believed that if I was attracted to men, that meant I was gay. It took me doing some reading and talking to other people who felt like I do, to realize that it's okay to be bi. I'm not in denial about being gay. I really am attracted to both men and women, and I enjoy having sex with both." His eyes dropped to my lips again. "And I've wanted to have sex with you for a very, very long time."

I could only stare at him. Had I fallen asleep? Was this some kind of crazy-ass dream fueled by too much alcohol and too many nights alone?

I held out my arm. "Pinch me."

He leaned forward. "I'd much rather kiss you." Then his lips were on mine again, and this time they weren't gentle. This time they were demanding, and my own parted for the invasion of his tongue. It twined around mine, and slick heat pooled between my legs. A helpless little whimper slipped out of me.

Cristo, the man could kiss. If this was a dream, I didn't want to wake up.

He drew me to my feet, then began unzipping the back of my dress, and I started unbuttoning his shirt. I pushed his shirt down his arms as my dress began to fall, and we released each other for a moment so we could drop the offending garments to the floor.

I took in the rich tan of his ripped torso with its sprinkling of black hair across his chest, his chiseled eight-pack, the perfect V of his obliques pointing down to the bulge still tenting his slacks. Javi had been a gym rat since college, but I hadn't known just how much time he'd put in there. I whistled. "*¡Ay, papi chulo!*" He grinned at me, making his pecs dance and flexing his biceps.

Then his eyes fell to my breasts, lingering there, and I couldn't get my black bra off fast enough. I let it fall from my fingers, and he dipped his head down, sucking one of my nipples into his mouth, his strong fingers tugging on the other and making electricity arc from each hard peak to my pussy. I hadn't been this turned on in a long time. When his mouth left my breast, I took his face in my hands. "Is this really happening?" I asked in all seriousness.

Javi broke into a grin. "*Sí, princesa*. It's really happening."

"Let's take this show into the bedroom."

Placing a hand on his shoulder for balance, I stepped out of my black stilettos, then I took his hand, giving it a little tug. He followed me into the bedroom, where he kicked off his shoes and went to work on his belt, the buckle jangling as he unzipped his slacks and left them in a heap on the floor.

Then he stepped forward, backing me into the mattress and urging me up onto it. I lay back, clad only in my lacy black panties, which he proceeded to strip off me. Dropping to his knees, he parted my legs, his lips traveling up the inside of my right thigh. I was quivering all over, and the closer he got to my pussy, the less I could control it. How many times had I fantasized about this? About Javi, the man I'd loved forever, making love to me? Being mine, in ways that went far beyond friendship?

He parted the lips of my sex, his tongue finding my clit and circling it. A throaty moan rushed out of me, and he gently sucked on that little nub, his tongue teasing me and making me writhe. He licked down to my entrance, spearing his tongue inside me, fucking me with it until I moaned. "More." He slid two fingers through my juices, coating them, before sliding them inside me, the sudden fullness making me gasp and rock my hips into his hand.

Keeping his fingers where they were, he rose up and leaned over me, cupping my neck with his other hand and drawing my mouth to his. I could taste myself on his lips. His tongue plunged into my mouth, mimicking what his fingers were doing below, and I cried out, coming apart on his hand.

I'd slept with three men since Daniel and I had broken up, and not one of them had made me feel like this, like I was shattering into a million pieces, but safe at the same time.

JAVIER

Arianna gasped into my mouth, her luscious body writhing beneath mine as she came, and I felt like the king of the world. I'd finally, finally done it. Finally manned up and gone after what I'd wanted for so many years.

I'd let Daniel have her because I'd convinced myself that I couldn't make her happy. I was gay after all. A gay man who weirdly lusted after his female best friend. And other women too.

By the time I'd realized what I really was, it had been too late. Daniel had swept her off her feet, and I couldn't even be that upset because at least the two people I loved most in the world were happy.

Even if I wasn't. Even if I secretly pined for them both. But I'd known when I'd met Daniel in college that he wasn't gay. He'd had a different girl in bed practically every night of the week. And after what had happened between us in Cancun… I knew he'd never go there with me.

For a long time, I'd resigned myself to never having what I wanted. But after Ari and Daniel had divorced, I'd vowed to myself not to lose her again.

The time hadn't been right for me to approach her; I'd wanted to wait until she was over Daniel, until the two of them had settled down and found a way to be around each other without tension filling the room.

But seeing her tonight, seeing her so damn miserable, broke something inside me. Ari was suffering, and it was time to make her see that losing Daniel wasn't the end of the world.

I just hoped I hadn't miscalculated. Was it too soon?

My heart pounding in my chest, my fingers still inside her, I released her mouth and waited for Ari to open her eyes, to look up at me, to let me know if this was going to go further. My aching cock was telling me to just keep going, but I wanted to be sure this was truly what she wanted.

She panted softly, her long, thick lashes fluttering against her tan cheeks, and I held my breath. Finally she looked up at me. "Well, what are you waiting for?" she asked.

"Just making sure you're still with me." My cock pressed into her hip, and she shifted against me, deliberately rubbing it through the thin cloth of my snug black boxer trunks.

"I'm with you. And I'm not done yet." She looked up at me at the same time she slipped a hand between us, her slender fingers grazing my cock.

I inhaled at the contact, and she started working the trunks over my hips. I pumped my fingers in and out of her again, and she moaned, the sound going straight to my already straining cock. Letting go of her, I stood and whipped off my briefs. I motioned to the nightstand. "Condoms in there?"

She opened her mouth to respond, then hesitated. Shit. She was reconsidering, and rightly so. I'd pushed too far, too fast.

Why did I think my being bi wouldn't be an issue? I should have given her time to think it over before taking her to bed.

"I'm sorry. I fucked up, didn't I?" I said, reaching for my boxers.

She sat up and shook her head. "No. I just—" Tears welled in her eyes again.

Oh *Cristo*. I promised myself I'd never hurt her, and look what I'd done. "Arianna—"

"I don't want to use a condom," she blurted.

I froze. "Why is that making you cry?"

"Because… because I want a baby, and I know it's not fair to ask you, and it's completely stupid, and I'm going to be thirty next year, but I wanted to have one by now…" The words poured out of her in a rush, punctuated by sharp inhales as she tried to suppress her tears.

"Shh." I folded her in my arms, rocking her gently. "*Corazón*, I really fucked up."

"No," she whispered against my chest, her warm tears sliding down my right pec. "I'm the one who's fucking up." She pulled back and wiped at her eyes, then she gave me a shaky smile. "The condoms are in the nightstand."

"You sure you want to do this?" I asked.

She nodded and reached down, wrapping her delicate fingers around my still-rigid shaft, which twitched in her hand. Jesus, the damn thing had always had a mind of its own. A one-track mind. And right now, it wanted to be buried inside this woman who made my heart want to beat out of my chest with one of her smiles.

Arianna Rodriguez was fucking luscious, from her bouncy tits to her curvy hips, and when she stroked my cock, her fingers squeezing me just right, every bit of common sense I had flew out the window. This beautiful, wonderful woman who I loved with all my heart wanted a baby. *My* baby. And it wasn't like I was planning to let her go.

What was the harm in making her happy?

What about Daniel? a voice in my head whispered. *She still loves him; he still loves her. What if they make up? Where does that leave you,* pendejo*?*

It's been almost a year. And Daniel was adamant that he didn't want children.

He'll never give her what she wants. What she needs.

But I can.

"You want that baby, *corazón*?"

She looked at me, her eyes lighting up. "You don't think I'm crazy?"

I laughed. "Maybe we both are. But I would love to have a baby with you."

She lay back on the bed, tugging me forward by my dick. And I was happy to follow.

I crawled up beside her. This *was* crazy. And stupid. And I couldn't stop grinning.

She smiled at me, then she wrapped her fingers around me again, stroking up and down, making me hiss this time. I wouldn't last long if she kept this going. How many nights had I beaten off to the thought of her touching me like this, back when we'd been teens and I'd had no idea what to make of my desire for her alongside my lust for Jack Anderson, the captain of the football team?

I grabbed her hand and pinned her wrist to the bed. "Enough, *corazón*, or that baby will have to wait a while longer." Grabbing the base of my cock, I moved over her, rubbing myself between her pussy lips, coating the tip in her juices. She gasped at the contact, spreading her legs and arching her hips, and then I was inside her, all that tight, wet heat making me groan. She fit me like we'd been made for each other, and I forced myself to go slow, to savor the feeling of her surrounding me. Then she crossed her legs behind my back and pressed down, forcing me back inside her with surprising power.

Apparently, all that yoga and Pilates hadn't just toned those muscles. She was a lot stronger than she looked.

And then she flexed the muscles surrounding my cock, and I about saw stars. "*Cristo*, woman," I panted.

She laughed and did it again, the sensation rippling from my shaft up my spine. "I like to keep in shape. *All* over."

"I'll show you in shape." I snapped my hips forward, thrusting into her hard, and she groaned, her fingernails digging into my back.

"Oh yes," she panted. "Harder."

I let myself loose, plunging into her without mercy, making sure I was pressing against her mound, and she arched, rubbing herself against me, her little gasps in my ear the fuel I needed to keep thrusting harder, faster, the tingling in my balls telling me I was close, so close, and then she shuddered beneath me, crying out my name, and I erupted inside her, my whole body stiffening.

I hadn't come that hard in years.

Collapsing on the bed beside her, I pulled her onto my chest and kissed her softly.

"You're the best thing to ever happen to me, Javi," she whispered.

"Same here, *corazón*." I wrapped my arms around her, enjoying how she snuggled into me like she'd always belonged there.

I'd held her a million times, but never like this.

Never like she was mine.

I'd finally manned up, finally claimed the woman I'd always wanted.

I was going to have everything I'd ever longed for.

Everything except Daniel.

A stone formed in my stomach. Daniel was probably going to hate me for this.

And it was probably going to destroy the company we'd spent the last decade building. The company that had been our dream way back since we'd organized that crazy spring-break trip down to Cancun for us and our entire college dorm. The trip that had made us campus legends.

The trip that had cemented our future.

That stone in my gut grew larger, and I hugged Arianna closer.

The future I'd just blown to smithereens.

DANIEL

Angry bees festered in my veins as I exited Miami International Airport. Or at least that's how it felt to me. I was riled up. Agitated. And horny as fuck. And who could blame me? I'd just spent two weeks in Tahiti with six insanely hot rock stars, two of whom were banging my new partner at Total Indulgence Tours. There'd been sex all around me, and I was going out of my mind with need.

I trudged through the parking lot and dumped my suitcase and laptop bag into the trunk of my silver Lexus. Inside, it was an inferno. I clawed at my tie, tearing it off and flicking open the buttons on my shirt while I waited for the air-conditioning to kick in. Beads of sweat snaked along my hairline, and I knew they weren't only due to the outside heat.

No. I was burning up inside. I angled the jet of air so it hit my face and leaned against the leather seat.

Get a hold of yourself, King.

I didn't want to give in to my need. I wouldn't.

Men didn't interest me. They never had, and they never would. Except when I got like this. When the memories from the past snuck up on me, tried to pull me back into that darkness. The only way I could breathe was to control them. To prove to the demons in my mind that I was no one's bitch. That I wasn't a scared kid anymore. That whatever I did, I did on my own terms.

Divorcing Arianna had only made things worse.

Had only made the nightmares more frequent. The loneliness more debilitating. What choice had there been, though? Once she'd started pushing for a baby, my brain had started to short-circuit, and all the insecurities of the past came back with a vengeance. I loved her more than life itself, but to survive, I'd had to let her go.

She could never know why.

Tomorrow, I'd have to go to the office and face her again. Face them both again. Arianna and Javier, my best friend and business partner since college. The man who'd introduced me to my ex-wife. The man who'd been in love with her all along. They'd grown up in the same Cuban community. Their mothers were friends. I didn't understand why he'd never gone after her. Sure, Javi was bi, though I doubted Arianna would have cared. The two of them were tight as ticks. But I was grateful that she'd picked me.

Javier didn't know that I knew, but it was hard not to notice the way he looked at her. The way his eyes lit up when she walked into a room, and the way his gaze traveled her generous curves and tanned skin.

I'd found it mesmerizing. Confusing. Fucking addictive.

And maybe I was a fucking masochist for continuing to work with both of them.

Today was her birthday, and for the first time in eleven years, I was missing her party. I could call her, but should I? I didn't want her to get the wrong impression, because we were never getting back together. I wouldn't hurt her that way. Not again.

She would be with her family tonight. With Javi. Happy.

He still looked at her like she was a goddess walking among mortals. And sometimes it pissed me off. Even though I couldn't have her, I still loved her. Other times, it *excited* me. I'd picture them in bed, their sweat-slicked bodies sliding together, their faces contorted in pleasure. His hands on her full breasts, her hands on his long, *hard* cock.

And then the fucking festering bees would return.

Goddamn it.

I fished my cell out of my back pocket and made the call that was the only solution that ever worked, even though it helped for only a while.

"Hello," a perky female voice said. "Diamond Escorts. How may I help you?"

"This is Daniel King. I'd like to book one of your escorts for a few hours this evening."

"Of course. Both Brandon and Diego are available. Any preference?"

I hadn't been with either man before, but… Javier's dark eyes and plump lips filled my mind. Fuck. I should pick Brandon. I knew from his photo in the company's online catalogue that he was the complete opposite of Javier, from his blond hair to his slim, small body. I also knew that he wouldn't do it for me. I cleared my throat. "Diego, please."

"Time?"

I checked my watch. It was eight. "Nine thirty at the usual place."

For years, I'd maintained a small bachelor pad in Fort Lauderdale. It was a place neither Arianna nor Javier knew about. My real home, the one

I'd purchased after the divorce, was in Coconut Grove, only a short drive from TI's headquarters and minutes away from the home I'd shared with Arianna. She still lived there, because I'd insisted she keep it. It would be perfect for her and Javier when he finally swept her off her feet and gave her the family she deserved.

"Very well, sir. I'll charge it to the card on file?"

"Yes."

I ended the call and drove the short distance to Fort Lauderdale, stopping only to pick up some pizza and a Coke. My fingers tap-danced on the steering wheel as I turned into the parking garage. I quickly found an open spot, and leaving my bags in the trunk, I headed up to my home away from home.

Since I always left some spare clothes here, I jumped in the shower and changed, then sat on my balcony to eat my dinner. I never drank when I was meeting with an escort. The scent of alcohol on my breath would make him think I wasn't in control when nothing could be further from the truth.

At nine thirty on the dot, the buzzer sounded. I walked over to the keypad. "Yes?"

"It's Diego."

"Come on up." I pressed the button to unlock the main entrance door.

A couple minutes later, there was a soft knock on my door. I opened it, and the breath left my body. *Jesus, fuck.* The man could be Javier's younger brother. He looked to be about twenty-five, five-ten, with a slender swimmer's build. His dark eyes shone brightly. He smiled, and the bees hummed louder.

I stepped back. "Right on time. Come in."

He walked into the living room and shrugged off his worn jean jacket, leaving him in a rib-hugging white tank top. His faded jeans sat low on his hips, held up by a black leather belt. There was a thick gold chain around his neck. My cock jumped at the sight of all that golden skin. I wanted to fall to my knees and kiss his stomach. Follow his treasure trail to what I was sure was a generously proportioned cock if the bulge in his pants was anything to go by.

But that wasn't how these encounters went. Not with me.

"Do you understand what's going to happen here?" I asked him.

He nodded. "Velma informed me."

Velma was the manager of Diamond Escorts. We'd ironed out the details long ago, and since they valued my business, they made sure to follow them to a T. "Let's get started then." I pressed Play on the playlist I'd created for these encounters. Liszt's "Dante Symphony" began to play, dark and brooding and matching my mood exactly.

Diego's smile dimmed a bit, but his fingers went to his tank top, tugging the hem out of his jeans and pulling it over his head. He placed it on the back of the couch as per my instructions. Next, he undid his belt, kicked off his shoes and socks, then slid his jeans off his hips, slowly to match the dramatic music. Each inch revealed more of him: his taut belly, his curved cock, his heavy balls.

My mouth watered even as my insides roiled. I wanted this, yet I hated it. I hated that I wanted it.

Like Dante, I was trapped inside my own inferno.

My life was like the nine circles of Hell. Only there was no chance of escape for me. No chance of Paradise. Because I was a wrecked, ruined man.

When Diego stood completely naked in front of me, I said, "On your knees."

He obeyed me. His eyes were wide, but he didn't seem afraid. And rightly so. I'd never hurt an escort. It was just that things had to go a certain way.

I stepped closer. I remained fully clothed. I lowered my zipper and freed my cock. It was achingly hard and already dripping. "Open your mouth."

His eyes on me, Diego parted his lips. I fed him my cock, the only part of me that would be touching him. My hips snapped forward, and I sank into his mouth. Fully. His eyes watered, but he didn't pull away. That was another requirement. The escorts had to be able to deep throat.

I thrust into his mouth as deep as he could take me, over and over. He reached out to touch me. I shuddered and froze. My stomach dropped.

"Hands on your lap!" My command was sharp. Desperate even.

Diego's eyes filled with concern, but his hands returned to his thighs, gripping them. Shame filled me. I hated that I'd let my desperation, my fear, slip into my voice. My erection flagged.

Damn it. I focused on his face, pictured someone else's. Someone I cared about. It was wrong and I knew it, but right now that didn't matter. All that mattered was exorcising the demons inside me.

When I felt I was getting close, I pulled out of his mouth and stepped away from him. "Bend over the armchair."

He rose and walked behind the chair, then leaned over it. His fingers clutched the threadbare fabric. I could no longer see his face, and that was exactly what I wanted. I picked up the condom I'd left on the coffee table after my shower and rolled it onto my cock. Then I tore open the packet of lube and slathered it onto my shaft. My instructions included that the escorts prepare themselves before coming over. An opportunity I'd rarely been afforded.

I stepped behind him. "Part your cheeks," I said.

He reached back and gripped one ass cheek in each hand, then pulled them apart. His puckered hole glistened. I gripped my shaft and positioned the head at his entrance.

"Brace yourself." It was my only instruction before I let loose. I rammed my cock into his tight ass, relishing in his gasp. The half-pained moan. I thrust back and forth until he relaxed enough that I could sink in all the way. I couldn't use the seatback as support because the risk of coming into contact with his arms was too high. Instead, I widened my stance and pistoned into Diego. His back arched, and I enjoyed the ripple of his muscles, the tightening of his glutes as he took me. Every inch of me. I wanted to slide my hand down his spine, feel the movement beneath his skin, but I didn't dare touch him. The one time I'd tried, years ago, before Arianna, the evening had ended with me heaving up my dinner in the bathroom.

So, I did what I always did: I used my imagination. In my mind, I ran my fingers over those sleek muscles, the narrow waist and slender hips. I dug my fingers into his hair and pulled his head back. Though it wasn't Diego in my mind. No, it was Javier. My best friend. But I could never do to him what I did to these men. To Diego.

I pictured myself kissing Javier while my cock drove into Diego's tight body, giving no care to his pleasure, only to mine. He was mine to do with as I pleased. Right now, he was an object. A sex toy. Someone who existed only as a receptacle for my cock. For my cum.

The thought set me off. Electricity jolted down my spine, through my balls and out the head of my cock. I rocked my hips into him as my body spasmed, releasing all the tension that had been building up inside me since the last time I'd fucked a man. Fucked anyone really.

When the aftershocks were done, I wrapped my hand around the base of my cock, holding the condom in place, and withdrew. Diego moaned softly, panting against the couch. He released his ass cheeks and pushed himself up. His cock was still hard, but I was done. That was also part of the instructions. The escorts weren't allowed to come. I'd learned over the years that the sight or scent of another man's cum could throw me into a flashback. And no one wanted to see that shit.

I grabbed some tissues off the kitchen counter to clean myself up and dispose of the condom while Diego got dressed. I reached into my pocket and pulled out a twenty. I handed him the tip. "Thank you."

"Ever thought about loosening up a bit?" Diego took the money, a sad expression on his face. "You might have more fun if you did."

After closing the door behind him, I grabbed the bottle of vodka stashed in the freezer. On my way to the balcony, I glugged down several mouthfuls and wiped away the drops that spilled onto my chin with the back of my hand. I sat in the cheap plastic chair and stared at the evening skyline as I drank more vodka and hoped it would numb the pain in my heart. Diego was right, but I couldn't loosen up, couldn't risk losing control.

I already hated that I couldn't suppress this fucking need. The need I had to control another man sexually. The need that had been put there by the sick fuck who'd warped me.

I needed help; I knew it. But how could I ever tell anyone what had happened to me when I didn't entirely understand it myself?

Chapter 2

ARIANNA

About an hour after Javier left, I pressed a hand to my temple and winced at the darts of pain as I opened my front door to more bright sunshine than should be allowed. Too much alcohol at my birthday celebration followed by a late night with Javier—and what a night it had been!—had left me a little hungover, a little tired, and very confused. Being in his arms had been the culmination of years of what I'd thought to be unrequited love, years of long empty nights filled with erotic dreams and broken hopes. Until I'd met Daniel, and then he'd mostly replaced Javier in my dreams and in my reality, though Javier had always been in my heart. It's true what they say: you never get over your first love, and Javier had been that for me… in spades. All through high school, even though he'd told me he was gay, I'd pictured us married, in a house filled with small happy children. And now to find out that he wasn't gay but bisexual? I didn't know whether I wanted to kiss him or punch him. All those wasted years.

But then you would never have been with Daniel.

And that was something else I wasn't sure how to feel about. I'd loved Daniel with all my heart. Hell, I still did. But his brand of love hurt. Deeply. We'd divorced almost a year ago, but I'd lost him long before that, and I still didn't know why. I probably never would.

So, it was more than time for me to move on. Last night had been a great step forward. But… My palm landed gently on my stomach, and I sucked in a sharp breath. Oh God. What had we done? Was I pregnant even now? No, it couldn't be. Okay, intellectually, I knew it was possible to get pregnant after only one night of sex. But really? What did I even want to happen? Did I want to be pregnant with Javier's child and walk into the sunset of happily ever after with him?

My thoughts wandered back to last night, to how he'd looked above me, how he'd felt inside me. I shivered. Yes. God, yes. I did want that.

With a little more bounce in my step, I let myself out of my house I'd shared with Daniel. My chest ached at the sight of my lonely Lexus parked in the driveway, one of a pair Daniel and I had bought together. I got in my car and set off for TI, the business helmed by Daniel.

There was definitely a pattern there. The man touched every aspect of my life, even a year later. What could I do about it though? The idea of moving or of leaving TI gave me hives. I'd spent years decorating my home and building up my part of the business. I was proud of the work I'd accomplished. The last thing I wanted to do was give it up.

Give Daniel up, you mean.

I sighed. Despite the divorce, we were still friendly. Not friends exactly, but cordial. Good business partners. I didn't want to go anywhere else. I didn't want Daniel completely out of my life. That didn't mean I didn't want more though. And Javier might be the man to give that to me.

Making a mental note to thank Javier for not letting me drive last night, I set off for work. A few minutes into the short commute, my cell phone, which I had yet to check this morning, rang. I directed my hands-free in-car system to answer the call. "Hello, this is Arianna Rodriguez, Chief Operating Officer at Total Indulgence Tours. How may I help you?"

"Finally!" an aggravated female voice barked out.

My brows lowered. "I beg your pardon?"

"Look, this is Greta Lindstrom at Exclusive Couples Counseling. I've left about fifteen messages between your direct number and the company number."

I glanced at my phone and saw that I did indeed have about ten missed calls. "I'm terribly sorry, Ms. Lindstrom. What did you want to speak to me about?"

"You mean you don't know?"

My stomach clenched. "Know what?"

"Jesus, what kind of a shoddy organization are you running over there?"

"Ms. Lindstrom, you seem very upset. Why don't you tell me—"

Her voice hardened. "Someone at TI leaked to the press that Monica Dashwood and Chad Winters will be attending our intensive relationship retreat in Santa Catalina."

"I can assure you that no one at TI—"

Greta cut me off. "It had to be someone in your organization. We've never had leaks before, and the only new factor in this equation is your company."

It was total bullshit. We'd dealt with some of the most famous people in the world over the years, and word of their whereabouts had never gotten out. I wanted to lambaste the woman, but while it would bring me a sense of satisfaction, it wouldn't solve the problem.

There was a loud sigh over the line, then Greta added, "We're going to need to move to a new location."

"What?" The retreat was scheduled to begin in less than a week. I'd been meticulously planning it for months, scheduling security, events, outings, none of which was easy when each place had to be reserved in advance and completely bought out to maintain the privacy of the retreat's celebrity couples. "There's no way we can—"

"There's no way we can have it in Santa Catalina now. The place will be crawling with paparazzi. My clients will be more concerned with the media than with repairing their failing relationships. No, it has to be moved."

The logistics, not to mention the expense, of moving the retreat at such a late date were staggering. And TI was no doubt going to have to eat the costs. Fuck. I was going to have to break the news to Daniel and Javier and brainstorm some solutions with them.

"Ms. Lindstrom, I understand. Give me the day, and I'll call you back this evening with some options."

"They'd better be good ones. Changing the event planner less than a week before the scheduled start of the retreat would be difficult, but I'll do it if I don't think you can pull this off."

What a bitch. I smiled sweetly to myself in the mirror. "We will prove to you that your faith in TI is not misplaced, Ms. Lindstrom. I'll call you this evening with a solution."

"I'm counting on it. Oh, and if we stay with TI, I expect Daniel to handle this retreat personally."

"Daniel?" While it was true that Daniel had been responsible for the early dealings with ECC to outline the initial contracts, I was the main point of contact for the actual retreat. There'd be nothing for Daniel to do there except maybe smooth Greta's ruffled feathers. He was good at that, smoothing ruffled feathers. Especially women's. Except my own of course.

"Will that be a problem?" Greta asked, her tone like shards of ice.

"Not at all." I cringed inside as I hung up. If Daniel came along, we'd be stuck together somewhere beautiful for two weeks. A week ago, hell, even a day ago, I'd have been happy for the opportunity to see if we could rekindle our relationship. Now I was terrified. What if he figured out that Javier and I had slept together?

Having arrived at TI, I slid into my parking spot behind the building and made my way inside and up to the fourth floor. I knocked on Daniel and Javier's doors as I passed by. "Emergency meeting in my office," I said.

Had the situation not been so dire, I'd have laughed. Both men narrowed their eyes at me, almost identical frowns furrowing their brows. Nonetheless, they got up and followed me to the meeting area next to my floor-to-ceiling windows. God, I loved my office.

"What's going on?" Daniel asked in a gruffer than usual voice as he settled into a chair, crossing his long legs at the knee. His dark dress pants tightened around his legs, showcasing his thick, muscular thighs. Despite it being only nine in the morning, he'd already loosened his tie, undone a couple buttons at his throat, and rolled up his sleeves, exposing his tanned forearms, the veins popping out and making my mouth water. Daniel might not have played tennis at a competitive level in over a decade, but he still looked like he could go out on the court at a moment's notice.

Javier entered a beat behind him. He eyed me cautiously. "How are you this morning, Ari?"

I smiled at him. "Good. You?"

"Good."

Daniel snorted. "Must have been some birthday party. You both look like you could have used some extra coffee this morning."

"It was, uh… really good. Mamá and Papá pulled out all the stops." Heat raced up my chest, hitting my face like a door as I stumbled through my excuse. Had we been so obvious that Daniel could tell what we'd been up to after only a couple minutes? Fuck.

"Happy belated birthday, Arianna." Daniel smiled, but it didn't reach his eyes. Didn't make those cute crinkles at the corners that I loved so much. In fact, he didn't look nearly as relaxed as he should have after two weeks in Tahiti.

Jane, our receptionist, walked into my office, carrying a tray of ice water and three tall glasses. Javier jumped to his feet to retrieve it. "Thank you, Jane," he said softly.

His low tone reminded me of last night, and I reached into my bag to hide my face. I pulled out the ECC file and set it on the table. "So, I got a call from Ms. Lindstrom at ECC this morning."

Daniel leaned back in his chair, a smirk on his handsome face. "How is the beautiful Greta?"

"Angry enough to spit," I deadpanned.

Again, both men frowned. I launched into my explanation of what had happened.

"So, she blames us?" Javier asked.

"Yep."

"Wasn't anyone at TI," Daniel said firmly. "If we got through the writers' retreat with Riley Kendrick and this Tahiti rescue mission with King's Cross without a leak, we can certainly get through a marriage-counseling gig."

"I know, but the damage is done, even if we could prove it wasn't us."

"We will prove it," Daniel insisted.

I rolled my eyes at him. When something riled him up, he was like a pit bull. "Regardless, we have to come up with an alternate solution that will satisfy and amaze so she doesn't cancel on us and move the business somewhere else."

"Definitely," Javier said. "I've already included the income from this event in this quarter's forecast. It will leave a big hole if we lose it."

"We won't lose it." Daniel flipped open my ECC folder and scanned the schedule I'd put together. "What are the initial constraints?" he asked. "Privacy and security for the guests is obviously number one."

"Right. It has to be a somewhat-secluded location. Preferably one that's small enough that we can buy it out, which will help greatly with the security and privacy aspects," I said.

"Fine. So, we pick a few resorts not in Santa Catalina, since that's out of the bag, and see which one can accommodate us." Daniel closed the folder and slid it across the table toward me.

I slid it back. "It's not that easy. When I was planning this retreat—months ago—all the high-end resorts in southern California were already booked. I only got this one in Santa Catalina because a huge wedding was cancelled."

"Does it have to be in southern California?" Javier asked.

I tapped a nail on my chin. "I was trying to keep it close to LA, since that's where ECC and, therefore, most of the clients are from. And I just assumed we should find a place nearby to make travel changes easier." Daniel was shaking his head. "What?" I asked, more than a little exasperation filtering into my voice.

"These people are loaded. Most have private planes. Find some place, any place. We'll pick up any travel expenses that ECC or its clients don't want to pay."

Javier's eyes bugged out. "Now wait a minute—"

"No, I'm serious." Daniel turned to Javier. "The fees for these retreats are in the mid-range five-digits. It's a big, money-making venture for us. If we can make ECC happy this go-round, we'll get more business like this from them and other similar companies."

"So, we take the hit this time and make up for it next time, that's your plan?" Javier said, more than a little skepticism in his tone. "Bit of a gamble, isn't it?"

"Have I ever steered us wrong?" Daniel asked, his gaze darting between us.

I shook my head. Javier said, "No."

"Okay then. Find us a location, and then set up a quick tour, some activities in the area. We'll buy out the venues whatever the cost."

"Jesus." Shuffling through my notes, I pressed two fingers to my temple. "You make it sound so easy."

"It *is* easy."

I narrowed my eyes at him. I really wanted to tell him off, but that wasn't how business partnerships worked.

"Daniel," Javier said.

"Fine. Okay, it's not that easy."

Javier turned to me. "What about northern California. A vineyard maybe? This isn't high season, so maybe—"

"That's it!" I jumped up and ran to him, squeezing his cheeks between my palms as I planted a smacking kiss on his lips. "You are a godsend."

He grinned. "Thank you. But… um… why?"

"My uncle owns a vineyard in Sonoma. They're closed for renovations, but they're supposed to reopen in November for the holidays. Maybe I can convince him to open early, in five days, to accommodate us."

"Ah… Uncle Manuel. The man never liked me much. Glad you're handling this and not me." Daniel stood and pushed his chair in.

"Not so fast, Mr. King. The beautiful Greta is insisting that you attend to this shitstorm personally."

Daniel gripped the back of his chair. "We'll send Javier instead. I'm sure you'd prefer that anyway."

What did he mean by that? "It doesn't matter what I prefer, Daniel. It never has." I flipped my hair over my shoulder. "Anyway, Greta sounded very firm on this point. She wants you… or rather… she wants you there."

Daniel dropped his head. "Fuck."

I chanced a glance at Javier. He widened his eyes. It wasn't like Daniel to get this worked up over a trip. "I get it, Daniel. This is going to be awkward for both of us. We'll both be going to a marriage-counseling retreat, only it's way too late to rescue our relationship."

Daniel straightened, his eyes on my face. He stepped toward me and slid a finger along my cheek. "That was always a forgone conclusion. We were just too blind to see it." His gaze flicked to Javier, then back to me. "I hope you find someone who makes you happy."

And without another word, he turned and left my office, walking straight into his, and closed the door quietly behind him.

Javier and I eyed each other warily. "Think he knows?" I asked.

"Nah." Javier forced a smile. "How could he?"

DANIEL

If I'd thought being in Tahiti with a bunch of hot rock stars was torture, it was nothing compared to being in the same room with Arianna and Javier again. Every time Ari moved, my eyes ate her up—the shimmer of her black hair when she brushed it out of her face, the bounce of her breasts when she walked across the room, the way she perched on a chair, so poised, so fucking perfect, my fingers flexed with the need to touch her. Add in Javi's toned and tanned body, the way his white teeth flashed at me whenever he smiled, the rock-solid feel of him when we'd hugged, his warm, spicy scent that always drove me crazy, and I felt as wound up as I had when I'd landed at the airport last night. Like I hadn't fucked Diego at all.

Somehow I made it through the meeting about ECC. And somehow I'd ended up agreeing to go to Sonoma with Ari and trying to placate Greta Lindstrom. With any luck, I'd only have to stay a day or two, and then I could slink back to Miami and pretend Ari didn't exist while she was on the job in California. Of course, Javi would still be at the office, but whenever Ari was gone, it was easier. I could pretend things were the way they'd always been. Javi and I the best of friends. Only friends. Nothing more.

For some reason, the three of us, that combination, brought out my desire for more.

A desire I couldn't fucking indulge.

I really was a goddamn masochist.

I checked my watch. Three o'clock. It was too early to quit for the day, but I was too wired to work. Probably the jet lag getting to me. I was running on fumes—too much booze, too little sleep, and certainly too much of Javi's Cuban coffee. He made it strong and sweet, and I was fucking addicted to it. Like the man himself.

I shouldn't be leaving the office early on my first day back, but what was the point of being CEO if you couldn't set your own hours?

But I didn't want to go home and stare at the walls, listening to the echoing silence and pretending Ari was just gone for the day. Pretending she'd walk in the door, give me that coy smile of hers, call me *mi amor,* and beg me for a kiss. I'd often liked to pretend she didn't deserve one, that she'd been a bad girl, and she'd always drop onto my lap, wrap her arms around my neck, and press light kisses to my cheeks, my eyelids, my lips until I gave in and kissed her. And that usually ended with us naked and sweaty. And happy.

So fucking happy. Until we weren't.

Since home was out, I packed up my briefcase and went to the next best thing to home. The Coconut Grove Women's and Children's Shelter, where my cousin, Jennifer King, volunteered on Monday afternoons when her restaurant was closed. She'd managed to rope me into volunteering there too, said it would be good for me, and it was. It gave me a reason to keep putting one foot in front of the other on the days when I'd rather curl into a ball. There was nothing like being needed, like helping other people change their lives for the better.

Jennifer was the only openly "out" person in the King family, and the only person in the world who knew what had happened to me. She'd been the one who'd figured it out, the one who'd ferreted the details out of me, the one who'd listened while I'd waded through my pain and confusion.

And she was the reason I'd stayed in Miami after giving up my tennis scholarship to Stanford. She owned a pizzeria near Florida International University. I'd started working there the summer after high school, finally making up my mind to go to FIU, and I'd ended up with Javi as my freshman roommate in Panther Hall.

If it wasn't for Jennifer, I'd probably be dead by now.

She was my favorite person in the world, after Javi and Ari. And I really, really wanted to talk to her. Get her opinion on the thing that had been niggling at me all during the meeting today with Javi and Ari. The thing I couldn't get out of my head.

Something had changed between them. I was sure of it. Then again, maybe I was seeing things that weren't there.

Jennifer would set me straight. She always did.

The minute I walked in the doors of the shelter, a half dozen kids came barreling at me. "Tío Danny!" Mateo was the fastest, and I scooped him up and gave him a hug. He was eight, and struggling with math. I'd been tutoring him for the past month while his mother worked on her English and tried to finish getting her GED. I gave hugs to the other kids as they crowded around, tugging on my slacks, and my heart felt ten times lighter.

I loved kids; I really did. I just couldn't be responsible for one of my own. Jennifer understood why, but I'd never been able to explain it to Ari.

Because then I'd have to tell her everything. And then she'd never see me the same way again.

And the last thing I wanted was to be fucking pitied.

"Tío, I want to show you something," Mateo said, tugging on my hand. I followed him into the kids' playroom and over to a cinder block wall plastered in hand-drawn pictures. He pointed to one of a tropical island sunset. "I drew this for you while you were in Tahiti. That's what it looked like, right?"

I gave him a grin and ruffled his hair. "Exactly." I pointed to the pinks and oranges he'd added to the sunset. "The colors are perfect."

He beamed up at me. "I looked at pictures on Mami's phone so I could get it right."

"You're going to be a great artist someday if you keep working hard at it."

Mateo loved to draw; he'd filled a dozen sketchbooks that I'd bought him and worn a set of pastels down to nubs. I'd have to pick him up another set soon.

Crouching down so we were eye to eye, I said, "Do you know where Tía Jenny is?"

He pointed to Admissions. "A new *mamá* and *bebé* came in an hour ago."

I patted him on the shoulder. "*Gracias*. I'll be back in a little bit. I need to ask her something."

"We'll work on my math homework?"

"Of course."

Another smile. "*Bueno*. Mamá just shakes her head when I ask."

She wasn't the only parent who didn't get the "new math." Thank God I'd always been good with numbers.

I headed over to Admissions and got lucky. Jennifer was just escorting a thin girl, maybe sixteen, out of her office. The girl was carrying a baby that couldn't have been more than a few weeks old. The girl looked tired, her eyelids red and puffy from crying. One of her eyes was black and blue, and I had to force myself not to show my anger. As justified as it was, it just made the women and children uncomfortable and reminded many of them of the angry, abusive men in their lives. Men who were supposed to care for them. Shelter them. Keep them safe.

Not beat them and abandon them.

Not abuse them. Not hurt them in ways no one should ever be hurt.

I pasted on a smile, tried to lower my shoulders, unclench my fists, and make myself as nonthreatening as possible. I must not have been that successful, because she turned away and Jennifer motioned me into her office. "Give me a sec."

I went in and took a seat, and Jennifer joined me minutes later, carrying two fresh cups of coffee. I took the cup, my eyes meeting hers, and she didn't even finish closing the door before she said, "Spill it. Something's bothering you. Something big."

I took a sip of the coffee. They made it strong and sweet here too, but it wasn't like Javi's special brew. Nothing was. "You always could tell when I've got something on my mind."

"You got a little too upset when you saw Teresa's injury."

I rubbed a hand over my face. "I was trying not to."

"I know." Jennifer set her cup down and leaned forward on crossed arms, her short pixie-cut blonde hair haloed by the sunlight streaming in behind her. "Maybe this place is too much for you sometimes. Hitting a little too close to home."

"Maybe. But sometimes this place is what gets me out of bed in the morning."

She picked up a paper clip and started bending it into a square. "So, what's bugging you? Didn't two weeks in Tahiti bliss you out?"

I snorted. "You'd think it would, but…" I paused, trying to figure out how much I could reveal. "Let's just say that two of the men there, two long-time friends, finally came to terms with their feelings for each other *and* the woman they're both in love with."

Her eyes grew round. "Are you saying it was Dev and Rod from King's Cross? They're lovers?"

I shook my head. "I can neither deny nor confirm that. I signed an NDA."

"Tease." She took another sip of her coffee. "So, two guys and a girl, huh?"

"Yep." I tried to relax, tried to act like this was all casual, just another day in my life.

"Hmm. After that whole thing with Paige and Riley and Carter, I would have thought that would be the one and only triad I'd ever hear of in real life."

"Me too."

A glint came into her eye. "And it's given you thoughts?"

I set my cup on the edge of her desk. "I hired someone last night. And it didn't fucking work."

She straightened, her brow wrinkling in concern. "Did you have a flashback?"

"No." I could hardly look at her. "I mean… it barely took the edge off. And then I was in this hour-long meeting with Ari and Javi today, and all I could think about was sex. With both of them."

She shrugged. "Well, they're both stunning. I don't even get hot for guys, but Javi…" She let out a low whistle. "Gorgeous *and* nice as hell. He could almost convert me to the other team."

I let out a sigh. "And I have to work with him every day. It's driving me crazy. They both are." I finally got to the point. "The two of them could barely keep their eyes off each other this morning. I think something happened between them."

Jennifer raised a brow. "Something?"

"It was Ari's birthday yesterday. She turned twenty-nine. It had to be hard for her. She had this whole life plan laid out: married by twenty-three, two or three kids by twenty-eight, loads of grandkids by the time she was sixty. And I fucked up her plan."

"So you think she and Javi hooked up?"

I met her gaze. "I'm not sure, but they both had that just-got-laid look about them. And they were just… attuned to each other, you know?"

"Assuming you're right about that, how does it make you feel?"

"Part of me wants to be furious. I still love her. I always will."

"And the other part of you?"

Butterflies swooped around my stomach, and I had to take a deep breath before I could speak. "That part of me wants to be part of it."

A corner of her mouth turned up. "Greedy little shit, aren't you?"

I grinned back at her, then I sobered, my gut knotting up. "But even if they wanted to… I just *can't*."

"Not even with Javi?"

I shook my head, pressing my lips together. "It's not possible."

She reached across the desk to me, and I took her outstretched hands. They were strong and calloused, and she squeezed my fingers reassuringly. "You're tougher than you think. And you've come a long way. But what you really need is professional counseling." She gave me a hopeful look. "Maybe you'll take my advice this time?"

The cramping in my gut intensified. "There's no point to it. It's not like I was good for Arianna anyway."

"Don't do that. Don't put yourself down."

"Well, it's true. I've brought her nothing but unhappiness. She should be happy, and I know Javi will treat her right."

Jennifer squeezed my fingers again. "You deserve happiness too. You pour all this energy into helping other people. When are you going to help yourself?"

I knew she was right. I knew it, but damn it, I was afraid of what would happen if I opened up that box I kept tightly locked inside myself. Would I be able to hold myself together anymore? Or would I just fly apart?

"Look at me," she said. When I did, she continued. "You know they both love you. The three of you… it's not out of the realm of possibility."

A lump crowded my throat. It was, as long as I couldn't fix myself.

And how the hell was I going to do that when the thought of telling someone made me want to vomit? How would I live with the shame of what I'd done?

But how long could I continue to hide from my demons? How long could I continue to let them rule my life before they destroyed every last bit of hope I had left?

JAVIER

"Wee! Again, Tío Javi. Again!" Tomás, my sister Clarita's youngest, squealed as I raced down the hallway, holding him above my head like a small airplane.

Elisa stomped her small foot and placed her hands on her hips. "No! It's my turn, Tío Javi." Two years older than Tomás, Elisa was the spitting image of her mother. Tomás had inherited his father's joyful spirit, though hopefully not his work ethic. Luis was a good father, but not a good provider, which was one of the many reasons he and Clarita were now divorced.

I set Tomás down and picked Elisa up.

"I swear to God, you're as young as they are," Clarita said, sticking her head out of her bedroom. "Come in here and help me get ready."

"But Mamá—" the children grumbled.

She rolled her eyes, but her mouth quirked as she tried to hide a grin. "Ten minutes. That's all I need. Then he's all yours."

"Fine." Elisa grabbed Tomás's hand. "Let's go watch TV until they're done."

I laughed as I joined Clarita in her room. "You're going to have your hands full with that one."

"Tell me about it. She tried to reorganize the pantry today. Said I was doing it all wrong."

My grin widened. "Not by size then?"

Clarita shook her head. "Apparently, it would be easier to find what we need if we stored everything by type. All the beans together, all the spices together, all the cereal together. You get the picture."

I rubbed my jaw. My sister was describing my own cupboards. "Well, she's not—"

Clarita held up her hand. "Stuff it. I don't want to hear how your system is better than mine. You've brainwashed my child. What will it be next, clothing by color?"

I looked away and smothered a grin. Little Elisa had stood spell-bound in the doorway to my closet the last time she and Tomás had been over.

"Anyway"—Clarita waved the entire subject away with a flip of her wrist—"I don't want to talk about that. Tell me how you're doing."

"Work's good. I think having Sky as a junior partner will be good for us."

Clarita nodded. "I'm glad to hear that Total Indulgence is expanding. But that's not what I was asking. How are *you*?"

I shrugged. "I'm fine." My ex, Sam, had taken a while to move all his belongings out of my home, but it was done now, and I was happy having my space back.

"You know what I don't get?"

"No, but I'm sure you're going to tell me."

"*¡Ay, chiquito*!" She boxed me lightly on the back of the head. "Why did you leave Sam? He was perfect for you. Cooking and cleaning. *Dios mío,* I will miss that potato stew of his."

I leaned against the wall and stared out the window. It was fall, but you couldn't really tell. Sometimes I wished I lived some place where the leaves changed colors. Then I thought about snow and cold, and I quickly changed my mind. "I already have a maid."

"Pfft. You're acting like a donkey's ass. The man was head over heels in love with you. I bet it broke his heart when you asked him to leave."

Sam had been upset, understandably so. We'd been living together for almost a year, but we both knew I could never give him what he truly wanted. My heart belonged to someone else, two someones. It always had. I sighed. "You know how conservative Mamá and Papá are. It wasn't fair for me to impose being closeted on him forever. If I came out, it would kill them. They'd never accept my being in a relationship with a man."

"Then find yourself a woman," she said, grinning cheekily. "Isn't that one of the bennies of being bisexual?"

Her comment and the look on her face had me cracking up. She walked up to me and bumped my hip with hers. "Zip me up, Romeo."

She turned and I dutifully closed the zipper at the back of her dress. "I slept with Arianna," I said.

Spinning around, eyes wide, she gawped. Then she smiled. "Finally!"

"Finally?" I sputtered. "What do you mean, finally?" I'd never shared my feelings for Arianna with anyone, especially not my sister.

She slapped a hand to her forehead. "*Ay, caramba*. Men can be so *estupido* sometimes. That poor girl has been in love with you forever."

No she hadn't. She'd been with Daniel for years, almost a decade.

I opened my mouth to protest, but Clarita's narrowed glare shut me down. "And don't think I missed those googly eyes you turn her way every time you're near her."

"You're crazy. *Loca*." I palpated her head. "Did you hit yourself at work today?"

She shoved my hands away but her smile never slipped. "Mamá and Papá will be ecstatic."

"Jesus." I rubbed my forehead. "Don't have us walking down the aisle just yet. I'm not sure she's completely over Daniel."

Clarita slipped a high-heeled shoe on her foot. She looked up at me, holding my stare. "And are you?"

"Wha—am I what?"

"Are you over Daniel?" She *tsk*ed. "Did you think you were fooling anyone with all that 'he's my best friend' BS?"

"Hey. He *is* my best friend."

"One you wish was so much more."

I focused on adjusting the strap of her dress so it lay flat on her shoulder.

"Javi?" she said, her tone gentle. "You look at him the way you look at her."

I closed my eyes. "Doesn't matter how I feel. It can never be."

When my eyes darted to her, she smiled softly with more than a touch of pity. "Still you wish it could."

Kicking off the heels, she rummaged through her shoes and selected a pair of sleek pumps. "If you could have Arianna or Daniel, which would it be?"

I groaned. How could I possibly choose?

She grinned. "I see. You'd have them both."

"Who wouldn't?" I chuckled. "But even if Daniel weren't straight, I couldn't. It would kill our parents. They'd never accept me with a man, and they'd never understand a threesome."

Clarita shrugged. "You can't live your life for other people. If I didn't go against our parents sometimes, I'd still be married to Luis."

I took the necklace from her hands and slipped it over her head. "They still refer to him as your husband."

"Yes." She sighed. "Our civil divorce is not recognized by the church or by our parents. If I ever have a boyfriend, they'll probably push for me to be excommunicated on the grounds of adultery."

I grimaced. "They aren't that bad."

Our eyes met, and we both laughed. "Yes, they are," we said at the same time.

I pulled her into my arms and hugged her. "I love you. Scarlet letter and all."

She pushed me away with her hands on my chest and a big grin on her face. She went back to the closet and retrieved the little velvet clutch I'd given her last Christmas. "Whatever you do or don't do with Arianna, don't, for all that's holy, get her pregnant until she has a ring on her finger. Our parents will accept a lot, but not that."

Pregnant. The blood drained from my head, and I was grateful she was packing her clutch and didn't see my reaction. Was Arianna even now pregnant? We'd only been together twice last night, but that could be all it took. I'd wanted that so much the night of her birthday. I'd wanted her. Wanted a life with her. But did I want a family with her if it meant giving up Daniel? I'd thought I was ready. Fifteen years of pining after a straight best friend was enough for anyone.

Except what about that look he'd given me today as he was leaving TI? Those beautiful blue eyes had been filled with heat and passion. But what did it mean? If Daniel suspected Arianna and I had taken our relationship to the next level, wouldn't he have glared at me? Wouldn't his eyes have been filled with hate and anger?

Maybe the look had meant something else. Something I'd been wanting forever.

Was Daniel finally ready to acknowledge the incredible chemistry that had always existed between us? The chemistry that went far beyond what was normal between friends, even "best buds." That long-ago trip to Cancun our freshman year had cemented it for me. Even though we'd both had girls with us, even though we'd both been balls-deep into them, it had felt as though we were the only two people in the room. His eyes had been as drawn to me as mine to him. They'd been hot and lust-filled. His cock had been hard for me. I knew it as surely as I knew my own name.

But then we'd kissed, and he'd panicked.

When he'd finally returned to our room the next morning, he'd acted as though the previous night had never happened. A couple times I'd tried to broach the subject. His face would tighten, and his eyes would get that dead look. Then after a few moments, the look would go away, and he'd continue whatever he'd been doing as if I hadn't said a word.

That look scared me. The possibilities of what could have happened to Daniel to put that it in his eyes scared me. I always wished he'd trust me enough to share, yet he didn't. Then again, it wasn't about me, was it?

After a while, I gave up trying and accepted that if I wanted Daniel in my life, I had to keep things platonic between us.

It had been difficult as hell.

Fuck, it had *been* hell.

And then he'd gone and married Arianna, and my hell had deepened. For five years, every aspect of my life was a reminder of what I didn't have. What I couldn't have. But now I had a chance to have some of it. With Arianna.

Clarita stepped past me. "Come on. Jaime will be here soon to pick me up."

Dutifully, I followed her to the living room and plopped down on the couch between Tomás and Elisa, who were watching a Disney movie I'd seen about ten times with them. I swear they watched it each time I came over.

"The phone number of Chez Antoine is on the fridge along with the pediatrician's number and poison control." She rattled off a few more instructions before I stopped her.

"Clarita, how many times a week do I babysit for you?"

She looked contrite. "One or two."

"And has anything ever happened that I couldn't handle?"

"No. I'm being a mother hen, and you're a wonderful brother. The best."

I smiled at that. I loved staying with my niece and nephew, so it wasn't a hardship. "Federico would be there for you too if he didn't have his hands full with Violeta." My little brother and his wife were expecting their first child in a couple months.

"She is rather high-maintenance, isn't she?"

"Tío Javier, what's high-maintenance?" Tomás asked, snuggling into my side.

I ruffled his hair. "Nothing you need to worry about, *niño*."

"It means Tía Violeta is a pain in the ass," Elisa said with an all-knowing tone.

"Elisa!" Clarita said. Her eyes drilled into me. "Where did you hear such a thing?"

Elisa glanced at me, a guilty look in her eyes. "Um… someone at school said it."

I winked conspiratorially, then gave Clarita my best smile. We weren't fooling anyone, least of all Clarita.

"Well, don't say it again," she huffed.

There was a honk outside. Her face brightened. "Jaime's here. Okay, be good for Tío Javi," she said, giving the kids a kiss on the cheek. Then she mock-glared at me. "And you be good too."

I bussed her cheek. "Always."

With a last wave, she left the house. I hugged the children to me and settled in to watch the movie. That's when it hit me: I might be a father soon. In nine months, I could have a child of my own. Arianna might be my wife. We might have a home together. A family.

Everything I'd always wanted could be mine in a just a few months.

Wow.

But Arianna and Daniel were going to Sonoma together. To a marriage-counseling retreat.

Ice filled my veins. What if they got back together? No. I couldn't even imagine it. Maybe I was a shit for going after Arianna, maybe it was a breach of the bro-code to go after your best friend's ex-wife, but Arianna had been my friend well before she'd met Daniel. Besides, he'd made it abundantly clear with the divorce that he didn't want to be married to her anymore. He didn't want children, and she did. I did.

I could make Arianna happy. At least two of us three should be happy.

God. I stifled a groan. I couldn't even think that without feeling guilty as fuck. I loved Daniel. I wanted him to be happy.

Even if it meant giving up Arianna?

I closed my eyes and pictured how she'd looked in bed next to me. Her long black hair fanned over the white pillow. Her slender leg curled around mine. The smile on her face as she'd pressed her lips to mine. No. I couldn't give her up this time. I wouldn't. Not without a fight.

Chapter 3

ARIANNA

I hadn't been alone with Daniel for this long since our divorce. Having him with me all day—through the long flight from Miami to Sonoma, and now the drive in our rental car—I was overly aware of him. How amazing he smelled, how comforting and familiar and distracting his presence was.

I'd been feeling shitty all day—headachy, sore, kind of crampy, like maybe my period was starting. Or maybe I was coming down with something. Of course, Daniel noticed right off, and he'd slipped into solicitous husband mode—taking care of everything, making sure I was as comfortable as possible, being so damn caring it made my throat ache and my eyes sting.

This would be so much easier if he was a proper asshole about our divorce. But he wasn't. He never had been. He'd just cleared out of my life as quickly as possible, hadn't even fought my ridiculous divorce demand for the house outright. He'd just nodded and signed the papers.

And he'd never explained why. Why he'd left. Why he'd said he couldn't do "this" anymore. Why he couldn't be my husband anymore.

Why he didn't love me anymore.

Except that he clearly did. Didn't he? He still remembered everything about me—how I liked my coffee, my favorite pastry at Starbucks when we'd gotten breakfast at the airport, the way I liked to curl into the window seat with two pillows and a blanket and make a little nest.

Daniel was so damn confusing. And so fucking sexy. All day I'd practically ached with the desire to touch him. Which was really weird, because I also longed to touch Javier. Aside from the night of my birthday, Javi and I had had only one quick tryst before I'd left, mainly because I'd done nothing but work nonstop on redoing this retreat, but damn it, now that I finally had him, I wanted more Javi. A lot more Javi.

It was going to be two very long weeks before I saw him again.

Two very long weeks with Daniel.

We pulled off the main road and turned onto the private gravel drive for Montero Vineyards. Daniel had rented us a Lexus—of course—and for a moment, it felt like nothing had changed, like we were out for a country drive or something, or off for a naughty weekend…

Could I stop thinking about sex for five damn minutes? Javi had woken up my libido, put it into overdrive, actually, and now I couldn't seem to stop my mind from wandering to sex. With Javi. With Daniel. With both of them…

Stop, chica. Just stop!

"What?" Daniel asked as he pulled up in front of the stone and timber façade of the main building.

"Nothing." Fuck, was I mumbling to myself out loud now? I really needed to get a grip.

Daniel put the car in park and set his hand on my shoulder. "Ari, I know having me along is difficult. I'll do my best to placate Greta tomorrow, and hopefully I'll be out of your hair in a couple days."

I nodded, but strangely my stomach sank at the idea of him leaving. "It's really not a problem." I reached up and touched his fingers. "You've been great today."

He squeezed my shoulder gently. "It's the least I owe you."

I stiffened. *Owe me?* I was just an obligation? Before I could open my mouth, he squeezed my shoulder again and spoke. "That came out wrong. What I mean is…" He trailed off, and I looked at him. It was odd seeing him struggle for the right words. Daniel was so good with them, so good at selling people on him, on the company, so good at knowing the exact right thing to say to get someone to trust him.

To get me to love him.

He cleared his throat. "What I mean is that I *want* to do those things for you. I always have. I always will. Not being your husband… it's really hard for me. I don't know how to turn that off." He paused. "I'm not sure I want to."

What the…? "What are you saying?" The words flew out of my mouth, my tone somewhere between breathless anticipation and irritation.

He shrugged and let go of my shoulder, and I missed the contact immediately. "I don't know. I don't know a damn thing when it comes to you, Arianna."

I stared at him openmouthed, then threw up my hands. "Then that makes two of us. The divorce was *your* idea."

"I know." He cleared his throat again and looked down at his lap.

He looked so… lost. I touched his hand and softened my voice. "Can you tell me why? Because you don't seem like you want us to be divorced."

He opened his mouth, and I waited, the moment stretching out as he continued to say nothing.

"Daniel?"

A movement in my peripheral vision caught my attention. My uncle, Manuel Montero, was coming out to greet us. *Bad timing, Tío!*

"We'd better say hi to Manuel," Daniel finally said, and the tension between us broke.

"I'm not letting this go, Daniel."

He sighed and reached for the door handle. "Later."

"I'll hold you to it."

He got out of the car and was opening my door before I'd finished gathering my purse and unbuckling my seatbelt. He offered me a hand out of the car, and I took it, not caring that I shouldn't. That I shouldn't want to. That I shouldn't encourage anymore confusion between us. And when his hand descended to the small of my back afterward, it felt right. Despite everything.

We stepped forward to greet Manuel, my mother's older brother. He was looking quite fit and younger than his fifty-five years, his dark hair only a little grayer than when I'd seen him last. The California life must be agreeing with him.

"Arianna, *cariña*, so good to see you!" he said, sweeping me into a bear hug.

When he released me, I reached up and rubbed his goatee. "This is new."

He stroked his well-trimmed mustache and goatee. "Sofia thought it would suit me for the new promotional photos for the website." His eyes twinkled, and I laughed.

"It does. You'll have single women flocking here."

His eyebrows wagged. "Óscar tells me I'll appeal to all the guys in San Francisco looking to hook up with a *papi chulo*."

I burst into laughter, especially at the baffled look on Daniel's face. "Sofia's brother Óscar is gay," I said.

"Oh." Daniel smiled, but it was tight for some odd reason. And then I realized Manuel hadn't even looked at him.

Sighing inwardly, I touched Daniel's shoulder. "You remember Daniel," I said to Manuel.

He shook Daniel's hand, his smile as tight as Daniel's. "I didn't expect to see you."

"I mentioned it to Tía Sofía," I said.

"She told me you were bringing someone. I thought it would be Javi."

Dios mío. Manuel hadn't exactly approved of Daniel when we'd married, and since the divorce, his estimation of Daniel had only gone down.

"Well, I should be here only a few days," Daniel said. "Greta Lindstrom asked for me personally after the change in plans."

Manuel rolled his eyes. "Greta. She's already *here*. We weren't expecting her until tomorrow morning when the rest of the ECC staff were supposed to arrive."

"She's here?" I asked.

He nodded. "You'll have your hands full with that one," he murmured.

"Fuck," I whispered. I'd wanted time to settle in and double-check things before I had to deal with her.

"I'll get our bags," Daniel said, starting for the car.

"Pull around back," Manuel called to him. "You can bring the bags in through the French doors off the terrace." He put a hand on my shoulder and steered me inside. "Sofía and Luciana will be so happy to see you."

We stepped inside the stone and timber great room that formed the lobby of the hotel portion of the vineyard. Sofía, my cousin Luciana, her husband, Brad, and their boys, Felipe, who was twelve, and Lucas, who was ten, were setting up furniture and hanging pictures and placing plants and other knickknacks around the lobby.

"We just got the new furniture and such delivered today. Had to beg and plead to get it early," Manuel said.

I reached out and squeezed his hand. "*Muchas gracias,* Tío, for making this possible. I don't know what I would have done without you."

He gave me a weary smile. "You're family, Ari, and for family, nothing is too much."

A tall blonde with creamy white skin rose from a table by the French doors leading out to the back terrace. I recognized her right away from the ECC website. Greta Lindstrom was even prettier in person, her willowy figure one I envied. She could have walked a runway and not looked out of place; the beige halter dress she wore flowed around her legs like it loved her.

But judging by the grimace on her face, she didn't love me. "Arianna Rodriguez?" she asked when she reached me.

I nodded and held out my hand. "Nice to meet you, Ms. Lindstrom."

She took my hand and shook it quickly, flicking a glance at Manuel. "Mr. Montero tells me you'll be ready for everyone tomorrow." Her tone expressed how dubious she thought that was.

"As I explained, the hotel is opening early for us. The pool and a few other amenities are still being worked on, but the Monteros are ready for our guests."

Greta crossed her arms and sniffed. "Our couples are used to five-star accommodations. That's what you promised." She looked around and waved a hand in the air. "Not this 'pardon our dust' nonsense."

Manuel stiffened beside me. "We'll be ready," he said. "As you'll recall, you weren't expected until tomorrow."

I placed a hand on his forearm and turned to Greta. "When Manuel Montero makes a promise, you can take it to the bank," I said. "By the time the couples arrive tomorrow evening, everything will be perfect."

"Except the pool. *And* the gym," Greta said. "Those are both very important to our couples."

"And they'll be ready in two to three days," Manuel snapped.

Greta shook her head. "Looked to me like two to three weeks."

What did this woman want? I'd managed to pull a secluded high-end location out of my ass at the last possible second. And all because someone at her damn company couldn't keep their yap shut—

I opened my mouth to give her a refresher on what we'd managed to accomplish when I felt Daniel's familiar presence by my side, his warm hand on the small of my back as he stuck out a hand for Greta to shake. "Good to see you again, Greta," he said, his voice smooth and even, and much calmer than mine would have been.

She took his hand, holding onto it far longer than she'd held mine. "I'm glad you're here, Daniel. I was just telling Ms. Rodriguez my concerns about the venue."

Daniel took his hand from my lower back and placed it atop Greta's, sandwiching her delicate fingers between his palms. "Everything is under control, Greta. I have full faith in the Montero family. They are very good at what they do. We wouldn't have moved the retreat here otherwise."

She took in a breath and gave him a tiny smile. "I suppose I'll have to trust you."

She'll trust Daniel, but not me? I wanted to light into her, but I needed to keep a lid on things. ECC could be worth a lot of money to TI in the future. But not if I let my temper loose.

And since when did Daniel think I couldn't handle a client on my own?

He steered Greta toward the French doors. "Have you seen the grounds? They're exquisite."

She shook her head. "I've been waiting for you to arrive."

"Let's take a look, then, shall we?" he said. "I just need a quick moment with Arianna first."

He left her by the door and came back to me. "What the fuck, Daniel?" I whispered. "I can manage her."

He leaned down and spoke in my ear, his warm breath washing over my neck and making me too aware of him again. "Please let me do this for you. You've been working on this day and night, and I know you're not feeling great." He gestured to the staircase that led up to the rooms. "You could lie down for a while. Might help that headache."

Well… damn. My anger drained away as quickly as it had risen. "Thank you."

"I'm here to help, Ari. You and the family have pulled off a minor miracle. Let me do my part to smooth things over." He gave me that dazzling Daniel King smile, the one that had charmed my panties off when I'd turned eighteen and he'd felt I was fair game, not just Javi's bestie. The smile that still did fluttery things to my insides. Then he was off and escorting my Swedish nemesis outside, turning that same smile Greta's way, and the butterflies in my stomach turned to razorblades.

Fuck. I was still hung up on my ex-husband. While I was sleeping with his best friend behind his back. I had no right to be jealous of Greta. I had no right to expect an iota of Daniel's attention.

And I certainly had no business feeling this way when I also ached for Javier.

I hadn't been this confused since I was a lovesick teenager pining for Javi, the guy who loved me but who I could never have.

What a mess.

Manuel, Sofía, and Luciana descended on me, Sofía and Luciana enfolding me in warm, tight hugs, and I forced myself to shift focus. I could worry about my screwed-up love life later.

"I'm so happy to see you," I said to them both. I looked around. "I can't thank you enough for all you've done. You really saved my bacon."

Luciana, a few years older than me but looking like she could be my sister, laughed. "Well, you should thank that gorgeous ex of yours for saving us all from Grumpy Greta."

I snorted and suppressed a laugh. "He's good at that sort of thing."

Sofía smiled at me, but I could see the concern in her eyes. "Tell me, *cariña*, are you and Daniel back together?"

I shook my head. "No. He's just here to help."

Sofía gave me a skeptical look, but it was Manuel who said, "I hope that's all he's here for. That man was never good for you. You should have been with Javier in the first place. He's a good man."

"He is." I wanted to tell them, but it was too soon. Besides, Javi and I had to figure out how to tell Daniel first.

"You look tired," Sofía said, touching my cheek. "Want to rest up after the plane? Your room is ready upstairs."

I took in the disarray around us, Brad and the boys scrambling around, trying various layouts of the lobby chairs and sofas. "I'm fine.

What can I do to help?"

Sofia gave me a grateful smile. "Well, we could use some help with the decorating and washing up all the new china and glasses that were delivered."

I took off the linen blazer I'd worn over my dress and draped it across my suitcases sitting by the back door. "I'm at your disposal. Point me where you want me."

I glanced out the French doors, catching a glimpse of Daniel and the Swedish harpy walking into the vineyard. She was leaning into him and laughing, and again I felt those razorblades in my stomach.

This was going to be a very long two weeks indeed.

DANIEL

"*Dios*, it's beautiful here."

Arianna and I were standing in one of the most beautiful spots on earth, Point Reyes, the vast Pacific Ocean at our feet, and all I could see was her.

"Makes you realize how very small we are," I said. Small and insignificant.

Ari was still trying to put together an exciting agenda for ECC and its clients. I kept trying to reassure her, but it was obvious she wasn't satisfied with what she'd come up with. She'd asked to drive out here to see if Point Reyes and its historic lighthouse would be a good day trip from the winery.

"What do you think?" She turned to me, a happy look on her face. "It took us less than two hours to drive out here, which is reasonable. We could add a stop midway out here and another on the way back to visit one of those cute little villages we passed."

I hated to disappoint her, but it was inevitable. I scratched my chin.

"What?" she said, attuned to me. "You hate it."

"I don't hate it. But… think about who we'd be bringing here."

"Shit. You're right. It's too unsecure here. Damn it."

"Let's sit for a bit and enjoy the view," I said, my eyes on her. As though of its own volition, my hand went to the small of her back. It was familiar and unsettling to touch her like that, to feel her heat against my palm. Jesus. I still wanted her so much.

I directed her to a bench, adjusting my slacks, which had gotten much too tight in the crotch. We sat, close. I cleared my throat. "What other ideas did you have?" If nothing else, I could help her with creating the activity schedule and enjoy her company while I did it.

"I was thinking maybe a kayaking and ziplining adventure on the Russian River. Greta said a high-adrenaline adventure would test the couples and maybe bring out some strong emotions for the counselors to work with." She waved a finely manicured hand and shrugged. "I don't know."

Greta had explained to us that the tour component of the retreat had to feed into experiences that would complement the therapy the couples were undergoing. "That could work. But do we know if everyone can swim? High adrenaline is one thing; outright terror is another."

"You're right." She rubbed at her temple. "My ideas suck."

"Still not feeling well?"

She shot me a wry look. "Nothing a good night's sleep won't cure."

Or a good fuck. It had been her go-to headache remedy in the past. Too bad we couldn't indulge again. Unable to resist the lure of her glistening locks, I reached out and slid the strands through my fingers. "Don't undervalue yourself. I certainly don't."

Her cheeks bloomed and she ducked her head. "Daniel."

"What about doing the Tough Mudder obstacle course? There's one right in Sonoma. They'd have to work in teams, and no one needs to know how to swim, and fear of heights wouldn't be an issue."

Her gorgeous brown eyes lit up. "Yes! And we could rent it out completely, so security would be easy to implement."

My heart warmed when I saw the excitement in her eyes. When we'd been together, I'd spent hours coming up with ways to draw that look from her. It seemed the divorce hadn't changed much in that regard.

We talked a while longer, the ocean spread out before us, and sorted out the last-minute details of the itinerary. Ari pulled me into a hug, and when I felt the hard points of her nipples against my chest, I had to grit my teeth to hold in a moan. Thank God she sat back quickly, her face glowing as she spoke. "Yes, this is perfect. We've got the Tough Mudder, horseback riding, a couples cooking lesson, hiking the Armstrong Redwood reserve, racetrack driving, and the safari trip. We've hit every one of Greta's 'experiential' requirements."

I couldn't keep my eyes off her. I loved seeing the tension lift from her, glad that I could help in some small way. "I knew you could do it."

"This is all going to be very expensive though." A cute little frown appeared between her perfectly shaped brows. I wanted to kiss it away. "Javi already said we'd be underwater on this adventure, and that was before all these extra expenses."

I stretched my arm along the top of the bench, my hand naturally going to her shoulder. Her breath hitched, and my cock jumped at the sound. "Don't worry about the money. If this goes well, it will open up a very lucrative business for us."

"Assuming Greta wants to hire us again."

I shook my head. "Greta or some other group, it doesn't matter. We'll have proved that not only can we can handle this type of event, but we can also offer something with the tour and adventures that no other company does."

"Talk about pressure," she said with a groan.

"No pressure." I slipped my fingers under her hair and massaged her neck.

She stiffened at my touch. "What are you doing?"

"Trying to relax you. I hate seeing you so wound up." I continued my massage. She dropped her head, and I felt her muscles soften. "That's it," I murmured.

"Tell me about Tahiti," she said. "How beautiful was it?"

My eyes caressed her slender neck, her smooth golden skin. "I prefer the current view," I said, my voice hoarse.

I moved my hands down to her left shoulder, digging my fingers into her tense muscles. "I'm sorry I missed your birthday." My hands went to her other shoulder, and I barely resisted the urge to pull her into my arms, to feel her body against mine, her breasts against my chest. Fuck. "I hope you and Javi had a good time."

Her gaze shot to mine, then she quickly turned her head away, but not before I spotted her flushed face. "Speaking of birthdays, didn't you celebrate Sky's in Tahiti? Vanessa said the guys from King's Cross sang a few songs a capella for her. That must have been cool."

Why was she trying to change the subject? "Ari?"

I waited for her to face me. When she continued to stare out at that ocean, I gently took her chin in my palm and turned her head. "What's going on? You seem uncomfortable about something. I thought we were past that."

"It's nothing." Her smile was as fake as plastic flowers. "I'm stressed out, that's all. This whole thing has gone to shit, and I feel like it's my fault. Greta thinks I'm incompetent."

"Hey, I brought in the business. I'm responsible for it. Things got a bit out of control in Tahiti, but it worked out in the end. This will work out too; you'll see." I took her hand with my free one and laid our clasped hands on my thigh. "I'm here to help you. You focus on the activities; I'll manage Greta."

Arianna grinned. "I'm sure you will."

"What do you mean by that?"

"Oh come on, Daniel. Have you seen the way she looks at you?"

"It's hard to notice anyone else when you're in the room."

"Bullshit." Arianna laughed. "I know how charmed you are by that

Swedish accent."

I deserved that, but I couldn't deny it hurt. "I know you won't believe this, but you're everything I ever wanted."

Her smile faded, and sadness filled her gaze. "I don't understand why we're divorced then."

I closed my eyes. "I don't understand it either." I opened my eyes and brought our clasped hands to my mouth, placing a light kiss on her knuckles. "I know this last year has been really tough for both of us."

She pressed her lips together in that way she did when she got emotional.

This time I did give in to the urge and pulled her shoulder against my chest. "I know we can't go back in time, but I'd really like for us to get back to how we used to be… how we used to just get along. Can we try?"

"What exactly are you saying, Daniel?"

"Hell, I don't know. I just know I can't keep going the way things are. It's too fucking hard."

She blew out a breath. "I don't like how things have been going either. We don't talk anymore unless it's about work."

And that was all my fault. I wanted to tell her what was wrong. Share with her what had happened to me, tell her about the escorts, about why I needed them. But what good would it do? She'd never understand why I'd had to betray our marriage vows, why I could never have children with her or anyone else. Admitting to the real reasons I'd left her would make me look weak in front of her, and that was one thing I'd never do. That didn't change the fact that my bed, my home, hell, my life—it was all so empty without my wife. Without Arianna. "I miss talking to you too." So damn much.

She rested her head on my shoulder. "How do we do this?"

I inhaled the scent of her hair, wishing I could bury my face in it. "Baby steps?"

"Okay. Let's give it a try."

JAVIER

Arianna and Daniel had been gone for less than a day, and the office already felt empty without them. And I'd pretty much had a permanent semi since I'd slept with Ari the night of her birthday. The quickie we'd worked in before she'd left had done nothing to quell my hunger for her. She was intoxicating to me in a way that no one else but Daniel had ever approached.

And now the two of them were off in California together. For two weeks.

I'd seen the way he still looked at her. The way she still looked at him. And though I didn't doubt her affection for me, part of me kept whispering that she was settling for me. If she couldn't have Daniel, I was the next best thing, right?

And he was there, with her.

While I was three thousand miles away.

Get over yourself, cabrón, and call your woman.

I dialed her number; it was around eight PM in California. She picked up instantly, her voice purring my name and making my semi a full hard-on in seconds.

"I've missed you, *corazón*," I said, rising and locking my office door. I sat down behind my desk and hit the button on the remote to darken my office windows. Just in case I couldn't stop myself from sneaking a hand into my pants.

"I've missed you too, *papi chulo*."

I smiled. *Papi chulo.* I suppose it fit, even if after all these years I sometimes forgot that I wasn't the chubby math nerd I used to be. Now I was a well-toned math nerd. "How are things going?"

"Daniel is being a bit weird."

I sat up in my chair. "Weird how? Do you think he knows?"

"I'm not sure what's going on with him. He was…" She paused, then said, "He was kind of flirting with me today. He hasn't been like that in years."

A stone formed in the pit of my stomach. Fuck. "You think he wants to get back together with you?"

"I don't know."

"Do you want to get back with him?" I winced. *Real cool, cabrón.*

"Nothing's changed, Javi. I still don't know why he left me."

"But you still love him."

She sighed into the phone. "I'm not going to lie to you, Javi. I do love him. I'm sure I always will. But that has nothing to do with anything."

The stone in my gut grew heavier. Well, since I'd already blown it in the staying-cool department, might as well go for broke. "So, where does that leave me?"

She chuckled. "I'm sorry, Javi. I'm an idiot. You know I love you too, right? Very much."

"Like a best friend."

"No. *Not* like a best friend. Not like a best friend at all. And you'd know that if you could see that dream you starred in while I was on the plane."

I liked where this was going, and my gut loosened up. I dropped a hand to my crotch, my fingers grazing the hard ridge of my cock through my slacks. "Tell me what I was doing in this dream."

"You were with me, on the plane. I was curled up under a blanket, asleep, but you kept touching me, under the blanket, kept making me moan."

I unzipped my slacks and took out my cock. "Did the other passengers notice?"

"Mmm-hmm." She purred the sound. "And then you suggested I join the Mile High Club with you."

"Did we meet in the bathroom?"

"Mmm-hmm." That purr again. "You tore off my clothes and set me on the sink. And then…" Her voice trailed off.

"Are you naked, Ari? Are you touching yourself, *corazón*?"

"Mmm-hmm."

"Spread your legs for me," I said, my voice deepening. "Show me that treasure between your thighs."

I heard a rustle of cloth and movement. "I'm showing you."

"You're wet? That pussy is ready for me?"

"Mmm-hmm. Very ready."

Fuck. I wrapped my hand around my cock, picturing her on the bed in the hotel, legs spread wide, her pink pussy glistening.

"Put your fingers inside. Imagine it's me, fucking you."

She moaned in my ear, and my cock twitched in my hand, that throaty sound tightening my balls. She wasn't even with me, and I was practically coming from the sound of her.

"I need you, Javi," she whimpered. "Need you so deep inside me."

"Fuck," I groaned, spreading my pre-cum over the head of my cock, fisting myself so fast and furiously I felt like I was sixteen again, jerking off to the thought of her with me, sucking my cock, or me with my face buried between her legs.

"I need you too, *corazón*. Need your pussy gripping me like a fist." I tightened my hold on my cock, the increase in sensation reminding of when I'd been inside her that first time, the way she'd surprised me by clamping down on me.

"Are you close, *princesa*?" I whispered. "Because I am. So close."

"I am, Javi."

"I'm inside you, *corazón*, fucking you so hard, and you're so damn tight."

"*Dios mío*, Javi. Fuck me. Deeper."

Jesus. I could picture her beneath me, the way her breasts had bobbed up and down the last time we'd fucked, the flush that had risen up her neck into her cheeks as she'd come… "Come for me, Arianna. Come hard."

Her whimpers in my ear took on new urgency, each one deeper and more desperate than the last, my own breathing harsh in my ears. And then I heard her peak, my cock erupting seconds later all over my hand.

"Fuck," I breathed into the phone.

She giggled. "I had no idea you were so naughty, Javi."

"I might be an accountant. That doesn't mean I'm boring."

She laughed, the sound husky. "No, you most definitely are not boring, *mi amor*."

Mi amor. Did she mean that the way I hoped?

I grabbed a wad of tissues off my desk and cleaned up. "When are we going to tell Daniel?"

"We'll tell him when we get back to Miami. The day after."

Two more weeks, then this would be settled.

Or would it? There was no predicting how Daniel would react. Would he be angry enough to destroy TI over it? To ruin our friendship over it?

I had to hope not, but if he was trying to rekindle things with Ari, it wasn't like we could wait forever.

And if I lost TI and Daniel but gained Ari in the process?

Well, that was a trade-off I was willing to make. I'd been on the outside of the two of them for too long, my nose pressed against the glass, and I wasn't going back there. I wasn't going to spend another decade alone.

Still, it couldn't hurt to know what was going on in Daniel's head. I'd call him tomorrow, feel him out a bit.

See if I could soften the blow somehow. If that was even possible.

And if it wasn't?

I had to be prepared for the fallout.

Chapter 4

ARIANNA

I adjusted the bodice of my dress, trying to stuff my swollen and achy breasts into the cups that seemed smaller than usual. Fucking PMS. I hated the bloat and headaches that came with my monthlies. At least the dress I'd brought along for the welcome reception wasn't my usual slim-fit style. Given ECC's clientele, I'd gone with something elegant and understated, thus the black and gray A-line dress and two-inch black heels.

Hearing a knock at the door, I inhaled deeply, then blew out slowly. Daniel and I had agreed to enter the reception together, a show of force for TI and the Monteros. My stomach was jittery, and not just because we'd be toe to toe with some of Hollywood's elite. It was also because of Daniel. The man confused me like no one else.

He was the one who'd walked away from us. Granted I'd given him an ultimatum, but he'd chosen to give up on us. And now? He wanted to get back to how things were before? What did that even mean? I was prepared to work on our friendship. I did miss him. Along with Javi, Daniel had been my best friend, not just my husband.

My early twenties had been filled with fun and laughter, my memories of that time all starring Daniel. But as I'd admitted to Javi last night, nothing had changed. If Daniel wanted more than friendship from me, he wouldn't get it. Not until and not unless he tore down the walls he'd put up between us.

And then there was Javi. He was everything I'd ever dreamed of and more. I wouldn't jeopardize our new relationship for a second chance with Daniel, one that was doomed to fail as spectacularly as the first had. My hand went to my belly. I wanted children, and I could have them with Javi. As far as I knew, Daniel hadn't changed his mind in that regard.

I opened the door and smiled at the man who'd once meant everything to me and who still owned a piece of my heart.

He eyed me up and down and whistled softly. His blue eyes were warm when they met mine, and he smiled. "Beautiful as always."

"You clean up pretty nicely yourself." Daniel looked gorgeous in navy slacks, a light blue shirt, a blazer with thin brown and blue stripes, and a brown tie with light blue squares. His sandy brown hair was thick and perfectly coiffed. I wanted to run my fingers through it, mess it up, so it looked like it did in the morning when he first woke up.

Memories hit me, one after the other. My throat swelled, and I stepped away to grab my purse and to hide the wave of regret, and yes, longing that washed over me. If I'd never issued that final ultimatum about having a baby, would Daniel and I still be together? Would he have relented eventually so that I might even now be pregnant with his—with our—child?

Daniel caught my elbow. "You okay?"

I offered him a wide smile I didn't feel. "Peachy."

"You don't have to go tonight if you aren't feeling well. I'll handle it."

I might not worthy of being your wife and the mother of your children, but I am damn well worthy of being your partner at TI.

Once again, irritation filled me. "This is TI business, Daniel. *My* business."

Even though I knew he was just being solicitous, a part of me couldn't deny that his words made me feel like less. Like I wasn't an essential part of TI, like I was dispensable and disposable. It wasn't what he thought. I knew that. There'd been numerous occasions over the years when I'd proved my worth to both Daniel and Javier, and I was a full partner in the business, just like they were. But still, it was how I felt. And yes, it was only a stupid cocktail party. No one would care if I didn't go. No one except me.

He touched my shoulder. "Hey. I never meant to imply it wasn't your business. What's going on?"

I brushed a strand of hair off my cheek and sighed. "Nothing. I'm sorry."

"Ari," he said, lowering his voice.

"I'm PMSing, okay?" I rolled my eyes. "You know how I get before my period starts."

"Should I run down and get you some chocolate?" He chuckled, eyes twinkling. The bastard.

I shoved him playfully. "Come on. We're going to be late to our own party."

When he angled his elbow out, I entwined my arm with his, and we left my room and headed downstairs. A few minutes later, we walked into the vineyard's newly renovated wine cellar. The underground space was lined with wooden barrels along one wall and tall round tables along the other. At the end was a long bar of dark walnut. The walls were made of exposed stone, and the dim lighting made everything cozy and warm. It was the perfect size for our small group.

"Daniel! You're here." Greta greeted us, or I should say she greeted Daniel, warmly, holding his face between her palms as she kissed him on both cheeks. In her heels, she was as tall as he was.

Daniel smiled, but immediately stepped back beside me. "The place looks great, Ari."

"Tío Manuel really pulled it off," I said.

"Let's hope the wine is good and that this isn't all for show," Greta said.

My spine stiffened. "I can assure you that Montero Vineyards' wine is top quality."

Greta's eyes flashed at me, and her mouth opened. Before she could speak, however, Daniel placed a hand on her shoulder. "Looks like your clients are arriving."

"Oh yes. Thank you, Daniel. Let's greet them."

She took his hand and dragged him to the door, where they and the ECC counselors formed a receiving line like in a damn wedding. Grunting, I turned away. Maybe if I asked nicely, Tío Manuel would give me a glass of his superb wine right this minute. Just enough to get me through this nightmare.

Luciana came in through a door to the right of the bar. She winked and beckoned me to her. "How's it going?" she asked when I hiked myself onto a stool at the bar.

"Daniel and Greta seem to be getting along."

My tone must have been more sarcastic than I'd intended because Luciana's brows arched. "Isn't that what you wanted him to do? Calm her down and get her off your back?"

"Yes, but not onto hers!"

Luciana's face slowly transformed into a grin, and her shoulders started to shake as she tried to hide her laughter.

"What the fuck is wrong with me?" I grumbled.

"I won't state the obvious." She glanced toward the back of the room, where no doubt Greta was finding every excuse to touch Daniel. Grimacing, Luciana set a wine glass in front of me and filled the bottom inch with a dark red wine. "This cabernet has been aging for ten years. If it doesn't make your world right, nothing will."

I raised my glass to her. "To divorce."

She frowned and her head jerked back. "What?"

I set the glass down. "Today is the one-year anniversary of when Daniel and I divorced. Daniel hasn't mentioned a word about it. I doubt he's even realized."

"Oh honey." Her hand covered mine. "I'm sorry."

"I don't know why this is even bothering me. I feel like everything bothers me lately." I must be missing Javier. That had to be the reason for all these sudden emotions. I was in a room filled with people whose marriages were on the skids, and my new lover was three thousand miles away while my ex-husband was making googly eyes with a woman who hated my guts.

Luciana studied my face for a moment, but then Tío Manuel clapped his hands for attention. He welcomed the guests to Montero Vineyards and explained how the wine tasting would go. He also gave a short history of the vineyard itself and the process of wine making. We'd be tasting wine from several of the barrels along the left wall. Tía Sofia and Brad began filling glasses, and Tío Manuel and Luciana went around the room handing them to the guests along with small bowls filled with pieces of dark chocolate.

Luciana set one in front of me with a wink. I abandoned the wine that I'd barely tasted and dove into the bowl of chocolate. I normally loved red wine, but I wasn't feeling it tonight. I'd have preferred some chamomile tea to go with the chocolate. Or maybe a huge glass of cold milk.

No wonder he doesn't want you anymore.

As the evening wore on, I forced myself to part with the bowl of chocolate and mingle with the guests. First, I met Branson and Malia Willet, a gorgeous African-American couple in their early thirties. Branson was a pro baseball player whom even I'd heard of. High-school sweethearts, they'd been married twelve years. I was surprised to see them here. Surprised and sad. Whenever I'd seen them on television, they'd seemed so in love. But now? Branson looked guilty as hell, and Malia was distant and withdrawn, two more victims of the high pressure and long hours that came with life as a pro athlete. I truly hoped ECC could save their relationship.

Joel and Rebecca Levin were both very successful Hollywood agents whose clients were among some of the most successful actors in the business. Rebecca already looked to be three sheets to the wind, while Joel was loudly exchanging raunchy stories with film director Darren Podesky. Darren's wife, film producer Ji-woo Park, was talking animatedly with Daniel, who looked decidedly starstruck. I wasn't surprised to see him in deep conversation with her. Ji-woo's films were some of his all-time favorites.

A-list movie star Monica Dashwood held center stage, flirting outrageously with Brad, who kept shooting worried glances at Luciana as she chatted with Monica's boy-toy husband. Twenty years Monica's junior, Chad Winters sat at the bar knocking back glass after glass of the Montero's expensive wine.

The last couple was country star Jay Samson and his choreographer wife Raven Monroe. They'd met on the set of one of Jay's music videos a few years back, and Raven had become Jay's second wife a month later. Despite the shambles of his private life, or maybe because of it, Jay was currently at the top of all the hit charts. His latest song, "Tall Tales," played constantly on all the radio stations.

Although not the group's only interracial couple, they were certainly its most striking one. Jay was a cowboy through and through, medium height, rough around the edges, and more likely to be happier with a Budweiser in his hand than an aged cabernet. Raven, on the other hand, was slender and lithe and supremely elegant. Her black hair was woven into tight braids interlaced with beads that went to her waist. But their good looks weren't why they were so striking. Rather, it was the way their gazes followed each other, the heat in their eyes, the love and lust that arced between them across the room.

What on earth were they doing at a marriage-counseling retreat? They looked so in love.

My eyes wandered around the room until I spotted Daniel. I jerked back when his hot gaze captured mine. Had he been watching me this whole time?

He said something to Ji-woo, then crossed the room to stand beside me. Brad hurried by with a tray in his hand, Monica trailing after him. Daniel grinned and snagged two glasses from Brad and handed me one. "Things seem to be going well."

"As long as your name isn't Brad," I said, laughing.

"Poor guy. Being chased after by a sexy movie star worth millions has to be hell."

"Maybe she should chase after you instead."

Daniel shrugged. "Rumor has it, she prefers married men for her trysts."

"Ah..." I took a sip of wine and grimaced. "No wonder Chad looks so morose."

"As long as the money keeps flowing into his bank account, I doubt he cares."

"Daniel!" How could he say such a thing? Chad looked so dejected, it broke my heart.

"What?" he said, wide-eyed. "It's true. He's only with her for her money."

Darren and Joel were getting louder with each new wine that was passed around. Inching closer to Daniel, I glared at him and raised my voice. "So, a guy in his mid-twenties can't possibly be attracted to a woman in her forties. Is that what you're saying?"

He leaned down so his mouth was close enough to my ear that I felt his warm breath on my skin. "I'll find you attractive even when you're eighty."

"Sure, because you'll be eighty-three!" I said, feigning outrage.

Someone bumped into my back, and I'd have fallen flat on my face if Daniel hadn't caught me against his chest. In the moment before he set me on my feet and let me go, I had a chance to take his scent deep into my lungs.

"Oh my gosh." Malia pressed a hand to her mouth as she teetered unsteadily on her heels. Tears filled her eyes. "I'm so sorry."

"It's okay. No harm done." I rubbed her upper arm.

Branson came up beside her and wrapped his arm around her waist. Big tear drops spilled over her lashes, making them spike. She closed her eyes, stiffened her shoulders, and pushed Branson away. "Don't touch me," she said sharply.

"Okay, okay." Hurt in his eyes, Branson raised his hands and took a few steps back. "Just calm down."

"I *am* calm," Malia said through tightly clenched teeth. She spun on her heels, and I held my breath, hoping she didn't trip. But no, she stalked off to the bar to talk with Chad. Branson shook his head and grabbed a glass from Manuel's tray as he walked past us. Daniel grabbed two fresh glasses and tried to hand me one.

"No thanks," I said. I was still longing for the big glass of milk.

He turned to set it on the table. Greta swooped it and took it from his hand. "Suit yourself," she said to me before taking a big gulp.

A commotion in the back of the room caught my attention. Rebecca was hanging off one of the counselors, a good-looking man about ten years her junior. He'd been introduced to me earlier. Rick something. Devlin. Yes, Rick Devlin.

He was talking to her softly. His hands captured hers, removing them from his chest. Joel charged across the room. "Get your hands off my wife!"

I couldn't hear Rick's response over all the chatter in the room, but I definitely heard Greta's. Her eyes lasered in my direction. "I knew a winery wasn't the best choice of venue for a group of people in an emotional crisis." She finished off her glass in one swallow and shoved it at me. "Maybe I'll start drinking after this myself."

Her heels clacking on the flagstone floor, she moved through her clients like a queen. The worst part? She was right. Fuck. I hadn't even thought about why any of these people were here. About the pain they must be suffering or about how a lot of people sought to drown their sorrows in a bottle. I should have though. Hadn't I done the same after Daniel left?

A warm hand cupped my shoulder. "Hey," Daniel said. "Don't listen to her. This was a great choice."

When he tried to pull me closer, I resisted. "She's right. I didn't stop to think about ECC's clients other than that we had to provide security for them because of their celebrity status. I never thought of them as *people*."

"Ari, what are you talking about? You did exactly what you were tasked to do."

"No. Even at the lighthouse, I didn't think about anyone being afraid of heights or not knowing how to swim when I proposed kayaking and ziplining as activities. But you did. Fuck, I'm a shallow bitch."

"The fact you even said that means you're not."

"Whatever." I shrugged. "What are we going to do about it?"

"Tell Manuel not to sell alcohol to ECC's clients?"

"Unlikely. I'm sure he's counting on those sales and on them telling their friends about the vineyard and the quality of the product to make up for the extra cost of finishing the renovations so quickly."

Daniel rubbed his jaw. "I hadn't thought about that. TI can't really absorb any more of the costs."

"No, we can't."

"I'm sure Greta was just venting." He looked around the room. I did the same and immediately wished I hadn't. All the couples were now arguing or crying or looking like they might cry, and the ECC counselors were flitting from one person to the other doing damage control.

I turned desperate eyes on Daniel. "Oh God, Daniel. We have to do something."

He nodded. "You look beat. Why don't you go to bed? I'll stick around and help Greta and her team take care of this, then I'll talk to her."

Feeling like I was about to melt down myself, I didn't even care that he was taking over again. "Thank you. I'm asleep on my feet."

He kissed my forehead. "Sweet dreams."

"You too."

He kissed my cheek and whispered in my ear, "They will be." A shiver ripped through me as his breath feathered my neck. "Because you'll be in each and every one of them."

Oh God.

DANIEL

It had been a long night, but the ECC clients were finally all calmed down and off in their rooms. And I was having a much-needed scotch at the bar. The Monteros kept a great selection of liquor on hand in addition to their excellent wines.

I took another sip of the scotch, letting it burn down my throat. What the fuck was I doing? Flirting with Ari like that, and on the one-year anniversary of our divorce to boot?

It was so easy to flirt with her, so easy to fall back into that kind of relationship. Too easy. And yeah, I could see she was bewildered by my behavior. I didn't understand it myself. And no doubt all the outrageous flirting I'd done with Greta wasn't helping either. But Greta seemed to like it, maybe even expect it.

I didn't blame Greta—she knew I was single, and I'd made no secret of the fact that I found her attractive. Her lilting Swedish accent and cool Nordic beauty were certainly alluring to me.

Truth be told though, Greta didn't hold a candle to Arianna in my mind. Sure, I could sleep with Greta—but would it get my mind off the woman I shouldn't be pining for? I doubted it.

But maybe I should try it. See what happened, see if this obsession with Ari could possibly wane. Then make my exit and head back to Miami before I fucked things up between Ari and me worse than I already had.

A hand slid up my shoulder and gripped the base of my neck. *He* had always grabbed me like that.

In a flash, I slid off the barstool and turned to confront him. Except it wasn't *him*. It was Greta. Her mouth was open, her hands raised to ward off a blow.

No doubt a reaction to the snarl on my lips. And the fists I'd raised.

I took in a deep breath to try to slow my pounding heart and lowered my fists, forcing my fingers to unclench. Fuck, fuck, fuck. Thank God I hadn't hit her.

"Greta, I—"

She cut me off. "No need to apologize. I snuck up on you."

"No, that was out of line. I overreacted." I could barely meet her gaze. "Just kind of tense, I guess."

"Kind of?" she asked, a brow raised.

I gave her a sheepish smile. "I guess this evening just kind of got to me." I gestured around. "It's the one-year anniversary of when Arianna and I separated."

Greta studied me for a moment. "Can we go for a walk and talk?"

"Sure." Anything to keep Greta happy with TI. Especially after I'd almost clocked her.

We walked outside. The vineyard's grounds were beautifully lit. The temperature was a bit crisp, but the cool air felt good against my overheated face. Maybe Jennifer was right. Maybe I did need to talk to someone.

I'd almost hit a client.

Gravel crunched beneath our shoes as we circled the main building. "I'm really, really sorry, Greta."

"I hope you don't mind me speaking frankly, Daniel."

Fuck. Here it comes. "Of course I don't mind."

"I've been doing this long enough that I've seen this reaction before. I know that you've had some kind of trauma in your past. Maybe even a sexual assault. Have you talked to anyone about it?"

When she said those words—trauma, sexual assault—my heart started to pound again, like I was about to be killed.

Like I was about to go through it all over again.

Answer the question. Tell her. This is an opportunity. Tell her.

I opened my mouth, but the words wouldn't come. I sucked in some air and opened my mouth to try again. "I don't know what you're talking about." The lie rose to my lips so easily. So automatically.

Heat flooded my cheeks. *Liar. Coward.*

Greta stopped in her tracks and turned to me, her face soft, her voice softer when she spoke. "We're here for the next two weeks together. If you want to talk to me, or if you want a referral to talk to someone else, any time, I'm here for you. I'm in room 410."

She looked so sincere. She sounded so sincere. But she'd wanted in my pants ten minutes ago. "Talk, huh? You gave me your room number so we could *talk*?"

She shook her head slowly. "Look, sex is off the table now. That's not the kind of attention you need."

I stepped closer to her, putting a seductive smirk on my face. I touched a tendril of blonde hair that had escaped her up-do. "You think you can give me what I need?"

She reached up and gently took my hand. "People who've been sexually abused, particularly when they were young, may use sex inappropriately to try to manipulate others. Because that's what they know."

I withdrew my hand from hers, a cold sweat breaking out on my back despite the chill in the air. Was that what I was doing?

"To answer your question, Daniel, yes, I can give you what you need. I know I can. But you have to want help. I can't force you to talk about it." She rummaged around in her clutch purse and then handed me a business card. "This has my personal number on it. Call me if you're ready. Or just knock on my door. I'm here whenever you're ready to talk."

We'd reached the back terrace of the building, and she headed inside. I watched her go, her card in my hand. I took a seat on a nearby bench, flipping the bit of cardstock around and around in my fingers.

The stars were out, just like they'd been that night not so long ago with Diego. He'd called me on my behavior, and he'd been right to do so. I knew I needed help. I knew it. Tears stung my eyes, and I blinked them back.

The last time with *him* had been fifteen years ago. I'd thought it would fade away. I'd thought when he died it would die with him. I'd thought I'd buried all this shit, locked it away, learned to cope.

The truth was, I was unraveling. Divorcing a wife I loved, drinking too much, nearly hitting a client, sleeping with escorts whenever the pressure built up too much, and that wasn't working anymore. None of it was fucking working anymore.

I wanted Arianna back. I wanted her, and I wanted my best friend too. But I couldn't have either one. Because I couldn't talk. Because I couldn't be honest.

And how much longer could I deal with the nightmares by continuing to have cold, brutal sex with escorts? Wasn't I just reenacting what had been done to me?

Why?

And how could I stop it, short of suicide, which looked really appealing some days?

I looked down at Greta's card. Opportunity was knocking, and I'd better answer the damn door. Before I ruined every last bit of my pathetic life.

I took a deep breath, my gut quivering. This was my chance. But was I man enough to take it?

JAVIER

I tossed my pen onto the printout of this month's balance sheet and rubbed at my eyes. I'd barely slept last night. I'd left Daniel a message yesterday morning, and he still hadn't returned my call. Was he ignoring me? Was he angry? Maybe he'd figured out I'd slept with Arianna and now he wanted to kick my ass.

Fuck! I shoved out of my chair and went to lean my head on one of the floor-to-ceiling windows that overlooked Miami's downtown, its tall hotels and condos seeking to reach the sun. The air-conditioning had cooled the window, and it felt great against my aching head.

When I'd fallen into bed with Arianna, high on love and lust, the thought of losing Daniel, while scary, had been nothing more than a distant threat. But now? It was all too fucking real. My insides quaked at the mere possibility of not having him in my life anymore. Of not seeing him on a regular basis. Of not working side by side with him on the business we'd built up from the ground together.

Are you over Daniel?

Clarita's question came back to me, cutting into my chest with laser-like precision. No, I fucking wasn't over him. I'd never be over him. Daniel had dug his claws into my heart freshman year of college, and he'd never let go. I would always be his, even if he didn't know it or want to acknowledge it. No other man would ever do. I compared every man I met to him and found them all lacking. That was the real reason things hadn't worked out with Sam. He'd been a great guy, but he wasn't Daniel. No one was.

No man had ever made me feel the way Daniel had that one night in Cancun, the sexual energy that had zinged between us even before we'd touched. And no man had ever broken my heart the way Daniel had, because I'd never let one in enough to be able to.

The only other person I felt as deeply connected with was Ari. The chemistry we had was every bit as strong as the chemistry I'd had with Daniel. The chemistry I think we still had, if those looks he'd been giving me recently were anything to go by. If only he could acknowledge what was between us.

Then what? Would you drop Ari for him?

Damn good question. Being with Daniel would be the fulfillment of a dream I'd been clinging to for over a decade. But being with Ari was one I'd had since discovering I liked girls.

Ari and Daniel were my best friends, and it would kill me to lose either one of them.

The phone on my desk rang, making me jump and bang my head on the window. "Shit!"

Rubbing the spot I hoped didn't turn into a bruise, I hurried over to my desk and picked up the receiver. "Javier Cordero. How may I help you?"

"You'll have to tell me, man. You're the one who left me a message."

My gut churned. There was a touch of humor in Daniel's voice, but something else too, something I couldn't pinpoint. "Hey, *hermano*. I just wanted to catch up with you. See how things were going."

"Everything's great." Daniel had never been big on small talk, but even this was curt for him.

"How's Ari?"

"You'll have to ask her that yourself."

I pulled the phone away from my ear and stared at it. What the fuck? I cleared my throat. "I did. She said she was okay, but I can tell she's not."

"She's a little under the weather. Probably just overworked herself putting all this together on such short notice."

"Okay, make sure you take care of our girl."

Our girl? Fuck, as soon as the words were out of my mouth, I wanted to inhale them back down, suck them right out of the phone line. They were way too close to some of the fantasies I'd been having lately. Me, Ari… Daniel. Bodies intertwined. And *that* thought had my cock hardening.

I closed my eyes and pinched the bridge of my nose. "How are things with Greta? Ari's really worried. She told me about the welcome reception…" I let my voice trail off.

Daniel laughed. "Yeah, that was something, all right."

"Is Greta going to make a stink over the venue? It's not like we had a ton of options after the leak to the press."

"I talked to her. I think it will be okay." There was a sipping sound as though Daniel were drinking coffee. Then he continued, "We need to figure out who talked. If it's one of our people, heads will roll."

Now here was something I could bring to the table. I'd set our IT guy, Zach, onto the case. "I've started looking into it. Zach's pulling reports from all our computers and phones to see if anyone has called or emailed *Entertainment Nightly*. If we find something, we'll have our guy or our girl."

"Zach can do that? Pull phone records?" Daniel's voice sounded strained.

"Yeah. Since the phones are all under TI's account, we can see every incoming and outgoing call, the number, the origin and destination cities, and the duration."

"Wow, okay. Let me know if you find anything."

"I will. I've also called the reporter and the editor at *Entertainment Nightly* to see if I can finagle any information from them on their source. It's a long shot, but you never know."

"Good work, Javi. Seriously. You already have a lot on your plate without adding this."

"If we have an in-house leak, we need to plug it, otherwise we have no credibility with our celebrity clients." I sat down in my chair and leaned my head back. The phone slipped in my sweaty palm, and I had to tighten my grip. "Ari says you guys decided to try to work things out."

"She told you about that, huh?"

"Well, she mentioned it in passing while we were discussing the budget for the retreat."

"Is that right? In passing?"

Oh shit. Daniel's tone was sharp and suspicious. I wanted to reassure him, but how could I do so without lying? On the other hand, maybe it wasn't sharp and suspicious, maybe it was cautious and guilty. Maybe Daniel and Ari were hiding something from me? "You'd tell me if something were going on between you two, wouldn't you, Daniel? I mean, not that it's any of my business," I backpedaled furiously. "Except as your partner, that is."

"You'd tell me the same, right?"

Fuck, fuck, fuck. I squeezed the phone between my fingers. "Of course I would." I hated lying to Daniel. The words settled in my stomach and twisted me up. I didn't want to lie to my best friend, but what choice did I have? Ari and I had agreed to tell Daniel the truth when she and Daniel returned to Miami. Right now, they already had enough to deal with.

"I know, man. I trust you," Daniel said. "Ari and I aren't trying to get back together. The issues we had haven't gone away. But, I do want us to get back to a better place. She and you are my best friends, and I miss her that way, you know?"

Yeah, I knew. I knew exactly. And a small, greedy part of me was thrilled to hear it. The only problem was, Daniel's behavior with Ari didn't match his words. According to Ari, he'd been very solicitous, had even flirted with her. That didn't sound like he wanted to only rebuild his friendship with her. No, it sounded like he wanted a lot more. And that scared the crap out of me. I'd fight for Ari this time, but I wasn't sure I could compete with Daniel for Ari's affections. Their relationship had been deep and intimate, and I knew they both still loved each other. It wouldn't take much to fan the flames back to life.

I needed to understand what was going on with Daniel. Why was he behaving so strangely all of a sudden? "Are you okay, *hermano*? You seem different somehow since coming back from Tahiti. Anything you want to talk about?"

Daniel snorted. "No. I'm fine. Right as rain."

"Fuck."

"What?"

"Every time you say you're fine, I know you're not."

Daniel sighed, the sound heavy over the line. "Seriously, bro. I am fine. We'll have a nice long chat over a couple six-packs and a pizza when I get back to Miami."

"I'm looking forward to it." And not only because I wanted to put an end to the lies and come clean about me and Ari, but also because something was definitely up with Daniel. Over the years, I'd seen him be down and moody from time to time, but never like this.

Something was wrong with him. I could feel it. But what could I do from three thousand miles away?

Chapter 5

DANIEL

I ended the call with Javier. Something was up with Javi and Ari. That "our girl" comment, and then him asking me if she and I were getting back together? Sure, it could be nothing, but something about the way Javi spoke about Ari had changed. Was he ready to make his move?

Or had he made it already?

Had I lost my chance to rekindle something with her? It would serve me right.

I was a fucking mess. I'd had no right to inflict myself on Arianna in the first place. And here I was, wanting to do just that all over again.

My stomach rumbled. I'd skipped lunch, and now it was dinner time. I should take Ari out—just as friends—and see if she was okay. It would be good practice for us going forward. I did want to at least rebuild our friendship. Even if we couldn't fix our romantic relationship, we could still be friends, right?

And maybe I could figure out where things stood between her and Javier. If he'd already made his move, I wouldn't get in the way.

I walked over to Ari's room and knocked. She answered right away, looking lovely without a bit of makeup on, if a bit less glamorous than usual. "What's up?" she asked.

"I wanted to see if you were feeling well enough to grab dinner with me."

"I'm having dinner with the family. Why don't you come along?"

And suffer the glares of Manuel and Sofia over divorcing Ari? No thanks. I could beat myself up enough on my own. "I'm not sure they'd want me there."

"It'll be fine. It's all of us. Luciana and Brad and the boys will be there."

Luciana and Brad had been unfailingly nice to me, that was true. And I think Brad in particular knew what I was going through regarding Manuel and Sofia. No doubt he'd gotten enough guff from them over the years for his "gringo" status.

"Okay." I offered Ari my arm, and we went down to the kitchen together. We were eating in a small dining room just off the big commercial kitchen, but the space had been decorated so nicely that it felt homey and warm. It should. This was the Montero family home, not just a business.

They'd made a big spread—fried chicken, corn on the cob, green beans, gravy and biscuits, along with pozole, and corn tortillas. I helped myself to a bit of everything, and Sofia smiled at me approvingly. "You need to eat more, Daniel. You're too thin."

I held up an ear of corn. "Don't worry. I'll eat my fill at your table."

"So, is Ms. Lindstrom still upset with us?" Manuel asked me.

I swallowed a mouthful of corn and wiped my lips with a napkin. "She's fine. I think the clients getting drunk like that threw her for a loop, but she admitted that it was okay. Kind of helped them start the therapy process early, and see where the major stresses were. She said clients tend to lie and dance around the issues at first, but at least this way the dirt started to come out early."

Manuel smiled. "*In vino veritas*."

I raised my glass of Syrah. "Here's to wine therapy." I took a swig while everyone chuckled. Then I raised my glass again. "And here's to family. You really came through for us, and I'll never forget it." I held Manuel's gaze for a moment, then Sofia's, then Luciana's, and lastly Brad's. All of their smiles were warm, and some of the tightness in my shoulders receded.

I might not be married to Ari anymore, but I still thought of the Monteros as family. They'd come through for TI when we'd needed it most, and I'd do my best to make it up to them. I leaned forward. "Did Ari tell you we're planning to put together an 'Escape to Sonoma' tour package with Montero Vineyards as the hub?"

Arianna gave me a look, her brows raised. I hadn't mentioned it to her, but she smoothly said, "Yes, we've been talking about it. Provided that you're interested," she said, turning to Manuel and Sofia.

"Of course," Manuel said. "That would be wonderful."

Brad picked up Luciana's hand and kissed the back of it, his eyes twinkling. She blushed and kissed his cheek. All night, the two of them had been making eyes at each other, like they were teenagers first in love, instead of a couple who'd been together over fifteen years.

A lump rose in my throat. That should be Ari and me. Would have been us if I hadn't fucked it all up.

Felipe and Lucas had been cutting up all during dinner, and Lucas tossed a kernel of corn at Felipe, who caught it in his open mouth. "Score!" Felipe crowed.

Luciana rolled her eyes. "What have I told you two about playing with your food? Eat it, or excuse yourselves to do your homework."

"Mom!" Lucas whined. "We were just having fun."

"And that means you're done eating. Go do your homework."

Lucas huffed. "It's math. Which one of you is going to help me?"

Luciana looked at Brad, who sighed. "I'll try."

This was something I could help with. I raised a couple fingers. "I've helped a lot of kids with the new math. I could do it."

Arianna stared at me openmouthed. "What kids?"

I turned to her. "At the shelter where Jennifer works. I've been volunteering there."

"Since when?"

"Since our divorce." The word hung there between us like a black cloud.

"I see," she said stiffly. "I thought you didn't like kids."

I touched her hand and shook my head. "I like kids just fine."

"But?"

Everyone was staring at us. "Not here, Ari. We can talk about this later."

She nodded, holding my gaze. Fuck. What was I going to tell her? I turned to Lucas. "Go get your math homework."

He ran off, and Luciana and Brad started clearing the table. Manuel poured us another glass of Syrah, and Sofia brought out some flan.

"Arianna," Manuel said, "I wanted to ask you something."

"What, Tío?"

Manuel eyes flicked to Sofia's, then back to Ari. "We recently had to fire our accountant. We discovered he was embezzling funds."

"*Dios mío*," Ari said. "Was it a lot of money?"

Manuel shrugged. "At least twenty thousand, maybe more. We're not sure. We were wondering if you could ask Javier for a favor. We'd like him—or somebody he recommends—to go over the books. We're not sure how much is gone."

"I'm sure Javi would be happy to help. It's the least we could do after all you've done for us. He might even be able to fly out in the next day or so. I'll call him tonight."

Fuck. Normally I'd have been happy to have Javi here. But if Javi and Ari had something brewing between them…

I bit my cheek. I had no right to interfere if they did. I had no right at all, and I needed to keep reminding myself of that.

We ate our flan, I helped Lucas with his math, and when Ari started yawning into her wine glass, I took that as our cue to leave.

"Come on, Ari. Let's get you up to bed. You look like you're about to drop."

She smiled at me sleepily and whispered, "Just want to get me into bed, don't you?"

Her voice was low and teasing. She'd definitely had a little too much Syrah. Not that I minded. Maybe nothing was going on with her and Javi after all. Maybe I was just being paranoid. But there was one way to find out, wasn't there?

I offered her my arm and walked her upstairs. As we approached her room, my heart started to pound, like it had the first time I'd ever kissed her. How many years had it been? Eleven now? I'd barely been able to wait until she'd turned eighteen. But there was no way I would have fucked things up with her back then. No way I would have abused her trust, or Javi's.

Arianna paused at her door, fumbling around in her purse for the card key. I put my hand on her arm, and she looked up at me. "What?"

I placed a couple fingers under her chin, angling her mouth up to mine, our lips meeting tenderly. Tentatively. So much like that first kiss. *Do you want this?* I wondered, moving my lips questioningly against hers.

She whimpered into my mouth, one of her hands going to my shoulder and clutching it. I took that as my cue to deepen the kiss, and she opened up to me and let out a soft gasp, her fingers digging into my shoulder. Then she stepped away and covered her mouth with the back of her hand, shaking her head. "We shouldn't have done that."

She grabbed her card key and started to insert it into the lock.

I put a hand on her bicep. "Wait. We should talk."

She looked up at me, her dark eyes flashing. "You never actually want to talk, Daniel. You say you do, but you really don't. What's changed?"

I started to open my mouth, but I didn't have an answer. What *had* changed?

Not a thing. Not a damn thing.

She crossed her arms. "Tell me this. Why did you divorce me?"

Again, I couldn't answer. Again, I gawped at her like an idiot.

Shaking her head, she frowned. "Just like I thought. This hotel is full of counselors. Maybe you should go find one and talk about whatever bullshit is in your head. I can't go through this again with you."

She inhaled shakily, her eyes bright with tears.

Oh fuck. "Ari, I'm sorry."

She leaned forward and poked me in the chest with a well-manicured nail. "You always do this, Daniel. You think you can kiss me, you think you can seduce me, and that will fix everything. But it won't. Sex isn't what we need. We need to be able to fucking *talk* for once."

A lump the size of Mt. Rushmore filled my throat. She was right. I couldn't argue.

And I still couldn't speak.

Tell her. Just tell her.

Bile rose in my throat, and I turned away and headed to my room before I vomited all over the woman I still loved.

DANIEL

Slap, slap, slap.

My feet hit the treadmill belt in a steady rhythm. I was running eight miles an hour, but it wasn't fast enough. Ever since I'd left Ari at her door, images of the past had been crowding my head. Sights, scents. My gut roiled ominously, even after the solid fifteen minutes of heaving I'd done in my room before heading to the resort's gym. Despite the ongoing construction, Manuel and Brad had fixed up a section with a few machines and weights for the retreat's guests and the ECC staff. I upped the speed to ten miles. Sweat dripped down my back, my face, my chest. My quads quivered under the strain. I could still smell it. Old Spice.

I swallowed convulsively and jabbed my finger at the console. Eleven. Even after all these years, I could still feel the heavy weight of his hand on my neck. Squeezing. Pushing. My chest contracted, and I stumbled off the treadmill. Air, I needed some fucking air. I ran outside onto the terrace, bent over at the knees, and tried to suck oxygen into my depleted lungs. Tried to remember everything I'd ever read about handling triggers. I focused on the here and now. On the cool breeze hitting my face, bringing with it the scent of roses instead of Old Spice. I filled my nose with it, my chest.

It calmed me. Marginally.

I still felt like fingers were scraping up my spine.

Like I was being crowded into a corner.

Like I needed to run. Away. As far away as I possibly could.

But nowhere was far enough. I could never outdistance the past.

If I were home, I'd call Diamond Escorts.

Yeah, and that had worked so well with Diego.

I could drive over to San Francisco. Find someone there. Someone who didn't look like Javier.

Maybe this time, instead of finding a man, I'd go for a woman. I didn't usually sleep with women when I was feeling this way. They weren't the answer. But maybe it was time for a change. Maybe this time, some pussy was what I needed.

Yeah. I'd drive to San Francisco, find a bar and pick up a chick with a big rack, a short dress, and an easy attitude. That's exactly what I'd do. Right the fuck now. I hurried back to my room, forgoing the elevator for the stairs, which I took three at a time. After a quick shower to wash off the sweat, I brushed my teeth, and hopped into a pair of comfortable jeans and a black T-shirt.

Minutes later, I sat in the rental car, my hand hovering over the ignition button on the dash.

And dropped my forehead on the steering wheel.

What the fuck was I doing?

I could sleep with hundreds of women or hundreds of men, and it wouldn't change a thing. It never had. The new faces could never stamp out the old one. The one that came back to me in the middle of the night, when I was sleeping. Or when someone touched me unexpectedly. Or when I caught a whiff of Old Spice on an unsuspecting grandpa. Sometimes it was a look someone gave me. An arrogant tilt to their lips. Sometimes it was a gruff note in someone's voice.

And the sight of cum. Every fucking time.

I avoided situations and people that I knew would affect me. But sometimes the memories blindsided me. Took my breath away. Made me feel faint. Made my skin crawl.

Until I wanted to disappear. Fade away. Fucking *die*.

Anything to stop the memories and the pain.

It didn't even matter that the bastard was six-feet under. He still controlled my present. He still impacted every aspect of my goddamn life.

The backs of my eyes began to burn.

I wished I could cry. Let the emotions flow out of me through my tears.

But I couldn't. I hadn't shed a single fucking tear since the fucker's death. Everything stayed stuck in my chest. Suffocating me as though my head were being held underwater by some unseen force.

Maybe this was my punishment. For years I'd kept the bastard's secret. Hell, I was the one who'd continued going back for more.

Shame filled my mouth with its bitter taste. I'd fucking enjoyed his attention. The nights of watching porn and drinking beer even though I was underage. But everything had had a price. And I'd paid and paid until I'd given him everything I had—my soul, my honor, and my dignity.

I should have known. I should have been smarter. Stronger. I should have resisted. Fought back. Been a fucking man.

But I hadn't. Instead, I'd sucked up the attention like I'd sucked up his cum, swallowing and swallowing. Like the little bitch I'd been. Like the little bitch I'd always be.

I grabbed for the handle, managing to shove the car door open right before bile spewed out of my mouth. I continued to dry heave until I thought I'd pass out.

Pitching myself back into the rental, I leaned back against the headrest. Nothing I was doing, nothing I'd done so far, held the answer. After all these years, it still felt as though it had all happened yesterday.

I was rapidly approaching rock bottom, and things were never going to change unless I did something different.

But what?

I tried to ignore the bomb ticking in my pocket. The card Greta had given me. The card I'd transferred from my suit pants to my jeans.

Greta was a therapist. She'd want me to talk about my past. Give voice to the boy inside me and let him tell his story. A story I'd only ever shared with Jennifer.

Could I do it? I didn't know, but I had to try. If I wanted any kind of future, I had to try.

I fished the card out of my pocket and palmed my phone. My heart pounded against my sternum as I dialed Greta's number with trembling fingers.

There were two rings, and then she answered. "Daniel?"

"I know it's late. But"—I took a deep breath and dug my nails into my thigh to keep myself from ending the call—"can we talk?"

ARIANNA

Damn Daniel King to hell and back.

After that kiss last night, I hadn't slept much. My dreams—the few I'd had—were full of Daniel and me making love, my heart so full it was aching, my body on fire for him. And then Javi would be there, and I'd go from Daniel's arms to Javi's, then back, then the two of them at once…

When I'd awoken for what seemed like the hundredth time and seen that it was six AM, I'd given up on sleep. My whole body ached, and I was horny as hell. And just as angry. Daniel had no right to stir things up between us. Not when he couldn't tell me what had broken us up in the first place.

And *Dios mío*, Javi. I was going to have to tell him about that kiss. At least I'd get to tell him in person. We were going to have to tell Daniel about us today, after Javi arrived. Daniel needed to know.

He needed to know it was over between him and me. Even if our stupid hearts didn't realize it yet.

I couldn't hurt Javi. He was too precious to me. He was my first love, and he didn't deserve to be second in my affections.

Daniel had had his chance. And it was clear he hadn't changed. How many times had he used sex to change the subject? To get us past a rough patch? To get me to stop asking questions he didn't want to answer?

He'd done it from the beginning, hadn't he? Again and again and again, and I'd fallen for it each time. I'd fallen for him so hard. But Daniel King was an illusion. Sure, he had it all together as a CEO, as a businessman. I couldn't fault him there.

But as a husband? As a partner in life?

He'd let me in only so far. He'd never let me get past a certain point. He could give me his body, but himself?

That he'd held back.

How many times had I begged him to tell me what was wrong when he woke up in a cold sweat? When he jumped if I came up behind him without announcing myself? When he'd have his black moods where he'd work out obsessively and barely speak to me? When he'd disappear, sometimes for a couple days, with no explanation?

I'd known well before we'd broken up that something was wrong. That's why I'd pushed him so hard about having a baby. I'd stupidly thought maybe if I pushed, he'd finally break, he'd finally tell me what was bothering him.

But he'd walked away instead.

Tears rose to my eyes as I dressed. Daniel didn't trust me. I'd been his wife, and he didn't trust me.

A sob burst out of my chest. I loved him so much. I'd thought I could fix him, could fix what was wrong. But I couldn't. Not if he couldn't trust me.

I calmed my breathing, wiped my eyes, and looked at myself in the mirror. I looked like hell, and I felt worse.

Well, fuck it. I didn't have to be perfect all the time, did I?

I stepped out of my room, making sure the door locked behind me, when I heard a door open down the hall. I looked up to see Daniel coming out of 410. Greta's room.

His normally neat hair was mussed up, like Greta had just been running her goddamn hands through it.

He started in my direction, then froze. Caught red-fucking-handed. He didn't move a muscle as I marched up to him.

"I see how much you meant that kiss last night," I hissed.

"This isn't what it looks like." There were dark circles under his eyes; no doubt they'd been fucking all night.

I held up a hand. "I don't want to hear it. I have work to do. Javi will be here this afternoon."

I tried to brush past Daniel, but he grabbed my arm. "You told me I needed to talk to somebody, and I did. I'm trying."

Was he serious with this bullshit? "So you picked Greta."

"She offered."

"I bet that's not *all* the Swedish princess offered." I sounded like a jealous bitch, but I didn't fucking care.

Daniel let go of me and crossed his arms. "This is part of the problem. You always make up your mind about what's happening, and you won't hear anything else."

Paz Santiago, one of the ECC counselors, was coming down the hall. She stopped a couple feet away. "I have an opening at ten, if you two would like to talk."

"We're not married anymore," I snapped.

"You both seem very emotionally involved with each other," she said, her voice calm. I envied her. "Maybe it's not too late to save things?"

I looked at her, then at Daniel, his face that stony mask I knew so well. "We're fine just as we are," I said, then shouldered past him to the stairs.

We are so not *fine. Dios,* would I even be able to work with him after this trip?

Of course, after Javi and I talked to him and told him about us, that might be a moot question. Who knew how Daniel would take that news? We might not even have a company after this.

My stomach lurched as I reached the bottom of the stairs. I avoided the public dining room and went into the kitchen to see if I could grab a little something in peace.

Luciana was plating up some bacon and eggs when I stepped inside. "You look like shit," she said. "What's wrong?"

I snorted with laughter. Luciana wasn't one to mince words. "What *isn't* wrong?"

"Is Daniel all right?" Luciana asked.

What an odd question. "What do you mean?"

"I delivered coffee to Greta's room twice last night. He was a mess. They seemed to be having some kind of really intense discussion. Is Greta upset about how things are going? I know the pool still isn't done. And we can't help the construction noise."

Oh fuck. Daniel hadn't been lying. My stomach cramped. He really was trying, wasn't he?

And I'd jumped all over him. No wonder he didn't trust me.

"I'm sure it's nothing like that, but I'll check with Daniel." *And apologize my damn ass off.*

I glanced at my watch. It was a little after seven. If Daniel was just going to bed, he probably wouldn't be up until after Javi arrived around noon. Damn it.

I'd just have to figure out a way to talk to him before Javi and I dropped our little bomb.

Chapter 6

JAVIER

Six hours after boarding the plane in Miami, I arrived in Sonoma, and thanks to the time difference, it was only noon when I drove my rental into the parking lot of Montero Vineyards, my stomach flipping as I stopped. How would Ari and I break the news about us to Daniel?

I took my time gathering my luggage from the trunk. It was quiet here, far quieter than Miami or even Coconut Grove. And the air smelled sweet. Maybe it was the scent of the trees and open fields and grapevines. Or maybe it was just the smell of clean country air. Either way, it was incredibly refreshing. I closed my eyes for a moment, inhaled deeply, slowly, and allowed the calmness to center me.

There was a sound, and when I opened my eyes, Arianna stood at the entrance to the resort. I could stand here and look at her all day, taking in her beauty, the flawlessness of her skin, the smile on her lips, and the love in her eyes. Or I could move my ass and go to her.

Grabbing the handle of my roller bag, I hurried across the parking lot and stopped in front of her. I wanted to kiss her so badly. I white-knuckled my bag to keep from folding her into a fierce hug and bending her backward in a passionate kiss. But that would have to wait until we were alone. Until we told Daniel about us. How did she want to play this? I'd let her take the lead.

When she held her arms open, I stepped right into them.

"God, I've missed you," I whispered into her hair.

Her hands squeezed me to her before she let me go. "I missed you too." She took my hand. "Come on, let's get you settled in."

I followed her inside and we were immediately waylaid by the Monteros.

"There he is. *Hola*, Javier." Manuel shook my hand heartily before pulling me against him for a hug and a kiss on either cheek. "How was your flight?"

"Long but otherwise uneventful."

Sofía crossed herself. "Thank you, *Dios*." She pulled me into a warm hug and kissed my cheeks. "You look good, Javi. But too thin. Isn't your mamá feeding you?"

I choked back a laugh. "She feeds me whenever I give her the chance."

"Which isn't very often, I hear," Manuel said with a wink.

It was true. I loved my parents, but dealing with their incessant matchmaking to every woman of marrying age in the community was difficult. Almost as difficult as my continued lying. Keeping my relationship with Sam from them had nearly killed me.

Luciana came over with her husband Brad and their two sons. I'd only met them a few times, but they'd always been friendly to me. I kissed Luciana and shook hands with Brad and the boys.

When I looked up, Daniel was there. My heart thumped loudly in my chest, skipping a beat. He looked rough. Really rough. Like he'd spent the night drinking. His clothes were impeccable as always, but he had dark circles under red-veined eyes. And the man who was always clean-shaven had a few millimeters of scruff on his chin and cheeks. His eyes darted to Ari before he came to me, hand held out. "Thanks for coming out on such short notice."

We did the bro-hug thing, one arm clasped while we bumped shoulders and clapped each other on the back. It felt utterly ridiculous, yet it was the only way I'd ever been able to touch Daniel. So no way was I giving it up.

As soon as we parted, Manuel grabbed my arm. "The books are in my office."

"Hush, you," Sofía said. "The man has just flown six hours. At least let him have lunch before you drag him into that stuffy office of yours."

"Stuffy?" Manuel said, feigning outrage. He turned to us. "The woman just spent two thousand dollars decorating it, and she calls it stuffy."

Luciana laughed, and Sofía grinned. She handed me a key card. "Room 425. Go settle in, and I'll have lunch for you and Arianna brought up."

Me and Arianna? My gaze slid over to Ari, who looked equally surprised. So, Sofía wanted to matchmake? I wasn't one to look a gift horse in the mouth. I took her hand and kissed her knuckles. "Thank you, Tía."

I turned to Daniel, who stood apart from everyone else. His gaze was fixed on Arianna. She, on the other hand, was looking everywhere but at him. What the hell was going on? Had something happened between them last night after I'd spoken with Ari? Was that the reason they were both acting so oddly?

Before I could ask Daniel to join me and Ari in my room, he raised a hand. "Have a good lunch. I'll talk to you later." Then he disappeared down the hall.

"What's up with him?"

Ari blushed, but she shrugged, a fake smile on her face. "Tired, I guess." She wound her arm through mine. "Let's go upstairs. I'm starved."

Sofia and Manuel sent us knowing looks as we passed by them. "Did you tell them about us?" I asked in a whisper once we were out by the elevators.

"No." The startled look on Ari's face made me believe her. Her eyes softened. "You know they've always liked you. The whole family has always thought we'd end up together."

The elevator came, and we stepped inside. I pulled her into my arms. "I always hoped we would too."

She frowned. "So, you wanted things between me and Daniel not to work out?"

"Not exactly."

The door opened, saving me from having to explain further. As soon as we were inside the room, I sat on the bed and pulled Ari onto my lap, her neck clasped in my hand while my mouth took hers. The kiss was deep and desperate, and I sank everything I'd been feeling since she and Daniel had boarded that plane together three days ago. She moaned against my lips, and her arms tightened around my shoulders.

"I want you, Ari. So fucking much."

"Wha-what about lunch?"

"Fuck the food."

I undid the top buttons of her blouse, enough so I could reach in and pull one lovely tit out of her lacy bra. My lips closed around a dark nipple while my hand went between her thighs. I was more grateful then for Ari's love of skirts and dresses than I'd ever been for anything before. I pushed her panties aside and toyed with the small tuft of hair at the top of her sex. She groomed it that way, while leaving the rest of her sweet pussy bare. I loved it, just as I loved everything else about her.

I slid my fingers lower, tracing her pussy lips, slicking her juices all around before plunging my index finger deep inside her.

She arched against me. "Oh Javi!"

I pushed a second finger inside her and rubbed her front wall even as I thumbed her clit, that little bundle of nerves that was so responsive to my touch. Her eyes widened and she moaned, her hips bucking as she rode my hand.

"That's it, *mi amada*. Give yourself to me. Let me see you come."

Her thighs parted even more and I pressed my fingers in more deeply. "Oh God, Javi. Yes. Oh fuck. Yes!"

She contracted her inner muscles around my hand and her entire body shook with her release. Arianna was so beautiful like this, her eyes closed, her neck stretched, her hair flowing down her back. I flicked my tongue against her nipple and she laughed, shoving my head away gently.

Arianna shifted on my lap. She unclasped my belt and lowered my zipper. When her fingers brushed my aching cock, I sucked in a breath. "Jesus, Ari."

She grinned, her fingers folding around my length. "You look ready for me."

"So fucking ready."

She lifted herself up, reached under her skirt, and then all I felt was warm, wet heat engulfing every throbbing inch of my cock. "Oh fuck!" I shouted.

My fingers gripped her hips, and I helped her find a rhythm that suited us both. I angled my head up and captured her lips with mine. My tongue slid into her mouth, tasting sweet heaven.

She rode me hard, her hips undulating in a sexy, mind-blowing wave. I would do this all day, except I couldn't. I was about to explode. "*Corazón*, I'm going to come. Let me pull—"

Ari pressed a finger to my lips. "Shh... give me what you've got. Fill me up."

Dios, she'd never spoken to me like that. And the dirty talk was hot as hell. A part of me knew we shouldn't be doing this. That things were too uncertain, but another part of me didn't give a shit. If Ari got pregnant, it would mean I'd have her forever. Or at least a part of her.

I took Ari's nipple in my mouth, bit it gently as I thrust up into her, my balls slapping against her ass with the force of it. She gripped my hair, pressed her tit into my mouth and screamed. Her orgasm took me with her, and I shot deep inside her, stream after stream until dots spotted my vision.

I fell back onto the bed and pulled her down with me. We lay there quietly for a few minutes with nothing but the sound of our breathing to mark the passage of time. It was peaceful. And everything I wanted. "I love you, Ari."

She raised her head a little, stared into my eyes, and smiled. "I love you too, Javier. Always."

Someone knocked at the door. "Room service."

I groaned, and Arianna laughed. "You'd better get that."

"Fine." I rolled her onto her back and gently pulled my half-hard cock out of her, wiping it off with a towel shaped like a swan that had been placed on the bed. "I'll be a fucking gentleman."

Ari's gentle laughter followed me to the door. I checked to make sure my cock was properly tucked away and that I'd zipped up my pants before opening the door. Luciana stood on the other side, a grin on her pretty face. "It's about time."

"What? It only took me a minute to answer the door." I took the heavy tray from her hands.

"True, but I've been standing out here for ten minutes."

The blood drained from my face, then returned in a heated rush. I had no idea how to respond.

She playfully punched my arm. "You did good, Cordero. Maybe now Ari will smile."

With a final wave, she set off down the hall toward the elevator.

I backed into the room and let the door shut behind me, then set the loaded tray on a small table by the window. Ari joined me. I was disappointed to see she'd rebuttoned her blouse. "Luciana heard us," I said.

Her face colored, but she shrugged it away. "We're consenting adults." When she lifted the lid on the tray, the scent of picadillo hit me. It smelled delicious. As did the rice and fried plantains. God, there had to be two thousand calories in the plate Ari set before me.

I waited for her to sit, then picked up my fork and tasted the picadillo, a mixture of ground beef, garlic, onions, sweet peppers, tomatoes, and spices. If I didn't have too much of the rice, I could have the picadillo and some of the fried plantain. Of course, I'd have to spend an extra hour on the treadmill. I heaped a forkful of picadillo with the rice this time and ate it, moaning as the mix of flavors hit my tongue. It would be so worth it.

Ari giggled.

"What?"

"You moan for food the same way you moan when you come."

I looked down at my plate, embarrassment making me avoid her eyes. Ari had known me when I was fat. Had loved me even then, I reminded myself. I forced myself to meet her gaze. Her eyes were soft, her lips curved.

I set my fork down. "Luciana said you haven't been smiling. Daniel looks like shit, you look tired, and don't think I missed the weirdness between the two of you. What's been going on here, Ari? Did you two have a fight?"

She sighed and took a sip of water. "I don't know what the hell's going on, to be honest." She took another bite of her meal and waved her fork in the air, using it to punctuate her words. "First Daniel kisses me, then I find out he's been getting counseling from Greta. I didn't believe him, but Luciana confirmed it. What could they have been discussing all night?"

"Back up," I said, sitting up straighter. "Daniel *kissed* you?"

The guilty expression on her face foreshadowed her answer. "Yes."

My gut clenched with a confusing combination of arousal and jealousy. "Did you kiss him back?"

She looked away. Her bottom lip quivered. I hadn't meant to upset her. "Ari." I took her chin in my palm and turned her head back to face me. "Look, I know Daniel is pretty irresistible."

Her forehead creased. "What are you saying?"

It took a lot of effort, but I somehow managed to keep my voice light, almost playful. "I'd kiss him back if he kissed me."

"Have you? Kissed him?" She arched a perfect brow.

"I tried once, back in college."

Interest flashed in her eyes. "Only once?"

I raised my shoulder and let it drop. "It didn't go well."

This time concern flared in her gaze. "What happened?"

"I've always had the sense that he's attracted to me, but for whatever reason, he won't act on it. When we were in freshman year, we went on spring break to Cancun. One night, things heated up between us. I mean the sparks were flying. Anyway, I guess I got his signals crossed, because when I kissed him, he got almost violent about it." I dropped my hands onto my lap. "Then the next day he pretended nothing had happened, and he's never said a word about it since."

"It's funny you say that, because I've always thought there's something more to his mood swings, but he won't say what it is. He's withdrawn from his family; he gave up his tennis career." Her voice dropped almost to a whisper. "Do you think maybe something happened to him?"

It was something I'd often thought about. There really was no other explanation, except… "I can't believe he wouldn't tell me. We've been friends for forever."

"Well, I was married to him." Ari's jaw hardened. "And here he is, talking to some woman he's known all of five minutes."

"Since he seems to be in a talking mood now, maybe it's a good time to tell him about us."

Ari shook her head. "We've made a lot of assumptions here, but we don't actually know anything, because as usual, he's said nothing to either of us. I think we need to play this by ear."

I understood what she was saying. She was right, of course. We had no idea what was the matter. I really wanted to tell Daniel about Ari and me. She was mine and I hated all the lies and obfuscation of the truth.

At the same time, I was terrified of telling him. What if he got pissed and turned on me, on us? Though it hurt like hell that Daniel felt more comfortable talking to a virtual stranger, even if she was a therapist, than he felt talking to me, I didn't want to lose him. I wanted to be there for him. To help him through whatever he was dealing with. I wanted to be his friend. I wanted to be his lover. If he'd have me. The truth was, I wanted them both, Daniel and Arianna.

"I think I'm going to try to talk to him. See if he'll tell me what's going on with him."

And maybe I could figure out how he'd react to my relationship with his ex-wife.

DANIEL

Why did I still feel like I'd been run over by a truck? A truck that had then backed up and rolled over me a few hundred times more?

I'd slept until just before noon, then slinked downstairs for lunch. Ari had been on her way over to my table—no doubt ready to deliver more of a scolding that I was absolutely in no mood for—when Javi had arrived and saved the day.

I'd been glad to see him of course, but the Monteros? They'd acted like Javi's arrival was the second coming of Jesus. Manuel and Sofia had rolled out the fucking red carpet, all smiles and hugs.

And I hadn't missed how Sofia had hustled Ari and Javi off to his room to have lunch. Alone.

Did Sofia know something I didn't? Was something going on with the two of them? Was that why Ari had gotten so upset when I'd kissed her last night?

When she'd kissed me back, I thought I'd had my answer. But now I didn't know.

After a lunch I had no appetite for, I'd gone back to my room, closed the curtains, and lain in the dark for hours, unable to fall back asleep even though I was a level of tired that went bone deep. I didn't want to interact with anyone. I just wanted to be alone.

And I especially didn't want to see Ari. Or Javi. Because if they were involved? God, I didn't even want to think about it. How was I going to see them every day at the office and smile and be happy for them when Ari had the half of my heart I hadn't already given to Javi?

If I thought this last year without her had sucked, it was going to be nothing compared to watching them together.

Could I do it?

My phone buzzed again. Greta had called earlier, but I'd texted her back and told her I was okay, just tired. No doubt this was Javi. Again. He'd been blowing up my phone for the last hour, trying to lure me out of my room for dinner.

But I couldn't be around people right now. Greta had warned me that I'd probably feel a little drained, but this was a level of exhaustion on par with having the flu.

I couldn't talk to Javi right now and pretend I was okay. And fuck, I definitely couldn't deal with Ari. I'd just order some room service and then go to bed early.

Someone knocked on the door. *Goddamn it.* I kept myself stretched out on the sofa.

More knocking. "Bro, I've brought you something to eat. Open the door."

Javi, of course. Maybe I could politely tell him to piss off. I scraped myself off the couch, opened the door, and before I could say a word, he barged past me, his arms full.

"Javi, man, I appreciate it, but I'm not feeling well, and I really can't deal with anything tonight."

He held up a six pack of beer and the pizza box he was carrying. "You can't deal with this?"

"Javi…"

Completely ignoring me, Javier walked over to the sitting area and plunked down the pizza and the six pack on the coffee table. He grabbed the remote and plopped his ass down on the sofa, turning the TV to the Miami Heat game. He patted the cushion beside him. "Bro, we're watching the game, having some pizza, and a few beers." He looked up at me. "That's it. You don't have to talk or anything. Just keep me company."

The pizza did smell good. Javi opened the box. "Got the supreme feast or whatever the hell they called it."

"Does it have sausage and black olives?"

"Dude, do I know what you like, or what?" He gave me that grin that always dazzled me, and I parked it beside him.

Javi, the game, pizza, and beer?

That I could deal with.

We dug into the pizza and started commenting on the game, Javi keeping it light, and I was suddenly really glad he was here. He always had my back.

Feeling full and nicely buzzed, I settled back on the couch. I was warm. Comfortably so. Javi smelled good, fresh from the shower, his cologne teasing my nostrils. My dick started swelling and tingling. I reached down and palmed myself, and I heard Javi clear his throat.

My eyes snapped open. I was leaning on Javi, my head on his shoulder. I'd fallen asleep. And my hand was cupping my rock-hard cock. Fuck!

I jumped off the couch, my heart pounding.

Javier looked up at me with wide eyes. "What's wrong, *hermano*?"

I ran a hand over my hair and sucked in a breath. "Nothing's wrong."

Real smooth, King. I'm sure *he bought that.*

Javi leaned back against the couch. "Bro, seriously."

"I'm fine."

"Ari might let you get away with that bullshit…" He paused. "Okay, I have too. But I think I shouldn't do that anymore."

I crossed my arms. "I'm fine, Javi. Just got a little disoriented."

It was Javi's turn to cross his arms. "Let's review, shall we? You were asleep, you moaned my name like you were about to come, then you touched yourself and jumped off this sofa like your ass was on fire."

Oh fuck. My face burned. "Man, I have no explanation."

He uncrossed his arms and leaned forward. "I do." His eyes bored into mine. "This reminds me of what happened in Cancun. When I kissed you."

I looked up at the ceiling, my crossed arms tightening, like I could somehow hold myself together that way. "You *had* to bring that up?" My stupid voice cracked, and I could have died.

Javier sat up, a dog-with-a-bone look in his eyes, and my heart started pounding again, a jolt of adrenaline hitting my system. How could I get out of this?

Javi continued. "We've never talked about it. About what happened. How you reacted."

"And we aren't going to now."

"Yes, we are."

I turned away from him and blew out a breath. "Look, I promise we'll talk about it sometime."

"When?"

"This is something I'm trying to work out."

"With Greta?"

I turned back to him. "Ari told you about that? I guess she believes me now."

"Ari and I… we're both concerned about you."

The way he said that made my spine prickle. Like he and Ari were a couple, something possessive about his voice when he mentioned her.

"Do the two of you have something to tell me?"

My question hung in the air for a long moment before Javi nodded. "Yeah, *hermano*, we do."

JAVIER

Daniel's entire expression tightened and he waved a stiff hand in my direction. "You want to talk, so talk."

The mistrust in Daniel's blue eyes fueled my apprehension. I could easily turn this around, reroute the conversation to something else. Of course, then I'd be adding to the lies, creating even more distance between me and my best friend. Me and the man I was in love with.

I had to hold on to the hope that maybe if I was honest about what was going on with me and Ari, about my feelings for the both of them, maybe we could find a solution that would allow us all to keep being friends and business partners.

C'mon, Cordero. You want to be a lot more than friends and business partners with both of them.

True, but I'd take what I could get. It was time to man up.

I met Daniel's hostile stare. "Ari should be here for this."

"Then call her."

Nodding, I turned away from him, put some distance between us, and dialed Arianna's cell. The tenderness in her voice when she answered reassured me that this was the right decision. "*Hola, princesa*. Come to Daniel's room. It's time."

She gasped. "Are you sure, Javi?"

"More than I am about anything else. Whatever happens, we'll still have each other."

"*Sí, querido. Ya voy.*"

"*Gracias.*" I ended the call. "She's on her way," I told Daniel.

We eyed each other uncomfortably while we waited. Just a few minutes ago, Daniel had been sleeping with his head on my shoulder, moaning my name as he rubbed his hard cock. Now he was bristling like a cornered badger.

When the knock on the door finally came, ending the tense silence, a mask fell over Daniel's face, making him even more impenetrable than usual. It was clear he expected bad news. My gut twisted. I didn't want to hurt Daniel. In fact, I wanted the exact opposite.

Daniel crossed the room to the door. His steps were heavy, his back stiff. He held the door open for Ari without speaking a word to her. She entered the room, her gaze swinging between and me and Javi. She swallowed and smiled awkwardly. "Hey guys. What's going on?"

Daniel arched a haughty brow. "I think that's the question I should be asking."

I looked at Ari. She gave me a small nod, and I held my hand out to her, pulling her down onto the couch beside me. With our clasped hands on my thigh, I turned to Daniel, who'd positioned himself on the other side of the room, perched on the edge of a small breakfast table, and forced myself to meet his stare. "Arianna and I have been seeing each other."

Daniel's nostrils flared as he sucked in a deep breath. "Since when?"

"Since her birthday."

Daniel looked pointedly at Ari. "And neither of you thought to tell me?"

I didn't want him to hold her responsible. I jumped in. "We wanted to be sure first."

He continued to stare at Ari. "Are you really certain about this? Because you sure as hell kissed me back last night."

"*Ay, Dios.*" Ari rolled her eyes and threw her free hand up in the air. "Between the two of you, I'm so fucking confused."

That's exactly where I want you, between the two of us.

The thought crashed over me like a category five hurricane. It left me flushed, my insides flipping madly, and my cock hard enough to break cement. This was the perfect opportunity to give voice to my wants, my needs. But did I have the balls to risk everything? To go for broke?

I looked at Ari and Daniel, took in the sexual energy coming off of them in waves. As though they'd been given a signal, they turned their eyes to me, and I was hit with the combination of their attraction to each other and their attraction to me. Blood thundered through my veins, all headed in a southerly direction. I could not pass up this chance.

My eyes on Ari, I said, "It doesn't have to be one or the other, does it?" I looked up at Daniel. "We could share."

Daniel's eyes burned with a fire that was so hot I feared being scorched by it. "What exactly do you mean?"

"I'm pretty sure you're attracted to me." I licked my suddenly dry lips. Daniel's gaze seemed to get even hotter. "God knows I'm attracted to you. It's never been a secret."

Ari let go of my hand and scooted her perky ass to the edge of the couch. Her eyes bounced between me and Daniel. "What's going on here?"

Daniel cleared his throat, but it did nothing to clear away the huskiness in his voice. "For the sake of argument, let's assume I am attracted to you."

Arianna inhaled audibly. "What?"

My heart soared at Daniel's admission, at his validation that I hadn't been crazy all these years. That my attraction to him had not been unreturned. Unable to tear my eyes off him, I reached blindly for Ari's hand.

Daniel continued. "For reasons I don't want to go into just now, I'm not sure I can act on it. But…"

My fingers tightened on Arianna's hand. *Please, please, please, don't walk away now,* I silently pleaded. Daniel might not have revealed his reasons for holding back, but just the fact that he'd admitted there were reasons at all was a huge step forward.

"But maybe we can agree to share Arianna."

Stunned by Daniel's words, I could only stare at him with my mouth hanging open.

Ari was not suffering the same paralysis. She released my hand and shot to her feet, waving her hands in my and Daniel's faces. "Hey! I'm *right here* in the room with you. Don't I get a say in this?"

Daniel blinked and slowly turned to Ari, a shit-eating smirk on his face. "Of course. What do you want, Ari? Two men doting on you? Two men showering you with attention? Two men pleasuring you in bed?"

"Yes," she said breathlessly. Her face was flushed, her big brown eyes glassy with desire. "I want both of you. I—I always have."

"Is that right?" Daniel shoved off the table and took a few steps closer. "In that case, let's put this to the test." He held his hand out to Arianna. "Get your luscious ass over here and kiss me like you mean it."

Daniel's voice, low and rough with arousal, almost had me coming in my pants. *Dios,* what this man did to me. Ari walked over to Daniel, her swaying hips perfectly outlined in the tight red dress she wore.

She stopped in front of Daniel and took his cheeks in her palms. Their eyes held for a moment, each searching the other's face, then they both smiled. Ari pushed up on her toes and pressed her lips to Daniel's. He groaned and caught her around the waist, pulling her flush against him. She angled her head, and when she arched her back, pressing her tits into his muscular chest, I knew he'd slipped his tongue into her warm mouth.

It was as though he were me. I felt her nipples rubbing my chest, her soft belly against my hard cock. I could taste her mouth, feel the hardness of her teeth and the softness of her cheeks. When Daniel's hands slid down to cup her heart-shaped ass, I felt those firm muscles in my palms.

I wanted to echo their moans, but I clasped my lips tightly together. This was their show, not mine. And what a show it was. My dick twitched, and the heat of pre-cum warmed my cockhead. Jesus.

If I was this turned on seeing the two of them kiss, how explosive would it be when I watched them fuck? I wasn't sure I'd survive it.

Daniel raised his head and gave Ari one last kiss. Then he stepped back and beckoned me over. "Your turn."

When I stood, I knew both of them could see my erection. Normally, I'd have tried to hide it, but fuck it. I wanted them to know how much they both affected me. How much I wanted this, the three of us together.

Daniel's eyes went to my crotch. His smirk widened, and holding Ari's hand, he offered it to me with a small bow, like a gallant knight.

Eyes shining brightly, Ari laughed. "I can't believe this is happening."

I swept her into my arms. "Oh, it's happening all right. And this is just the beginning."

My mouth descended on hers, capturing her lips, her tongue, her essence. I couldn't kiss Daniel, but I could enjoy his taste on her. Enjoy the taste of both of them combined. Sweet. Delicious. Irresistible.

I slid my hands up and down her back, caressing her hips, her ribs, her shoulders. She moaned into my mouth and thrust herself against my cock. The friction electrified me. I shuddered and slid my thigh between her legs. She rode it like I wished she was riding my cock. "Yes, *corazón*. Like that."

Her fingers tightened in my hair. "Oh, God. Javi."

She pressed her face into my chest. I had to know how Daniel was taking this. Was he angry? Excited? Jealous? If he was jealous, this wouldn't work.

I looked over at him, above Ari's head. And sighed with relief. Daniel's gaze was firmly planted on us. His chest rose and fell rapidly, his lips parted, his eyes hooded. I wished I could take a photo. Keep it under my pillow. The last time I'd seen Daniel like this had been in Cancun.

A pang gripped my gut. Would tonight end the way that night had?

Chapter 7

ARIANNA

I couldn't stop trembling. Being in Daniel's arms, then Javi's again while Daniel was watching was overwhelming. Javi's hands slid down to my ass, and he pulled me closer, his hard cock pressing into my belly. I glanced at Daniel. His eyes were glued to us, his chest heaving as he pulled in air. I looked down at his crotch and saw the bulge there. Yep, he was definitely into this.

Just hours ago, Javier had been inside me, and now… now I was going to have both of them. Was this really happening?

Javi leaned down and kissed me again, and I moaned into his mouth. I couldn't help it. I wanted him; I wanted Daniel. But could I really have them both?

Daniel's heat pressed into my back, his mouth on my neck, and I felt like I'd died and gone to heaven. Javi loosened his hold on me, and Daniel spun me around into his arms. His mouth crashed down on mine, his kiss wild, frenzied, his hands on me crushing our bodies together.

Dios mío. What the hell was I doing? Shouldn't I stop this? It could only end in disaster.

I must have frozen, because Daniel released my mouth and pulled back. "Look at me." When I did, he said, "I can't promise you that this is going to work out." He glanced at Javi, who smiled at us and palmed his erection through his pants. Daniel touched my jaw, bringing my attention back to him. "But I think we should try this. Try sharing you. Because none of us are all that happy with how things are right now. Something has to change."

His gaze on me was intense, his blue eyes darkening as they bore into mine. Something was different about Daniel; he was changing. He was trying.

Maybe this could actually work.

I slid my arms around his neck and glanced over at Javi. "I want to try this." Then I looked back at Daniel. "But if…" My voice started shaking. "But if this doesn't work…" I closed my eyes, not wanting to say it, but needing to. I opened them again to see Daniel staring at me with concern. "If this doesn't work, I want your blessing to be with Javi."

Daniel said nothing for a long moment, then he nodded, a muscle ticking in his jaw.

"I need to hear it, Daniel," I said, keeping my voice soft but firm.

"If this doesn't work," he said, his voice rough, "you have my blessing to be with Javi." He cleared his throat and looked at Javier, then at me. "I want you to be happy, Ari. I've always wanted that. And I'm so sorry—"

I pressed a finger to his lips. "I know. So am I." I rose up on my tiptoes and pressed my mouth to his, my tongue swiping along his bottom lip. He opened to me, and his hold on me tightened, then he scooped me up into his arms and deposited me on his bed.

Javi started to join us, but Daniel held up a hand. "I don't think I'm quite ready for all three of us in bed together. How about we take turns?" He looked down at me. "That okay with you?"

My gaze darted between them. Javier nodded, and I took a deep breath before nodding myself.

We were really doing this. *I* was really doing this.

If this was a dream, I didn't want to wake up.

Daniel sat back on the bed, his fingers going to the buttons on his shirt. I just lay there, watching as Javi took a seat in the chair in the corner, both of us rapt as Daniel started revealing his tanned chest and that chiseled torso that had always made my mouth go dry. He was perfect, so fucking perfect.

A corner of Daniel's mouth lifted up, his eyes twinkling as he unbuttoned his shirt cuffs, his eyes moving from me to Javi. "I feel like I should have some stripper music in the background."

I giggled. "Our own private Magic Mike."

He tossed his white button-down aside, and his hands dropped to the fly of his slacks.

"Boom chicka wow wow," Javi said, cracking us all up as Daniel started sliding his trousers off his narrow hips. He was already barefoot, so nothing obstructed them as he stepped free. He'd taken off his boxers

at the same time, and his erection sprang free, standing proudly at attention.

It had been a year, more than that really, since I'd last seen him naked, but I hadn't forgotten a millimeter of his body.

I was so slick between my legs, so ready for him. For Javi. For whatever was coming.

If this all blew up in our faces, I wouldn't regret it. I wouldn't regret this chance with Daniel again.

He crossed his arms, that sexy half-smile on his face, and raised a brow, staring down at me. "Well?" His eyes roamed up and down my body, my breasts swelling and tingling under his gaze, and he wasn't even touching me.

I sat up and swung my legs over the edge of the mattress. I'd put on one of my tightest dresses—why, I didn't know, except that I guess I wanted to please Javi. And maybe, just maybe, make Daniel regret leaving me.

I toed off my heels and stood, presenting my back to Daniel. "Give me a hand?" I asked, gesturing to the zipper.

He stepped up behind me, his warm breath washing over my neck. He bent down and pressed a kiss to the base of my neck, then undid the hook at the top of my dress. Ever so slowly, he slid the zipper down, the metallic noise it made so loud in the room, his fingers grazing my back, the barely-there touch making me shiver.

I helped the dress over my shoulders, and it slid down to my hips. With a wriggle, I dropped it to the floor, and Daniel's hands immediately went to the clasp on the back of my black lace bra, his mouth on my neck, his tongue caressing my sensitive skin and making me moan.

Daniel knew everything that turned me on. He knew my body in ways Javi was just discovering.

And yet, this time with Daniel felt new. Because Javi was here with us. Watching.

Raising my eyes, I met Javi's across the room. One of his hands was on his crotch, but his pants were still zipped. I smiled at him. "Why don't you show us how much you like this?" I said, surprising myself. I hadn't meant to say the words, but Daniel chuckled and so did Javi.

Daniel pushed my bra off my shoulders, and Javi started unzipping his slacks. My eyes were glued to Javier as he took out his erect cock and wrapped his fist around it.

"This what you wanted to see, *corazón*?"

I nodded, my mouth dry as Daniel shoved my panties over my hips and I stepped out of them. He yanked me against him, his hard cock pressed into my low back, his hands going to my aching breasts, his fingers tugging my nipples and sending electric sparks straight to my pussy. I groaned and arched into his touch.

A flood of moisture between my legs made me press my thighs together. Daniel bit my neck where it met my shoulder and inhaled. "I can smell how turned on you are, Arianna."

My cheeks heated, and I gasped when he bit me again, his fingers tugging harder on my nipples, my pussy suddenly needing to be filled.

I moved a hand to touch myself, and he shoved it away. "That's mine right now. Until it's Javi's." He ground his hips against me, his erection pressing insistently into my back, and I swear I went even wetter. *Cristo.* Somehow, he knew, he always knew, what would drive me higher. When I needed that edge of possession, of dominance.

"Then do something about it," I whispered.

He nipped at the nape of my neck, and I shuddered. "I'll do something about it when I feel like it," he growled. "And you'll like it that way."

I smiled, my gaze meeting Javi's. He was fisting his cock, his eyes eating us up.

Daniel dropped his left hand to my hip and repositioned his cock with the other, rubbing it against the crack of my ass. I moaned. Was he going to take me that way?

I enjoyed that too, but I wanted him in my pussy again after all this time. I put a hand over his on my hip. "Daniel, I want you inside me, but—"

He bit my neck again, my gasp cutting me off.

"But not that way," he finished for me. He licked the spot he'd bitten. "No worries, baby. I'm just teasing you. I want that tight little pussy."

He let go of his cock, and his right hand finally, finally moved down between my legs, his fingers grazing my patch of pubic hair, and I writhed in his arms, wanting his touch, needing it, so damn bad.

Daniel's fingers parted me, spreading my juices over my swollen clit and stroking it, the touch making me cry out in relief. Javi groaned and squeezed the head of his cock.

Dipping into my moisture again, Daniel ground the heel of his hand against my clit, his fingers invading me, making my hips roll forward, trying to give him more access. He positioned his thumb to work my clit, his breathing speeding up as mine did. I wound my arms around his neck, pulling his head over my shoulder for a kiss.

I loved him so much; I'd never stopped. And now—now he was giving me this. This second chance, this expanded chance at happiness. With him and Javi.

Still kissing me, Daniel started walking us to the bed. When we reached it, he pushed me down onto my butt so that I was perched on the edge, my legs spread wide, his hands on my inner thighs holding me apart, baring my glistening pussy to his gaze and Javi's.

Dropping to his knees, Daniel licked me from my entrance to my clit,

his tongue sweet torture. "God, I've missed this," he said.

"Me too," I moaned as he did it again and slid two fingers inside me, making me cry out in pleasure.

Reaching down, I clutched Daniel's light brown hair, grinding myself against his tongue, his fingers, my hips moving of their own accord, my eyes seeking out Javi. The molten heat in his gaze catapulted me over the edge, and I came with a high-pitched cry, shuddering all over.

Daniel surged up between my legs, his broad cockhead nudging at my entrance. Then he abruptly stepped back.

"What's wrong?" I asked.

"Need a condom," he said, going over to his suitcase and rummaging through it.

I almost said he didn't, but I didn't know who he'd been with in the last year. And I wasn't on birth control.

Didn't stop you from having unprotected sex with Javi, did it?

I looked over at Javier, and our gazes locked. Yeah, we hadn't told Daniel that tidbit, had we? But now wasn't the time.

Daniel returned to me, his cock sheathed in latex, and he looked from me to Javi. "Still with me, baby?" he asked.

I lay back on the bed and beckoned him to me. "Always."

He bent over me and pressed a kiss to my mouth, his tongue curling around mine, his hard cock drilling into my belly.

"Fuck me, Daniel," I whispered when he pulled back. "I need it. I need it so bad."

He thrust into me, and I could have wept in relief. It felt like it had been forever. Forever since we'd been joined this way.

His hands gripped my hips, pulling me closer, and I wrapped my legs around him, my heels pressing into his firm ass, urging him in deeper.

Javi groaned, and my eyes flew to his.

"Look at me," Daniel said, and I turned back to him, clutching his shoulders. "You know Javi is watching us. You know he's waiting for his turn. You know he wants to be right where I am."

God, did I know. And I wanted that too. "I know." I stared up Daniel, his face tightening with effort as he sped up his thrusts, his blue eyes locked on mine.

"But right now, it's my cock inside you, Arianna. Mine." His low voice was a dark growl. A warning.

I shivered at the possessiveness in Daniel's tone, in his gaze. Could this really work? Could he really turn me over to Javier when he was finished?

I clutched him harder to me, aware of Javi's gaze on us. "If you don't want to share, if you can't—"

Daniel cut me off. "I want to see him make you come. I want to watch him fuck you, get you off." He punctuated his words with his thrusts, his pace growing frenzied. He was breathing hard now, and so was I, pleasure coiling inside me, building toward a climax. "I want us both to have you." He thrust into me savagely, his cock bumping against something inside that made me cry out, my orgasm rushing over me. "I want us all to share this," Daniel said between clenched teeth before coming with a groan, his body convulsing, and I held him tightly to me, his breath blowing in hot gusts over my throat.

He held me for a minute as his breathing slowed, and I felt like something had shifted between us. Between the three of us.

Daniel pulled back a bit and glanced over his shoulder. I followed his gaze to Javi, who'd stilled, his hand on his fully engorged cock.

Then Daniel looked back at me. "You want him, don't you? You want him inside you?"

I held his gaze. "Yes, I want that."

He pressed a tender kiss to my lips, then withdrew and stepped away from the bed. He beckoned to Javi, who rose from the chair.

"She's all yours."

Javi grinned and stepped forward, his eyes lighting up as they darted from Daniel to me, like he still couldn't believe this was happening. I shared the feeling, unable to stop staring at the man who'd owned my heart for so long I couldn't remember a time before that.

Daniel's eyes were eating up Javier the way mine were. This was a side of Daniel I'd never guessed at.

How many other things didn't I know about the man I'd married?

He slipped on his slacks, then traded places with Javi, settling into the chair, his eyes meeting mine as Javi strode toward me.

Daniel King, after all these years, was still a mystery to me.

But maybe this time he would finally let me in.

DANIEL

I sat in the chair watching Arianna undress Javier. I hadn't seen the man fully naked since that night in Cancun. The night that had changed everything, because until then, I'd actually thought I was getting better. That I could have a relationship with another guy. I'd wanted that so badly with Javier. He was everything I wanted in a man and then some.

My mouth literally watered when Ari undid the buttons of Javi's shirt and slipped it over his broad shoulders and down his muscled arms. His stomach was so cut, I could count each ab. Eight in all. Christ. His biceps rippled as he reached up to card his fingers through Ari's long hair. And when she trailed her tongue down the center of his chest, following that thin line of dark hair to the waistband of his pants, I wanted to be right there licking along with her.

But even back in college, I'd had it bad for my chubby and socially awkward roomie. The way he'd fumbled through conversations with both guys and girls had been endearing. And so fucking frustrating. Because I'd wanted him all to myself. I'd wanted to tuck him under my wing and protect him from the world. I hadn't done that though. Instead, I'd fucked anything in a skirt. When that hadn't worked to keep the nightmares at bay, I'd started fucking men.

And that's when I'd known that as hot as I found Javi, I could never have him. I could never do to him what I'd done to all those men. What I still did.

I shifted, uncomfortable with the truth.

As Ari fell to her knees at Javier's feet, I shifted again, uncomfortable for a wholly different reason. My cock, which should have been resting flaccid against my thigh given that I'd just had Ari, the only woman I'd ever loved, for the first time in well over a year, was once again perking up. Thickening. Hardening.

I wanted to be on my knees too. For him.

I wanted to see his cock. Feel its weight in my hand. On my tongue.

But just the thought of smelling his cum, tasting it, had me gagging.

Shit. Could I do this? Why the hell had I started this if I couldn't see it through? Closing my eyes, I inhaled deeply. I held the air in my lungs, counted to ten, then slowly released it. When I opened my eyes again, Ari and Javi had moved to the bed. She was straddling his lap as he sat on the edge of the mattress, her body hiding his cock from me.

Christ, they were beautiful. Individually and even more so together.

Their smooth brown skin, perfectly matched. Ari's firm, high tits with their peaked nipples fit in Javi's hands like they'd been made for him. She was soft everywhere he was hard.

Her hands stroked his arms, his shoulders, his chest. She bent her head down and tongued his tight nipples. When she bit him, revealing her white teeth, she shot him a knowing look. He threw his head back and groaned. The sound, low and guttural, had my cock pulsing against my zipper.

Did I want her to do that to me? Or did I want to be the one doing that to him?

Did I want to feel the hard pebble of his nipple on my tongue, between my teeth, against my lips?

Fuck yes. I spread my thighs and rubbed my palm on my aching cock. I didn't care if they could see how turned on I was. That was the whole point of this, wasn't it?

I tracked Javi's hand as it glided over Arianna's hip and slid between her legs.

"Oh!" Ari's eyes widened. Her fingers dug into Javi's shoulders. I was sure she'd leave a pattern of half-moons on them. She'd done the same to me many times over the years. I'd always considered them a badge of honor.

Javi's arm moved and Ari hitched her hips up, thrusting as she rode his fingers. Next time, I wanted him to do that to her in a position where I'd have a better view of his fingers sinking into her, fucking her deep.

I shivered and a wet spot appeared on my trousers. I undid the button and zipper and slid my hand inside.

Ari clutched Javier's neck. "Oh, Javi. I'm—"

"No," he said, removing his hand. "You aren't. Not yet."

She thrust her bottom lip out. "*Cabrón.*"

Javi laughed. Amusement danced in his warm brown eyes. The look in them so full of love for her, I felt like an intruder. But then he turned to me and winked. And his eyes were full of the same amusement and warmth. The same… love. For me? Oh fuck. I'd always known Javi was into me. Hell, he'd made it abundantly clear. But love?

Of course, he loves you, dumbass. Why else would he have stuck around all these years?

Javi lifted Ari off his lap and quickly turned, showing me his gorgeous ass. Firm, round globes that made my palms itch. His back, with all its muscles, each so well defined, was a work of art. I knew he worked out a lot, but I'd had no idea he was hiding all this magnificence under his silk work shirts.

I was no slouch myself, but the muscles I'd had during my competitive tennis days were a distant memory.

Bile rose in my throat.

Shit, shit, shit. Don't think about that. Think of something else. Quick.

With my eyes closed, I did a few more deep breathing exercises, and when I thought I had the budding panic attack under control, I opened my eyes to find that my prospective lovers had climbed onto the bed. Ari was facing me, on her hands and knees. Javi sat on his heels behind her. There was the sound of a condom wrapper being opened followed by the snap of latex. Then Javi rose onto his knees and gripped Ari's hips in his big hands.

"Ready?" Javi asked. He was looking at me, but he was speaking to Ari. Wasn't he?

"Yes," Ari snapped, pushing her ass back against Javi. "I've been ready since we started, damn you."

I smiled at her sass. It had been the thing that had first attracted me to her. She was no shrinking violet, and I found nothing sexier than a woman who stood up for herself.

My gaze swung to Javi's face. He arched a questioning brow. Was he seeking my permission? If so, why? He was the one Ari was dating, not me. I was the third here, not him. Didn't he see that?

When a second brow joined the first, I nodded. If Javi needed my permission, he had it.

He lowered his gaze, then slowly pushed his hips forward. I watched Ari's face, watched pleasure suffuse her expression as he filled her inch by slow inch. Had she looked like that when I'd been inside her?

She dropped her head between her shoulders, her long hair covering her face. When Javi bottomed out, she moaned. "*Ay, papi chulo*. You fill me so good."

He pulled back, putting a good distance between them—was his cock really that long?—before slamming back into her. She shouted. He threaded his fingers into her hair, wrapping a hunk of it around his hand, and jerked her head up. Her full tits swung wildly.

"Like that, woman?"

"*Sí. Damelo duro*!"

"Oh, you want it harder, do you? Naughty girl." He grinned and smacked her ass.

Her eyes shot to mine. Surprise was etched in them, but something else was too. Something I'd never seen in them when we'd been together. Did she enjoy this side of Javier? The dominant side I'd never have imagined in a million years?

He smacked her ass again. She hissed, but her mouth curved into a smile. Her gaze never strayed from mine. "*Sí, papi*. I want it hard. Fuck me like you mean it."

Christ. Her echo of my words rocked through me. I trembled inside and pre-cum dripped from the slit in my cockhead. I slid my hand over it, coating my dick with it, and slowly stroked my shaft. I'd known they'd be hot together, but I'd never imagined I'd enjoy it this much. I'd been certain jealousy would rear its ugly green head.

But whatever I was feeling right now, it definitely wasn't jealousy.

"What do you say, Daniel? Should I give her what she wants?"

Javi's eyes danced with humor, and I was so fucking happy he was including me in this I could have kissed him. I stroked my cock in my pants, once. Twice. "I don't think she asked nicely enough."

"Hey!" Arianna's eyes narrowed playfully. "No tag-teaming me."

"No?" I quirked my lips, shooting her a teasing grin. "I thought tag-teaming you was what this was all about."

Her eyes closed and slowly opened as a moan escaped her throat. Her body undulated, a sensual motion that had both me and Javi groaning. When she looked at me again, her eyes were burning pools of mocha. "Oh God. Please, Javi. Please, Daniel. I need this. Please."

Still Javi waited. His face was as tight with need as my balls felt. "Do it, man. Give the lady what she's begging for so prettily."

"This is from both of us," Javi told Ari as he plunged into her. His hips pistoned back and forth. From my position, slightly to the side of the bed, I had a great view of them from the front and of Javi's side. I could see the cheeks of his ass, hardening, hollowing out as his glutes contracted. Christ, the man was a vision.

Their bodies moved together. Ari rocked back and forth, her arms shaking, her breasts swaying. Strands of dark hair clung to her face, and drops of sweat slid between her tits. I wanted to slide under her, to take each dusky peak into my mouth. To roll them on my tongue and see them glisten with my saliva as Javi continued to pound her pussy.

I was pretty sure neither of them would object.

So what was keeping my ass glued to the chair?

Why didn't I just get up, strip, and join them on the bed? It's what we all wanted.

Their movements got more frantic. Ari pushed back against each of Javi's thrusts, fucking herself on his cock. Her throat was stretched out, her eyes half-closed. The hair on Javi's chest, matted with sweat, shone in the room's light. I'd never be able to look at this bed again without seeing the two of them on it, their faces contorted with pleasure.

Without imagining myself in Javi's place. Snapping my hips and driving my cock into Ari's sweet pussy.

"*Voy a venir*!" Ari cried.

"Come, *querida*. Come with me."

Ari's head dropped forward. Javi's dropped back. Her fingers gripped the bed's thick comforter and Javi's gripped her hips. His pelvis snapped forward, his muscles locked. He was still for a moment, and then his body convulsed.

And in that moment, it was me in Ari's place. My ass impaled on Javi's hard cock. Feeling him deep inside me. The bulbous head of his cock pushing past the tight ring of muscle. The slide of his shaft as he thrust in and pulled out. The sharp all-encompassing pleasure as that thick head rubbed just right against my prostate.

My hand jerked my cock. A rapid up and down. My legs shook. My eyes closed.

I imagined the heat when he came inside me. The smell of his—

Fuck, fuck, fuck!

My throat filled with bitter-tasting bile.

I doubled over, caught in that all-too-familiar dark place between coming and puking.

Oh Jesus. I was back there. In that place. In Coach's office at the high school. In his living room. In his bedroom. Shit. And it wasn't Javi fucking me. It was *him*.

Goddamn. *Pull it together, man. Don't let them see you like this.*

I breathed through my nose, blew out through my mouth. Pushed the memories into their box at the back of my mind where they were supposed to stay. Fuck Greta for making me unlock that box. I hadn't been hit with a flashback this intense in years.

But maybe that meant the therapy was working?

Shit. I just wanted to be normal. To be there for Ari and for Javi. To enjoy sex in all its forms without the past sneaking up on me like a stalker in a deserted alley.

I breathed some more, and when I finally had myself under control and was no longer in imminent risk of upchucking the pizza I'd shared with Javi, I adjusted my slacks and sat up. Javi and Ari had both dressed and were quietly holding hands while sitting on the edge of the bed. They wore identical worried expressions. "Are you okay?" Ari asked gently.

I forced a smile I was most definitely not feeling. "Just exhausted. Two orgasms in a row is a lot for an old man like me." It was a lie, but the only explanation I could come up with for why I'd been doubled over for so long.

"Daniel, *hermano*." Eyes dark with concern, Javi tilted his head to the side, clearly not buying my lie. And why should he? We'd been in a similar place before.

I shoved to my feet. I couldn't fucking do this to Javi again. Or Ari. I wouldn't hurt either of them again. I'd told Ari something had to change, and I'd meant it. I'd do whatever I had to do to get over this. To get over my past. I was sick of being this way. Sick of hiding. Sick of being sick.

"It's cool, guys." I moved to the door.

"Where are you going? This is your room."

It was, wasn't it? Fuck, I was so turned around I didn't even remember where I was.

Something had to change, and that something was me. I looked away from them. "I—I'm going to make some more appointments with Greta."

"I love you, Daniel," Ari said, tears in her voice.

"We both do," Javi added.

Jesus. They were killing me. I wanted to say it back, but the words, like so many others, stuck in my throat.

DANIEL

Why the fuck couldn't I get over this? Why couldn't I think about Javi fucking me without freaking out? Javi wasn't *him*.

I knocked on Greta's door and heard her call out. "Coming." She opened the door seconds later and ushered me inside. We took chairs in her suite's sitting area, and she leaned forward. "You look like something's bothering you."

I raked a hand through my hair, tugging at it and closing my eyes, letting my shoulders slump forward. "I thought after I told you, I'd be better. Like the poison would be gone. But it's still there."

"Tell me what happened." Her light blue eyes met mine. I saw no judgment there. No worry. Just calm.

A calm I really needed to see right now.

"Javier and I have tentatively agreed to share Arianna."

Greta raised an eyebrow. "And is Arianna party to this agreement?"

I nodded. "We already tried. And it went really well until…" I trailed off.

"Tell me what you were feeling and what specifically triggered it."

I closed my eyes. "We agreed to share her, but one at a time. I didn't think I could… perform if Javi was in bed with us. So, he watched while Ari and I had sex. And then I watched them." I stopped there, my heart starting to speed up again.

"Did you have any problems during that?"

I shook my head. "Not until I started fantasizing about Javi taking me the way he was taking Ari."

"And how was that?" Greta asked, her voice soft.

"From behind. The way *he* used to."

"And then?"

"And then I fucking freaked out and practically had a goddamn panic attack in front of them."

"That's only natural."

"No. It fucking isn't!" I snapped.

"It is, after what you went through."

My gut cramped, and I crossed my arms, bending forward, taking deep breaths. God, I felt like vomiting. A cold sweat broke out all over me. If just the thought of it made me feel like this, how could I ever get past it?

"I shouldn't have started this. I *knew* I shouldn't have. I've resisted Javi all this time because I didn't want to hurt him. And then I had to suggest we try."

"Back up a bit," Greta said. "I thought you only agreed to share Arianna."

"Well, yes, but…"

"But you want more?"

"And I know Javier wants more too. And I feel like I'm leading him on with the promise of that." I ground my teeth together. "A promise I can't fucking deliver on." I swallowed hard. "Because I'm a fucking mess. A fucking freak."

"Daniel." Greta's voice was gentle. "Those things you're saying about yourself aren't true. The way you're reacting—it's one hundred percent normal. There is *nothing* wrong with you."

"Then why can't I get over this? I've tried to be intimate with a man, and I can't. Not the way I should. Not the way I want to be with Javi. I just want to be normal."

"What's normal?"

"Not what I've been doing." I thought of Diego, my skin crawling with shame. I'd used him. I'd used all those escorts.

The way *he'd* used me.

Like a piece of meat.

A fuck toy.

And I could never do that to Javier.

To anyone again.

"You had a coping mechanism that was working for you," Greta said.

"I can't do that anymore." I rocked back and forth in the chair. "I won't. I hate that I did that. I hate that I was so harsh with those men. So cruel." I blew out a breath. "Why would I do that?"

"Sometimes when a person has been abused, they have a hard time functioning normally when it comes to sex. The sex and the abuse become tangled in their minds."

"I hate this. I need it to stop."

"Were you ever this way with women?"

I shook my head. "Never."

"That's good."

"Whenever I tried to be normal with a guy, I couldn't. I'd freak out." I stared at the floor. "I could only do it if I shut myself off."

"Dissociation after a trauma is common."

"I want the sex, but I don't. I'm turned on, but I'm not. I'm afraid, but I'm numb too."

She nodded. "That's all normal."

I took a deep breath. "It is?"

"It is. All of it. It might help you to read some other survivors' stories online. You'll see that everything you're feeling is normal."

"Okay." My heartbeat started to slow. "Then how do I get past it?"

"We can treat this through several different therapies that will help your mind move past the emotional trauma—EMDR and lifespan integration may be helpful. I'll explain those in more detail when we try them."

"Will those treatments help with my panic attacks?"

"They should. But it would also help if we treated this like any other fear. The more you're exposed to a fear in small controlled amounts, the easier it is for you to overcome it."

"You mean like some kind of conditioning?"

She nodded. "If Javier is willing, the two of you could try some gradual physical intimacy. But…"

"But?"

She held my gaze. "He's going to need to know what happened to you. Arianna too. They both need to understand what happened and why you might have a hard time with some things or react in certain ways."

Fuck. "I *have* to tell them? Everything?"

"The more you disclose, the better. It will help them understand."

"And they'll look at me like I'm some pathetic mess."

"They won't. I assure you." She smiled. "You are incredibly brave, Daniel. They'll see that."

Would they though? The whole time they'd known me, I'd never let them see me like this. Like the disaster I was. If they knew, if they really knew, could they trust me with the business?

Could they trust me with themselves?

And could they look at me as a man?

I didn't see how that was possible. Their view of me would change, and not for the better.

There was no way I could let that happen. Now that we'd finally moved closer, I wasn't going to risk what we had.

I'd do the other therapy Greta wanted to do, and that would have to do the trick.

Because telling them? That wasn't going to happen.

Chapter 8

JAVIER

Just as I parked the rental car outside the venue for the Tough Mudder obstacle course, my phone rang. It was Zach. Maybe he'd made some progress on the investigation into the leak of the retreat's original Santa Catalina location. "Hey, Zach," I said. "Give me a minute."

"Sure thing, boss."

Not wanting any of the clients to get an inkling that we were looking into the leak, I told Daniel and Ari I'd meet them inside. Daniel sent me a closed look, then slung his arm around Arianna's shoulders. "Come on, Ari. I'll help you get everyone organized."

I walked to the far end of the parking lot before unmuting the speaker. "Zach."

"I've got some news for you," he said.

My gut clenched. I couldn't tell by Zach's tone if it was good news or bad. I didn't think a TI employee was responsible for the leak, but I didn't *know* it. "I'm listening," I said cautiously.

I heard the clacking of a keyboard. "I'm sending you the report of the phone record search," Zach said.

Almost immediately, my phone pinged, a notification of an incoming message. "How about you give me the executive summary right now?"

"I didn't find any evidence of a leak in the phone records. I also searched all the outgoing emails and chats, still nothing."

Relief flooded me. "Great work, Zach."

"What do you want me to look into next?"

"I don't think there's anything else we can legally do."

"That sucks, man. This was kind of fun."

I laughed. "Sorry you didn't find anything juicy."

"Oh, I wouldn't say that," Zach said, and I could hear the smirk in his voice.

"What? You did find something?"

"Nothing related to the leak. But yeah… I did."

"What is it? What did you find?"

"It's in the report I emailed you."

I blew out an impatient breath. "We're about to start a 5K Tough Mudder race, and my phone will be locked up in the glove compartment for the next three or four hours. You can't keep me in suspense like this, Zach."

Zach laughed. "My bad, boss." There was more clacking of the keyboard. He cleared his throat. "I'm not sure I should be telling you this, but it's in the report… so…"

"Come on, Zach," I practically growled.

"Okay, okay. Let me see. Um… on October first, that's the day Daniel returned from Tahiti, he placed a call to a place called Diamond Escorts."

What the hell? Daniel had called an escort service? "Maybe it was a wrong number."

"The call lasted five minutes."

Okay, so not a wrong number. "Are there any charges from Diamond Escorts to Daniel's TI credit card?"

I held my breath as I waited for Zach's answer.

"No."

Jesus. Thank fuck. "Then it's none of our business."

"Got it," Zach said. "So, for now I sit tight?"

"Yep. If I think of some other plan of attack, I'll let you know."

"Good luck with the race, not that you'll need it."

"Why do you say that?"

"I've seen you on the treadmill. Three miles is just a warm-up for you."

He was right. I'd already run ten miles that morning in the vineyard's gym. "All right. I'd better go before they start without me."

We said quick goodbyes and I hung up. My mind whirled with the news Zach had just given me. Why would Daniel call an escort service? Why would he need to?

I jogged across the parking lot and rejoined the group. We were at Sears Point in the southern Sonoma Mountains, and I turned around in a circle, taking in the hilly, arid terrain. Our group contained six ECC counselors, three TI staff, and ten ECC clients battling ourselves and our demons to traverse the three miles and thirteen obstacles in the course laid out for us. I couldn't fucking wait.

Beside me, Daniel stretched his legs, and Ari bounced on her toes. Their faces were bright and eager. Those two were always up for a challenge. I grinned at them.

"What?" Ari said.

"Think we can beat the other teams?"

Ari scoffed. "Other teams? I'm gonna beat the two of you."

Daniel smirked. "You sure about that, cupcake?"

Her face darkened. "Cupcake? I'm no cupcake. I'm a fucking crème brûlée, and don't you forget it."

Daniel winked at me, then held his hands up. "My mistake, ma'am."

"*Cabrón*!" Ari rolled her eyes and stomped off to the start line.

I nudged Daniel's shoulder. "I don't think she quite gets the concept of this race."

We'd divided everyone into groups of three, with each client couple accompanied by an ECC counselor, and Greta floating between the couples, which left the three of us to form one team. Greta had also emphasized to everyone that the goal of the exercise was to build a sense of teamwork, of community. We were all supposed to help each other and reach the finish line as a group.

Daniel chuckled. "Nothing's changed over the years. Arianna's always been very competitive."

The Tough Mudder staff herded us toward the start line. It was actually a giant arch with the word "start" on it. We would run under it when the race began, but first, it was time for the national anthem. As a group, we stood, hands on our hearts, and sang the familiar words.

"Have a great run, everyone!" shouted the organizer. We all whooped as we charged under the arch. Ari was, of course, in the lead.

The first obstacle was the Kiss of Mud. It was a forty-foot crawl under barbed wire in what looked like thousands of gallons of mud. I shuddered. I fucking hated being dirty. Daniel squeezed my neck. "Come on, dude. Man up."

I pulled out of his grasp. "You're on."

We dove under the barbed wire. Using my elbows, knees, and toes, I wiggled and slid my way through the obstacle. Mud coated my face and every inch of my front. Fucking gross.

When I reached the end, Daniel was already standing there, calm and collected. But oh so dirty. His blue eyes shone even more brightly in his face, darkened by the wet mud. My breath caught in my throat. He was so damn sexy. I wanted to kidnap him, take him to the showers and wash every inch of him clean, first with my hands, and then with my mouth.

My cock hardened, and I thanked *Dios* I'd chosen to wear compression trunks under my basketball shorts.

Smiling, Daniel crouched down held his hand out. I grabbed it, and he tugged me to my feet. "Where's Ari?" I asked.

He pointed down the path. "But we'll catch up to her."

I looked at the others in the group. A few of the women were still on the other side, clearly complaining about getting dirty. Chad stood several feet away from us. His arms were crossed as he waited next to Jay Samson. Chad's eyes never left his wife, Monica, one of the women who hadn't crossed over yet. He laughed darkly. "She hates getting dirty. Fuck, last week Monica fired an assistant because a drop of coffee landed on her pants when the woman handed her a cup of takeout coffee. It wasn't even her fault. The cover hadn't been put on right."

"That's harsh, man," Jay said. His own wife, Raven, had kept up with Ari and was even now almost to the next obstacle. As a choreographer, she was slim and fit and clearly quite competitive.

"No shit. Maybe this race will take her down a notch."

Rick Devlin, one of the ECC counselors, clearly having overheard, came to stand beside Chad. "Remember what we discussed. You're supposed to offer your spouse words of encouragement. We're one team."

Chad groaned. "Fine. Come on, Monica," he shouted. "It's just mud, but unlike the mud in those high-end spas you love, it won't cost you an arm and a leg."

Monica waved him away. "That's the problem with you, Chad. You're so pedestrian."

"Whatever." Chad gave her his back and proceeded down the path. Jay stayed in step with him.

"Well, that went well," Daniel whispered next to my ear. His warm breath brushed my skin, making me shiver.

"We'd better do something."

"Let's go back. Maybe if we go in behind them, it will help."

We doubled back. When the women saw us, they brightened. Monica sidled up to me. Her finger trailed down my chest. I hoped Chad was too far off to see this. My eyes searched out Daniel's. He'd been similarly trapped by Rebecca.

We cajoled the ladies and pretty soon we had them all in a line. I was in front, leading the way, while Daniel took up the rear.

"That's it, ladies. Almost there," I called out.

Monica's hands kept "accidentally" stroking my calves. At one point, she was almost on top of me. I was sure only the threat of the barbed wire kept her from climbing me completely.

Nothing had ever felt as freeing as that first breath I took on the other side. I slithered out from under Monica, stood, and helped her to her feet. Rick joined us and led her away. I could have kissed the man.

A few of the husbands had stayed behind. They helped their wives to their feet, then along with their ECC counselors, they headed to the next obstacle. I waited for Daniel. When he finally emerged from the Kiss of Mud, he was even dirtier than the first time. I couldn't help laughing. "You look like the mud monster in that movie we used to watch in college."

Daniel's eyes lit up. He raised his hands and began stalking me, his legs stiff and his feet plodding. He growled deep in his chest, and God help me, I was turned on, so fucking turned on. "You'd better run, little boy." he said darkly. "If I catch you, I'm gonna eat you!"

I snorted. I'd love nothing better than to have Daniel eat me. But I couldn't say that. Instead, I pretended to shriek. "No, no. Help me! Someone help me!"

Greta smiled warmly. "You guys are crazy. Thank you, by the way. I feared we'd be stuck on the first obstacle all day."

I bent at the waist in a courtly manner. "Our pleasure, Ms. Lindstrom."

She laughed and wound her arms around mine and Daniel's. "Come on, you two. I'm sure we'll need your help again at the next obstacle."

We chit-chatted along the way about the Tough Mudder and what she hoped it would do to advance each couple's therapy. She and Daniel seemed very comfortable with each other, and while I was thrilled that he'd found someone to talk to about his issues, I was also a little hurt that I wasn't his confidant. That he didn't feel he could share with me whatever it was he'd been telling her. It was selfish and self-centered, I knew. But I couldn't help the way I felt.

The next obstacle was the Devil's Beard. A huge rope net had been hung over some very muddy ground. The goal was to crawl under the netting, about twenty yards, to the other side.

When Daniel and I reached Ari, she was already on her hands and knees, her gorgeous ass sticking out as she tried to wiggle under the heavy rope. "*Corazón*," I half-laughed, half-sighed. "You'll never make it to the other side like that."

She brought her head back out. "What's your suggestion then, oh smart one?"

I eyed Daniel. We'd been friends for so long that a look was usually all it took for the other to understand. Daniel nodded, and in sync, we each grabbed the edge of the net and lifted it up onto our shoulders as we stepped underneath it.

Ari walked under the net in the area we'd raised. "Great idea, Javi," she said, her face beaming. But how do we keep pushing forward?"

Daniel whistled and caught the attention of the others. "Chad, get your ass over here and help us."

When Chad grumbled, Branson, standing beside his wife, Malia, laughed. Daniel waved them both over. "You too, Branson."

The men crouched under the rope. "Get a little ahead of us and put the rope on your shoulders," I instructed.

The other members of the group came over to see what we were doing. Ari quickly moved to the front, followed by the women, and told the men where to stand to lift the rope. We leapfrogged each other like this to the other side. Ari, of course, was the first one out. She jumped and cheered. "We did it!"

"We, huh?" Daniel said, his eyes bright with humor.

God, I loved that look on him. It was one I'd rarely seen in recent years. I hoped that I was at least partly responsible for it.

Ari winked at him. "Maybe you helped… a little bit." She danced on her toes. "Come on. We need to get to the next obstacle."

And with that, she turned and disappeared down the muddy path. "So much for teamwork," I said.

Daniel just shook his head. We set off down the trail, Chad and Branson walking behind us. I could hear them talking softly. I edged closer to Daniel, being sure to keep my voice low. "So, Zach."

Daniel shot me an alarmed look. "Did he find the leak?"

"No, but he did find something interesting."

"Oh yeah? What's that?"

"Ever hear of Diamond Escorts?"

Daniel stared straight ahead.

When he remained silent, I added, "He sent me the phone records. You called them the night you got back from Tahiti."

He shrugged. "So what if I did?"

"So nothing." We walked in silence for a bit. Ari had already reached the next obstacle. The closer we got, the more I felt the pressure. I wanted him to tell me why, but I couldn't ask him directly. I also didn't like that I'd upset him. "I'm surprised you have to pay for it," I teased. "I guess you've lost your touch."

Daniel turned to me and grinned predatorily. "Is that right? Arianna seems to enjoy my touch just fine."

"That she does, my friend. That she does."

We passed a water station, and I grabbed a cup for each of us. I turned to hand it to Daniel when it was snatched from my hand. Monica stood grinning. "Thank you, darling."

I narrowed my eyes. "It wasn't meant for you."

"Maybe so, yet I'm the one with it now. Just like… maybe you aren't meant for me, but"—she looked around, caught Chad's eyes, and returned her gaze to me—"I'm the one who has you now." She hooked her hand around my neck and rubbed her tit along my arm. What the hell was she up to? "I haven't been with someone like you in a long time."

"Like me?" I asked as I tried to remove her arm from my neck. "Latino?"

"No. Big, strong. In charge."

That last bit she directed at Chad. I couldn't help but feel for the guy. Monica was a good twenty years older than him; her career had been set when he'd still been in elementary school. How could he come into her life and make a place for himself when she was so fierce and independent?

Chad approached, his eyes shooting daggers at his wife. He gripped her wrist and snarled. "Stop making a fool of yourself."

She jerked back as though he'd slapped her. "No, that's your job, isn't it?" Turning, she ripped her wrist out of his grasp and flounced off after the others.

Chad sighed. "Sorry about that, Javier."

"Hey, man. No worries. It's a tough time."

"Well, it's about to be over."

"What do you mean, over?" Daniel asked, his posture suddenly stiff.

"I'm just saying I'm glad the first location was leaked because now this farce of a fucking marriage can be over."

"I don't understand. Wasn't it over anyway?" I asked.

He pursed his lips. "The studio threatened to make us pay back all her earnings from her current film if we didn't keep a lid on our marital problems until six months after the launch. We've still got four months to go."

"So," Daniel said, his fingers picking at the drying mud on his cheeks. "Now that the story of your troubles was leaked, the cat's out of the bag, so to speak, and the studio has nothing to hold over you?"

Chad raised a shoulder. "That's pretty much it. It's public knowledge now. We can get a divorce if we want to."

"Do you really want to?" Daniel asked, his voice gone unusually soft. "A divorce is one thing that's really hard to take back."

My heart broke for Daniel. Everything in his expression said he'd love to take back his decision to divorce Arianna. Something that would leave me exactly no-fucking-where.

Chad hung his head. "I don't know, man."

"You still love her?"

When Chad raised his head, his eyes swam with pain and anguish. "I do. God help me." He swallowed as though the words themselves hurt.

"Then fight for her, okay?" Daniel said.

He sniffed and wiped at his reddened eyes with the back of his hand. He looked sheepishly from me to Daniel. "Thanks, guys."

I angled my head toward the next obstacle. "We'd better get going. I have it on good authority that the next obstacle is the Hero Carry. I'm sure those ECC counselors are sick of lugging everyone up the muddy hills."

"Yeah," Chad smiled and jokingly flexed his biceps. "They need some fit young men to save the day."

Daniel shot me a look behind Chad's back. It took me in. All of me, from head to toe. He licked his lips, and his voice was unusually gruff when he said, "We all do."

JAVIER

When we got to the final part of the Tough Mudder course, I turned to Daniel. "What do you say we teach a certain someone the value of teamwork?"

A glint came into his eye. "Are you thinking what I'm thinking?"

I grinned at him. "You and me teaming up to give her a night she'll remember."

Daniel nodded and started to say something, then stopped.

"What is it, bro?" I asked.

"I'm not ready for any stuff between you and me," he said, his face going red.

I couldn't say I wasn't disappointed, but I shrugged to hide it. "I'm cool with whatever happens. Or doesn't happen." And I was. The last thing I wanted was to make him uncomfortable.

"You sure?" he asked. "I just…" His voice trailed off, and then I realized.

I lowered my voice and leaned close. "You're a virgin when it comes to guys?"

He shrugged. "Not exactly, but I might as well be."

Okay… "Care to elaborate?"

He looked around at everyone racing past us. "Maybe later."

"When you're ready," I said, crouching down to offer him a leg up over the wall.

He looked at me for a long moment. "You're a great friend, Javi."

I straightened and pretended to buff my nails on my mud-spattered chest. "I try."

He laughed, and I crouched over again, bracing myself for his weight as he placed a foot on my back and reached up for the top of the wall. He scrambled over, then leaned down to give me a hand up. I took it, and when I reached the top, I said, "And you're a damn good friend too, Daniel."

He nodded and looked away, then hopped down to the ground, charging toward the muddy water and the jungle-gym like structure over it. Ari was already halfway across, easily swinging from bar to bar, and I shook my head at her retreating figure.

I wish I knew what was going on with Daniel, but I'd eventually find out. He was starting to open up, ever so slowly, and he had no idea how patient I could be.

I'd waited forever to get to this point. I'd keep nudging him—and Ari—bit by bit. Because this *had* to work between us.

I couldn't imagine going back to how we'd been before.

We bombed through the obstacle to meet a grinning Ari at the other side. "In your faces!" she crowed, pumping her fists in the air and dancing around in a circle while shaking her hips and her very fine ass.

I cracked up and grabbed her around the waist and hoisted her up over my shoulder as she pounded on my back and shrieked at me to put her down. I just patted her ass.

"Your room or mine?" I asked Daniel.

"Yours," he said.

Ari smacked at my legs. "The Hero's Carry is over. Put me down, you troglodyte!"

"Not a chance," I murmured and kissed her hip.

I carried her over to the outdoor showers where the three of us rinsed off the worst of the muck. The Tough Mudder folks helpfully gave us some plastic seat covers so we wouldn't trash the rental car.

Daniel slipped into the driver's seat and Ari took shotgun. I got in behind Ari and leaned forward, speaking in her ear. "*Corazón*, you are going to pay for leaving us behind."

"Not my fault you two couldn't keep up."

Daniel reached over and put a hand on her thigh. "We could have. We just chose to watch your exceptional ass jiggling in those shorts."

"My ass doesn't jiggle!"

Daniel chuckled. "Okay, it bounces."

She crossed her arms. "I have a great ass. A very firm, very toned ass. I've worked damn hard on it."

"You definitely have, *corazón*. That's why we could hardly take our eyes off it," I whispered in her ear. "And it's why you're going to show it to us in my room."

She gave me a dark look. "Oh, am I? Who says you two deserve it?"

Daniel slid his hand up her thigh until he was just barely touching her crotch. "We do."

"And I have no say in this?" she huffed.

He brushed his fingers against her, and I leaned forward and kissed her neck. "Do you want to say no?" I asked.

She huffed again. "No. But it's the principle of the thing."

"You just want to be contrary," Daniel said, and I laughed.

"Did you know her sisters called her Contr-Ari when she was little?" I asked him.

She whirled around and pointed at me. "Don't tell him that!"

Daniel grinned. "Oh, now I'm going to have to call you that."

"No, no, you do not," she said.

He took his hand off her thigh and offered me his fist to bump.

Ari shook her head in disgust. "You two are such… frat bros sometimes."

We bumped fists again. "Yeah, and so?" Daniel said.

"I feel like you're ganging up on me."

We pulled onto the gravel drive for Montero Vineyards. "Oh, you know you like it," I said in her ear. "And you're going to like what we have in mind."

She flipped her damp hair at me. "We'll see about that."

I met Daniel's gaze in the rearview mirror, and we both said "Challenge accepted" at the same time.

We hustled ourselves upstairs and into my room, all three of us starting to strip and calling dibs on the shower. "I should go first," Ari said. "I take the longest."

"It is big enough for three," I said. It really was.

Gloriously bare, a streak of mud on her cheek, her hair spotted with it, Ari held out her clenched fist. "Rock, paper, scissors."

She threw a rock, I did paper, and Daniel did a rock.

I grinned at the two of them. "All three of us in there."

Daniel scratched at his chin. "You think it's that big?"

He really was uncomfortable with he and I being too close, wasn't he?

"Or, she could go first, and we could take turns supervising. Make sure she doesn't miss any spots," I said.

Ari rolled her eyes. "You two."

"You might miss the spot behind your ears," I said, following her to the bathroom, Daniel behind us.

"I'm pretty sure that's not the spot you're concerned with."

She stepped into the natural stone enclosure. The end opposite the showerhead was open, and the wall facing the rest of the bathroom was clear glass. Daniel parked himself on the closed toilet lid while Ari started the shower. When the spray was warm enough, she stepped under it and moaned as she let the water run over her.

That sound woke up my half-hard cock. I glanced through the glass to see Daniel responding as well.

I picked up a bar of soap and started lathering my hands, then ran them over Ari's back, kneading her shoulders as I did, then cupping her ass and massaging it. I parted her cheeks and ran my soapy fingers up and down her crack, making her shiver and press into my hands. I circled my fingers around her hole, and she moaned. I hadn't been sure if she liked anal play, but apparently she did. I fingered her a bit as she braced herself against the wall, water cascading over her shoulders, her little whimpers making me as hard as the stone surrounding us.

I wanted to take her that way someday. But not today.

I turned her around under the spray so she was facing me, then I soaped up her front, paying special attention to her full tits. I skirted around her pussy until her hips were rolling, then I touched her there until she was panting. But I didn't want to let her come just yet. I released her and she pouted at me. I quickly soaped myself up while she rinsed out her hair. When she was finished, I traded places with her under the spray, and when she started to walk out, Daniel rose.

"Just a minute," he said. "I'm pretty sure you missed a spot." He crowded her back inside and into a corner so I could step past without touching him.

I was dying to. All that smooth tanned skin, those rippling muscles, and that jutting cock begged for my hands. But I kept them to myself. He'd made it clear he didn't want that.

At least not yet.

I grabbed a towel and started to dry off. Daniel had herded Ari into the corner that had a stone seat built in, and he urged one of her feet up onto it as he sank to his knees in front of her.

He parted her legs and licked her pussy. She gasped and widened her stance for him. He shot me a grin over his shoulder. "You definitely missed a spot."

"Definitely," she murmured, and I laughed.

Daniel went back to his task while I finished drying off, my eyes glued to them, eating up the way she fisted his hair and arched into his mouth. He took her to the brink, then rose.

"You're stopping?" she said, her voice rising with indignation. "Now?"

He nodded and stepped under the water.

She cast him a withering look, and he grinned. I gave him a thumbs-up. We hadn't planned to edge her, but now it was game on.

Her gaze flicked between us. "You're bastards, both of you," she said and stomped out of the shower.

"Not so fast, *princesa*." I handed her a towel and barred her exit from the bathroom.

Daniel quickly washed up while she toweled off, her eyes flashing sparks at me. "If you two think you're going to just toy with me—"

"Hush, Contr-Ari," Daniel said as he shut off the water and stepped out, grabbing a towel off the rack and crowding up behind her. He forced her closer to me, until she was sandwiched between us. "We'll make this more than worth your while," he whispered as he dropped a kiss to her shoulder.

She glared up at me. "Will you?"

"*Ciertamente*," I murmured, my hands going to those glorious tits of hers once again. I cupped them in my hands, my thumbs stroking her hard nipples, and she moaned, closing her eyes.

Daniel finished drying off and ran his fingers through his hair, pushing it off his forehead. "Let's get her somewhere more comfortable," he said, using his head to indicate the bedroom.

We followed him to the bed, and he motioned Ari up onto it. "On all fours," he said.

"Am I a performing seal?" she asked, but she started to get into position. He grabbed her jaw and when she opened her mouth to protest, he stuck his thumb in her mouth. She closed her lips around it and sucked.

"You'll perform the way we say," he said, his voice low and commanding. "And if you're good, you'll get to come."

My cock twitched at his controlling tone. I liked this side of Daniel. A side I hadn't seen before. Yeah, I'd seen flashes of it the other night, but this was different.

And Ari softened right up for him.

There was history here, something I hadn't guessed at. I thought I knew her so well, but there was so much I still had to learn.

She continued sucking on his thumb, her eyes locked on his, and I tamped down a rush of jealousy. Of course they had history.

Daniel grinned at me and motioned to Ari's unoccupied back half. "I think she could use some tag-teaming, don't you?"

I wasn't going to say no. I crawled up behind her in time to see Daniel withdraw his thumb from her mouth and replace it with his cock.

Fuck. My dick was suddenly very jealous. She swallowed him, bobbing up and down on his shaft like it was her favorite thing in the world.

I was torn between wanting to trade places with him and wanting to trade places with her.

But I had a different job to do, didn't I?

Teasing our very contrary Ari.

I urged her legs apart so I could see that pretty pussy. God, she was gorgeous. I should probably take her ass just to teach her a lesson, but I'd go easy on her. I started stroking her slit, my fingers dipping into her juices and spreading them around her clit. She arched her back and moaned around Daniel's cock.

He groaned, and I rubbed her faster, until she was whimpering, and he was panting. Then I withdrew my hand. She whined in protest, starting to sit back from Daniel, but he gripped the nape of her neck and held her in place.

"All good things come to those who wait," he said, looking from her to me.

His burning eyes met mine, and I flashed back to Cancun, to the way our eyes had met as we'd each fucked our girls. That connection arced between us again, and I suddenly needed to be inside her. Now.

I gestured to the nightstand drawer by Daniel. "Help a brother out?" I said.

With one hand still holding onto Ari's neck, he opened the drawer and grabbed a condom packet, then tossed it to me.

I suited up. Ari and I hadn't been using protection, but I didn't want to explain that to Daniel.

Hell, I didn't know when or exactly how to bring that subject up. But that was a topic for another time, when Ari wasn't writhing between us and trying to back up onto my cock while I teased her entrance with it.

Without warning, I plunged inside her, and she groaned around Daniel's shaft. He started rocking his hips, his grip on her neck visibly tightening. I slammed into her, pushing her forward, and she moaned again, then pushed back against me. We had her suspended between us, and she had no choice but to let us do what we wanted.

She clenched herself around me, and it was my turn to groan. "*Princesa*, you don't play fair," I murmured, and she gave me the finger, making me snort with laughter. Daniel and I fist bumped over her shoulder, then I started fucking her in earnest.

After a few minutes, Daniel stiffened and came with a shout, shuddering as he shot down Ari's throat. She held his hip and swallowed him down, then he released her and stumbled over to the chair in the corner and sat down, his eyes on us. I put a hand on her back and urged her to arch her ass in the air for me. She was breathing hard and whispering, "*Por favor*, Javi."

I took pity on her and reached between her legs, finding her clit and stroking it while angling my cock to hit her G-spot square on.

She let out a throaty moan and fisted the sheets. "*Dios*, Javi."

That just spurred me on, and I snapped my hips forward, driving into her. I looked up and saw Daniel watching, his eyes boring into me. He was hard again and touching himself, and I knew, I knew he was thinking about me.

About us. Together.

I imagined him in Ari's place, his hands fisting the sheets, his groans in my ears, and I came with a roar, Ari clenching around me as she shuddered beneath me and cried out.

I slumped over her and kissed the nape of her neck. "Was it worth it, *corazón*?"

I pulled out of her and she collapsed facedown on the mattress. "You know it was."

Chuckling, I looked up at Daniel. He was still gazing at me intently, his hand gripping his cock.

I plucked a tissue out of the box on the nightstand and removed the condom. Daniel looked away for a second, but after I'd disposed of it in the trash, his gaze snagged mine again, and his fist pumped his cock.

I stepped over to him and stopped, my own cock starting to wake up like I was eighteen all over again. I put a hand on the arm of the chair and leaned a bit into his personal space. "I could take care of that for you," I said.

He just stared at me and said nothing. Did he want it or not? I dropped to my knees beside the chair, making my intent clear, and touched his knee. He sprang out of the chair, a fist swinging dangerously near my face, and I reared back.

"What the fuck, Daniel?" Ari said.

He froze a couple feet from both of us, his chest heaving, both hands clenched into fists, his knuckles shining white beneath his skin.

"Yeah," I said, settling back onto my heels. "What the fuck, bro? I thought you wanted it."

He stared at me wide-eyed, then he shook his head. "I do. But I *can't*." His voice cracked on the last word.

I rose, but decided to sit in the chair to appear as nonthreatening as possible. "Why can't you?"

He looked from me to Ari and shook his head again, closing his eyes.

Ari got off the bed and cautiously approached him. "Daniel, *mi amor*, you can tell us anything. You know that."

She touched his forearm, and he shuddered, then suddenly he wrapped his arms around her, his body trembling. They stood like that for several moments, she rubbing her hands in circles on his back and murmuring, "It's okay. Whatever it is, it's okay."

Finally, he let go of her and swallowed visibly. He looked from her to me. "There's something I need to tell you." He reached for his shorts. "But I'd be more comfortable if we were all dressed."

I stopped them from putting on their damp, dirty clothes and handed out items from my suitcase, the whole time my mind asking the same question.

What the hell had happened to Daniel?

I was about to find out.

DANIEL

We settled in the seating area of Javi's room, he and Ari on the couch, me across from them, pretty much exactly as it had been the last time we'd had a big talk. And I was just as fucking nervous. Which was stupid, because I'd already spilled my guts to Greta. This was no different.

Liar.

I perched on the edge of the armchair and dropped my head down. It was a lot different. Javi was my best friend, the only man I'd ever loved, and Ari, she'd been my everything for so long. I didn't want them to judge me, to judge me and find me lacking. It could happen though. They weren't like Greta. She was impartial, uninvested. But Ari and Javi had spent decades as my friends and more. They weren't impartial. I didn't want to lose them.

Despite that very real fear, I had to come clean with them, if we had any hope of pursuing our arrangement. The cards would fall where they did. And I'd go on with my life, the same way I always did.

I stiffened my spine and my resolve. These were my friends. If they loved me as much as I hoped they did, as much as I loved them, they'd understand.

But will they see me the same?

I'd know soon enough. Hate I could deal with. But pity? I shuddered. That was something I never wanted to see in their eyes. Ever.

I cleared my throat. "When I was in high school, I played on a competitive tennis team."

"You were a state champion," Ari said.

I nodded. "Throughout all of it, I had a coach, C-coach Wilkins. I was in gym class one day out on the tennis court. We were doing racket sports that semester. Anyway, Coach Wilkins walked right up to me in front of the whole class and told me that I should join the tennis team." I smiled at the memory. "I felt so special when this man who clearly knew his stuff said I had potential. That with proper equipment and a lot of training, I could be someone. A great player like Andre Agassi or Pete Sampras."

I shifted on the seat and rubbed my jaw before continuing. This next part was the hardest. I hoped I could get the words out. "I joined the team, and he started coaching me. By the time I was fifteen, I was playing on a national level. It cost a lot of money, and my parents were working their butts off to pay for it all. I pushed myself really hard because I couldn't let my parents down and I couldn't let Coach down."

I raised my eyes. Ari clutched Javi's hand. Her nails dug into his skin, but he didn't seem to even notice. Their faces were strained as they listened intently to my story. "It started slowly."

Ari gasped. I pressed my lips together and looked away. I had to get it all out. Get the whole story out, then I could deal with the fallout. "A hand on my shoulder. An innocent brushing of fingers against my ass as he helped me perfect a stroke. He'd often come talk to me while I was showering, usually when no one else was around. One day, he invited me to his house. I thought the whole team would be there, but it turned out that it was just me. At first, I was scared. I wanted to leave. He convinced me to stay, and we had pizza and soft drinks, watched a movie on pay-per-view. He didn't touch me once." I shook my head. I'd been so fucking naïve. "I thought that meant I'd imagined the whole thing."

"Oh, Daniel," Ari said, tears in her voice. She reached out to me.

I moved away. "L-let me finish."

She nodded. "Of course."

"When he invited me again a few weeks later, I went eagerly. My family was spending so much on my tennis that we didn't have any money left for stuff like pay-per-view or even renting movies at Blockbuster. Spending the evening with Coach was a luxury. That night, he offered me a beer. I remember being shocked. I was just fifteen, didn't he realize that? He laughed at me and told me about how he and his friends had started drinking beer when he was even younger than me. I felt so grown up."

The closer I got to the ugly part, the deeper into the story, the faster my leg bounced. I pushed down on it with my elbow and relished the sharp pain. "A few weeks later, a couple days after my birthday, he invited me over again. We had beer and pizza, but instead of a movie, he put on some porn. I'd seen a magazine or two, but I'd never seen an actual porno. I was embarrassed as fuck when I got a hard-on. I tried to leave. Coach assured me it was normal. I was a healthy young male. Didn't I masturbate?"

His voice was still in my head along with his fucking Old Spice. Swallowing hard, I looked up at Ari and Javi. "Alarm bells went off in my brain then. Why was my tennis coach asking me if I masturbated? Adults didn't talk to kids about that. But he had an answer for everything. 'I'm only asking because it's not good for your game if you get backed up. You won't be able to concentrate with a stiffy in your shorts.'"

I'd remember that line for the rest of my life. It was the lure he'd used to suck me into his depraved game. "I don't know if it was the alcohol or the teenage hormones, but when he reached into my shorts and pulled my cock out, I didn't even resist. He jacked me off and when I came, he told me I'd play even better the next day." An acrid taste filled my mouth. I had to close my eyes. The memory was too much.

"It's okay, Daniel," Javi said, his voice low and gentle. "You don't have to tell us anything more."

"No," I insisted, "I do. I have to tell you everything." I looked up and met Ari's gaze. "Both of you."

"Okay," she said. "But take your time. We're here for you."

"I don't know why, and I don't know how, but the bastard was right.

The next day, I had a match against a really tough opponent, and for the first time ever I beat him."

"Do you think he paid the other kid to lose?" Javier asked.

The question was so startling that for the longest time, I could only stare at Javi. Finally, I barked out a humorless laugh. "You know, that's probably exactly what the fucker did. Because I won, I believed him. I believed that if I let him touch me, it would somehow make me a better player. I'd win my matches and my parents' sacrifices wouldn't be for nothing."

I pushed to my feet and ran a hand through my hair as I paced behind my chair. "I'm sure you know where this is going. I started going to Coach's house two or three times a week. Sometimes, usually on the weekends, we'd have some beer. Sometimes, we'd watch porn, but every time, he'd touch me. Until we ended up in division finals. And then he started making me touch him. He said the stakes were higher now. I had to put more effort into it if I wanted to keep winning. The first time he made me jerk him off, he came in my face. Then he grabbed me by the hair, scooped up his cum, and made me eat it. 'The protein is good for you,' he'd said."

I remembered everything, clear as fucking day—the sight of his cum, the taste, and, oh God, the smell.

I gagged and ran into the bathroom. Bent over the toilet, I spewed out the contents of my stomach. I imagined it was my body trying to expel the memories that were bombarding me.

When I was done, I moved to the sink and rinsed my mouth. Javi had some mouthwash on the counter. I gurgled some, spit it out, and did it again. Then I splashed some water on my face. I looked at myself in the mirror as I dried off the water. My eyes were sunken and… haunted. I couldn't do it, couldn't tell them the rest. They'd have to assume it.

"Daniel?" Ari said from the other side of the door. "Are you all right? Do you need something? Should I call Greta?"

The barrage of questions, especially that last one, had me smiling. I knew how hard it had to be for Ari to mention Greta after everything that had gone down between them in the last few weeks.

I opened the door and smiled at Ari. At least I hoped it was a smile. "I'm okay."

We returned to the sitting area, and I dropped down into the armchair. "I-I won't go into detail about the rest. I just…" I broke off and pressed my lips together. "I just can't."

"You don't have to, Daniel. You never have to," Javi said. From the look in his eyes, I knew he meant more than the current conversation. He was telling me I never had to be intimate with him, but damn it, I wanted to be. *Fuck.*

"Suffice it to say that things progressed even further. We had a sexual relationship for years. At the time, I didn't understand what exactly was happening. I was actually flattered by it. By all the attention I was getting from him. I—I enjoyed most of it." That was so fucking hard to admit. Even now. Especially now. "I was young and naïve. I thought I was special. I thought he cared about me. I thought…" I swallowed hard.

"I thought he loved me." I smiled grimly. "Problem was, as I got older, I started to understand that what we had wasn't healthy. The power imbalance was too great. He was my coach. A teacher at my school. I started to understand that he was using me." I grimaced. "A-abusing me. I wanted out. Senior year, I told him that we were over. That's when the threats started."

"He threatened you?" Ari said, looking scandalized.

"Said if I told my parents or anyone at the school, that I'd start losing. That I wouldn't get a scholarship to a big tennis school like I wanted, and I'd never make pro. He had a lot of connections in the tennis world, and I knew he could get me blackballed. They'd believe him over me, a stupid kid blaming his coach because he stopped winning."

"You told your parents anyway, though, right?" Arianna asked.

Javi took her hand. "I don't think he did, *corazón*. Daniel didn't want to lose the scholarships after everything they'd given up for him." His warm brown eyes turned to me.

I nodded.

"But you never did go to Stanford. You turned down the scholarship," Javi said.

"I'd decided to tell my parents everything. I was going to tell Coach he couldn't scare me. That I'd rather clean toilets for the rest of my life than let him continue to manipulate me. It took me weeks to gather up the courage. I went to his office one morning before school started. I was going to tell him. I was going to be free of him forever. But Coach wasn't there. The principal was. Coach had been killed the night before in a car accident."

"So you *were* free of him," Ari said.

I pressed a hand to my chest. "Not in here. I never got to face him, to tell him to fuck off. He died knowing I was his." I pressed my hand harder against the spot. "I'll never be free of him. Not in here."

"I'm sure it's left you very confused," Javi said with understanding eyes.

Ari looked at him. "What do you mean?"

"Sexually, *bella*."

Her eyes widened. "Oh. So you've never"—she waved her hand vaguely in front of herself—"with another man?"

Javi arched a brow. I'd kind of let slip on that one already.

"I have actually, but not…" I shoved to my feet. The chair couldn't contain my jumpy body. "Man, this is really hard to say."

"It's okay, Daniel," Javi said. "Only tell us what you want us to know."

"You do need to know this, both of you." I leaned against the wall. "Over the years, I developed a sort of… coping mechanism. Whenever the pressure built up too much, whenever I felt like I couldn't take it anymore, I'd have to be with a man."

I pushed off the wall and stopped in front of Ari and Javi. I met Ari's eyes, then Javi's. "I *use* men. The same way Coach used me." My gaze switched back to Ari. I could see her processing my words.

"When did this start?" she asked.

"Toward the end of college. I tried to have a few relationships before then, but it always turned out like it had when…"

"When I touched you," Javi said. He looked devastated, and it ripped my heart. Had I made a mistake in sharing this with him, with them?

"In college," Ari said, her tone hard. "So, that means, you were sleeping with men when we were together?"

"I *fuck* men, Ari. I use them. It's a need. A need to dominate. To do to someone what was done to me. It's sick. *I'm* sick."

"No," Javi said. "You aren't sick. That fucker who hurt you was sick. You've just been dealing with a raw hand."

"Who's to say the same didn't happen to him?" I asked. I was sure Diego and all the others would say I was almost as bad as the man who'd abused me.

I heard Greta's voice in my head. *Not true. How you've acted is normal.*

"Anyway, I can't do it anymore. I won't. That's why I started talking with Greta. I want to be better."

"You slept with these men while we were engaged?" Ari's voice rose. "While we were married? You cheated on me while we were married?"

"I know you're angry, Ari. And for that I'm sorry."

She jumped to her feet, fists clenched at her sides. "But not sorry you did it? Not sorry you cheated?"

I knew Arianna. And I knew that her anger was a cover for her pain. I'd hurt her. I'd wounded the woman I loved. Deep in her soul where it did the most damage. The turmoil in her dark eyes and the sheen of tears told me how deeply this was cutting her. I didn't know if she'd ever forgive me, but I did want her to understand.

"I never meant to hurt you." I raised my hand to touch her arm, my shoulders dropping when she stepped out of reach.

"That hardly makes it better."

I closed my eyes and rubbed the lids with my thumb and forefinger. What could I say to that? She was right. I'd broken my vows to her. "I don't know how better to explain it."

Her face softened. "I wish you'd tried to explain it then. Maybe I could have helped you somehow. Done for you what those men do."

God no. "I'd *never* do that to you. Besides, I've never had any issue with women." I rubbed my chest again and tried to verbalize how it felt. "There's an ache, a pressure, in here. In my chest. Some days, I want to crawl out of my skin, leave my body behind and become someone else. Someone who hasn't been tainted. Soiled. Sullied."

"And these men do that for you? Help you escape the pain?" She blew out a breath and turned her face toward the window. "I still don't get what they could do for you that I couldn't."

"It only works with men. Nothing you could have done would have helped."

"Oh God," she rolled her eyes.

"What?"

"Don't you dare say 'it's me, not you.'"

"In this case, it really is me, not you."

She mulled that over for a moment. Her eyes closed, and I thought maybe I had her. That I'd convinced her that although I had hurt her and I knew it, it had not been my intention. But then her shoulders straightened. Then she looked at me, her long lashes framing her flashing brown eyes. "I don't know if I can get past this, Daniel. I trusted you. God, I was so in love. So fucking naïve. All those years you cheated on me, and I didn't have a damn clue." She bit her trembling lip and looked away.

I gripped her chin and forced her gaze back to mine. "They weren't men I met in clubs, sweetheart. They were escorts. Prostitutes. I *fucked* them, and then I paid them. There were never any feelings involved."

My eyes slid to Javi. Not like there would have been had I given in to my feelings for him.

"Oh my God!" Ari's hand went to her mouth. "Did you… did the two of you—"

"No!" I shouted. "I never slept with Javi. Although God knows I've wanted to. From the first fucking day he walked into our dorm room." I lowered my voice, whispered, "I couldn't."

"Because you care about me," Javi said. His expression was soft and open. And… so fucking hopeful.

I couldn't do anything but share that hope. Maybe Greta was right. She had been about everything else. Maybe I needed Javier's help. Maybe he could help me work through my fears. He cared about me. He didn't want to hurt me. I knew in my bones that he'd never do anything to harm me. Greta's treatment idea might not work. And I might be worse off than before I'd started. But wasn't Javi worth trying for?

I reached out and very hesitantly, laid my hand on his shoulder. "I do. And I'm hoping you'll agree to help me."

"Whatever you need, *hermano*. Whenever."

"Not now, but maybe soon."

Chapter 9

ARIANNA

Daniel had cheated on me. From the very start of our relationship.

And always with men.

The way he was looking at Javi now, the love in his eyes—*Cristo*, had Daniel ever really loved me?

He said he was sexually confused by what happened. Could that mean that he was gay? That he'd be happier with Javi? That maybe he never should have been with me at all?

He wanted *Javi's* help. Not mine.

Never mine.

Daniel had fucking divorced me rather than tell me the truth. Rather than ask me for help.

Why the fuck was I still standing here, watching them?

I turned to go, not sure where I was going, only that I couldn't look at Daniel right now. A lump filled my throat and tears stung my eyes. I loved him. I loved him so damn much.

And I wasn't enough for him. I'd *never* been enough.

His hand wrapped around my bicep. "Ari—"

I shoved his hand away and kept going, unable to speak. And I sure as shit did not want him to see what he was doing to me.

I yanked open the door. I started for my room, but one of them would just come after me. I turned for the stairs instead. I was wearing one of

Javi's white button-downs over a pair of his black boxer trunks, and I didn't fucking care who saw me. I just needed to get the hell away from Daniel. From them.

From the *two* of them.

They wanted to be together. And they didn't need me in the middle.

Dios, I was an idiot. Pining for two men who loved each other.

I was stepping off the bottom stair when I heard Javi's voice. "*Corazón*, stop."

The tears started falling in earnest now. I couldn't do this. I couldn't.

I raced across the slate floor of the lobby and out the French doors to the back terrace, Javi right on my heels. I hadn't taken more than a step or two outside when his arms went around me, pulling my back tight to his chest, his warmth enveloping me, and a sob ripped out of my throat. "Let me go," I pleaded, trying to keep my voice steady but failing miserably.

"Never," he said into my hair, his voice thick. He nudged me over to a table and chairs on the terrace and tugged me down onto his lap, and I couldn't help it. I sobbed all over his shirt. His large hands stroked my back, his voice a soft murmur in my ear. "It's okay, *mi amor*. Let it out."

"Why couldn't he tell me?" I forced out. "I would've helped him. I would've understood."

"We're talking about Daniel. And you. Two of the proudest, most stubborn people I've ever met."

I wiped my eyes and took a deep breath. "So? I'm not heartless."

Javi brushed the hair out of my eyes and smiled. "Of course not. But you're telling me you would have understood what he was going through when you were eighteen and he was twenty-one?"

I shrugged. "I don't know. Maybe. But he never even gave me a fucking chance. He chose to cheat on me instead of being honest. Instead of admitting he needed help."

"He regrets that. You know he does."

A thought occurred to me. "He was trying to break up with me practically from the moment we got together."

Javi frowned. "I wouldn't say that."

I shook my head. "We were so up and down, remember? How many times did we break up? And then I had to put my foot down about him marrying me or leaving me for good. I should have never put up with that bullshit. I forced him to marry me. I couldn't take the fucking hint."

"*Corazón*, he married you because he didn't want to lose you."

"He married me because he didn't want to admit that he was gay. That he wanted to be with *you*." My voice broke on the last word, and I had to wipe my welling eyes again. I'd thought Daniel couldn't hurt me anymore. I was wrong.

Javier shook his head. "He's not gay. Just like I'm not." He smoothed a hand over my hair, his voice so soft. "I love you, *corazón*. And so does he."

I wanted to believe that, I did, but… "He *lied* to me, again and again, Javi. And then when I pushed him about having a baby, he divorced me. *That's* how much he loves me. I didn't matter more to him than his pride. I didn't matter enough for him to tell me the truth. I didn't matter enough for him to fight for me. For us. He broke my heart, and he fucking walked away. How can I trust him now?"

Javi clucked his tongue at me, slowly shaking his head. "Let's back up a bit. I know your heart is bruised." A hint of a smile crossed his lips. "And probably your ego too." I lightly punched him in the chest, and he laughed, then his amusement faded away and he hugged me tighter. "What happened today—that's Daniel trying *now*. That's him trying to heal, trying to fix what's broken, trying to fix what he's done to himself, to all three of us. And you need to recognize that."

Dios. Javi was right. I was making this about me. And it wasn't. I wanted Daniel back. I wanted to fix things between us.

How many times had I wished he'd confide in me? How many times had I asked him what was wrong? And now he was telling me. He was giving me what I'd asked for. What I'd begged for.

I took a deep breath. "I'm almost thirty, and I'm still a baby, aren't I?" Javier stroked my cheek, his warm brown gaze locked on mine. My eyes welled again. "What he went through, Javi… it fucking scares me. What if he can't get past this? What if we can't make this work?"

Javi cupped my chin and pressed his lips to mine. The kiss was tender, sweet. Then he pulled back. "Have faith, *corazón*. Open your heart to him. And if—*if*—this doesn't work, we'll get through it. You and me."

A hard truth hit me then. "I owe him an apology." Javi smiled, and I steeled myself for what I needed to say next. "And you can't be there, Javi. I need to spend some time with Daniel. Alone."

That beautiful smile of Javi's faded, and he nodded. "I love you, Javi," I whispered. "But I love him too. And I need to see if he and I can be with each other again."

I was trying to see this from Daniel's side. I really was. And my heart broke for the boy he'd been back then. But he'd been an adult when we'd gotten together. And he'd lied to me. He'd betrayed me.

But… he'd been struggling with something, and I'd known it all along.

I'd never tried hard enough to understand what was going on with him. I'd never opened my heart to him. I'd never just listened without pushing. Without worrying about myself.

It was time for me to be the partner to Daniel I always should have been.

JAVIER

Goddamn fuckers like Manuel's previous accountant were the reason accountants got such a bad rap. But I had to hand it to the guy. He'd very cleverly disguised the missing amounts as business losses in the ledgers. Small amounts that over the years had added up to a sizable amount, larger than the twenty grand Manuel had originally estimated.

Lucky for the Monteros, the guy had gotten greedy and had started increasing the loss amounts to a point where Manuel and Sofia had noticed that although their earnings had continued to rise, their profits had fallen. And that had started them looking.

I'd spent the whole day doing a painstaking comparison of the handwritten ledgers that Manuel kept against the vineyard's QuickBooks data, and that was when I'd started to notice a pattern. I entered a few more numbers into the calculator and the final loss estimate was heartbreaking, especially considering all the money they'd just poured into the renovation.

The door to Manuel's office opened, and the man himself entered. He held the door for Sofia, who was carrying a tray with two coffee cups and a plate of cookies. "You're working too hard, Javi. It's time for a break. I've brought you some refreshments."

"You're an angel," I said, eyeing the homemade cookies, *torticas de morón*. My stomach growled. I loved Cuban sugar cookies. Only problem was that my waistline didn't.

The office had a small seating area with a low coffee table, a loveseat, and an armchair. Manuel sat on the loveseat. I took the armchair and sipped on the coffee Sofia handed me. It was dark and strong and hot and perfect. "No one makes coffee like you, Sofia."

Manuel patted her hip. "Wait until you taste her *torticas*." He picked up the plate and offered it to me.

"I'm sure they're delicious, but…" I patted my stomach and shot her an apologetic smile.

She swatted my shoulder. "Nonsense. You're a young man. Strong. You need to eat."

Manuel grinned, patting his own not quite flat belly. "You'll never win with her, Javi. It's how she shows love."

I was all too familiar with the food-as-love mothering philosophy. My mamá was one of its most ardent followers. I grinned at Sofia and took a cookie. I'd just have to add a couple miles to my run later. I bit into the sugary goodness and had to close my eyes against the almost orgasmic joy rushing through my body. "God, this is good." I grabbed another cookie and mentally added four miles to my run.

When Sofía headed for the door, I frowned. "Won't you be joining us?"

She hugged the tray to her chest. "I leave the money problems to Manuel. If I worry about it, the worry tastes in my food."

Huh. Okay. "I'll see you later then. Thank you."

The door closed behind her and Manuel set his cup down. "Have you found anything?"

I finished off the second cookie, wiped the crumbs from my shirt, then leaned forward. "Your suspicions were well-founded."

He groaned and dropped his face into his hands. "How much?" he asked, the question muffled.

"Seventy-five thousand, five hundred and twenty, give or take a few cents."

"*Hostia puta.*" He rubbed the back of his still-lowered head. "That's a lot of fucking money."

"I'm sorry."

He raised his head, splaying his fingers so his index finger rested over his top lip and the others curled around his chin. "Not your fault, *hijo.*"

I gave him a sad smile. "I know. I'm still sorry you were taken advantage of. What are you going to do?"

Shrugging his shoulders, he slumped against the back of the couch. "What can I do?" His brows rose. "Unless you have some hard evidence?"

"There's definitely evidence. If you wish to pursue this matter legally, I can refer you to some very good forensic accountants. They can help you build up a strong case that should stand up in court."

Manuel nodded. "Thank you. I'll discuss it with Sofía. I'm not sure she will want to take legal action."

The corner of my mouth curled up. Based on what she'd said about her worries changing the taste of her food and with the resort just opening up, I'm sure she would want to avoid anything that would jeopardize that. Still seventy-five thousand was a lot of money for a small business.

"Whatever you decide, I'll support you in any way I can," I said.

"I appreciate that." Leaning forward, Manuel picked up his cup of coffee and took a sip before setting it back down. "Enough of that. Tell me about my beautiful niece."

Now there was a subject I could sink into. I bit back a groan and crossed my legs to hide the growing bulge in my pants that just the thought of her brought on. "What about her?"

"I saw you two out on the terrace. She seemed very upset, but it didn't seem to be with you. What's Daniel done now?"

I could feel my hackles rise at the accusation. "Why do you think he's done anything?"

He chuckled dryly. "It seems he's always doing something to upset her. The *niñita* who used to run around trying to catch butterflies with the biggest smile on her face disappeared the day she met Daniel King. That man has put Ari through the wringer."

"No disagreement is one-sided. Both of them did things that led to the divorce."

Manuel cocked his head and narrowed his eyes. "I thought you and Ari…?"

"We are." God, that felt good and terrible to say at the same time. I was so torn, it was killing me. If this threesome with Daniel and Ari didn't work out, I didn't know what I was going to do. I crunched on a cookie, then stared at my hand in surprise. When had I picked it up? Shit. Stress always made me eat too much. I set it on a napkin beside my cup of coffee.

"Why are you sticking up for him then?" Manuel asked, clearly, and thankfully, not understanding our crazy situation.

Seeing as my erection had wilted away, I spread my thighs and leaned forward, resting my elbows on my knees. "Look, I love Ari. I always have. But Daniel is my friend. My best friend actually, and the guy, well, he's been through hell. It doesn't excuse all his troubles with Ari, but it sure as hell explains some of them."

"Huh. I wasn't aware that anything had happened to him. He's intelligent, successful, good-looking. Walks around like he owns the world. Just like every other *gringo*."

Oh man. That description of Daniel was so far off from reality, it wasn't even funny. Was that really how the family saw him? "Daniel is nothing like that. He's really a great guy." I held Manuel's gaze and looked deep. "You know, you and the rest of Ari's family haven't been exactly easy on him."

Manuel's jaw tightened, but other than that he didn't react. "I don't know what you mean."

"Come on. None of you were happy she married him."

"That's true."

"Why not?"

"It's simple really." He smiled. "We wanted her to marry you." He leaned across the coffee table and lightly tapped my knee. "And now she can."

I sucked in a harsh breath. Hell, I'd wanted nothing more for years. But now… what if this relationship between the three of us was successful? I meant what I'd said to Daniel yesterday. I'd be happy to keep things exactly how they were. I wanted to hold him and touch him and taste him and, oh God, so much more, but I'd accept the status quo, because at least that way, I had a small part of him. It wasn't him and Ari, or me and Ari, it was him and me and Ari. And I honestly loved that combination the best.

But fuck, what about our families? Daniel's family was pretty much out of the picture. Now that I knew about his past, I understood his reasoning for completely distancing himself from them: he didn't want them to feel guilty. Which was *muy estupido*, and I'd be sure to tell him so at some point. His family loved him, and the knowledge of what had happened to Daniel wouldn't change that for them anymore than it had changed my feelings toward him. He was still the strong, intelligent, independent man he'd been before.

My and Ari's families were another story. We'd have to tell them something. I might have been able to play straight with my family in the past, but that was mostly because there'd been no one I'd really wanted them to know about. But Daniel and Ari? I wanted everyone to know. And really, I doubted people could be in the room with me and them and not *see* how I felt. I wasn't the best at hiding my feelings. Unless I ate them. I stared at the empty cookie plate and the crumbs on my shirt. Fucking stress-eating.

I'd have to tell my family I was bisexual. But if I did that, if I told them, other than Clarita, the rest of them would flip their shit. I looked up at Manuel, who was watching me like a hawk. I was so tempted to tell him everything. To say, "Hey, Manuel. By the way, I'm bisexual. Still want me to marry your niece?"

I knew what his reaction would be: exactly what the families had done to Daniel—that cordial shunning, that freezing out that stung like a bitch.

I'd never hurt Ari and Daniel like that though. It wasn't my place to out them. Hell, I'd never even outed myself.

So instead of telling Manuel the truth, I simply held his gaze.

Manuel's gaze narrowed, and then his brows rose as if in surprise. He cleared his throat. "Uh… Sofía has a younger brother, Óscar."

"She does?" I thought I'd met all of Manuel's in-laws at some point or another.

"He doesn't come around much for family reunions." He looked down at his hands clasped loosely between his legs. "Óscar is gay. He lives in San Francisco, and we see him every few weeks." He looked up at me. "We love him just fine."

"Uhhh… that's really nice, but why are you telling me this?"

Manuel snorted and shook his head. "I love you too, Javi. So, if ever there was something you wanted to tell me about you and Arianna and…" He paused. Glanced down at his hands, cracked the knuckles. "And *Daniel*, you can. I don't have anything against Daniel. I just didn't like that he'd made Ari unhappy."

"But—"

He held up his hand. "No, no. I get it. And you're right, I'm sure that they both contributed to their marriage troubles. If they are moving past all that, then I'm happy for them." His eyes bore into me. "I'm happy for all of you." He touched his chest. "Me and my family, we're a safe place. We see you. We accept you."

His words shook me to my core. I'd known Manuel a long time and sure, he lived close to San Francisco, but *still*… I'd never expected this from him. *I'm bisexual and I'm in love with Ari and Daniel, and they both want me.* The words clung to my lips. Never in my entire life had I wanted something more than to come out right then. To finally be able to be myself, to stop the lies. To end the hiding.

Dios, it was so close. The life I'd always wanted was within reach. If only I had the *cojones* to see it through.

Touched more than I could say, I simply slow blinked and swallowed hard.

Manuel smiled, then his smile turned sad. "We accept you, but your family and Ari's? They won't take it well, *hijo*."

My spine lost its stiffness and a heavy weight returned to my shoulders. "Like I don't already know that."

ARIANNA

My heart in my throat, I knocked on Daniel's door, hoping he'd be there. I'd taken a shower and changed into a blouse and flowing skirt, though I'd hated washing off Javi's comforting scent. But this had to be about Daniel and me. Just the two of us.

Sure, Javi had always been an effective buffer between us. And no doubt he'd continue to play the part without complaining. But Javi deserved better than that. He deserved two partners who had their shit together. Who could work things out like functioning adults.

The door opened, and Daniel stood before me, all six glorious feet of him. His eyes were bloodshot and haunted, and his gaze flicked away from mine. "I need you to know, Arianna, that I never wanted to hurt you. But I did." He swallowed, looking at me. "And I'm so sorry."

I reached up and touched his cheek. "I know. And so am I. May I come in?"

"Of course." He motioned me inside and closed the door. My pulse sped up, and I was all too aware of him behind me, my body practically aching for his touch. But we needed to talk first.

I walked over to the sofa and took a seat, and he sat at the other end, both of us turning to face each other. Only a few feet separated us, and it was tempting to bridge the gap by scooting over and pressing myself against him. To let sex paper over the hurt, the way it had so many times before.

But that would be shortchanging both of us. And it wouldn't solve a damn thing.

I clasped my bent knee with both hands and leaned forward. "Javi set me straight." I mock-rolled my eyes. "As usual."

A corner of Daniel's mouth curved up. "Set you straight how?"

"My reaction was all about me. *My* fears. *My* hurt. And you'd just told me about something terrible that had happened to you. And I pushed it away." My voice started to tremble, and I took a steadying breath, my heart speeding up again. "Because I'm scared. I'm scared that I can't deal with this. That I'm not right for you. That I'm too much of a child to support you the way you need. But I'm going to try."

He started to speak, but I raised a hand to stop him. "Daniel, you were always the strong one, and I wasn't that person for you.. The whole time we were together, this fear lived in me. That you didn't really love me. That I was just chasing you. And I pushed and pushed because I wanted to see if you'd stay or if you'd run."

"And I finally ran." His voice was rough, thick.

I nodded. "And you broke my heart." I sucked in a breath, willing the tears not to start again. "But you ran because *I* wasn't ready to hear what was wrong, and you knew it." The fucking tears welled up anyway, but I forced myself to keep talking. "I was a shitty partner to you. I thought you were perfect. I never let you lean on me. I was always the one leaning on you. You needed me to be patient and supportive, not demanding and scared."

"Ari, you're being too hard on yourself. You did try. You tried and tried, and I shut you out." He rubbed his forehead. "How you reacted—it's understandable. I was hiding so much from you, and you knew it. Of course you were scared and didn't quite trust me. How could you?"

I looked down. "That's true. But…" I blew out. "You were part of my agenda, my life plan. Handsome husband. Check. And the fact that I knew something was weighing on you, I kept pushing that away, kept closing my eyes to it. Because I didn't want to fuck up my plan. Husband by twenty-four, kids by twenty-six…"

"World domination by thirty." He smiled at me. "I loved all that about you. You knew what you wanted. I *wanted* to be part of your plan.

I wanted to be with someone who knew what the fuck they were doing. Instead of me, who was running scared ninety percent of the time." He locked eyes with me. "I thought if you knew, you'd dump me."

I slowly shook my head, my eyes on his the whole time, then I was up and moving across the couch and into his arms, straddling his lap. "Never, *mi amor*. Never." I cupped his face in my hands, rising up on my knees. "You are so fucking brave. So fucking strong. You didn't let that bastard crush you. You kept pushing. You built TI. It was your vision that made us a success. Your heart. Your determination." I pressed my lips to his. "I admire the hell out of you, Daniel King. And I love you. And I swear I'm going to be the partner I should have always been to you."

He drew me closer. "And I'm going to do the same. No more lies. Nothing but the truth between us. Because you deserve that."

"We both do," I said, my heart so full I was on the verge of tears again. This man I'd loved so long, this man who'd stolen my heart and never given it back—he had the power to break me. And he'd done it once. But I'd survived. I was stronger than I knew. I was strong enough for both of us. I knew that now.

We could do this. We could move forward, no matter how rough the road.

Daniel raised an eyebrow and gave me that seductive smirk I knew so well. "Now how about you give me that sugar I've been craving?" His gaze dipped to my lips, and I smiled.

"You have a bigger sweet tooth than Javi," I said.

Daniel's smirk broadened into a grin, and he thrust his hips up against my crotch. The bulge between his legs grazed my pussy through the thin fabric of my panties. "It's bigger, huh?" he said, his voice a deep burr.

Giggling, I kissed him. "Oh, I don't know about *that*." I parted my lips, letting his tongue explore my mouth, his hands descending to my ass and squeezing as he urged me to grind against him, not that I needed much persuasion. The hard ridge of his cock in his jeans pressed against my swelling pussy, forcing the fabric of my panties to rub against my aching clit. I moaned, and Daniel stuck two fingers in his mouth, then pushed my loose skirt up my thighs and yanked the crotch of my panties aside so he could touch my slick flesh.

I shifted restlessly, trying to impale myself on his fingers, my hands going to the fly of his jeans and taking out his stiff cock.

"You want it, baby?" he murmured.

"Uh-huh."

He rubbed circles around my clit, then pressed his fingers inside me, his thumb continuing to rub my most sensitive place. I was panting, my eyes locked on his, the mixture of lust and tenderness in his gaze warming my heart.

I wrapped a hand around his cock and stroked, wanting that steely length inside me. Wanting *Daniel* inside me.

When I twisted my fingers around the head of his cock, he grunted in appreciation. "You want to come on my cock, baby?"

"You know I do." I started to position him, but he wrapped a hand around my wrist.

"Just a sec." He let go, then grabbed his wallet off the end table and took out a condom. He held it up. "Trying to keep prepared."

Should I tell him about me and Javi, how we hadn't been using them?

Daniel raised an eyebrow. "Something wrong?"

I shook my head. "No. Not at all." Javi should be there when we told Daniel. When we talked about that subject again.

Kids.

I still wanted them.

And Daniel didn't.

Unless that was another thing that had changed. But this was a conversation for another time.

He suited up, then I rubbed myself against him, coating the tip with my juices, making both of us moan in anticipation before I descended on him.

I loved the tension in his powerful body as I straddled him, the way his breath hitched when I swiveled my hips, and then how he took control and pulled me down atop him, his hips rising to meet mine, his engorged cock hitting that spot inside that I loved. I rose up again on my knees, and he yanked me back down again, fucking up into me and forcing groans of pleasure from both of us.

I'd wanted to make this slow and tender, but I should have known better. With Daniel, it was always urgent, always a hard, fast drive to the finish that left both of us breathless and soaring.

I wanted that too. But I wanted slow and sweet for once.

I rose up again, resisting when he tried to pull me down. "It's not a race, *mi amor*."

"You drive me crazy."

I leaned forward and kissed him, softly, sweetly, and he let me. When I pulled back, he held my gaze. "You drive me crazy too," I said. I swiveled my hips slowly, placing my hands on his shoulders for balance, his muscles solid granite beneath my fingers. His blue eyes held mine, a lock of his light brown hair falling onto his forehead. I smoothed it back as I rose up again.

I loved this man. I loved him so damn much.

And maybe, just maybe, he'd actually be mine again for good. I had to hope so. I had to fight for us.

Daniel reached between us, his thumb grazing my swollen clit. "I want you to ride my hand and my cock, Ari. I want you to ride them hard. I want to watch you come." He stroked my clit, the touch making me shiver.

I smiled. My darling, dirty Daniel always had the best ideas. I rocked forward, grinding myself against his thumb, pleasure coiling inside me. If he insisted on being in charge, who was I to resist?

We could always have slower and sweeter a little later.

Neither of us was going anywhere. Right?

Chapter 10

DANIEL

"Okay, Vanessa," I said. "If you get me a social media marketing plan by morning and we snag the Alpine Skiing account, I guarantee you a promotion."

"Yeah? So I wouldn't be an intern anymore?"

"Nope. You'd be a full-time permanent member of the TI family. How does that sound?"

"OMG, Daniel! I'll have a plan for you that's so fantastic, Alpine Skiing will be begging to sign with us."

I chuckled. "If anyone can do it, it's you, Vanessa."

I ended the call and hopped back onto the treadmill. It was barely seven AM, and I'd already put out three fires. This time, one of our potential new clients, Alpine Skiing, was insisting on a full-blown social media marketing plan for a high-end luxury skiing trip in the Alps we were proposing to them. They would provide the guides and we would provide everything else, including the clients.

Paige and her team had already designed a multimedia marketing plan, which Alpine Skiing loved. But, on the social media side, they wanted something much more organized and focused than anything we'd done in the past. I'd assigned the task to Vanessa because I knew that she could bring us the youth and excitement we needed to wow the clients. Besides, it was high time we offered the girl a job before some other company snatched her up. Vanessa was a handful, but she was worth every headache.

When my phone rang again and the caller ID indicated it was one of my staff calling, a sense of dread came over me. Fuck. I was too wound up. There was no way I could spend the entire day firefighting and doing damage control. What I needed was some air, some exercise, and a friend.

I typed a text and sent it to Javi.

Daniel: Let's play hooky. Meet outside in twenty. Bringing hiking gear.

Javi:

Ninety minutes later, I was pulling into a spot in the parking lot of the Armstrong Redwoods Preserve. "Hey, man." I glanced over at Javi in the passenger seat. "Thank you for doing this."

He grinned. "Don't mention it. I was just as eager to fly the coop as you."

Last night, Ari and I had made up. We'd had some of the most tender, emotional sex we'd ever had. It had been so different. She'd been so different. It was like she'd turned the tables on me and become the aggressor. Although she hadn't been aggressive at all. No, she'd been loving, and caring, and giving.

A small part of me had wondered if it had been out of pity. But then afterward, when we'd been lying in bed together, snuggling, I'd looked in her eyes and what I'd seen there had most definitely not been pity. And while I should be on cloud nine about it, I was actually even more confused than I'd been before.

Because when I'd looked in Javi's eyes just now, I'd seen the exact same look. And the flip in my belly? Yeah, that was exactly the same too.

How could I be both attracted to him and repulsed by him? I wanted to do to him all the things I did to Ari. I wanted him to do to *me* all the things I did to Ari. But when I tried to imagine them, that's when the panic would set in.

My fingers grew white around the steering wheel. I quickly turned off the ignition and got out of the car before Javi could notice. We went around to the trunk and got our day packs out. When I'd told Luciana to let Ari know Javi and I were heading out for a hike, she'd insisted on packing each of us a lunch.

We got our packs on our backs and headed over to the visitor center. There we could look at the trails and pick one.

In my peripheral vision, I saw Javier frown. He cleared his throat. "Want to talk about it?"

"It?"

He waved his hand. "Whatever's bugging you."

I snorted. "Nothing. Everything. I don't know. I just really needed to get out and do some exercise."

Javi patted his flat stomach. "Tell me about it. I feel like I've gained ten pounds since I got here."

"Dude. It's only been four days."

"Tell that to my ass."

I stared pointedly at Javi's ass. It was firm and round, and fuck did I want to sink my teeth into it…

Your teeth? Yeah right, King.

Javi crossed his arms. "What?"

"Your ass looks pretty good to me."

A blush colored Javi's cheeks. He also looked ridiculously pleased. He batted his lashes at me. "I bet you say that to all the boys."

"Fuck no." I laughed. "Just you."

"Wow." He pressed a hand to his chest. "Flattery will get you everywhere, Mr. King."

I gripped his shoulder. "You're such an idiot, Cordoba."

"At least I got you to smile."

We arrived at the visitor center and checked out the various hiking trails. "What are you up for?" I asked Javi. "Three miles? Five?"

"Don't they have something longer?"

Javi was gnawing at his bottom lip in a way I'd rarely seen him do since college, and his comment about his ass came back to me. Was he really still worried about his weight? Fuck. I knew he worked out a lot and that he had to be careful what he ate, but I didn't think it was still a struggle. I took in his whole body then. *Had* he gained weight, or was he just being paranoid about it?

I pointed to a trail on the map. "Says here it's a strenuous nine-mile hike with a fifteen-thousand-foot climb. That enough for you?"

His face lit up, and oh fuck. My breath caught in my throat. He was so damn beautiful. "It's perfect," he said.

"Yeah. It is." My eyes were on him.

Javi blushed again. "Daniel."

"Come on," I said, hitching up my pack and moving toward the start of the trail. Javi came up behind me and then we continued to walk side by side.

The trail took us into the grove, and the majesty of the redwoods took my breath away. I stopped walking and turned in a slow circle, my head up as I tried to see the tops of the trees. "Wow. This is really impressive."

"It's amazing. Feels like we're in church."

I immediately knew what Javi meant. Given that it was mid-October and that it always rained a bit in the rainforest, we were pretty much the only people around. The air was hushed under the canopy of the ancient redwoods. "The brochure said the trees are on average between two hundred and two hundred and fifty feet tall, and that they are between five hundred and a thousand years old." I touched the base of one next to me. It had to have a diameter of at least ten feet. I'm not sure Javi and I could have made a ring around it with our arms. "Can you imagine the changes it's seen?"

"Not to mention that some of these trees will still be around in a thousand years. Long after we're gone."

"Makes you feel kind of insignificant in the big picture of things, doesn't it?" I mused aloud.

"A little. But it also makes me feel like we're all a part of something so much bigger. That we need to not worry about the little things, because our lives are too short to waste on things that don't matter."

Was he talking about himself or me?

We started walking again. "So, uh, I should thank you for talking with Ari after my big reveal. She was pretty upset about… yeah."

He carefully stepped over a large root that bisected the trail. "I had to tell her what I thought. It's the only way this thing with the three of us will work."

"Do you want it to work?" I held my breath as I waited for him to answer. Bastard took his sweet fucking time.

"Do you?"

"Don't answer a question with a question. I asked you first."

"Fair enough. Okay, yes. I do want it to work. But like I said before, I'll take whatever you're comfortable giving me, and if that's only friendship, then I'm happy with that."

"I want to give you more."

He looked back at me, his eyes going round, and he tripped over a fallen branch. I lunged forward and grabbed his elbow, helping him find his balance. "Careful."

"Fuck. It's your fault."

I released his arm. "Too honest?"

"Too surprising."

"Really?" I was sure my attraction to him had always been written all over my face even though I'd been trying to deny it for years.

"No." He grinned. "Not really. But hearing you say it?" He shook his head. "I don't know if I'll ever get used to it."

"You should get used to it, because you'll be seeing and hearing a lot more of that from me."

He stopped walking and turned to face me. "Is that right?"

"Mmm-hmm." *This* was the reason I'd been tied in knots all morning. After getting Javi's agreement to help me yesterday, I'd spent the night thinking about how I was going to ask him and how we could even try this thing without him getting hurt. In the end, I'd decided to just go for it. He was a big boy. He could decide for himself if he could handle the risk or not.

I fished my water bottle out of my pack and cracked it open, sipping on it as I started walking again. "So, as you know, Greta and I have been talking about my… my past."

"Yes. I'm so grateful to her for helping you."

Fuck, the guy had a big heart. "She says that there are some therapies that can help me. EMDR and lifespan integration. I don't know too much about them yet, but they're supposed to help people deal with emotional trauma."

"That's great, Daniel." Javi's soft, encouraging voice had my throat tightening.

I took another sip of water. "They can be very successful, but they take a long time."

"You've been suffering from this trauma for years, Daniel. However long the therapies take, it's worth it, isn't it?"

I shrugged.

"You don't think so?" he asked.

The air left my lungs in a rush, and I stopped walking. "I don't want you to have to wait that long. It's not fair to you."

"Fuck me."

"I'd like to."

Javi spun around and stared back at me wide-eyed. I'd meant it as a sort-of joke, but now that I'd said it out loud, it didn't sound so funny. Because it was so much the goddamned truth.

He blinked, wet his lips. "But…"

"But I fucking can't." I inhaled deeply. "At least not yet."

"Right. Maybe after you've completed those therapies you mentioned. Or maybe never."

"No." I shook my head. "Please, God. It can't be never."

Javier stepped forward, putting us only inches apart. "It won't change how I feel about you."

"I hope you're right about that, because Greta also suggested something else. Something I'll need your help for."

"Anything you need," he said with such solemnity that I knew he meant it with everything he was.

Now it was my turn to be as honest as I could. To make myself vulnerable to him in a way I never had before. I forced myself to look him in the eye. "She said that we might be able to treat my… uh… panic attacks. I need to be exposed to my triggers in small doses. That way I can learn to handle them and maybe overcome them eventually."

"Okay." Javi indicated a log placed alongside the trail. "Let's sit for a bit."

I nodded and followed him mutely to the log. Once we were seated, he clasped his hands between his knees. "I want to help you, Daniel, any way I can. So, you tell me what you need."

Javi was a smart man, and I was sure that based on what I'd told him about Coach yesterday, he'd already figured out what my triggers were. He seemed calm enough. Maybe a bit hopeful. For my part, I was scared shitless, and more excited than I could remember being in a long time. If this worked, I'd finally be able to touch Javi. To let him touch me. God, just thinking about it gave me goosebumps.

"I-I want to touch you. Can I?"

"Of course."

"Just uh… keep your hands on your knees."

When Javier nodded and his fingers were cupped around his kneecaps, I lifted my hand and lightly brushed his cheek. I could feel the stubble already pushing through his warm skin. It rasped against my fingers. I shivered. "You're so beautiful."

He swallowed, and his Adam's apple bobbed in his throat. I trailed my fingers over it. Javi's heartbeat pulsed beneath my fingertip.

"You don't have to say things like that, Daniel. I know that I'm not a gay wet dream."

"Shh." I pressed two fingers over his lips. "Stop putting yourself down. You're gorgeous, and I hate myself for ever making you think you weren't."

Javi looked startled. "You didn't."

"You never thought I didn't pursue you because you were chubby when we met?" I asked him, knowing full well that what I was saying was the truth.

"Call it like it was, Daniel. I was well beyond chubby. Fuck, I'd probably be morbidly obese today if I hadn't met you and started working out. You saved me."

"Now that's fucking bullshit."

"No, seriously. All I did was eat back then."

"Do you know why?"

"I didn't then, but I do now." He looked away. "I hated lying to my parents, my siblings, my friends. Only Ari knew I was gay."

"But you aren't gay."

"Well, no." He laughed, the sound harsh and bitter in the quiet of the rainforest. "I was so messed up back then. I didn't know if I was gay or what, but I sure as hell knew I wasn't straight."

I kicked a stone with my foot. It bounced off the trunk of a tree. "We both kept secrets."

"And I ate through mine."

"Yeah, well, I fucked through mine."

"But you never fucked me."

"No."

"Exactly. Because I wasn't attractive enough. I wasn't good enough. I wasn't—"

"Stop." I covered the hand on his knee with my own. "You've got it all wrong. I didn't fuck you because I could never do that. I could never hurt you. Even then, I cared about you too much."

He faced me, his eyes sad. "I would have let you."

"I know, and that's exactly why I didn't. Not because I didn't think you were hot. You're gorgeous. Sexy. Cut like a bodybuilder."

Javi scoffed. "Hardly."

I brought a shaky hand to his belly. I watched his face, and when he gave me a small nod, I pressed my hand to his hard muscles. "I've seen this eight-pack."

And I fucking want to lick it.

The heat of his skin, the movement of his abs when he drew in a sharp breath had my head spinning. I'd never touched a man like this. Want surged inside me, and I couldn't look away from his face. His jaw clenched and his hot eyes filled with lust. Energy seemed to arc between us. This was a connection we'd never quite had before. I'd never had my hand on him like this. Even better, I didn't feel like puking up my breakfast.

Maybe Greta's idea really could work.

"You know," I said slowly, moving my hand back to his face and brushing his bottom lip with my thumb, "I've never kissed a man."

"Never?"

I shook my head. Coach had never kissed me. That should have been a clear sign that he didn't love me. That he'd just been using me. Looking on the bright side, at least that was one thing that wasn't tainted. One thing I had left to give.

"When you tried, in Cancun, that was the first time a guy had tried to kiss me, but I wasn't ready." I dropped my gaze to his lips. "I want my first to be with you."

Javier moaned and licked his lips, his tongue bumping up against my thumb.

"Fuck." I shuddered as arousal curled in my belly, the need sharp and immediate. Leaning forward, I pressed my mouth to his in a soft tentative kiss. I didn't want to dive in and trigger a panic attack. So I took it slow, discovering the curve of his lips with the tip of my tongue. I pressed gently with my teeth, and when he whimpered, my cock started to harden.

We hadn't even opened our mouths yet, and already it was the best kiss I'd ever had. His scruff scratched my cheeks. The skin above his top lip felt rough against my mouth. I ran my tongue over it, testing the texture and enjoying it.

Javier groaned, the sound low and growly, and his lips parted. My cock filled even more. I was painfully hard from just a kiss.

I pressed my tongue into his mouth and *fuck*! It was hot and wet and so fucking good. I moaned and angled my head to taste him more deeply.

A finger touched my neck, and I bolted off the log, my hands up in a defensive position.

"Oh shit! I'm so sorry," Javi said. White-faced, he remained seated on the log, his hands once again cupping his knees. "I just got so into it and forgot for a moment." He stopped talking and dropped his head. "I've fucking ruined everything."

My heart was pounding in my veins, the panic attack waiting for me to let it in. But I wouldn't. Not this time. The devastation in Javier's voice was killing me. I had to prove to him and to myself that this was only a minor setback. "Don't say that. It felt really, really good."

Javier's head lifted, his expression cautious but optimistic. "Yeah?"

"Definitely."

"For me too."

"How about we walk some more and maybe try again later?"

Javier agreed. We put our daypacks back on and walked in a comfortable silence for a couple miles. When the path turned into a lookout area, we took our backpacks off and decided to have our lunches there. The view was extraordinary.

"Do you think we should have brought the group here?" I asked.

His brows shot up, a look of utter horror on his perfect features. "Today? With us?"

I laughed at his reaction. I hoped it meant he was happy to be alone with me. To be testing the waters with me even though I'd freaked out when he'd touched me.

"No, not today," I said. "I'm glad it's just you and me."

"Oh yeah?" Javi's voice grew husky. I was started to recognize that it got that way whenever he was turned on.

"Can we try again?"

"Now?"

I looked around. We are all alone, unsurprising since we'd picked the hardest damn trail in the place. I stood up and turned to face him. "Right fucking now."

Javi blinked, and a moment later, he was on his feet, arms at his sides. "Ready when you are."

I held his face in my hands and kissed him. Hard. The way I'd always wanted to. It was so different from kissing a woman, from kissing Ari. We were about the same height for one thing. He also smelled different. He smelled like a man, all clean sweat and spicy cologne.

I laid one hand on his shoulder and touched his chest with the other. His heart pounded against my palm. In a strange way, that reassured me. He was as nervous about this as I was. He was also very turned on. When I pulled back, he gulped air into his lungs and his chest heaved with the effort. I glanced down to see what effect I'd had on him, and I was certainly not disappointed.

Something was off though. His arms were dangling uselessly at his sides. I chuckled. "Is that as uncomfortable as it looks?"

Javier palmed his crotch. "Christ. You've got me so fucking hard."

"I was talking about your arms, asshole."

He grinned. "Sorry."

"No, you're not."

He pressed the heel of his hand against his cock and groaned. "You're right. I'm not."

"Come here," I said, yanking him closer. I grabbed his wrist and pulled the hand off his crotch, settling it instead on my waist. I placed his other hand on my hip. "Better?"

His eyes were pools of molten copper and just as heated. His breath feathered my lips when he whispered, "Much."

Just being this close to him was driving me crazy. I was as hard as he was. My cock tented my sweatpants in a way that I was sure could get me arrested for indecent exposure. Like a moth fluttering around a flame, I was drawn to him. How desperately I wanted to be burned by his heat. I moved the inch that brought our mouths together in a fiery kiss that made the other two seem like child's play. My hands were all over him. I touched his shoulders, his spine, his hips. His muscles rippled under my palms, and he kept making the sexiest little sounds. His fingers dug into the flesh of my hips. But he never let go.

God, I hoped he'd never let go.

When we were both out of breath and insane with desire, I broke the kiss and pressed my forehead to his. "Wow," Javier said.

"I want to do everything with you," I whispered against his mouth.

His hands squeezed my waist. "You have no idea how long I've waited to hear you say that."

"Since the first day of freshman year?"

He laughed softly.

"I meant it when I told you that yesterday. You need to believe it."

"I'm starting to."

"Good."

"I… uh… I think we should stop now."

I squeezed his nape and lifted my forehead off his. "We'll never be able to get back to the car if we don't."

His hand slid off my hip and he palmed himself. "Jesus. Maybe I'll just slip behind a tree. They're big enough to shield me."

"Don't you fucking dare."

"Why? You got a better idea?"

"Yeah. Let's go back to the winery and pick things up again with Arianna."

Javier grinned. "I like the way you think, *hermano*."

JAVIER

Daniel had fucking kissed me and gotten turned on. My mind was still replaying every moment of our time in the Armstrong Redwoods Preserve as we headed to Ari's room. He'd called ahead, telling her to strip before we got there.

He'd kept a hand on my thigh as he'd driven us back to the winery, and both of us were sporting hard-ons. I was glad we'd managed to avoid everyone else as we headed to Ari's room.

She answered at Daniel's knock, discreetly keeping herself shielded behind the door. As soon as we were inside and had the door closed, Daniel and I started undressing. Neither one of us was in the mood to wait a second longer for relief.

Ari chuckled at our haste, the two of us tossing clothes everywhere. "What got into you two?" she asked.

Daniel's eyes met mine, and he grinned. "I managed to kiss Javi without losing my shit."

Ari smiled. "I wouldn't mind seeing that."

I wouldn't mind a repeat either. But would it be too much too soon? Because we were both naked this time, our cocks jutting into the air. I raised my brows at him in question.

His eyes roamed me up and down, then he nodded and beckoned me forward. We were only a few feet apart, but it felt like a mile as I crossed over to him, my heart thudding. I reached for his waist, then hesitated. He stepped closer, his hard cock grazing mine and making me shudder. He closed his eyes for a second, and I did my best not to react otherwise. I didn't move a muscle, keeping my eyes on his, waiting for him to make the next move.

He reached up and grabbed my shoulder, urging me a bit closer. He stopped me when we were close enough to kiss, but not pressed together from head to toe. His cock brushed mine again, and I bit my lip, resisting the urge to tug his crotch against mine. His eyes closed again, and he let out a long shuddering breath, going utterly still.

I thought my heart would thrash out of my chest. Was this happening too fast?

Opening his eyes, he placed a hand on the nape of my neck, and then we were kissing again, his tongue slipping into my mouth, and I gripped his waist harder, fighting not to close the gap between us. I wanted us pressed

skin to skin, our cocks sliding together, but that would have to wait. *Baby steps, Cordero. Baby steps.*

Daniel broke the kiss, and when I opened my eyes, he gave me a grin that was so hopeful I thought my heart would break.

Then his eyes flicked to Ari. "Was that too weird?" he asked her.

She slowly shook her head and stepped forward. "No, *mi amor*. That was fucking hot."

He took her in his arms, and they kissed, both tender and fierce, pressed tightly together, his hands kneading her luscious ass, and I was mixture of jealous and turned on.

Was it just my imagination, or had they forgotten I was in the room? The way they came together was different this time. And then I saw why. They were relaxed with each other. Familiar with each other.

I guess Ari's apology had gone well. Really well.

I took a breath. Someday, hopefully, Daniel and I would get to the same point. I just had to be patient.

Daniel whispered something in Ari's ear, and she glanced at me over her shoulder, then nodded, a sexy smile curving her lips. She walked over to the nightstand and pulled out a condom and tube of lube.

"Up on the bed," Daniel said to her. "Ass in the air."

She obeyed quickly, positioning herself near the edge of the bed, then she crooked a finger at me. When I got close, she reached for my cock and opened her mouth, her pink tongue slipping out to lick around the crown. "*Dios*," I murmured, a shiver moving over me. What this woman did to me. One touch, and I was lost.

Behind her, Daniel flipped open the lid of the tube and coated his fingers. Then he started running those fingers between Ari's ass cheeks. I knew when he penetrated her tight little hole because she gasped around me, her tongue swiveling faster around my shaft.

I rocked my hips forward, my cock disappearing between her lips, feeling her shudder as Daniel caressed her. When her hips were moving in slow circles and she was moaning continuously around me, he withdrew his fingers and sat down on the edge of the mattress, then tugged her onto his lap. She let go of me with a protest. "I wasn't finished."

Daniel looked at me and grinned. "Javier will get his. But right now, I need his help."

"How so?" I asked.

Daniel rubbed his cock between Ari's ass cheeks, and she shivered. "Our girl likes to be fucked in the ass, but she needs her clit touched while it's happening. I thought you could help us out."

He positioned his cock at her entrance, and she sank down onto him, ever so slowly, her breath coming out in little hitches as he breached her. Her nails dug into the thick muscles of his thighs, her whole body tensed as she took him, her dusky nipples spiked, and I couldn't resist tugging on them. She gasped and arched her back, shoving her tits into my palms.

When Daniel was fully inside her, he spread his legs wide and hooked hers over his thighs, forcing her legs apart and baring her slick pussy to my gaze.

I sank down onto my knees before them and looked up at her, then him, waiting for his nod to make sure he was okay with my face being so close to his dick. Maybe he'd wanted me to do this differently, but I wanted to make Ari feel good and to push the envelope with Daniel a bit.

He held my gaze for a second, then he nodded, his hands holding Ari tight as he raised her a bit, his hips moving as he thrust up into her.

I dove into the feast before me, Ari's pussy wet and glistening. I circled my tongue around her clit and she gasped, one hand twining in my hair. "*Dios*," she cried, her hips rolling as we both worked on her.

I speared my tongue inside her, wishing Daniel was taking her there so I could lick his shaft as he did. Instead, I had to settle for watching him slide in and out of her, a sight that was making my cock twitch and beg for attention from my own hand.

Ari rode my tongue, her fingers pulling on my hair, whimpers falling from those lush lips. "Don't stop, Javi," she moaned.

Daniel chuckled and pinched one of her nipples. "She likes this, doesn't she, Javi?"

I nodded, then moved my attention back to her clit, sucking on it gently and provoking another gasp from her. Then I had a brilliant idea. I stopped for a second and stuck two fingers in my mouth, getting them good and wet, before I went back to her clit and worked those fingers inside her pussy.

We all groaned when I did. I could feel Daniel moving inside her, and he could feel my fingers as well. Ari's toes curled and she whimpered. "Fuck, Javi," she panted. "Keep doing that. Don't stop."

All I could think about was the sensation of Daniel's cock moving inside her, how I could almost touch it, what it would feel like if we both took her at once… I tightened my grip on my dick, fisting myself harder.

Ari was shaking, and I tongued her faster, pleased to hear her cry out in that low, throaty way she did when she came. She was clutching my hair so hard I thought she might rip some out, but I really didn't care. I wanted to make her come. Her *and* Daniel. When he was ready to let me assist in a more direct way.

I added a third finger, and Ari swore, grinding faster on my hand. Daniel pumped into her harder, and I was sure the added pressure was the reason. Again, the thought entered my head: What would it be like if we were both inside her at the same time, Ari sandwiched between us, our cocks nearly touching, feeling each other fucking her? That familiar tingle in my balls started, and I grabbed my shirt and wrapped it around my dick just before I came, my cock pulsing as my climax rocketed through me.

With a few fierce strokes, Daniel slammed into Ari's ass, then let out a low and guttural groan. I sucked hard on Ari's clit, and she shuddered again, her thighs tensing as she writhed. She tried to close them, but Daniel held her legs apart, and I kept at it until she swore again and begged me to stop.

I sat back, panting, and looked up at my two lovers. Daniel let Ari's legs close, but he held her tightly to his chest, both of them breathing hard, his eyes meeting mine as he kissed her neck.

"You are one surprise after another, Cordero," he murmured.

Ari nodded and laughed. "I'm not sure I'll be able to walk after this." I rose and took her into my arms when Daniel let her up. Her legs wobbled, and she sagged against me with a giggle. "The two of you are going to kill me." She pressed a kiss to my mouth. Then she touched my cheek. "But what a way to go."

Indeed.

Daniel stood and came up behind me, planting a kiss on the nape of my neck, the touch so fleeting I almost thought I'd imagined it. He didn't linger before continuing to the bathroom.

I wanted more, but this was progress. Maybe someday I really could have everything I wanted.

And for the first time, the hope I'd carried so damn long didn't hurt.

DANIEL

"Arianna," Greta said. "I've got to hand it to you. This safari was a stroke of genius."

Greta was right. We'd only arrived in the early afternoon, but already I sensed a difference in the couples. The wonder of the safari, of the wild and beautiful animals, was breathtaking, and it made you look at your life and your problems a little differently. At least it did for me. We'd just finished an amazing meal of grilled meats and vegetables and some very good wine from local wineries, all eaten al fresco with the sound of the animals all around us. I could hear the chatter of monkeys in the trees not too far away and the occasional braying of a zebra or lowing of a water buffalo. I couldn't recall a more magical evening. And now, we were all gathered in small groups around a bonfire. Some people were standing while others were seated on logs, the heat keeping us warm as we enjoyed a nightcap or two.

Ari beamed as she accepted Greta's compliment. "I figured it would be a treat for everyone and make up for needing to relocate the retreat." It was only then that I realized how drawn her face had been in the days prior. Whether it had been the stress of the leak and having to replan the entire retreat, or whether it had been because she'd caught some bug, she seemed fully recovered now.

Ari's attention shifted to Javier. She lowered her voice. "Any news on that front?"

"No. Zach's investigations didn't turn up anything suspect coming out of TI." Somehow, he managed not to stumble on the lie. Of course, now he understood why I'd had to use Diamond Escorts.

Greta grimaced. She looked around, then leaned in. "ECC has conducted an extensive investigation as well, and we've also come up empty."

"I'm sure we'll figure it out eventually." My gaze met Javier's. He nodded. We'd discuss my suspicions later. But for now, it was time to celebrate. "A toast," I said, raising my glass of Syrah. Once the others had followed, I continued. "To ECC and TI Tours and to a long and mutually beneficial partnership."

"Here, here!"

Greta smiled and clinked her glass against mine, then against Ari's and Javi's as well.

Jay and Raven stopped by and started chatting with Ari and Javier. Greta stepped closer to me and rested her hand on my forearm. "How are you doing with"—her eyes flicked over to Ari and Javi—"everything?"

My lips curled into a jaw-splitting smile. "Really well."

"Yes?"

I nodded. "Definitely making progress."

"I'm so pleased to hear that. But…" She paused.

"But?"

"Just… take it slow, all right? Give yourself time to absorb and adjust. Your issues won't go away overnight."

"I appreciate your advice, Greta."

Her lips kicked up at the corner. "You don't think it applies to you?"

"Thirteen years is taking it plenty slow."

Concern filled her narrowed eyes. "You can't rush your recovery, Daniel. It will take the time it takes."

"I hear you," I said.

"Good. Now try to understand too." She smiled and stepped back. "Call if you need me."

"I will."

Greta was right, of course. Yet an urge inside me pushed me to go faster. I wanted Javi. So badly. Hell, I'd wanted to be with him for what seemed like a lifetime, and that taste of him I'd had yesterday had only whetted my appetite.

Feeling his hot skin on mine, the tension in his muscles beneath my palms, and the crispness of his hair on my fingers.... God, it had been even more exciting than I'd thought it would be.

When he'd held me in his strong arms, I'd felt like I'd come home. His voice had rumbled in his chest and vibrated against mine, so deep and manly.

And his mouth. That first kiss had blown my mind. I loved the rub of his square jaw against mine and the roughness of his stubble on my cheeks. When he'd gotten on his knees between my legs to eat Arianna's pussy, fuck, he'd been so close to my cock. His shoulders had brushed the hair on my thighs. And then he'd looked up and our gazes had met. And held. I couldn't have looked away if my life had depended on it.

He'd looked so beautiful then. As beautiful as Arianna, and I wanted them equally. I wanted to give him the pleasure I could so easily give to her.

As I observed them laughing together in the firelight, my heart swelled, filled with joy. Christ, I was being a sappy motherfucker.

Javi turned to me then. "Did you know that Raven isn't only an accomplished choreographer, but she sings beautifully as well? Or so Jay says."

Mr. Top of the Country Charts Jay Samson couldn't tear his gaze away from Raven. It was very clear they still loved each other so much. If there was one couple I was rooting for, it was this one.

"I didn't know Jay had any competition at home," I said, coming to stand between Javi and Ari. I smiled at Raven. "Would you sing something for us?"

She swallowed. "Now?"

"A little music is exactly what this party is missing," Arianna said, her face radiant, so gorgeous. Emotions bubbled up strong and powerful in my chest. Thankfully, her attention was on Raven and Jay, and she didn't notice the hitch in my breathing. When I chanced a glance at Javi, his eyes were on Arianna as well. They burned with so much intensity, my first reaction was jealousy, and that stopped me cold.

The last time I'd caught him watching her, I'd been overwhelmed with possessiveness, a feeling of "Ari's mine." This time was different. While there was still the possessiveness, there was also envy. I wanted Javi to look at me that way too.

Jesus. Be careful what you wish for.

I'd wanted to deal with my past and explore my attraction to Javi. I hadn't accounted for the fact it might be more than physical. Javi was my best friend, but what if—I inhaled deeply—what if he was also something more?

Assuming I could get past all my intimacy hang-ups, could I handle being in a relationship with a man? Did I want to?

Jay began to strum a guitar, drawing my attention back to the bonfire. I squinted to see the guitar better and realized it was one of his own. I guess he'd brought it along with him. Seated next to him, Raven began to sing in a clear voice.

It was a popular song, one I remembered hearing recently on the radio. When she sang the chorus, Raven raised her hands, inviting everyone to join in.

Ari's arm circled my waist. She smiled up at me and sang along. I wasn't much of a singer, but I could carry a tune. So at Ari's urging, I sang with everyone.

Soon, all the ECC counselors and clients gathered around. Some of the couples were clearly taking full advantage of the chance to rekindle their relationships in an exotic and romantic setting.

The safari seemed to have melted some of Malia's frostiness. She and Branson stood side by side, singing along, their gazes colliding and holding. Darren and Ji-woo were singing along and laughing, his arm around her shoulders. Chad and Monica were on opposite sides of the gathering. She was, of course, trying to be the belle of the ball and vying for everyone's attention by attempting to out-sing Raven.

Chad, looking sad and lonely, watched her every move. The poor bastard was still very much in love with his wife. It was so obvious to me now. As obvious as the fact that I was still in love with Ari.

I pulled her closer to my side. She smiled up at me. I leaned down to whisper in her ear, "What do you say we grab Javi and head over to your cabin?"

"Now?"

I waggled my eyebrows.

"Oh!" Her bright brown eyes turned sultry. She licked her lips in a subconscious gesture. "What did you have in mind?"

"Mmm… let me see. I haven't finished this great article I found in the *Financial Times*, and then there's—"

She lightly smacked my arm. "You think you're so funny, don't you, Mr. King?"

"I have my moments."

"This isn't one of them."

"No?" I stared into her eyes, letting every dirty thing I wanted to do to her show on my face.

She gasped. Her eyes locked on mine. "Oh wow. Yeah… let's…"

Chuckling, I pulled her closer, loving the feel of her tight body against mine. "Christ, I've missed you."

"I can tell," she said, a smirk in her voice.

I laughed and let her go. Everyone had assumed Ari and Javi were a couple, and I didn't want to do anything to make them doubt their conclusions.

Ari turned and grabbed Javi's hand. He was sitting on a log and pulled her between his knees. She whispered something to him. He looked at me, then shot to his feet, and with his arm going around her shoulders, they headed into the darkness toward their cabin. I followed close behind.

We passed my own cabin, a double I was sharing with Tyrell Jackson, one of the ECC counselors. Good thing they'd signed NDAs because he'd no doubt soon realize that I was seeing someone, and maybe he'd even figure out who. Hell, probably everybody would, since our "cabins" were actually big, glammed-up tents with hardwood floors and some wooden framing, and those thin canvas walls weren't much of a sound blocker. Still, no amount of discomfort would make me alter my evening plans.

Tonight, I wanted to be with Ari *and* Javi.

Javi unlocked the door, and with a saucy smile and a swing of her hips, Ari skipped into the room. I followed close on her heels. I couldn't wait to get my hands on that round ass, hugged so seductively in her skin-tight yoga pants. Paired with heeled boots and a long tan blouse with a thick belt at her waist, it was Arianna's version of safari-wear, and it was sexy as hell.

As soon as the door closed with a snick behind us, I circled her waist with my hands, stopping her in her tracks. I dropped to my knees and lowered her pants in one swift move, nipping a trail over her ass cheeks.

She squealed and tried to squirm away, but I held her tight. Javi chuckled. "Great minds think alike, I see." He stood in front of her and began undoing her belt and the buttons of her blouse. Moments later, she was naked between us, except for her boots.

I kissed her long legs, down one and up the other, biting gently when I reached her thighs.

"Oh God." She moaned and jutted her ass out. I looked up to see Javier's head buried between her breasts. When her hands gripped his hair and pushed him down, a rumbling laugh escaped my throat.

Javier peeked at me around her hip. His lips were reddened and wet, and he was grinning ear to ear. "Let's rock her world, eh, *hermano*?"

Fuck. He was so damn hot. I had to pull my tongue back in my mouth before I could respond. "You got it." My voice was so rough I sounded like a two-pack-a-day smoker.

I edged Ari's legs open and palmed her ass cheeks, exposing her pink bud to my view. I'd been inside that tight hole just last night. I shivered at the memory.

Pressing forward, I drew the flat of my tongue up her crack from her wet pussy to the base of her spine. She shivered in my hands.

"Oh fuck. Oh shit." Arianna pushed her butt into my face, and I had to stifle a laugh.

I pointed my tongue and circled her hole, gently probing it after each revolution. The taste was clean and slightly musky and exactly perfect. Just like the rest of her.

As I was about to spread her with my thumbs, Arianna turned in my hands. She cried out, then groaned when my mouth landed on her pussy.

"Ari." Javi's deep voice seemed to echo in the cabin.

She froze for a moment. I looked up at her, then over to him. A look passed between them. She bit her lip, nodded, then smiled at me. "Come here, *mi amor*."

I grinned and squeezed her ass. "I'm pretty happy with where I am right now."

She shook her finger at me and *tsk*ed. "Dirty boy."

"Dirty, huh?" I nuzzled her pussy and used the opportunity to lap at her clit.

"Oh. Oh. No, stop."

Frowning, I sat back on my heels. "What's wrong?"

"Nothing, it's just that…" Her teeth sank into her bottom lip and she cast another uncertain glance at Javier. Something passed between them again.

"What's going on here?" I asked. I felt left out and I hated it.

Her hand on my shoulder tightened. "We want tonight to be about you, Daniel."

About me? "I don't understand." Lately, I felt like everything was always about me and my fucking insecurities. Focusing on them helped me forget about my fucked-up past even if it was only for a few hours.

She tugged on my hand. I rose and waited uncertainly.

"We"—her eyes included Javier—"want to make you feel good. Will you let us do that?"

I could handle anything from her, but… My gaze swung to Javi. I bit my lips and swallowed in a nervous habit I wish I could get rid of. "What do you have in mind?"

"A kiss like before, or"—he shrugged—"or maybe something more. Whatever you need."

Whatever I needed? Christ, I needed everything from him, but the better question was what could I handle?

Ari pulled on my hand. "Why don't we get on the bed?"

I blinked and slowly nodded my assent, but my movements were stiff as I sat on the edge. She set one knee on the mattress, fluffed up the pillows, then patted a spot in the middle. "Scoot up here."

Still fully dressed, I turned and crawled to the spot she'd indicated. I sat with my back against the headboard. She straddled my lap and grasped the hem of my T-shirt. "Let's start by getting rid of this, okay?"

"Okay," I mumbled.

She pulled it over my head. Javier folded it and placed it on the dresser at the foot of the bed, then removed his own shirt. My gaze was riveted to his broad back, all that tanned flesh stretched tightly over cut muscles that flexed and rippled as he moved.

"Mmm," I moaned appreciatively.

"Oh yeah," Ari said. "Our Javi is one sexy *papi chulo*."

Papi chulo? I choked on a laugh, but couldn't quite manage to hold it in when Javier's face turned bright red.

"Ari," he scolded.

"What?" She grinned. "It's the truth, isn't it, Daniel?"

My eyes drank him in, from the top of his silky brown hair to the bottom of his long muscular legs. "Oh yeah." Holding his gaze, I deliberately licked my lips and smirked lasciviously.

"Ooh-la-la." Ari fanned herself.

"Is it hot in here or is it—?" I started to ask.

"It's definitely you," Javi cut in, his hot eyes boring into mine.

Ari swung her leg over me, her hands going to the buttons on my khakis. "Let's take these off. I want to see you, *mi amor*."

"Oh yeah?"

"Yeah." She unzipped my pants and when I raised my hips, she tugged them and my boxers down my legs and over my feet, tossing them over her shoulder. Javier caught the bundle. He carefully folded my clothes and set them on top of my shirt.

"You too, Javi," I said, my voice cracking.

His face tightened, and his eyes blazed. He slowly pulled his pants down his narrow hips and over his firm ass. My mouth watered. Christ, he was a sight.

Ari whistled loudly, and Javi blushed again. My cock twitched. I wanted him. I held my hand out. "Come here, babe."

His eyes widened, whether at my gesture or at the term of endearment, I wasn't sure. His throat worked as he swallowed. I could see in his face how much he wanted this, and how tightly he was restraining himself. I curled my fingers, beckoning.

He gave a small smile and slowly walked around the bed. "Tell me what you want."

"Lie down beside me."

He settled on the bed, close to me, but not touching.

Ari walked on her knees to the foot of the bed and started to massage my feet. She lifted one of my legs, and I groaned when she sucked on my big toe. "Jesus, girl. Warn a guy before you do that." Pre-cum dripped down the side of my throbbing cock.

Javier stared at it, hunger etching his face. I wrapped my fingers around my hard length and lazily stroked it from my balls to the tip, rolling my palm over the darkening head to smear my juices around. "You want this, babe?"

"Fuck, yeah." Javier's voice was raw, like he'd swallowed rocks.

I groaned. "Kiss me. Fucking kiss me… please."

He didn't move except to raise his head. I rolled onto my side and propped myself up on an elbow. My pulse thundered in my veins as I coiled my fingers in his soft hair and pulled his mouth to mine. He sighed against my lips, a heartfelt little sound that heated my blood.

Arousal tightened my belly. "You feel so good," I murmured into his mouth.

Javi moaned and closed his eyes. His tongue danced around mine, and I saw stars. Whether that was because of Javi's kiss or because Ari had managed to work her way up my legs and had popped a ball into her mouth, I couldn't say.

"Oh fuck," I cried out, falling onto my back.

Javier leaned over my chest. "May I?" he asked softly. Not daring, or maybe more accurately, unable to speak, I simply nodded, and watched, my mouth hanging open, as his lips closed over one of my nipples.

Arianna released my ball and sucked in the other. "Oh God."

Javier caught my nipple between his teeth and grinned up at me. Christ, the sight of him, of them. Both focused on me, on my pleasure. It was too much. I groaned loudly. Javi released my nipple and pressed tiny kisses on my chest, down the center of my abs. His tongue swirled around my navel, dipped in. I inhaled sharply at the curious sensations. He continued downward, and I held my breath when he nipped my treasure trail, then hovered over my cock.

His eyes pleaded with mine. "Please," he begged. "Let me do this for you, *cariño*."

Fuck, I wanted to let him do it. Ari moved up beside me, cradled my head against her chest and stroked my hair. "I'll be right here with you, Daniel. If you need him to stop"—she took my hand in hers—"squeeze my fingers."

I searched her face for some indication of something… God, I didn't know what. But this had to be fucking strange for her. I didn't want to hurt her again. Nothing was more important than that. "Are you sure you're okay with me and Javi…?" I swallowed and let the question hang between us.

She brought my hand between her legs and rocked against it. "See for yourself." She was wet and swollen.

I stretched my neck and gave her a quick kiss. "You're an amazing woman, Arianna Rodriguez."

She stroked her long red-tipped fingers along my jaw. "No more amazing than you and Javi."

I nodded. "Okay, let's try this."

Javier closed his eyes and blew out a breath. The stream of warm air bathed my cock, and a shiver shook my entire body. He opened his eyes and kept them on my face as he first kissed my cockhead, little pecks all around, up and down my shaft.

My pulse quickened, but I forced my fingers to relax around Ari's. She smiled and kissed me, a slow tender kiss that did wonders toward relaxing me. I sighed in pleasure and sank lower onto the pillows. "Ride my face, sweetheart," I said.

She glanced at Javier over her shoulder, then nodded to me. With my hands on her hips, I steadied her while she straddled my chest and edged up on her knees until her succulent pussy was poised within licking distance of my mouth.

I inhaled deeply, taking her scent into my lungs. My hands palmed her ass and tugged her forward so I could taste her again. Savor her. Eat her out.

Warm wet heat engulfed my entire cock and the head butted up against something soft. "Jesus!" I yelled, bucking my hips up.

I heard Javier gag and tried to pull back, feeling like shit. A strong masculine hand rested lightly on my thigh. It wasn't meant to hold me in place, only to reassure.

"It's okay, Daniel. Javi's okay. Do you want to stop?"

I looked up the length of her body, her slim waist, her gently curved belly, firm full tits, her concern-filled face. I assessed my reactions. I wasn't panicked. I shook my head.

"Good boy." She gripped my hair and tugged. "Now let me fuck your face."

I barked out a much-needed laugh. "Come here, you vixen."

As Javier sucked my cock with long slow pulls, I pressed my tongue inside Ari's sweet pussy. I thought I was going to lose my mind. My mouth was full of her. His mouth was full of me. It was heaven.

Javi increased his rhythm, bobbing up and down my shaft, my cockhead repeatedly bumping the back of his throat. Ari squirmed and rubbed herself on my face. My fingers dug into the flesh of her hips as she rode me. Her moans told me she was close and, fuck, so was I.

"Javi," I said in warning, only seconds before I arched off the bed, Ari's pussy impaled on my tongue, my cock deep down Javier's throat.

He swallowed around me and my body spasmed. Colors exploded in my eyes, white-hot heat raced up my spine, and one of the most powerful orgasms I'd ever experienced barreled through me.

I shuddered as cum shot out of my dick and down Javi's throat. It had been a long time since I'd come in someone's mouth. Since I'd come in Ari's mouth. And that I was experiencing this with Javi now made it so much more special.

Above me, Arianna stiffened. Her body arched beautifully as her release came. She called out my name and ground herself against my mouth. I flicked her clit with my tongue until she stopped moving.

Javi's lips and tongue laved my cock deliciously. I shivered and tried to rock my hips, but I couldn't move. They'd fucking killed me. I lay sprawled on the bed, dragging air into my lungs, trying to catch my breath and regain my senses. Much to my amazement, I didn't feel even an inkling of panic or revulsion. Fuck, maybe I was cured. Finally fucking cured. And all because of my two best friends. My lovers.

After a few moments, Ari shifted off me and lay down at my side. Javier sat up, his face still tight with arousal. "Hey, babe." I nodded at his stiff cock. "Let me give you a hand with that."

He frowned. "You don't have to."

I smiled. "I know. I want to." He'd already given me so much, helped me so much. I could do this for him. I *needed* to do this for him.

Javier lay next to me. I rolled to my side and wrapped a hand around his cock. It was hot, the skin tight and dark. Long and thick, his cock was beautiful. He groaned as soon as I started to stroke him.

"This won't take long," he said. His eyes were glassy, heavy-lidded, his lips puffy and wet.

I wanted to kiss them and fuck them again. Instead I smirked and firmed my hold on him. "I know."

Arianna pressed herself against my back. Her presence was reassuring and exactly what I needed.

"Faster," Javi said.

I grinned. "Yes, sir."

"Oh God, Daniel." Javier thrust into my hand, my fist tightly squeezing his shaft.

I stared in fascination at the cum pooling in the slit. Stared as it shifted from clear to creamy. He groaned, then after another couple of frantic thrusts, he pushed his head back into the pillows. Ropes of cum erupted from his cockhead to coat my hand and his abs.

My stomach roiled.

I jackknifed into a sitting position and scrambled off the mattress, desperately wiping my hand on the bedding as I went.

Fuck. Bitterness filled my mouth. Oh fuck. I was going to puke. It was too much. The sight of his cum. The smell.

"Goddamn it," I shouted and slammed my hand against the frame of door to the en-suite bathroom. I screwed my eyes tight and sucked in breath after breath. I refused to give in to the panic. I refused to let Coach and what he'd done to me continue to control my life.

"Daniel?" Ari stood a few feet away from me.

"Why the fuck can't I do this?"

"It's okay, Daniel. Maybe we just went too far too soon," she said. Her words echoed Greta's. I knew she was right, but I couldn't accept it.

"No. I wanted this. I wanted to do this for Javier. So fucking much."

"It was good though, wasn't it, for a while?" Javier asked in a gentle voice.

I ducked my head, but snuck a look at him, hoping, praying, the nausea wouldn't return.

He'd cleaned himself up, and he was Javier again. My best friend. A man who would never hurt me. A man I could trust, did trust, with my life. A man who'd been there for me every day since we'd met. I nodded. "Yeah, it was more than good, right up until you… uh… until you"—I swallowed and dropped my gaze to the floor—"until you finished."

Javier's smile was warm and loving. "So next time we'll use a condom."

"That simple, is it?"

"Yep."

In my experience, life was never that simple.

Chapter 11

JAVIER

Daniel had been quiet all during this morning's safari, a sharp contrast to his excitement the day before. He had a real soft spot for animals—he was one of those people who never passed a dog or cat without trying to befriend it—and he'd been like a little kid during yesterday's safari, excitedly pointing out the various animals we'd encountered, his eyes nearly as sharp as our guide's.

Today, Daniel seemed barely engaged. And I knew why. He was still focused on his "failure" the night before. I'd known we were pushing it, and I should have had the restraint to say no, to wait a bit longer before I let him jerk me off. But I didn't.

Now it was up to me to turn this around, to get Daniel smiling again. And I had an idea how I could do that.

I pulled our guide aside after we clambered down off our safari jeep back at the main buildings. Our guide's name was Ryan, and given his hippie-ish, laid-back demeanor, I was pretty sure he could deal with any unusual displays of affection he might witness if my plan succeeded.

"Ryan, I've heard there's a tour where we can see the cheetahs up close. Could the three of us"—I pointed to Daniel and Ari chatting by themselves—"do one of those tours now? Daniel's feeling a bit down, and I thought it might cheer him up. He loves cats."

Ryan scrubbed a hand over his light brown beard, then tightened his blond-streaked man bun, his hazel eyes holding mine. He looked from me to Daniel, then Ari, then back to me. "Yeah, sure. It's two hundred. You can have up to four people if you want."

I thought about inviting Luciana, but she was talking with Greta—the two had managed to become quite friendly—and I figured it was best to keep our group small so Daniel wouldn't feel inhibited. "It'll just be the three of us. Add it to my tab."

He nodded. "Will do."

I gathered up Ari and Daniel and explained the opportunity. Ari's eyes lit up, and Daniel mustered a tight smile. Not exactly what I was hoping for, but it would have to do.

We followed Ryan to the cheetah barn. He let us inside and stopped us near the entrance. "Cheetahs don't look as fierce as lions or tigers, but they are wild cats and they definitely can hurt you. So don't try to pet any adult cats, and keep your voices soft. No flash photography. We don't want to stress them out."

We all nodded, then Ryan grinned. "You're in luck. We have a litter of cubs around two months old, and they're quite friendly, so you might be able to pet them if you're patient. Would you like to concentrate your visit there?"

"Yes!" Ari said and she turned to Daniel. He smiled, and this time it looked more genuine. Maybe this would do the trick.

Ryan led us through the barn to an open-air enclosure at the back. We hadn't seen this during our safaris through the park. "We keep the cubs here so that they don't get stressed by too many people being around."

We walked up to the wire fence and peered in. Three cubs gamboled through the short grass toward us. A layer of thick, tawny fur covered their backs, standing up kind of like a lion's mane. The hair wasn't spotted like the rest of them.

Daniel crouched down. "What's that weird fur on their backs?" he asked, taking the question out of my mouth.

Ari and I crouched beside him, getting down to eye level with the cubs, who'd stopped a few feet from the fence, their tails twitching as they studied us.

"That fur is called the mantle," Ryan said. "It helps hide them when they're young, and it possibly convinces other animals that the cubs might be badgers—something other animals don't want to tangle with."

"Clever," Daniel said, sticking his fingers through the fence. Ari gasped and touched my arm, gesturing for me to stop him.

Ryan laughed. "It's okay to let the cubs sniff you. They probably won't nip, unless you get them really excited."

Daniel gave Ari a smirk, and she reached across me to smack his arm. "Fine, lose a hand for all I care."

"I won't lose a hand." He wiggled his fingers, and one of the cubs came up and sniffed them, then rubbed against Daniel's fingertips. "You're so soft," he said to it, his voice hushed, a genuine grin breaking out on his face.

The cub made a noise that sounded exactly like a bird chirping. "Why is it chirping?" Ari asked, looking over her shoulder at Ryan.

"It's technically called chirruping. They make that sound a lot. So do the adults. It's a way to announce their presence and find each other."

The cub did it again, stepping away from the fence. Daniel's face fell. "Am I disturbing it?"

Ryan shook his head. "No, man. Just wait a sec. It'll be back. That one's Bouncer. He's the bravest of the three. But easily distracted."

Bouncer, true to his name, bounced away for a minute, chasing the other two around the enclosure, the three of them hopping over a boulder and dashing around a clump of logs.

"Are they all boys?" I asked.

"Two boys and a girl. The other boy is Lightning, and the girl is Zara. She's the smallest."

"How do you tell Bouncer and Lightning apart?" Daniel asked.

"Personality, mostly, at least at first glance. Bouncer has six rings at the end of his tail. Lightning has four. And if you spend long enough around them, you start to notice differences in their spot patterns."

Bouncer raced back over to us, stopping just shy of Daniel's outstretched fingers, then the cub stepped forward again and rubbed against them.

Ari looked up at Ryan. "It's really safe to touch them?"

Ryan grinned. "Yeah. They might nip, but they're not aggressive or trying to hurt anyone. They're very playful at this stage."

Ari nodded, then stuck her fingers through the wire. Lightning and Zara had come closer, the two of them hanging back a bit while Bouncer circled around and around in front of Daniel, who was talking to him in a low murmur. "That's my boy," he said as Bouncer finally stood still, allowing Daniel to scratch the top of his head.

"Zara," Ari called, also keeping her voice low. "Come here, girl."

Zara's ears pricked forward, and she took a cautious step toward us. "That's it," Ari said. "Will you let me pet you, pretty girl?"

With a chirrup, Zara stepped closer. Lightning followed at her side, then jumped up and nipped at her ear. That set the three of them off, and they chased each other around the enclosure several times before coming back.

Daniel made a chirrup sound, and Ryan grinned. "Keep doing that, and they'll definitely investigate."

When Daniel did it again, all three cubs came closer, advancing slowly, sniffing the air as if to figure out whether Daniel was a cat or something else. Bouncer suddenly jumped forward, going right up to Daniel and sniffing. Bouncer chirruped at Daniel and he did it back, a wide smile on his face.

"They're adorable," Ari said when Zara finally got close enough for her to touch.

I reached through the wire, and Zara sniffed my fingers, then allowed me to touch her. She started purring as she rubbed her muzzle on my hand.

"The black 'tear' marks that flow from their eyes around their muzzles are also unique," Ryan said, "but the definitive way to identify cheetahs is by the markings on their legs and tails. Those are often the most distinctive."

"When do they lose the mantle?" Daniel asked, running his fingers over the ruff of fur covering Bouncer's back.

"Around three months. At that point, they start getting more independent."

"How long do they stay with their mother?" I asked.

"About eighteen months. She teaches them to hunt during that time, then the cubs form a sibling group that will live together once their mother leaves. Around two years after that, the females will go out on their own, but the males will usually stay together for life."

Ari looked at me, then Daniel, and grinned. Daniel met my gaze, and I put a hand on his shoulder. "Thanks," he said to me. "This was a really good idea."

I squeezed his shoulder and glanced up to see Ryan studying us, his expression shifting to a smile when our eyes met. He gave a slight nod, as if to say he'd figured out what was up with us, and I let out the breath I'd been holding. I leaned over and kissed Daniel's cheek, and he whipped his head around to look at Ryan.

Ryan held up his hands. "It's all good with me," he said, stepping back to give us a bit of privacy.

Daniel pressed a kiss to my lips. I looked at Ari, who was watching us, then gave her a kiss too, glancing up at Ryan as I did. He raised an eyebrow, then gave me a grin. Thank goodness. I hadn't been sure how he'd react to our threesome, but it turned out I'd read him right.

Ryan checked his watch. "Okay, folks, it's time to go. We don't want to disturb the cubs too much. They're pretty easygoing, but we like to leave them be most of the time."

Daniel gave Bouncer one last scratch, then all three of us rose. We followed Ryan outside, where he shook our hands. I slipped him a twenty. "Thanks, man," I said.

He grinned at me. "My pleasure." Then he lowered his voice and said, "You appear to be a very lucky guy."

I beamed at him so widely my cheeks ached. "Yeah, I am."

Daniel, Ari, and I headed back to our cabins. Just before Daniel split off for his, he stopped me. He looked from Ari to me. "I'm sorry I was so mopey earlier."

"It's okay, Daniel," Arianna said. She stroked his arm.

"That's nice of you to say, but I didn't mean to let my mood overshadow the day." He shifted his focus to me. "Thanks for the cheetah encounter. That was..." He smiled, seemingly at a loss for words. "It was amazing. Something I won't forget."

A lump formed in my throat. It was great seeing Daniel smile—really smile—again. I hadn't seen a whole lot of those during the past year.

He took a deep breath, then met my eyes. "I want to try again." His gaze flicked to Ari's. "If you two can put up with me."

I shook my head. "Stop that. I'm not upset. Ari isn't either," I said, and she nodded. "We understand. This is going to take however long it takes."

"And what if it doesn't get better?" Daniel asked.

"It will," I said with a firmness that was part bravado. But Daniel had come a long way already, and I had to believe he could get comfortable with me, with all the things we could do together. And even if he never got as relaxed with me as I hoped, the fact that he *wanted* to, that he wanted to try, that he wasn't giving up?

That gave me more hope than anything.

DANIEL

After stopping by my cabin for a quick shower and change of clothes, I said goodbye to Tyrell and hurried over to Ari and Javi's. I wanted to try again with Javi. For the first time in my adult life, I felt "normality" in reach. Yeah, yeah. I could hear Greta's voice in my head telling me I *was* normal, that my reactions to what had happened to me were normal. It was all fine in theory. But I didn't *feel* normal. Normal was Javier. A guy who was sexually attracted to other men, who could give a guy a blow job or a hand job without being nauseated. Who could fuck a man or be fucked by one without having a panic attack. Who could see and smell cum, taste it, and fucking enjoy it.

I didn't know if I'd ever reach that point. Christ, just the thought of having cum in my mouth had me dry heaving. What I did know was that I wanted to try with Javier, more than anything.

Having arrived at their cabin, I knocked on the door and shifted from foot to foot. Would I be interrupting something? It wasn't reasonable of me to think they'd be completely hands off when I wasn't around. I'd slept with Arianna just a few days ago. Besides, they were a couple as far as everyone was concerned. They were sharing a room. If she and I had been sharing a room, I'm pretty sure my cock would be deep inside her right now instead of pressing against my zipper.

Arianna opened the door. Her face was flushed and she wore a huge smile, but she was fully clothed. Javi on the other hand, looked fresh from the shower. He stood in front of the mirror, a towel around his waist, water dripping down his gorgeous chest. Beads of water glittered in his short dark hair. My tongue felt like it had swollen to twice its size. I could barely speak.

Ari's knowing chuckle brought my gaze slowly back to her. She arched a brow. "Right?"

I cleared my throat. "Fuck."

She took my arm and tugged me inside and closed the door behind me. "He wanted to get all clean for you." The way she emphasized the word "all" had Javi turning bright red. I choked on the implication. Did he mean it that way? Did she? I looked from her to him, then back. Uncertainty gripped my belly in a tight hold.

Christ, could I do this in front of them again? What if it went bad? What if it went worse than yesterday? I didn't want to look weak in front of Ari. Neither of them really, but especially her. Maybe it was some macho bullshit left over from my youth, but I just couldn't do it. Not in front of her. My gaze went to Javier. He stood in all his half-naked glory, an understanding look in his eyes. I knew then that I if I fell apart in his arms, he'd put me back together and never see me as anything less than manly. He'd proved it over and over again, hadn't he? The guy was my fucking rock.

I pulled Ari to me. Hugged her tightly. "Ari," I whispered. "I need to do this with Javi. Do you think you can give us a little time? Alone?"

Her smile fell. "Why? Yesterday, I—"

"Ari," Javi said sternly.

She looked at him. Swallowed and nodded. "You're right. Sorry." Without looking at either of us, she grabbed her purse off the dresser. "I'll go see Luciana. We'll have some girl time."

When she passed by me, I touched her arm. "Ari, I'm so—"

"No." She shook her head. "You do what you have to do. I'm a big girl. I'll be okay."

Still, I hesitated. "You sure?"

Finally, she looked up at me. Her eyes held hurt and disappointment in them. But then she smiled and her eyes cleared. "I get it," she said softly. "Javi needs to be the one to help you through this. I'll see you both later, okay?" She rose on her toes and kissed my cheek.

"Thank you, Arianna. I love you."

"I know you do." She stepped outside and quietly closed the door between us.

I started at the glossy wood. Was I doing the right thing, or had I just damaged my relationship with her? Again. *Fuck.*

A warm hand landed on my shoulder. "Daniel?"

Slowly I turned to face Javi. When I saw his open arms and loving expression, I stumbled into them. They closed around me as he hugged me against his warm, solid chest. I rested my head on his shoulder and let out a relieved breath. No one had ever hugged me like this. No one had ever made me feel safe like this. And it was exactly what I needed right now. Javier was what I needed.

I raised my head, cupped his cheek with my palm, and kissed him. I sought to express all that I was feeling in that moment, to thank him for all the comfort and strength he was giving me.

His arms brought me closer against him, brought our hips together. I could feel his cock, not exactly hard, but also not exactly soft, against my own. It was a curious sensation. I pressed into him. Into all that heat.

Javier moaned and his cock twitched. I felt it against my own. "Wow," I said in wonder. "That feels…"

He stilled. His brows rose.

"Good. Really fucking good." I rocked into him, my own cock hardening.

"Oh God." He buried his face in the crook of my neck. "Tell me what you want. Tell me what I can do for you."

I brought my hand up to the back of his head and let my fingers sink into his silky hair. "Thing is, I want to do something for you."

He drew his head back. "Oh yeah?" His expression was a funny mix of uneasy excitement and loving concern.

"Yeah." I walked him backward to the edge of the bed. When his legs touched the mattress, he stopped and looked at me warily. I winked and unknotted the towel at his waist. It dropped to the floor. I took a step back and kicked it toward the bathroom, managing to get it through the narrowly cracked door.

"Show off," Javier teased.

Grinning, I buffed my nails on my shirt. "When you got it, you got it." That brought my attention to Javier's body. He certainly had it. His cock stood out, long and thick, from a small patch of neatly trimmed pubes. Without conscious thought, my hand went to his belly. I touched it lightly before going lower to toy with the nest of dark hairs. Javier sucked in a breath, but didn't move. His eyes burned as he silently took in my every touch.

I lifted my other hand to his shoulder and pressed lightly. Catching my hint, he sat on the bed. I followed him down and lower still until I was on my knees between his legs. His eyes widened at my position. "Daniel. We don't… I can…"

I reached up and stopped him with two fingers of my free hand on his lips. "It's okay, babe." I pulled a flavored non-lubricated condom out of my back pocket. I grinned. "It's banana flavored."

For a second, he didn't say anything. Then he tipped his head back and roared with laughter. "How fitting."

"I thought so." I carefully tore the foil packet open with my teeth and got the condom out. Javier hissed as I tightened my grip on his cock and stroked him firmly a few times before placing the condom over the weeping head. I pinched the latex with two fingers and used my other hand to roll it down his shaft.

He hissed and pressed himself into my grip. "Jesus. Keep stroking me like that and I'm gonna come in thirty seconds."

I released his cock.

He frowned down at me. "Hey now."

My hands shook, so I grabbed hold of his thighs and opened them wider. His frown turned into surprise, but he let me do what I wanted. His fingers curled into the bedding behind him as he relaxed into the support of his arms.

Jesus. He was very clearly offering himself to me. I had six feet of hot, tanned male at my disposal. Before I could second-guess myself, I leaned over him and licked around the head of his cock. The taste of artificial banana filled my mouth. It wasn't great, but it wasn't unpleasant. Javier's hiss and sigh of pleasure made it all worthwhile.

I worked my hand under his balls. They felt full and heavy in my palm. I rolled them gently between my fingers as I used my lips to nip down the side of his shaft. His fingers clutched at the bedding, but he didn't move a single other muscle. Until I rose above him and took the head of his cock in my mouth.

His back arched and he groaned loudly. "Fuck, Daniel. I can't believe you're—"

I swallowed more of him then. Half of his shaft. He gasped and cried out. His thighs became slabs of marble, cradling me between them.

When I'd imagined this, I'd thought I'd feel trapped by all his thick muscles, by the power in his legs, which could wrap around me and force me to do his bidding if he so chose. But I didn't feel that way at all. I felt protected. Coddled almost. All that strength and power was mine. To be used for me and not against me.

I raised my eyes to him, to that beautiful face that regarded me with love, that had always regarded me with so much love. I brought my lips off him slowly. Then I smiled. "I love you, Javier Cordero."

"Jesus, Daniel. I love you too." His cock twitched and bumped my chin.

I laughed and stuck my tongue out to lap at the head.

Javi squeezed his lids together. "Fuck, *cariño*. I'm dying here."

I rolled my eyes playfully. "Fine." I opened my mouth and took him in as deeply as I could without gagging. It wouldn't do to remind my body of what I didn't want it doing.

Javier moaned. "Oh fuck, yes. Faster, please."

I gripped the base of Javier's cock with one hand and his balls with the other. I moved my hand up and down his shaft in time with the bobbing of my mouth, swirling my tongue around the head with each upstroke. He moaned and writhed beneath me, and I felt exactly the same joy and power I did when I got Ari off. *I* was doing this. *I* was bringing Javi this pleasure. He wasn't controlling me. He wasn't forcing me. And I wasn't forcing or controlling him.

It was mutual, consensual pleasure. The way sex was supposed to be.

The realization freed something inside me. Unlocked a door that had been welded shut for so damn long. My cock hardened, lengthened. And fuck, I was enjoying this too.

Javier brushed my cheek lightly. "Can I touch you?" he asked. I hated the hesitancy in his voice, but I understood it. Neither of us wanted to ruin the moment. "I won't push or pull or anything." His voice broke. "I just need to feel you."

There was a jab of fear in my gut, but then I met his gaze and took in his guileless expression. I had nothing to worry about. This was Javier.

I nodded, and keeping my eyes on his face, I took him back into my mouth. His fingers petted my hair softly. It was soothing. I opened my jaw a little wider and took more of him in.

"Oh fuck." Javier's guttural cry was like a top-shelf aphrodisiac. My cock pulsed and pre-cum soaked my boxers. "I'm coming," he shouted. I braced for his fingers to tighten, to claw at my scalp.

But they didn't. They gently continued to stroke and soothe. And my love for this man grew.

The head of his cock swelled, and I knew that if it were me, I'd be jackhammering into his mouth, fucking his face for all I was worth. But not Javier. He continued to sit still on the bed. The only movements he made were with his fingers in my hair.

I felt his cock pulse in my mouth. Cum filled the tip of the condom. His thighs trembled against my shoulders, and then he fell back onto the bed with a groan. His hand left my hair and fell across his flat stomach.

For a few minutes, I remained there on my knees, happy to watch his chest rise and fall with his heavy breaths. His spent condom-covered cock rested against his thigh. I stared at it, almost daring myself to react. I swallowed and assessed myself. All I tasted was banana with a faint hint of latex. My stomach didn't roil. I didn't feel disgusted. I lowered my eyes to the bulge in my pants. My cock didn't have any issue with the current situation or the sexy man lying on the bed right in front of me.

Rising to my feet, I placed my hands on his thighs. Javier cracked open an eye. His brow arched. "Everything okay?"

"Better than okay." I licked my lips. "I want more."

JAVIER

For several moments, all I did, all I *could* do, was stare at the hopeful, eager look on Daniel's face. His blue eyes were bright, for once free of the shadows that had plagued him since we'd first met. Was it crazy that I was super proud that Daniel wanted to face his fears with me? That he trusted me, above everyone else, to be there for him when he was at his most vulnerable?

I looked up into his face, let my love for him shine through, and I smiled. "Do whatever you want, Daniel. I'm yours."

His answering smile took my breath away. Literally took it away. I gasped and inhaled deeply. Daniel's eyes were fixed on my lips. He lowered himself slowly, until all his weight was on me, and kissed me.

Fuck, I loved having his big strong body press me into the mattress. His pelvis settled against mine, his cock hard and long, and even though I'd just come, my cock twitched with renewed interest. What would he ask of me? Did he just want to frot, or did he want to fuck me? As an image of that floated in front of my eyes, I shuddered with need. I'd take whatever he wanted to give me, and I'd take it happily.

Daniel continued to kiss me. He angled his head, and I opened for him as he deepened the kiss. His hips ground against mine and his breathing quickened. After a few minutes, when we were both breathing rapidly, he released my mouth and ran a hand through my damp hair. "Do you think—" He stopped. His eyes lowered. He swallowed. "Do you think maybe we could try… fuck."

"Try… to… fuck?" I asked with a teasing tone. Inside, I was on high alert.

His head popped up. "Would you?"

"Would I let you fuck me? Hell yeah. Jesus, Daniel. I've been dreaming of that from the moment I first saw you sprawled on your bed in our dorm room."

"I don't know how it's going to go." Anxiety leached into Daniel's voice and his eyes, dissipating some of the joy that had been there only moments before. I wanted it back.

I brought my hands up and lightly cupped his cheeks. "It doesn't matter. You do what you can. What feels good. And if at any point you're uncomfortable, just stop."

"Yeah?"

"It's your show. You're in total control of what does and doesn't happen between us."

"Why are you being so good to me? I'm not sure I deserve you."

"Are you kidding me right now?"

"No, it's true. What I'm asking of you, it's… fuck." He shook his head. "It's too much."

"Hey," I said, as calmly as I could. I didn't want him to back out before he tried just because he was worried about hurting me somehow. "I *want* to do this, for you, but also for us. I want to be able to hold you and kiss you and make love to you."

"And Arianna?"

"What about her?"

"Well, where does that leave her?"

I gently moved Daniel to my side and sat up. He followed suit. "I love Arianna. And yes, in the past, I stepped aside so the two of you could be together. At the time, I thought it was what would make you both happiest."

Daniel closed his eyes. "I figured that's what you'd done."

"I didn't fight for her."

Daniel's shoulders slumped.

"And I didn't fight for you either," I added.

His head jerked up. He frowned. "What do you mean?"

"I've always wanted both of you, but I didn't think I could have you. Now I know better. Believe me, I'm going to fight for what we have."

"We?"

"The three of us. I think our triad is good for all of us. I don't want to lose Ari to you, and I don't want to lose you to her. I'm sure she feels the same about us." I let the silence grow, then nudged his shoulder. "What about you, Daniel? What do *you* want? Where do you see this going?"

I held my breath as I waited for him to answer. He clasped his hands between his thighs and seemed to be thinking really hard. Fuck, had I pushed too far? Had I just ruined everything with my fucking incessant need to know where I stood?

Finally, after what felt like forever, he turned his head and looked at me. "I want both of you too. I want each of us to have our own relationships with each other, but I also want us to have a relationship that's the three of us. Know what I mean?"

"Yeah." I smiled and cupped his knee. "I know exactly what you mean."

"Right now, though," he continued, "the weak link is us." He waved his hand between our bodies. "You and me."

"But you think you're ready to change that?"

"Fuck yeah."

"Okay then." I rubbed my hands together comically. When he cracked a smile, I said, "How do you want me?" I remembered what he'd said about the escorts, how he always took them from behind. I put myself into the position he'd described: feet on the floor, shoulder-width apart, hands on the bed, ass up in the air. I looked back at him. "This is how you usually do it, right?"

He nodded. "Yeah."

I pointed to my bag beside the dresser. "There are condoms and lube in my bag."

I tracked him as he riffled through my clothes, found the supplies and dropped them on the bed: lube and two condoms. Would he undress, or would he remain clothed, like he had with the escorts? I'd prefer him naked, but if keeping a barrier between us helped him deal with all his memories and emotions, I was happy for him to keep his clothes on.

Daniel took a shaky breath and removed his T-shirt. Even though we'd been naked in front of each other before, even though we'd kissed naked, I understood that this time, things were different. This time, we'd be doing something that his coach, his abuser, had done to him.

I forced myself to stay in position. To keep my body relaxed. I'd hoped to keep my cock out of the equation, but seeing Daniel slip his pants and boxers off his slim hips was making me hard.

And Daniel's erection hadn't flagged at all.

He stepped behind me and picked up the lube. I watched as he popped it open. His eyes went to my ass, then back to the tube of lube. He frowned. "I—I've never actually done this part. C-c… *he* rarely allowed me to use lube."

Goddamn that fucker. If he weren't already dead, I'd kill him for what he'd done to Daniel. My heart broke for the young man who'd been so roughly violated over and over.

Masking my reaction, I held my hand out. "I'll do it." Daniel squeezed some lube onto my fingers. His gaze followed my hands as I pulled a cheek to the side and quickly slicked my hole. I inserted a finger, wincing at the bite of pain. I was far better at doing this for my partners than I was at doing it for myself. Once the intrusion of my finger became comfortable, I added a second, carefully pushing it in. Fuck, I was tight. I glanced over at Daniel's big cock and flinched. That was going to fucking hurt.

I forged on, scissoring my fingers, stretching myself. When I pulled my fingers out to add a third, Daniel gently brushed my hand aside. Moments later, three thick fingers filled my hole. I grunted at the slick pressure. He'd clearly added more lube to his fingers before penetrating me. He moved slowly, finger-fucking my hole. Somehow, he elicited sensations I'd never experienced before. I shivered and moaned. Arched my back to ride his fingers. And when he curled them inside me, grazing my prostate, I shouted and almost shot my load right then and there.

"Fuck. Fuck. Fuck." Frantically, I scrambled for one of the condoms on the bed, ripped open the package, and rolled the latex over my cock. Only then did I let out a relieved breath. "Holy shit." It was all I could think to say.

Behind me, Daniel laughed. His body shook against mine. I glared at him over my shoulder. "What?"

"I think you're ready." His tone was mirthful.

"What gave it away, Sherlock?"

He slapped my ass, shocking the fuck out of me. "Hey!"

"Stop giving me sass."

"Then fucking fuck me already!"

"As you wish." He gripped my hips, and I felt the bump of his cockhead at my hole.

This was it. We were really going to do this. He pushed in a bit. The pressure grew. And grew. And grew. Jesus. Just as I was about to tap out, the ring of muscle gave way, and Daniel's cock slid in. I grunted and dropped my head.

Daniel stopped moving, and I thought it was to give me time to adjust. But after a minute, when he still hadn't moved, I looked back. His eyes were glued to my ass, to where his cockhead was stretching my hole. And his face was pale. Too pale. "Daniel?"

As though I'd jerked him out of a dream, or a nightmare, he blinked and his eyes refocused on me.

"Are you okay?" I asked.

He frowned. "I am… and I'm not."

I gulped. *Please don't call it quits.* "What do you need?" I asked evenly.

"I don't like seeing you in this position. I thought it might make things easier, but"—he shook his head—"it's not. You aren't like those other men, like the escorts. You're Javier. I want to see you. I want to look at you and know you're the one with me."

"Oh God, Daniel. The things you say to me." He withdrew from me, and I straightened and turned around. I loved that we were the same height. That we could look into each other's eyes as I looked into his right now. "You are *mi alma*, my soul. No one except Ari has ever made me feel the way you do." I touched his cheek. "May I kiss you?"

Daniel opened his mouth to respond, but when nothing came out, he nodded. I pressed my lips to his. It was a soft kiss, a confirmation of everything we'd said, everything we were feeling for each other. Of the love we shared. "Make love to me, Daniel," I said.

He pressed me back onto the bed. I lay down, opened my legs, and held them up with my hands behind my knees. Daniel's face tightened, need evident in the sharp line of his jaw, in the intent focus of his eyes. Keeping his feet on the floor, Daniel pressed on the back of my thighs and lined up his cock with my entrance. His hips rocked forward and his cock slid home.

We both groaned as he filled me, as his cock inched deeper and deeper until he was fully seated, his balls slapping heavily against my ass.

"Fuck, yeah," he whispered.

"Give, give me a sec," I said, needing a minute to let the pain abate. It wasn't excruciating, but it was uncomfortable.

Daniel's brow furrowed. "Am hurting you? You're tight as hell."

I averted my gaze. "It's… uh… it's been a while."

"Since you've bottomed?"

"Yeah."

"Javi."

"Yeah?"

"Look at me."

I met his gaze.

"How long?"

"Not since college."

"Jesus." Daniel rubbed his hands over the sides of my legs, the light touch making me shiver. "You sure you really want to do this?"

"For you, I'd do anything."

"Even bottom?"

I snorted. "It's hardly a hardship."

Daniel rolled his hips, causing his cock to slide a little deeper. "Yeah?"

"Oh my God, Daniel. Fuck me already."

His eyes darkening, Daniel gripped both my thighs and pulled his cock almost all the way out before plunging into me in one swift, brutal stroke.

Jesus. "More," I begged.

No one had ever made me beg before.

He took me deep and hard. His thrusts grew shallower and faster as I hung on for dear life. It was so fucking good. And it was Daniel.

It was *his* fingers digging into my legs. It was his groans in my ears. His gorgeous face in front of me. And his cock inside me. I wanted him there forever.

But the way we were going, it would all be over soon.

"Fuck, Cordero. Your tight little hole is squeezing my cock so good."

Daniel's eyes glazed over, a sure sign he was on the edge. And I was right there too. Already my spine tingled. Heat surged in my belly.

He shifted slightly and his cockhead pegged my prostate.

The impending orgasm lit up my veins with surging lava. "Daniel," I shouted.

He lowered himself between my legs, his body completely covering mine, completely enveloping mine. I wanted to wrap my legs around his hips, but I didn't dare. Instead, I held him loosely, my hands on his shoulder blades.

"Thank you," he whispered in my ear, over and over, as he pistoned into me. I shot over the edge and tumbled into an exquisite orgasm. My body convulsed under Daniel's as I shouted his name.

Daniel jerked, then stiffened, and his cries joined mine. We held each other through the aftershocks, and I'd never been happier.

After a few minutes, I rolled away from Daniel and went to the bathroom to dispose of the condom and clean up. I got a warm washcloth and brought it back to the bed. As I got rid of Daniel's condom and wiped him down, he watched me in wonderment. "We did it," he said, his voice barely louder than a whisper.

I tossed the towel toward the bathroom. "No." I kissed his cheek. "*You* did it. You're so fucking brave, Daniel. I'm in awe of you."

"Ha! I'm not the one who risked getting puked on."

I knew what he was doing. Injecting some levity into a heavily emotional situation. If that's what he needed right now, I was more than happy to help him out.

"Or the one who risked having blue balls if you decided to end things midway," I said.

Daniel grinned. "There is that."

With a sigh, he snuggled against my side, his head on my shoulder, his hand playing with the hairs on my chest. "I couldn't have done this with anyone else, you know that, right?"

"I do."

"I love you, Javier. And no matter what happens with the three of us, that's not going to change."

"I know that too." I kissed him softly. Not in a sexual manner, just a loving one. I had always loved Daniel and I always would. But as to what would happen if our threesome didn't work out? I had no fucking clue. I only knew that we'd all be hurting.

ARIANNA

I knew Daniel loved me. I knew Javi did too. Still… it was a little hard for me not to feel left out as I walked away from the cabin in search of Luciana.

This isn't about you. It's about Daniel.

I had to keep reminding myself of that. Daniel was trying really hard to make all of this work. I just wished I could be a part of the process. That *I* could help him. Not Greta. Not Javier.

Me.

Yes, we'd been divorced for a year. My head knew this, but my heart?

My heart still thought of him as my husband. The man I'd pledged to be with through thick and thin.

But what about Javi?

I didn't want to give him up either. He was mine, and in a way that Daniel had never been. Javi was my friend. My best friend. With Daniel… there was still a wall. His need to not have me there today proved it. We'd broken down some of it, but a lot of that damn wall still remained. I had to hope we'd eventually dismantle it entirely.

But Javi was right. Daniel and I—we were both stubborn. And full of pride.

I knocked on the door to Luciana's cabin. We'd invited the whole Montero family to come to the safari too as a thank-you gift, but Manuel and Sofia wanted to stay back and watch over the final work on the pool and the gym—and get some peace and quiet, I suspected. Brad and the boys had done the safari a few months ago without Luciana, so Brad had urged her to go on her own and take some "me" time.

And now was my chance to make sure she enjoyed herself.

She answered at my knock. "Ari, what's going on?"

"I've got the afternoon to myself. Want to have some girl time? I figured we could get massages, and have some chocolates and some wine. My treat. What do you say?"

She held up the book in her hand, her eyes sparkling. "As good as my book is, I won't say no to all of that."

"Excellent!" I whipped out my phone and made the arrangements, and thirty minutes later, our masseuses arrived, followed shortly by a couple bottles of wine and an array of sweets, including one of my favorites, chocolate-dipped strawberries.

Luciana and I stripped down to our undies behind the towels our masseuses held up for us, then we got on the tables facedown. I would have preferred two hunky guys working on us, but it was probably for the best that they were women instead. My dirty mind didn't need any more encouragement.

I hadn't realized how sore I was until my masseuse, Sandy, went to work. After all the hours I'd put in getting this retreat rescheduled, then doing the Tough Mudder course, and then all the time I was spending in bed between Javier and Daniel, my poor muscles were screaming.

"You're very tight," Sandy said to me as she kneaded my shoulders.

"Lots going on," I said. I looked over at Luciana, who gave me a wink.

"Same here," she said. But the knowing grin on her face made me wonder. Had she figured out what was going on with Daniel, Javier, and me?

Shit.

"You're tensing up," Sandy said. "Relax."

I tried, but if Luciana knew, would she be able to keep it to herself? The last thing I needed was a lecture—or worse—from her parents. Or mine.

I'd have to tell them some time. If things worked out.

Dios, how would I ever tell my parents the truth? And how would they take it?

Mamá would probably faint, and Papá would probably have a heart attack. And then my grandparents…

"Relax," Sandy repeated, her voice firmer than before.

I took a deep breath then released it, trying to clear my mind, but no dice. What the fuck was I doing? Maybe I should call Paige. I had to smile, remembering how blithely I'd told her to go for it with Riley and Carter.

You can talk the talk, but you can't walk the walk, can you?

If Paige could do this—prim, proper Paige—couldn't I? And she'd been outed in the press, for God's sake. I wasn't facing anything like that.

Just, oh, a ton of Catholic guilt and disapproval and being shunned by my entire family.

"Take another deep breath and blow it out," Sandy said. "Relax. You'll enjoy this much more if you do."

I did as she said and grinned to myself. Sandy was right. I would enjoy *all* of this if I could relax.

But I just hated the unknown. I hated not being in control.

It was bad enough being in a relationship with one person, even if that relationship was sanctioned by your family and society. But being in a relationship with two people, in a situation that other people thought was impossible at best and perverted at worst?

Cristo. What had I gotten myself into?

The time flew by, and our masseuses finished up and left us sitting in a pair of white fluffy robes with a tray of sweets and two bottles of wine, a pinot gris and a Syrah.

"Which would you pair with the chocolates?" I asked Luciana.

"Let's start with the Syrah." She poured glasses for us both, and we clinked them together.

The wine was lovely, but I choked when Luciana said, "So what has your panties in a bunch?"

"Nothing," I spluttered, trying not to spew wine on my robe.

She stared at me. "Arianna, seriously, *chica*. You've been in Javi's *and* Daniel's pockets the whole time you've been here. Until today."

I shrugged, trying to look nonchalant. "They wanted some bro time."

Luciana picked up a strawberry and bit into it. "Bro time. Is that what they call it now?"

My cheeks grew hot. "What do you mean?"

"Daniel, and Javier, and you. The walls of these cabins are mostly canvas."

I put a hand over my eyes. I couldn't look at her, my blush spreading down my neck. "Does everyone know?" I asked, peeking at her between my fingers.

She laughed and wagged an eyebrow at me. "I'm teasing! But… Papá did say something to me."

"*Manuel* knows? How?"

"He's pretty sharp. Apparently Javi sort of admitted it when they were talking a couple nights ago."

"And Manuel didn't fall dead on the spot?"

Luciana shook her head. "Papá's had to loosen up a lot since we came here. He's spent a lot of time with Óscar, and many of the guests who come to the vineyard are gay, and they certainly don't hide it."

"Why didn't you say something earlier?"

"Why didn't you?"

I stared into my glass, the ruby red wine winking back at me in the lamplight. "I wasn't sure what you'd think."

"I love you, Ari. So does the whole family. We just want you to be happy."

"With Javi, you mean."

Luciana drained her glass and poured herself some more Syrah and topped off mine. "That would probably be easiest, for everyone involved. But, I've seen how Daniel looks at you. And how he looks at Javi. How the three of you are together. There's a lot of love there."

My heart started pounding. "Does Sofía know? Does Brad?"

She nodded. "I don't think Mamá is quite ready to embrace Daniel being part of the family again—she doesn't really trust him not to run off—but she wants you and Javi to be happy. And Brad thinks you're nuts wanting to have that much testosterone in your life. He's already seen how crazy he and the boys can make me. I love Felipe and Lucas, but sometimes I wish one of them was a girl."

I laughed, my heart slowing. "Brad's probably right about all the testosterone. The two of them—sometimes I feel a little on the outside, you know?"

Luciana shook her head. "I can imagine." Then she grinned. "So why are you hanging with me, when you could be with your *two* gorgeous hunks?"

How to answer? I couldn't say a word about Daniel's past. That was his story to tell, not mine. "They wanted some alone time."

"And you're feeling a bit left out?"

"Yeah." I let out a breath. "I'm trying not to make this about me." I made a wry face. "Javi recently pointed out to me that I have a tendency to be a bit self-absorbed."

She finished another chocolate, her brown eyes twinkling with mirth. "He said that?"

I nodded, my cheeks heating again.

"I hadn't realized Javi had gotten so brave."

I tossed the small pillow behind my back at her, and she batted it to the floor with a peal of laughter. "You *know* he's right," she said.

"I know." I retrieved the pillow and put it behind me again. "I think it's why my marriage failed."

She sobered and set down her wine. "You really think so?"

I nodded. "I pushed Daniel a lot instead of realizing he had good reasons for hesitating about getting married, about having a baby. I guess I kept thinking he was just being difficult."

Luciana shrugged. "He can be a handful. I've seen him when he gets something into his head. It's his way, or no way."

"And I'm the same."

She picked up her glass again and took a sip. "Poor Javi," she said, her tone teasing.

I chuckled. "Poor Javi is right. He's been the peacemaker between Daniel and me since the moment we met." I finished my wine. "But that's not fair to him. Daniel and I are trying to work on that." *And I'm trying to give him the space he needs to work through his issues.*

I had to. Daniel had to get through this. If he didn't, I didn't see how the three of us could go forward. It would be hell on Javi if he had Daniel so close, and yet out of reach.

And Javi had suffered long enough. Too long.

"Sounds complicated," Luciana said. Then she smiled. "But it's worth it, right?"

"It is. It so is." My throat tightened, my voice warping. "I love them both, so much."

She got us fresh glasses and poured some of the pinot gris for each of us. "To love," she said, holding her glass out.

"To love," I said, clinking my glass against hers.

Our love was messy, and complicated, and sometimes hard. But I wanted it to work.

I could be happy with Javi—I knew we'd be good together. But the three of us?

We could be great together.

I just hoped Daniel would continue making progress. Even if I couldn't be part of that.

Above all else, I wanted Daniel to have some peace, some happiness. *Dios* knew, he deserved it.

And so did Javi.

Chapter 12

ARIANNA

I left Luciana's cabin with a bit more bounce in my step. The girl talk had set me straight. Butterflies still fluttered in my belly, but this time it wasn't so much with nerves as with excitement.

Daniel had needed this time with Javi to begin working through his issues, and as much as I would have liked to be the one he needed, I wasn't.

I was starting to accept that Javi really loved Daniel, and I was happy Daniel had Javi. I was happy they had each other. I just hoped they didn't suddenly realize that neither of them needed me.

As I approached the cabin, I got my key out of my purse and climbed the short set of stairs to the strangely magical place I shared with Javi. It was like a tent with a door and screened windows, gorgeous hardwood floors, cute furniture, and soft lighting. I unlocked the door and held my breath. What would I find inside?

God, I hoped I wasn't interrupting. On the other hand, what a sight that would be. Watching Javi and Daniel together the day before had been so fucking hot, my deep dark fantasies come to life. Why should Paige and Sky have all the fun?

Swallowing a snort, I quietly entered. My eyes searched the darkened room and landed on my two gorgeous lovers, laid out on the bed, their arms around each other. Their eyes were open, and they tracked my entrance.

"*Buenas tardes, corazón*," Javier said. With his ruffled hair, lazy smile, and blissful expression, he looked so well-fucked, my pussy clenched jealously.

My gaze slid over to Daniel, who seemed to be watching me with a defensive air. Was he worried I'd think less of him because he'd been with Javier? It certainly wasn't true. I admired both of them for daring to follow their hearts despite the many obstacles in their way.

I smiled at him reassuringly. "So, it went well? You both look"—I paused for dramatic effect—"satisfied."

The defensiveness faded from Daniel's gaze, leaving behind only pools of pure blue. The two men exchanged an intense look. Daniel stroked Javier's hip lovingly. "Javier was amazing." He leaned forward to kiss him, and Javier smiled against his lips.

My heart hammered in my chest. I'd never seen either of them look at anyone else that way, with so much love and tenderness, with so much focus.

Except me.

Over the years, they'd both looked at me that way from time to time. It had been a gift that I'd cherished, because it had made me *feel* cherished. Like they were really seeing me and loved me still.

Javi and Daniel separated from their kiss and as one, they turned to me. My breath caught, seeing the same loving look on both their faces. But this time it was directed at me.

"Oh!" I pressed my fingers to my lips. My eyes welled with tears.

"Sweetheart," Daniel said, his voice thick. "Come join us."

A whimper escaped my throat. I kicked off my shoes, then dashed across the room and walked right up onto the bed, falling forward into their arms. Laughing, they caught me between them and showered me with kisses. Two sets of hands relieved me of my clothing.

"We missed you," Daniel murmured into my neck.

"Really?" I asked, hating that my heart still needed the reassurance.

Javier nuzzled the other side of my neck. He nipped my earlobe. "We have plans for you, *princesa*."

"Oh?"

"*Sí*. We want tonight to be all about you."

"About me?" I parroted.

Daniel chuckled. He wrapped a few of my curls around his fingers. "Do you have any fantasies, Ari?"

Could I tell them? Should I? My face heated with embarrassment, and I snuggled deeper between them, hiding my face in Javi's armpit.

Since he'd always been insanely ticklish, Javier laughed and tried to twist away from me while Daniel pulled me against his hard chest. "Don't hide from us, Ari. If this is going to work between all of us, we have to be honest. That means no secrets."

A sobering pang of guilt twisted my gut, and I could have sworn I felt the heat of Javier's stare on my belly.

I hadn't yet been completely honest with Daniel. We, Javier and I, hadn't told him we'd had unprotected sex the night of my birthday and a couple times since. I opened my mouth to blurt out the truth, but Javier gave a slight shake of his head. I snapped my jaw shut.

"What is it?" Daniel asked. "Tell us your fantasy."

"Well, I…" I licked my dry lips. "I've always wanted to have both of you, at the same time."

His brows rose. "You mean both of us inside you at the same time?"

I swallowed. "I've read up on it, even…" Shit, this was embarrassing. "Even watched some double penetration porn. It looks… interesting."

Javi chuckled darkly. His hand slid over my butt, his finger lightly touching my hole. "I'm assuming you mean you want one of us in your pussy while the other fills your ass?"

"Is there any other way?" I asked, seriously curious.

Both men nodded. "Some people like two cocks in their pussy or—"

Javier cut in. "—in their ass."

I felt my eyes grow wide. "At the same time?" I winced. "D-do you?"

Javi's gaze flicked to Daniel's. "I've never been on the receiving end of that. But…"

I rolled my eyes. It was like pulling teeth. "But?"

"But I have fisted people. It's along the same lines."

Two cocks were bad enough, but a whole fist? "And they… they liked it?"

His face lit up. "Oh yeah."

"Mmm…. maybe some other time," I said, strangely intrigued. "But for now, let's stick to front and back DP."

Javi reached across me and touched Daniel's arm. "Is this something you want to try, Daniel?"

"Want? Hell yeah. But you'd have to be on the bottom."

Javier stretched out on the bed, his hands locked behind his head. A Cheshire cat smile split his face.

I surveyed his long muscular body, noting the small red love bites along his thighs, and his eager cock pointing straight up, a long thick obelisk. Already pre-cum leaked from the tip. Hopping off the bed, I retrieved a couple condoms and the lube Javier kept in his bag.

When I returned, Daniel had scooted down to the foot of the bed and was sitting on his heels. He reached out a hand to help me onto the mattress. He took a condom from me, but instead of covering his own cock, he slid the latex over Javier's.

Javi sucked in an audible breath and groaned. "Fuck, Daniel. I love your hands on me."

His tone made it clear that having Daniel touch him was a dream he'd never thought would be realized. Yet here he was. Here *we* were.

Daniel gave him an extra squeeze and winked. "I love my hands on you too." Releasing Javi, he moved out of the way and tapped Javi's thigh. "Climb up, cowgirl."

I swung my leg over Javi's hips, so I faced away from him, and wiggled around until the head of his cock teased my clit. I moaned and leaned forward, bracing my hands on his legs.

Daniel handed Javier the lube, then rolled the second condom over his own cock. He straddled Javier's lower legs and faced me. Touching my jaw, he searched my face. "You're sure you want to do this?"

I pressed my cheek into his palm. It was warm and felt so good on my skin. I couldn't wait to have them both heating me up, front and back, inside and out. "I'm sure."

Holding my jaw, he kissed me. It started out sweet. His teeth tugged on my lower lip in a way that had always turned me on, and when his tongue slid out to lick where he'd nipped, I moaned.

Javi took advantage of my distraction to ease a lubed finger into my ass. I gasped at the sensation. It was always a bit odd and uncomfortable at first. But then, Daniel gripped the side of my face and forced me to angle my head. He deepened the kiss, pushing his tongue into my mouth. He teased my gums, my palate, and my tongue with his own.

Javi pressed a second finger into my hole. The pressure grew. I whimpered softly. Daniel pulled his tongue back and lapped gently at my lips. His hands smoothed down my sides, my hips. One went to my breast, to tweak the nipple, the other parted my pussy lips and unerringly found my clit.

"That's it, baby. Relax that pretty hole. Let Javier in."

I blew out a breath and used my muscles to push back. Javier's fingers slid in all the way. It felt good. The stretch was indescribable, yet I knew more was coming. He thrust his fingers in and out a few times, coating me liberally with lube, before adding a third finger. I clutched Daniel's shoulders and stared into his eyes.

"Breathe," he coaxed.

When I inhaled sharply, he smiled. "That's a good girl."

After a moment, Javier moved his fingers, stretching and stroking, while Daniel rubbed circles on and around my clit.

Need curled in my stomach.

I jerked my hips, alternately grinding against Daniel's hand and pushing back onto Javier's fingers to get them deeper into my ass. "Fuck that feels good."

"He's not even in you yet," Daniel reminded me.

Javi chuckled. "Neither are you, *hermano*. But it's time we changed that."

"Ready?" Daniel asked me.

I bit my lip, but nodded. "Ready."

Javi removed his fingers. I heard the click of the cap on the lube, the shlick-shlick of him coating his cock with it. Daniel's hands reached around me to palm my butt cheeks. He parted them.

Javier groaned and the head of his cock touched my hole. Slowly, he pressed into me. Our Javi was not a small man, and neither was his cock. The pressure against the tight ring of muscle guarding my back entrance grew until my nails dug into Daniel's shoulders. He winced slightly, but just around his eyes.

I bore down, there was a popping sensation, and then my butt seemed to suck Javier inside.

"Ah… yes, *corazón*. I love how your body welcomes mine. It's so fucking hot and tight."

Javier and I had not yet engaged in anal sex. He was slightly bigger than Daniel, so the fit was a bit snugger. Still, once the burn dissipated, and the bite of pain became one of pleasure, I moaned. "Yes, Javi. Oh God. You fill me up so good."

Daniel used his hold on my hips to lift me almost all the way off Javier. When we both groaned in complaint, Daniel chuckled evilly before dropping me. Gravity did its thing and Javier's cock impaled me as we both shouted out hoarsely.

After that, I couldn't hold still. Taking advantage of the reverse cowgirl position, I rode Javi's cock and stroked my clit. Anxious, needy moans fell from my lips in a constant stream.

Daniel, the skin on his face tight with arousal, watched us. His pupils were blown, his nipples hard. The temptation proved too much for me. I leaned forward and caught one between my lips, using my teeth to secure it in place.

Daniel cried out. "Oh fuck." His hands clamped on my head. He didn't push me away though. Rather, he kept me there, where I could continue to play.

I loved how responsive he was. I moved to his other nipple, laving it gently, swirling my tongue around and around. When it peaked beautifully, I bit down.

Daniel gasped, and this time, he did push me away. "Lie back on Javi," he instructed in a guttural voice so different from his usual tenor.

Javi's hands closed over my breasts, and he eased me down until I was lying on his chest. We were at a slight upward angle, so he must have pushed a pillow behind his back. He kissed my neck and toyed with my breasts, pinching and tugging on the nipples while he hooked my legs over his spread knees.

Daniel maneuvered himself in the space Javier had made for him.

When his thighs touched mine, he ran a finger up my slit and brought the finger to his mouth. His eyes locked on me, he sucked it into his mouth. "Mmm... you taste so fucking good, sweetheart." He moved over me. "But you're going to *feel* even better."

His cock bumped against my entrance. He pushed in. I was so turned on, so wet, there wasn't much resistance.

Except for Javier's cock in my ass.

I was full. So goddamn full. With each inch Daniel slid in, the three of us moaned. The room filled with our chorus, with the sounds of our pleasure. The guys adjusted their rhythm so one was pulling out while the other was pushing in.

"Oh fuck. I can feel you, Daniel," Javi said.

"I can feel you too. Jesus. I knew from when you'd fingered Ari while I was in her ass that this would feel good. I hadn't counted on it being this fucking incredible."

One of Javi's arms closed around my waist, the other went to Daniel's shoulder. "I can feel you too, *mi alma*." He kissed my neck. "What's it like for you?"

"Oh Javi, Daniel. It's so much better than my fantasy. I feel so completely taken, so used—"

As quickly as the word left my mouth, I knew it was the exact wrong thing to say.

Daniel's body went ramrod stiff.

"Daniel, I-I didn't... shit!" Frustrated, I clenched my fists and punched the mattress. "I didn't mean anything by that."

Still Daniel stared at me as though frozen. His eyes took on that distance. That blankness.

I dug my fingers into his hair and brought him down on top of me. I was certain Javier couldn't breathe. I was also certain he didn't care. "Daniel, *mi amor*, listen to me. I meant used in the best possible way. I love having you and Javier use my body for your pleasure. It's a huge turn-on for me to be there for you and Javi like this."

The distant look began to fade and Daniel's usual gaze, so full of piercing intelligence, returned. He studied my face, a small frown on his forehead. "You enjoy humiliation, sweetheart? That's new."

He arched a brow at Javi.

Before Javi could say anything, I jumped in. "No, of course not. But there is a small part of me that thinks it's sexy... exciting... to be at your disposal... for both of you to take me at your pleasure. Lord knows I'm a bossy bitch most of the time. But sometimes..." I looked away. "Sometimes, I like to be..."

"Used," Daniel said flatly.

"But," I rushed to add, "only by you and Javi." I narrowed my eyes.

"And only in bed."

Daniel slowly nodded. His frown turned into a grin. "I can live with that."

Javi's sigh reverberated through me. Daniel kissed me. And then they both started thrusting into me again. It was hard and rough and, oh fuck, I was so close. They pounded into me, one pushing, one retreating, until we were all on the verge of losing our minds. Then the rhythm changed and they were in sync, filling me together.

"Oh shit," I cried out, stretched to capacity. "Yes!"

Javi's hand snaked between my and Daniel's bodies. He pressed on my clit, circled it with a finger. "Come for us, *corazón*."

"Show us how much you like being fucked by both our cocks, sweetheart."

"*Fuck.*" My orgasm ripped through me, stunningly strong. I saw literal stars. My body convulsed as my vision faded out, and in the distance, I heard the catch of breath, the short grunts and long moans that signaled that Javi and Daniel had followed my lead.

A while later, warm wetness on both sides of my neck woke me out of my stupor.

"Hey, babe. You're back." Daniel grinned proudly at me.

"Was never gone," I muttered. "Right here all along."

Behind me, Javi chuckled. "I think you blacked out for a minute, *princesa*."

I blinked at Daniel. "Really?"

"Yes. Did we meet expectations?"

"Oh, I don't know," I teased.

Right on cue, he frowned.

Javier's hand stroked my hair. "Did we hurt you?"

Laughter burst out of my chest. "Oh God, you two. It was so far from my expectations, it's not even funny. You two blew my fucking mind. I'll never be the same again."

Daniel clasped Javier's hand in his as though needing the extra security. "How so?"

I winked at him and pushed back onto Javier. "I'm going to expect you to always outperform fantasy Daniel and fantasy Javier."

Javier surged up, rolling both me and Daniel onto our sides. He propped himself up onto an elbow. "If that's a challenge, Ms. Rodriguez, Daniel and I accept."

Daniel's eyes rounded. "We do?"

"Hell yeah, *hermano*." He held his hand out for a fist bump. "We're a team, right?"

Looking far too serious, Daniel bumped Javi's fist. "Fucking right. Bros before h—"

"Watch it, King!" I cut in sharply.

Daniel grinned. "I'm going to teach you a lesson, wench."

"Oh yeah?"

"Yeah. You can't give me a heart attack like that."

I hooked my hands around his neck. "How about just a heart?"

His eyes darted between me and Javier. They stopped dancing and the blue seemed to melt.

"I love you, Daniel. I never stopped."

"Do you forgive me? Really forgive me?"

Tears flooded my eyes and I cried for Daniel and the child he'd been. "Of course, I do. And I'm so glad to have you back." I reached behind me and hooked my arm around Javier's neck as well, pulling them both into me. "To have you both. I want you both. I want this… whatever it's called… to work. Because, honestly, I could never choose between you. I wouldn't want to, and I won't. Never again."

They kissed me, and my emotions, already pretty confused, soared. I'd never felt so loved. So complete. So exactly where I wanted to be.

My life was finally perfect.

ARIANNA

I still couldn't believe I'd had both Daniel and Javier inside me at the same time last night. But my body wouldn't let me forget. Despite my massage yesterday afternoon, I was sore all over, that delicious kind of sore from really, really good sex.

I kept flashing back to it, to the sensation of being between Javi and Daniel, being loved by them both. And even though the three of us were in public right now, standing together at our cooking station at the back of a class being led by Chef Louis in the cellar of the winery, surrounded by all the ECC couples, I just wanted to kiss both of my men, put my arms around them, tell them how much I loved them…

I could do that with Javi, and no one would bat an eye. But adding Daniel to the mix? *Dios* knew I wanted to…

But I wasn't Paige. I wasn't brave like her. I wasn't ready to be "out." Nor had the three of us discussed it.

Javi slid an arm around my waist, his lips hovering at my ear. "Something on your mind, *corazón*? You've gone all quiet."

"I'm fine." I smiled up at him, then gave him a quick peck on the lips. I glanced at Daniel and squeezed his hand under the edge of our station.

It seemed so weird to hide my affection for him, after so many years of showing it. It felt… wrong.

We needed to talk about it. And soon. Before one of us made a mistake.

Chef Louis picked up his wine glass and clanked a knife against it. "Everyone," he said, raising his voice. "Please open the coolers beneath your stations."

Daniel bent down and pulled out the small cooler and opened the lid.

"We're preparing a three-course seafood meal," Chef Louis said. "Raw oysters, steamed mussels, and poached salmon."

Ah… that was why Sofía had asked everyone about allergies a few days ago. I'd left the planning for this part of the retreat up to her, since the winery regularly offered cooking classes onsite.

The chef instructed us on how to open the oysters and talked about how to garnish them. Daniel and Javi quickly opened the six raw oysters in the cooler and lined them up in front of us.

I took a look at my two oysters, their grayish flesh glistening under the lights. Javi squeezed a lemon over them, the light citrus scent thankfully covering the briny smell of the oysters.

I swallowed hard, feeling queasy all of a sudden. I normally loved seafood, but for some reason, my stomach was rebelling at the idea.

Javi and Daniel picked up their oysters and slurped them down, and my stomach turned over. "Don't you want yours?" Daniel asked.

Staring at the oysters in front of me, I tried to imagine eating one, and my belly started to cramp. I shook my head and pressed a hand to my stomach.

"You don't look so good," Javi said. "You okay?"

Daniel was opening the bag of mussels and pulling out the salmon, and though everything was fresh, the odor of so much raw seafood made me gag. I pressed a fist to my mouth and backed away, hurrying out to the hallway.

Javi followed me, Daniel on his heels. I stopped out in the corridor and took a deep breath, trying to clear my sinuses and push down the nausea. I'd been a little tired all day. Maybe I was coming down with something?

"Ari, are you okay?" Javi asked again, and Daniel placed a hand on my back.

I nodded, finally feeling like I wasn't going to hurl. "I think I need to lie down. I've been a little off today."

"You're not getting sick again, are you?" Daniel asked.

"Maybe. I don't know."

Javi's lips pressed together. "When we get back to Miami, I think you should see the doctor."

I nodded. "Or maybe I should get some more sleep?" I gave them a teasing look, and they both smiled.

Daniel touched my hair. "Wearing you out, are we?"

I grinned at him. "Well, the two of you are a lot of man between you."

Javi nudged me lightly and kissed me on the cheek. "I seem to remember a certain someone gloating about how she kicked our asses during the Tough Mudder course."

"I *did* kick your asses." I rose up on tiptoe and gave them each a quick kiss. "But I think I'm going to make it an early night and catch up on my beauty sleep. I'll order something light to have in my room."

"You want me to go with you?" Javi asked.

I shook my head. "No, you two stay and enjoy yourselves."

"You'll call if you need us?" Daniel said.

"I will." I left them and climbed the stone steps up from the cellar and into the lobby, taking it slow. My stomach seemed okay now, but every time I thought about those oysters, the nausea started again.

I headed over to the kitchen, not wanting to put Luciana to the trouble of bringing something upstairs for me.

She and Brad were clearing away the evening meal, Felipe and Lucas at the dining table doing their homework. Sofía and Manuel had already left; no doubt they'd probably done most of the meal prep.

Luciana looked up when I entered. "Everything okay?"

"Yes. I just felt a little off, you know? Thought I'd grab some toast and tea and see if that would settle my stomach."

Brad grinned. "Did the oysters get to you? I can't even look at them."

I nodded. "Yeah. It's weird. I've had them before, but today—just the smell of them—" I had to stop talking and swallow down a bit of nausea again.

"Sit," Luciana said, pulling out a stool at the bar for me. "You look white as a ghost."

I sat, gripping the edge of the granite-topped bar. "*Dios*," I murmured. "I really must be sick."

Luciana bustled around the kitchen, bringing me a cup of chamomile tea and a plate with a couple pieces of toast and some strawberry jam. "Maybe if you get a little something in your stomach you'll feel better."

The toast and jam did smell good. I took a few cautious bites and sipped the tea while Luciana and Brad finished cleaning up.

Brad went over to the table to help the boys wrap up their homework, and Luciana came to sit with me with her own cup of tea. "Better?" she asked.

"*Sí, gracias.*" I took another sip from my mug.

"You weren't feeling well when you first got here," Luciana said.

I nodded. "Yeah, I thought it was because—"

Because my period was supposed to start.

And it hadn't.

"Because what?" Luciana asked.

"I thought my period was going to start when we got here."

"And?"

I shook my head. "It *should* have."

"How late are you?" Luciana's voice was hushed.

I thought back. "It was actually a bit late when we got here, but I'd chalked that up to stress."

Or maybe it was from the night of my birthday…

"Is there any chance you could be pregnant?" she whispered.

I couldn't be. Not from just one night…

Except it *hadn't* been just one night. We'd had sex several times with no protection, twice the night of my birthday alone.

Fuck, fuck, fuck. We still hadn't told Daniel. I hadn't known how to broach the subject, and I didn't think it would really happen so soon. Most women I knew had to try a few months at least. I'd thought we'd have time to talk it over with Daniel, to settle how things were going to work between the three of us first.

Bringing a baby into this, right now? Talk about terrible timing.

"Ari?" Luciana asked, touching my hand.

I looked at her. "Where's the nearest pharmacy that's still open?"

I'd take a test in the morning. That's when you were supposed to do it, right?

And between now and then I'd pray that this was just a little stomach bug, and not something that could blow the three of us apart.

JAVIER

What a glorious morning.

The air was crisp and cool, the sky a perfect, cloudless blue, and everything was quiet except for the chatter of birds in the trees, the buzz of insects in the bushes, and the steady thump of my running shoes hitting the packed gravel path that looped around the vineyard's grounds.

Even though it had been hell to leave Daniel's warm bed, the need to move, to burn off the calories from the wine and the seafood we'd cooked with Chef Louis, had been stronger. I wanted to look good for him, for both of them. I looked down at my belly and my thighs, and grimaced when they jiggled. How many fucking squats and quad presses and sit ups did I need to do to combat the effects of age and gravity? I upped my pace and topped the hill that would bring the path back to the main building. The Monteros had built something really special here.

As I was considering another run around the grounds, my phone dinged with an incoming text. I slowed my steps and dug the phone out of my running belt, snagging my bottle of water at the same time. I gulped down several long swallows of the cold water and wiped my forehead with the hem of my running shirt before checking my notifications. The text was from Ari. I clicked on it.

Ari: Come see me—alone

Alone. Huh. What could she want to talk to me about that she didn't want to share with Daniel? If she was still unwell, Daniel would want to know. He'd want to be there for her too.

Figuring I'd find out soon enough, I quickly texted back.

Javi: thirty minutes

I ran up the stairs to my room. I was far too sweaty and ripe to go see her without first taking a shower. My phone dinged again.

Ari: No. Come now. Please, Javi.

Standing at my door, I reread her text. Cold slid down my spine like an icy finger tracing each vertebra. *What the hell?*

I looked down the empty hall toward Arianna's room. Moments later, I stood in front of her door. The sheen of sweat on my skin had cooled. I shivered and stuffed the bottle of water I hadn't realized I was still holding into my running belt before knocking.

Ari threw the door open. "Did you come alone?" She poked her pale face into the hallway, checked left then right, then grabbed my shirt in her fist and hauled me inside.

I practically tripped over my own feet trying to keep up. "Jesus, Ari. Give me a second."

She let go of my shirt and went over to the window. Her shoulders and chest heaved from the deep breaths she took.

My stomach flip-flopped. Fuck, what the hell was going on? "Ari, what's this all about?" I asked, struggling to keep the anxiety out of my voice.

She turned to face me. "You need to sit down. I have something to tell you."

A bitter taste filled my mouth. I forced a smile. "So tell me."

"Sit."

"Fine." I sat on the edge of her bed. "Now talk."

She held up a brown paper bag. "I went to the drugstore earlier."

"Are you still sick?" I jumped up and had her in my arms before I knew it.

For a moment, she rested her head on my chest. The heat of her breath warmed me, but her forehead and face didn't feel unusually hot. She placed her hand on my shoulder and took a step back, bringing up the bag I'd crushed between our bodies. She pulled out a rectangular box. "This is a pregnancy test."

I flushed hot, then cold, then hot again. "A pr-pregnancy test?" Holy shit. Was I going to be a father?

She nodded mutely.

"Are you…"—I swallowed, my mouth suddenly dry—"are you pregnant?"

"Fuck, Javi. I don't know. I haven't taken the goddamn test yet." Immediately, she looked contrite. "I'm sorry. I didn't mean to snap. This is just so…" Her eyes flooded with tears, becoming wet and shiny. "Overwhelming."

"Shh. Come here, *corazón*." I drew her back into my arms. She came willingly. "I'm here now. You're not alone. Never alone."

"I know." She gulped down a sob. "I'm just so scared."

I rubbed her back. "Take the test. We'll figure the rest out afterward."

Looking up, she nodded. "You're right."

She walked to the bathroom and left the door ajar. I heard the sound of the box being torn open, the rustle of plastic, then tinkling as she peed. The toilet flushed, and Ari came out holding a plastic stick in her hands. "The instructions say to wait about three minutes."

She set it on a tissue on the table and we stared at it.

"What should we see?" I asked.

"One line means not pregnant; two pink lines means pregnant."

I wanted to take her hand in mine. I needed the comfort, and I'm sure she did as well, but she held her arms firmly crossed over her middle. Her face was tight, her jaw sharp as her eyes remained fixed on the plastic stick. I shifted my gaze to the stick as well. A second light pink bar began to take shape.

Ari gasped. "Oh my God." A trembling hand covered her mouth.

A well of happiness I didn't know I was capable of feeling filled me. I felt lighter than air, buoyant, like a helium-filled balloon. I let out a whoop and swung Ari up into my arms. "Jesus, *corazón*. We did it! We're going to have a baby." I set her down and hugged her close, only then registering the stiffness in her shoulders. The way her hands pushed against my chest.

"Javi, let me go," she said, her voice flat.

I dropped my arms to my sides. "It's mine, right?"

"Of course it is."

"Aren't you happy?"

She closed her eyes, and a sob shook her thin shoulders. I wanted to hug her, but everything about her screamed not to touch her. When she opened her eyes, they were red-rimmed and full of fear. *Mierda*. She didn't want this child. "Are you happy about this, Javi? Really happy?"

"Why wouldn't I be?" I'd always dreamed of having a child, of being a father. I just hadn't wanted to do it with anyone other than her. "Isn't this what we decided we both wanted, what was it, two weeks ago?"

"Three," she said, looking away. "It seems like a lifetime ago. So much has changed since then."

That's when it hit me, the missing piece of this puzzle. The reason for Ari's decidedly *un*happy reaction to the test results. "Oh fuck. Daniel."

"Yeah, exactly." She laughed dryly. "All my life I dreamed of having a baby. Of holding that small person in my arms and knowing that he or she was a part of me." Her eyes rose to meet mine.

"Then why aren't you happy?" I asked, in a voice barely above a whisper.

"This isn't what I had planned." Her voice started to rise as she paced the room. Hands in the air, she said, "Don't you get it, Javi? I'm not married. This baby is illegitimate. How do you think my family will feel about that?" A dark smirk creased her face. "As if it wasn't bad enough that I'm divorced, now I'm going to be a single mother too."

"I'm fucking *here*, Ari."

"And so is Daniel. And that means you and I can't get married." Her bottom lip trembled, and a tear slid down her cheek. She raised her face toward the ceiling. "Oh God. These past ten days have been some of the best of my life. I knew it was too good to be true."

"No, it wasn't. I love you. Daniel loves you. You aren't alone in this."

She rolled her lips between her teeth as though holding back another sob. The sob won. It burst through her lips and shook her shoulders. She waved her red-tipped fingers between us in vague circles. "This whole thing with you and Daniel, that… that… Fuck." She turned big brown eyes made glassy with tears to me. "H-how can I raise a baby in that kind of relationship?"

"We'll make it work."

"My parents would freak." Her lips curved into a trembling smile. "They *will* freak. I'm an abomination. Oh God. My baby will be an abomination." Her breath hitched, and she fell onto the bed. "Why couldn't this have happened when Daniel and I were still married? Everything would have been okay then." She buried her face in her hands and her body was wracked with tears and great heaving sobs.

In all the years, I'd known Ari, I'd never seen her like this.

Her words kept playing in my head on a loop. *Why couldn't this have happened when Daniel and I were still married?* That hammered the truth home. I was Arianna's second choice after Daniel. I'd been nothing more than a back-up plan, and now that Daniel was back in her life, she wanted her first choice back.

I was a stupid fucking dumbass. I'd believed Arianna, listened to her when she'd been drunk. Gone along with her plan when I should have known better. When I'd known she still loved Daniel. Not only that, but I'd kept on making the same damn decision. We'd made the choice to have unprotected sex, not just that once, but over and over again, whenever Daniel wasn't with us.

Arianna was going to have this baby. She was too Catholic not to. But would it be mine too? Would she let me be a part of its life?

Jesus Christ. I'd screwed the pooch on this one. Arianna couldn't stand to look at me, and when Daniel heard about the baby, he'd fucking hate me too. I'd wrecked everything.

How could I have made such a big goddamn mistake? Even worse, how could I survive the aftermath?

Chapter 13

DANIEL

I hadn't seen Javi or Ari all morning, and now it was lunchtime. I called Ari, and she said she was fine, but still a little under the weather and was going to stay in her room. She sounded tired, but okay. She told me she thought Javi had gone to the gym, so that's where I went in search of him.

I heard someone running hard on the treadmill before I even reached the door. Whoever it was was going all-out.

I stepped inside and saw Javi on the treadmill, flat-out running. His shirt and skin were drenched in sweat, his damp hair flopping onto his forehead, his face dark with exertion.

All of sudden, he slammed the stop button and jumped off the machine, racing over to the trash can and heaving up his guts.

Oh fuck. Now Javi was sick too? Was it from the oysters?

Except… Ari hadn't eaten any. And I felt fine.

Maybe it was some stomach bug. Or maybe it was something else. I'd seen Javi do this before. Push himself too hard at the gym. Push himself to the point of vomiting.

Something was wrong.

I waited until he finished, then I approached. Javi pulled up his gray T-shirt and used the hem of it to wipe his face, then went back to the treadmill and grabbed his bottle of water and rinsed his mouth.

He was breathing hard, so hard I was concerned.

And he wouldn't look at me.

"Javi, what's wrong?"

He shook his head, still not looking at me.

"Is it Arianna? Is she okay?"

He nodded, but his eyes welled with tears.

Oh fuck. "Did something happen between you?"

He nodded again, then he shook his head, pressing his palms to his eyes.

I placed a hand on his damp shoulder. "Javi, talk to me."

He opened his mouth, then closed it, still shaking his head. Finally he said, "I've made a terrible, terrible mistake, and I've wrecked everything."

I squeezed his shoulder. "It can't be as bad as you think. We'll fix it."

He stared at me, his eyes red, then shook his head again. "There's no fixing it." Then he pushed past me, walking fast through the lobby and jogging up the stairs.

I stayed tight on his tail, not wanting to let him get away from me without an explanation. What the hell had happened?

Javi opened the door to his room, and I crowded in behind him, not giving him the chance to keep me out.

And that's when I saw it. The floor and the duvet were covered with candy and junk food wrappers. Obviously he'd gone nuts with the vending machine downstairs.

When we were in college, Javi would binge whenever he got upset. And then he would work out until he dropped.

I thought he'd stopped that years ago.

"What caused all this?" I asked, sitting down on the chair at the desk while Javi hurried around the room gathering up wrappers and shoving them in the trash. He was still avoiding my gaze, and he hadn't answered my question.

"Did you and Ari fight?"

He paced over to the window and put his hands on his hips. "No."

"Then what? What's got you so upset?"

He rubbed his forehead, still not looking at me. "Maybe I'm just a mess."

"What are you talking about?"

"I'm a mess, Daniel." He finally looked at me.

"A mess how?"

He pulled off his T-shirt and dropped it to the floor, then gestured to his finely toned torso. "You know what I see when I look at myself?" He walked over to the mirror above the dresser and looked at his reflection. "I see that fat, confused kid who didn't know how to tell the truth about himself. The kid who still, to this day, hasn't told his parents the truth about who he is. The kid who ate all his feelings." He motioned to the wastebasket. "The kid who still *does*."

"Javi, what's going on?"

He turned to me. "When I met you—*Cristo*, I about *died* when I saw you. You were fucking perfect. *Are* fucking perfect. I thought you wouldn't want to have a thing to do with me, the fat accounting nerd who got tongue-tied talking to a pretty girl. Or you. But *you*"—he choked on the word, then forced himself to continue—"you were so fucking *nice* to me. You were kind. You took an interest in me. You showed me how to work out, what to eat. Fuck, you even played *tennis* with me, and now that I know how difficult that must have been..."

He slumped onto his back on the bed, placing an arm across his eyes.

Where was this coming from?

I walked over to the bed and sat down on the edge, one leg on the floor, the other folded up on the mattress, and touched his shoulder. "Javi, you said you made a terrible mistake. What are you talking about?"

I waited, watching his breathing hitch like he wanted to cry. I stroked his arm, not sure what to do.

"I believed her when she said she loved me. And maybe she does, but..." He rolled over, turning his back to me. "I'm just the third wheel. Like I always have been."

I shook my head even though he couldn't see me. I reached for him to roll him back over, tugging his shoulders up onto my lap. "You're not the third wheel at all, Javi. *You* brought us all together, and we both love you. You're the glue."

He took a deep breath, then slowly let it out. "The glue, huh?"

"Yeah. The glue."

He craned his neck to look up at me. "You're such a fucking romantic, King."

I grinned at him and chuckled. "I do have a way with words, I've been told."

I leaned down to kiss him, and he reached up and grabbed the nape of my neck. I stiffened, and he immediately let go.

"Fuck," he whispered. "I'm sorry."

I took a breath, then placed his hand on the nape of my neck again. "I need to get over that. I need to make better memories." Then I touched my lips to his, keeping the kiss gentle, and he caressed the hair at the base of my skull, his touch light, reverent.

My heart ached, it was so full of love for this man. This sweet, tender man who still somehow didn't know how goddamn wonderful he was.

If I managed to do nothing else with the rest of my life, I'd show Javi how much I loved him. How amazing I thought he was. I owed him that.

We kissed softly for a while, then I sat back. "You okay now?"

He nodded, but he still looked troubled about something.

"You know, when we met," I said, "I really needed a friend. Even though I couldn't talk about what was going on with me, I just needed someone who'd be there, you know? And you were that someone. You made me feel needed. Useful. Worth something. I'd disappointed my whole damn family. I'd given up the career I'd worked so hard for, that my parents had sacrificed everything for. But you didn't know any of that. You didn't see me as a failure, or a disappointment. And I really, really needed that."

My eyes were welling up, and I sniffed hard. "You saved me, Javi, and you didn't even know it. And we made such a great team. When we pulled off that Cancun trip, I just knew we could build something together. And that gave me hope."

"We saved each other," he said.

I touched his cheek. "We can get through anything." I paused, holding his eyes. "Now how about you tell me what set all of this off."

Javi sighed and sat up, and the look he gave me was so sad my gut clenched. Something was still seriously wrong.

"There's something we need to talk about. But Ari needs to be part of the conversation."

I nodded, and as Javi reached for his phone, my stomach balled up.

What bomb was about to drop?

ARIANNA

Dios. I twisted my clenched hands in front of me as I walked down the hallway to Javi's room. The narrow, dimly lit hallway made me feel like a defendant going to stand before a judge, certain to be found lacking. I lifted my hands in front of me. I'd held heaven in them just a day ago. Before I'd peed on that stick and my life was changed forever.

Why had Javi asked me to come talk to him? Did he want to brainstorm on how we'd break the news to Daniel? Or did he want to pressure me into something… Oh God. Did he want me to have an abortion? No. I squeezed my fingers. Javi would never do that. He'd been happy when the second pink line had appeared. He'd twirled me in his arms, and just for a moment, I'd let myself feel joy. I'd let myself imagine a perfect future. And then I'd seen Daniel in this perfect picture, the three of us caring for this baby, and I'd known it could never be. Daniel didn't want children. He wouldn't want to be with me, or Javier for that matter, if a baby were part of the package. I'd learned that the hard way. And it was a lesson I'd never forget.

My hand went to my belly. I stroked it softly, imagining the beginnings of the child inside me. Imagining what he or she would look like when we met in nine months' time. I hiccupped a sob. God, this was so fucking hard. I had everything I'd ever wanted: Daniel, Javier, and now a baby.

Only, I wouldn't be able to hold onto it.

Once Daniel found out about the baby…

The door to Javier's room opened before I even knocked. Javi looked ravaged. Utterly destroyed. His face was drawn. Pale. His eyes were red and scared. "Come in. Daniel's here too."

Daniel got up from the bed. A candy wrapper tumbled to the carpet. He stood behind Javier. "Hello, Ari."

Javi's eyes searched mine. He closed his mouth, his lips forming a thin line, and his eyes grew shiny.

My heart broke in the face of all that fear. All those dying hopes and dreams. It broke for Javi and for me, and for Daniel too, but most of all, it broke for this child. I wasn't stupid. I knew why I'd been summoned to Javi's room. Again. We were going to have a big talk. *The* talk. The one where Daniel was going to walk out on me, on *us*, again. Nausea rose in my throat. This was so not what I had envisioned the night of my birthday when Javi and I had decided to try for a baby.

His back still to Daniel, Javi took a big breath. He held his hand out to me. I took it, and he led me into the room, and over to the couch in his sitting area. All the conversations we'd had here raced through my mind. I felt like I was going to be sick again, and my hands started to shake, so I shoved them under my thighs. Was this what Daniel's PTSD felt like?

My eyes sought him out, snagged on several cans of soda on the coffee table. How long had Daniel been here with Javi? I checked my watch. Daniel had called me about two hours ago. *Mierda.* Had Javi already told him about the baby? What the hell was I walking into?

Daniel sat on the couch beside me and dug one of my hands out from under my legs. He pressed my fingers to his lips. "Are you feeling better, sweetheart?"

I swallowed hard and turned to Javi sitting on my other side. His eyes implored me. "We have to tell him, Ari."

Ari. Not *corazón*. Not *princesa*. Just plain Ari. Oh God. Had I already lost him? I gnawed on my lip. At least he hadn't already shared our secret. At least he'd waited for me to do it. Even if I wasn't ready. "Yes," I said, my voice a barely whisper. God, I didn't want to lose Daniel when I'd only just gotten him back.

"Guys." Daniel's voice was tight. "One of you had better start talking. Now."

Javi cleared his throat. His nail scraped at a spot on his thigh. With his heel, he pushed an empty chip bag under the edge of the couch. He didn't look at me or at Daniel. He just stared at that spot. "Remember we told you that Ari and I had gotten together on her birthday?"

Daniel nodded. "Go on."

"Well, we… uh… slept together that night."

Daniel's face seemed to relax, even as my gut clenched. "I'd surmised as much."

Javier whimpered. It was such a forlorn sound. One I'd never heard from him before. Without giving it a second thought, I did what I'd been wanting to do since he'd opened the door, looking so lost and hurt and scared. I took his hand and cradled it in my lap. "Something else happened that night," I said.

"Oh?"

"Javier agreed to help me make my dream come true."

A cautious glint seeped into Daniel's eyes. "What dream was that, Ari?"

Had he already gleaned the truth?

Javi squeezed my hand, his touch giving me some much-needed strength. "Having a baby. We had unprotected sex," I admitted.

"I see."

"Do you, Daniel?" Javi asked softly.

His body went rigid, and he gritted his teeth. "Spit it the fuck out."

Javi nodded. "Ari's…" He stopped and gave a small cough. "Ari's pregnant."

I held my breath, knowing the fireworks were about to start and I'd have a front-row seat, exactly like I'd had a little more than a year ago now when I'd given Daniel the ultimatum about a baby. An ultimatum that had ended in our divorce. Would he do as he'd done then? Get up, pack a bag, and walk out? Except this time, he'd be walking out on Javier too.

Daniel stood. He crossed his arms, hunched his shoulders. I wanted to cry. Fuck. I already was. When had the tears started? I sniffed and wiped at my wet cheeks with my free hand as I watched Daniel. He went to the window, stared outside. After a long, tense minute, he turned back to us. A fake smile on his lips, he nodded. "Congratulations. When's the wedding?"

"Wedding?" I gulped. "What are you talking about?"

He gestured with one hand while keeping his other arm snug against his body. "Neither of your families will accept this situation if you're not married. I don't have to tell you. You both know this."

Javi's eyes went to that spot on his thigh. His finger went back to picking at it. "We don't want to lose you."

"We're business partners. I'll be around."

I gasped. The words were a dull knife to my already bleeding heart.

"*Business* partners?" Javi said in a small voice. "That's all we are to you?"

I released Javi's hand, stood and went to Daniel. I got right in his face. Last time, I'd let him slink away… but not this time. This time I'd fucking get some answers. "What's going on with you? Why don't you want to have kids?"

"Ari…" Daniel said in that hard voice meant to shut me up.

"No, Daniel. This time you're going to talk. You've never explained it to me, and I think"—I motioned to Javi still sitting on the couch—"we'd both like to understand what's going on with you."

His eyes flared and he blew out loudly. "I can't do this right now." Before I could stop him, he'd crossed the room, opened the door and left.

"*Madre de puta*," I said. *Motherfuck.*

Javi snorted and shook his head. He leaned forward with his elbows on his knees and pinched the bridge of his nose. When he looked up, his face looked like I felt. "Ari, do you really want to have this baby? It's my fault this happened in the first place. You'd been drinking and I should have been the one to make us stop and think about our decision before we acted on it."

"No." I sat next to him. "It's not your fault. We both participated. And kept participating. And I…" I paused and really examined my feelings. My palm went to my belly. I smiled. "I do. I really do want this baby."

"Even if it's not Daniel's?"

Startled by his question, I simply stared at him, and slowly, I put two and two together. The candy wrappers, the chip bags, the soda cans. They'd all been Javi's, and if I wasn't mistaken, there'd probably been many others. I laid my hand on his arm. "Where's this coming from?" I asked gently.

His eyes settled on my face. He pressed his lips together, then looked straight ahead. "I've seen how much you love him. That's why I waited so long to go after you. But I don't think I waited long enough. It was a mistake for me to try to change things."

"Javi, I—"

He continued as though I hadn't said anything. "Daniel was your first choice. He always has been. Fuck, I've known that from day one. *Que idiota he estado.* I've just been the back-up plan all along, haven't I?"

"No. You've got it all wrong, *mi amado.*" I held his face in my palms, forcing him to meet my eyes. "You were my *first* love. My first choice. Always. Never forget that. I love Daniel, I do, but you, you're my rock, Javier. I'll never not love you."

I leaned in closer. My mouth hovered over his. His warm breath brushed my lips with each exhale. I stared into his eyes, trying to convey my love for him. The depth of it. The strength of it. The persistence. "I love you, Javier. And I'm so sorry if, for even one minute, I ever made you feel like I didn't."

He closed his eyes, and I pressed delicate kisses on his lids. A choked sound escaped his lips.

"What is it?" I asked.

"In your room earlier, you said some things…" His voice broke. "Fuck, Ari. You said 'Why couldn't this have happened when Daniel and I were still married?'"

"Oh, Javi." Tears slid down my face. "I didn't mean it. I was shocked and upset and I didn't even know what I was saying."

"You also said the baby… my baby… would be an abomination."

"No. Oh God, no, Javi." I swung my leg over his thighs and straddled him, then pressed my forehead to his. "I meant in the eyes of the church. Of my parents. Not mine. *Never* mine." I pulled back and tried to smile. "How could he be when he's a part of you? You are so very special to me."

"He?"

"Well, maybe she. A *gordita* with my eyes and your smile." I could picture her and the image made my heart soar. "She'll be the perfect mix of us both."

He choked back a laugh. "Christ, don't wish that on anyone, especially not our *bebé*."

"What?" I said, widening my eyes. "Any baby of ours will be gorgeous."

"That, he or she will get from you," he insisted.

I remembered all the wrappers I'd seen. I surveyed the room, noticing even more. "Javi, I loved you when you were a chubby kid with glasses. You have a fantastic body now, but that's not what draws me to you." I took his hand and brought it between my legs. "It's not what gets me wet."

He groaned and thrust his hips up. "What does?"

"You. Your heart, your soul. The way you take care of the people you love. The way you've always taken care of me." I winked. "Don't think I haven't noticed that we always have plenty of those black pens I like or the colored folders or the—"

He laughed. "Okay, okay. I've been found out."

I kissed him again. A little more insistently this time. "You never have to worry about how you look. I want you to be healthy and happy, and whether you do that at a hundred and seventy pounds or at two hundred, you'll always be my *papi chulo*."

"You were always my first choice, too, Arianna," he said, suddenly serious. "*Siempre*."

Hearing my earlier words said back to me made the tear-machine start up again. Was this the result of pregnancy hormones? If so, I was going to be a giant mess by the time nine months were over. I smiled through the tears. "And Daniel? Where does he fit now?"

Javier's long fingers dug into my hair, pushing it off my face. He dried my cheeks with his thumbs. "I love you, I'll always love you, and I'll do my best for our child, but…" His eyes held mine. "I love Daniel too, and I need him. I think you do too." When I nodded, he pressed a sweet kiss to my quivering lips.

"I love who we are when we're all together. I think we all make each other better." I wanted what Javier wanted. But I'd been burned in this particular fire before. I looked at him. "If Daniel can't come back to us, can you be happy with it being just you and me?"

Javi nodded. "Of course, *corazón.* We'd already made this decision, remember?"

I smiled to hide my relief. "I remember."

I didn't want to admit how much I'd needed to hear Javi confirm it. Because Daniel… Daniel was going to wreck us both, wasn't he? Even though he'd made a lot of progress lately, he still couldn't tell me why he was so opposed to having a child—so much so that he'd left me.

What was to stop him from leaving us both?

DANIEL

My mind wouldn't stop reeling. *Arianna is having Javier's baby.* The baby she'd always wanted to have with me.

The baby we *should* have had. If I had any goddamn guts.

My stomach was one huge knot. They were having a child. And for some reason, they still wanted me in the picture.

Why? I sure as shit wasn't going to be any goddamn help. Especially when the thought of it, the thought of a *baby*, was practically giving me hives.

I couldn't do it.

I couldn't be part of it.

I couldn't pretend I was okay.

I paced down the hallway, my feet automatically taking me to Greta's door. I hoped she wasn't busy with someone else. I needed her to talk me off the ledge here, to calm me down, to tell me the turmoil inside me was somehow normal.

Even though I knew it wasn't.

I should be… happy, right? Happy that Javi could give Ari the thing I couldn't. Happy that they were going to be parents. Happy that a new life was coming into the world.

Instead of scared shitless.

I knocked on Greta's door, so relieved to hear her answer that I laughed. But the amusement left me as soon as she ushered me inside.

She took one look at me—at my hunched shoulders, my crossed arms, my overall state of "oh fuck"—and asked me what happened as we took seats in the living area, me on the couch, she in the armchair. I didn't want to say the words, to make this whole thing real.

"Daniel?" Greta said.

Man up, King. Just say it. "Arianna's pregnant."

"And you're the father?"

"It's Javier's."

She looked at me for a second. "And you're not happy about that."

I shook my head. "I'm not upset. Surprised, but not angry."

"I take it this was an accident."

Again I shook my head. "They sort of planned it. They agreed to try before I came back into the picture."

"Ah. And how do you feel about that?"

I thought for a moment, trying to sort out my emotions. "I'm not sure. Upset with myself, I guess, that I couldn't do that for her."

"Considering everything you've had going on, it's not surprising you didn't want to take on a child."

"They want me to be part of their relationship. To help raise the baby."

"Is that what you want?"

A lump grew in my throat and tears stung my eyes. "I *can't* be part of it."

"Because you're not the father?"

"It's not that. I don't care about that."

"Then?"

"I can't be responsible for a kid."

"Why not?" she asked.

I wrapped my arms around myself. "I'm a fucking mess. What kind of role model am I?"

Greta's brow creased. "I've seen you with Luciana's boys. You were helping Lucas with his math a few days ago. You seemed to be having a great time."

"That's different."

"Why is it different?"

"I'm not responsible for Lucas."

She held my eyes. "Daniel, what's at the root of this? You seem almost… panicked."

Panic. That was a good word for how I felt, my heart racing, my gut in a knot, my brain screaming at me to run, to leave, to go to San Francisco and disappear, do something stupid, like try to pick up some random guy in a gay bar. But how would that work? I could let Javi touch me, but someone else? Some stranger?

I doubted it. I was still overreacting and flashing back sometimes, even with Javi.

But I needed to do something. Something to make this clawing, gnawing beast inside me go away.

"Daniel, why is the idea of having a child, of being responsible for one, bothering you so much?"

My eyes burned and my throat ached. I drew in a breath, willing myself to say the words. "My parents loved me, so much." I wished I could just fucking cry and let it all out. But everything remained stuck. "And they couldn't stop me from getting hurt."

"Is that why you divorced Arianna?"

I nodded. "I just… I couldn't do it. I couldn't be a father."

"So, did divorcing Arianna fix anything?"

"Not really." I sighed and rubbed my eyes. "It solved the immediate problem. But I just ended up more miserable."

"Isn't it better to take the risk, then? Out of the three of you, something terrible happened to you, but Arianna and Javier came through their childhoods just fine. You'll be attached to this child no matter what you do, because you're attached to them."

"It would just kill me if something like that happened to their child."

"Wouldn't you be better placed to help protect that child if you were part of its life?"

What she was saying made sense. I knew it did. But… "Kids are so helpless. They need so much."

"They do. But that child will be better off with three people looking out for it."

"I'm so fucking scared, Greta."

She leaned forward and took my hand, giving it a gentle squeeze. "Every parent is."

"So, you're saying this is normal?"

"More or less. Maybe not your specific fear, but everyone gets hit with the enormity of the challenge at some point." She smiled. "And everyone freaks out."

Maybe they did. But the fear doing loop-de-loops in my gut?

It wasn't going away.

Chapter 14

JAVIER

Despite Daniel's ongoing distant attitude, I had to admit I was psyched for today's adventure. We pulled into the parking lot of the Simraceway Performance Driving Center where we'd have the chance to drive an actual sports car around the track. I couldn't wait, and maybe it would be just the kind of incredible, adrenaline-pumping experience we all needed to shock us out of the jumble our minds were in.

When the bus stopped, I looked down at Ari, who'd fallen asleep with her head on my shoulder. She looked so innocent, so trusting. My heart swelled with love for her and the child she carried. Not because it was mine. I'd love the child even if it were Daniel's. I already loved it because it was a part of her.

Dark smudges marred the delicate skin under her eyes, and her long lashes cast shadows on her cheeks. Her condition stirred something inside me, a need to protect. To provide. I wanted to wrap her up in cotton. To keep her warm and safe. To keep *them* warm and safe.

I hated to wake her, but I also didn't want to leave her alone on the bus. I ran a finger along her cheek, her jaw. Her lids fluttered. She moaned and snuggled deeper into my arms. I kissed her forehead. "Wake up, *princesa*. We've arrived."

"One more minute," she said.

I chuckled. People were already standing up and preparing to get off the bus. I knew she'd want to be in front, leading the group. "Come on, *corazón*. We have a job to do."

"Slave driver," she grumbled. After a moment, she stifled a yawn and sat up, stretching her lush body.

My cock hardened. I wanted to take her right here and now. But we weren't alone. And when I glanced up, Daniel was there. Ari and I had sat in the front row since she'd feared getting motion sick. When we'd sat down, Daniel had continued walking, all the way to the back. It had hurt me, it had hurt Arianna, and I knew it had hurt him.

Yet here he was. A big silent mountain. Arianna's bag was over his shoulder.

"Daniel," she breathed.

His face remained impassive. He held his hand out. "Let me help you."

Nodding, she took it, stumbling groggily as she rose. He steadied her with a hand on her waist and led her down the narrow stairs. I wasn't sure how to take that. Was he thawing? He hadn't said a word to me or Ari during breakfast at the winery. He'd simply watched us from across the room where he'd sat with Greta, sipping cup after cup of coffee.

He hadn't looked angry or upset during breakfast, and he still didn't. No, it was much worse. He looked blank. As though he didn't feel anything at all. Like he'd shut off his emotions, and seeing him like this carved a big aching wound in my chest. Fuck. Just yesterday, Daniel had held me in his arms. We'd kissed. He'd told me he loved me, and like a fool, I'd believed him. Because, God, I'd so wanted to believe him. Hadn't I been dreaming of having him love me back for over a decade?

Today, he kept looking at me like I was a stranger.

I swallowed my emotions, gathered up my belongings, and stepped down from the bus. I was going to forget about everything, just for a few hours. I loved racing. I watched it whenever I could and even drove up to the Daytona International Speedway several times a year to watch the races. Those were some of my most cherished memories.

Especially the times when Daniel had gone with me.

Fuck. I shoved him out of my mind. Again.

As a group, we tramped into the hospitality center that overlooked Turn 1 of the raceway. Several members of the staff were talking with Arianna. Daniel stood off to the side. Our gazes collided. His eyes blazed heat and hunger for a moment. Desire coiled in my belly even as fear and anger sizzled in my veins.

Then as though a curtain had been drawn, the heat and the hunger in his gaze were gone. All that remained was that god-awful blankness. And I was left feeling bereft, and strangely drained.

Fortunately, before I could dwell on it further, one of the Simraceway staff called everyone to attention. Because we'd booked only a half-day event, we were given a crash-course in how to handle the site's KTM X-Bow race cars rather than a full classroom lecture. The cars, called KTM Crossbows, were sleek and came in two color combinations, red and black or white and black. After the course, we were teamed up with an instructor, who got us suited up with a race jacket, gloves, and, of course, a helmet.

When I emerged from the dressing room, Arianna was seated at the window with Luciana and Brad. Brad was in full gear; the women were not. Frowning, I told my instructor Sean that I'd be right back. I went to Ari. "You aren't participating, *princesa*?"

She excused herself and led me off to the side. "I'm not sure it's a good idea. You know… because of the…"—she lowered her voice to a whisper—"baby. I'm also still feeling nauseated."

"Of course." I smacked myself on the forehead. "Should have thought of that."

"We'll get the hang of it soon enough." She rose on her toes to kiss me. "Have fun out there."

"I will." I led her back to the others, and when I turned to get back to my instructor, I once again came eye to eye with Daniel. My stomach tightened. He'd watched our entire exchange. With a tight nod, he spun on his heel and walked out the door that led to the track. I couldn't help the irritation that was taking root in my gut. What the hell was his problem? We were the same people we'd been yesterday or the day before. Hell, I was still the same insecure kid inside I'd been when we'd first met. "He'd better get the fuck over it and quick," I muttered to myself as I fell in step with Sean.

"What's that?" he asked.

"Nothing. Sorry." I cleared my throat as I tried to clear my head. "Tell me how this is going to go."

"Sure thing, Mr. Cordero. Do you drive manual?"

"Yep."

"Great. So, we're all going to get in our KTM X-Bows. For the first few laps, the instructors will be driving. I'll explain everything as I'm doing it. That way, you'll get to see it and hear it. Then, because you know how to drive a stick shift, once you're comfortable with the speed and the vehicle, we'll trade places."

My eyes widened and excitement sparked in my chest. "I'm really going to get to drive it?"

"Absolutely."

I rubbed my hands together. "I can't fucking wait. Can I go fast?"

"As fast as you dare." He laughed. "There are rules though."

"Okay, sure. What are they?" I could live with a few rules as long as I got to go flat out for a bit. Fuck, I needed to feel the air whizzing past me.

I needed to feel like I was flying. I needed to forget, just for a little while. Just long enough to catch my breath and remember that I'd get through this, we'd get through it, just like we had gotten through everything else in our lives.

"Okay, so first, you have to listen to me. We're going to be going fast. Faster than you've ever driven before. You won't see everything that's going on around you, but I will. So, if I say go right, you go right. If I say slow down, you slow down."

"Got it."

"Second rule: don't pass anyone on a curve. You're all novices, and we don't want any accidents."

"Makes sense," I said, giving him a nod.

"Third rule: no showboating."

That one made me snort. "Dude, I'm an accountant. I don't showboat, ever."

Sean clapped me on the back. "Then we're going to have a great time." He stopped in front of a gorgeous white and black race car. My pulse quickened at the sight. "This one's ours. Hop in."

We climbed in and did up our seatbelts. Sean checked to make sure my helmet was on properly and then he started up the vehicle. The noise was overwhelming and the vibrations went all the way through me. "Oh fuck. This is really happening."

"You bet," Sean said. He put the car in gear and off we went, driving slowly as he explained the controls. "This baby goes 0 to 60 in 3.9 seconds, so be mindful of the acceleration when you press the gas. It's made of ultra-lightweight carbon fiber and only weighs 750 kilos or about half of what a regular Toyota Camry weighs. You'll feel it in the turns."

After that, he floored it. Gravity pushed me back in the seat, and I let out a whoop of pure joy. Jesus, this was the life. As we came up to a curve, he slowed down a bit, hugging the edge of the track, and then accelerated. It was beautiful, and I couldn't wait to get behind the wheel and try it for myself.

Fifteen minutes later, Sean slowed and pulled into a designated spot to the side of the track. He turned to me. "Ready?"

"Hell yeah!" I unbuckled my seatbelt and was out of the car in seconds.

Sean followed a little more sedately. When we were both in our seats with our belts buckled, he said, "Okay, Mr. Cordero. Let's see what you can do."

I checked over my shoulder and eased onto the racetrack when the way was clear. The vehicle was amazingly responsive. Since Sean had been considerate enough to get off the track right after the curve, I had the entire straightaway to test the speed before hitting the next turn. I pressed the gas pedal, shifted, and, fuck! There was just something about all that speed, all that power in my hands. My veins buzzed, and my heart hammered in my chest. I pushed the speed until we were doing one sixty.

About an eighth of a mile from the curve, Sean instructed me to reduce my speed. I downshifted and engaged the turn exactly as he'd shown me. Once I'd straightened out again, I took off. "This is so fucking awesome!" I shouted. We had microphones and speakers attached to our helmets, so he could hear me even if I spoke normally. I was so damn excited though, I had to shout.

I slowed for the next turn, hugged the edge of the track, and then sped up. As I engaged in the next curve, I heard the rumble of a car behind me. This was followed by a high whine as the car zipped past me. "Hey, didn't you tell me—" My jaw snapped shut when I realized Daniel was at the wheel.

"Damn it," Sean ground out. "There's always one idiot who thinks the rules don't apply to him."

I swallowed the immediate defense that rose to my lips. What Daniel had done was dangerous. I tracked closely behind him while Sean spoke to Daniel's instructor. "Damn it. When you get in front of the welcome center, make him stop."

There was one turn left, and even I could see that Daniel was approaching it with too much speed. Jesus. He whipped around the curve and— "Oh shit!" I cried.

A car was pulling onto the racetrack.

Fear flooded my entire body. Christ no. *No!*

Daniel tried to swerve around the other car, but the back of his X-Bow fishtailed and then—

"Fuck, fuck!" I shouted.

Daniel's car started to spin. The whole while, I'd been slowing down, my heart in my throat. I took the turn and prayed.

God, don't let him hit the wall. Please keep him safe.

God must have been listening, because Daniel's car skidded to a sideways stop about a foot from the barrier, smoke rising from the tires. I followed Sean's instructions and pulled off the track before stopping. We quickly climbed out and ran over to Daniel's car. Even from a distance, I could hear the instructor bawling him out. I had plenty to say to the shithead too.

Behind us, people were running and shouting. Sean and I reached Daniel first as he was climbing out. "Fuck, Daniel," I said, coming up to him. "What the *hell* were you thinking?"

"I had everything under control," he said, not even looking at me.

"Is that right?" Ari slid in between us. She was pale and out of breath. Her eyes were shining with tears she was fighting not to let spill. "So, you *meant* to almost crash into the wall? Kill yourself and your instructor?

Destroy the car? That was your plan, really?"

"I'm sorry, okay?" Daniel bowed his head and plowed through the growing crowd. He slipped down a pathway that led God knew where.

"I'm going after him," I told Ari.

She grabbed my arm. "I'm going with you."

As quickly as we could without running, we traced his steps, and found him just around the corner, out of sight of everyone. His hands were on his hips, his shoulders rounded, his chin touching his chest. He was breathing heavily. When he heard our arrival, he sighed. "Go away."

Go away? I'd had enough of Daniel's bullshit. "*Oye*, dickhead," I shouted as I grabbed his shirt and pushed him up against the wall. "You have a death wish or something? Because what I saw out there wasn't *my* Daniel. It was some stupid-ass teenager in an adult body. You're better than this."

He stared at me wide-eyed. "You always thought I was, but I wasn't. I'm not." He laughed darkly. "You have no idea how many times I've wanted to just fucking end it all." His eyes reflected all his pain, all his misery. And I'd added to it. Arianna and I had both added to it.

"Goddamn it, Daniel." My voice broke, but I forced myself to continue. "I won't let you do this to yourself. I fucking love you."

Daniel's eyes misted over. "The two of you don't really need me." His voice was raw, broken. He looked away.

I grabbed his chin. "You're wrong."

Ari came up beside me. She stroked his cheek. "You are so wrong, *mi amor*." She smiled, then her expression crumpled and she burst into tears.

Daniel shot me an alarmed look. I responded with a glare. He was the one doing this to her.

Ari looked from Daniel to me. "I don't know how any of this is going to work out"—her words came out in short staccato bursts through her many sobs—"but I can't see myself being happy without both of you."

I crushed Daniel to my chest. He came easily, almost as though he'd needed the comfort too. "We can't do this without you, *hermano*. We don't want to. You're an essential part of this. Of us."

His arms came around me and he hugged me tightly, burying his face in my neck. "I want to. Fuck, I want to so badly. But…" His thought went unfinished as his arms dropped to his sides.

I stumbled back, an ache growing in my chest. I was losing him. We were losing him. How could I fix this? I had to find a way.

Ari slipped between us. She grabbed Daniel's arms and shook him, as much as she could, given her size and his. Her ferocity had me smiling even though I was dying inside. "Haven't you been happier this last week than you have in a long time?" When he finally looked at her, she held his blue gaze with her own piercing one. "I've seen a change in you."

That was the crux of it. We'd all changed a lot, but had we changed enough, or were we still the same scared kids we'd been before? The ones who'd loved and lost from a distance, too frightened, too influenced by society's opinion of us, to give voice to our true desires?

DANIEL

Arianna's question lingered in the air. "You're right," I said. "I've been happier this past week than I have been in a long time. Hell, I'm happier than I've ever been, period."

But I still had a rock in my stomach that seemed to weigh a ton.

Ari's face softened. "Then what's the problem?"

"You know why I never wanted to have kids?"

She shook her head. "Why?"

I closed my eyes and looked away, my heart speeding up and my chest heaving as I pictured what could happen to my child. "I never wanted a kid of mine to go through what I did." My tight throat warped my words, and tears stung my eyes. "It *wrecked* me. Coach fucking wrecked me."

I could have been a tennis star. I could have paid my parents back for all the sacrifices they'd made for me. I could have remained close to them. I could have stayed married to Ari all this time, could have had children. Could have been with Javi so much sooner. I could have been someone who'd been happy, who hadn't destroyed almost every close tie I'd ever had.

I'd lost so much. So many dreams. So many relationships. So much time.

And I'd never get any of it back.

I'd never be that boy with so much promise again.

I was damaged goods. And now I was inflicting that damage on Ari and Javi.

"I'm no good for you," I said, the words strangled, my eyes flooded with tears. "I'm no fucking good." A sob ripped out of my throat, and I turned my face to the wall, trying to hold the tears back, not wanting them to see me like this. Not wanting them to know what a fucking disaster I was.

"No, no, Daniel," Arianna said, her soft hand on my back. "You've got it all wrong."

I couldn't look at her, didn't want to see the pity on her face. "Just walk away from me." I wiped at the tears streaming down my cheeks, but they didn't stop. They wouldn't stop.

Javi's strong arms came around me, and he pressed himself tight to my back, pulling me away from the wall. "I've got you, Daniel," he whispered in my ear, the words thick with emotion.

Ari slipped in front of me and pressed herself to my chest, her arms going around me as well. "We've got you, *mi amor.*" She was sobbing too, tears rolling down her face and onto my chest.

I hadn't cried like this since I was a child. Greta had warned me it would come out sometime, but I hadn't believed her. Ari let out a sound that was so full of pain, I grabbed onto her, hugging her tightly. I'd hurt her so badly. I'd cheated on her. I'd ruined our marriage.

And still, somehow, she loved me.

"I don't fucking deserve you," I choked out. "Either of you."

Javi pressed his cheek to the back of my neck. "That's where you're wrong. So goddamn wrong I don't even know how to say it." He squeezed me tightly, his warm breath gusting over my neck. "You're the best thing that ever happened to me. You changed my life."

"Mine too," Ari said, and she too squeezed me tighter.

"But I wrecked everything. I'm a fucking mess. I wreck everything I touch. I ruin everyone's life." I shut my eyes. "That's why I can't be a father."

Ari shook her head against my chest. "No, *mi amor.* You are an amazing, wonderful person. You always have been. You'll make an excellent father."

God, I wanted that. I wanted to be a dad someday. But could I really do it?

I took a deep breath, then another, slowly letting them each out, getting the sobbing under control, the tears finally drying up.

Could I do this? Should I?

Javi slid a hand up to touch my cheek. "*Hermano,* you're the strongest person I know."

I snorted. "Really? *I'm* the strongest person you know?"

"You are. You started TI, and you've been goddamn fearless in steering us. You just have to trust in that."

He had a point, but that was different. That was business. "When it comes to my personal life, I've been letting fear take the wheel for a really long time."

Javi squeezed my shoulder, his touch comforting. "And doesn't it feel good now that you're starting not to do that?"

"It does, but—"

Ari put her arms around my neck. "Then trust in *that* feeling. Trust in *us.*"

Could I do it?

Fuck "Could I"—I *had* to. I had to, or life just wasn't worth living.

I nodded, wiping off my cheeks, taking one last deep breath before I looked at her. "Okay, I'll try." I tried to turn to look at Javi, and they both loosened their grips on me, but Ari took hold of my hand, her fingers curling around mine. I gave her fingers a squeeze, then I met Javi's steady gaze, his hopeful smile. "But I think we need to work on the one thing I still haven't been able to do."

Arianna released my hand and started to step away from me, but I caught her wrist. "I'm going to need you to be there, Ari."

Her eyes glistened again with unshed tears. "Always, *mi amor*. Always."

DANIEL

Was I really, truly ready to do this? Ready to let another man take me again?

Even if it was Javi?

My pulse had been racing off and on since I'd made the decision back at the racetrack. Now that we were at the winery, in my room, my heart was pounding.

I'm not ready.

I looked from Javi to Ari. I loved them both, so much. They wouldn't let anything bad happen to me. I knew this in my head. I knew it in my heart.

But my body wouldn't listen.

All I could do was stand there, frozen, until Ari turned to me and said, "Nothing has to happen until you're ready. You can try, and then change your mind. You can try a million times, or never, and that's okay."

A lump filled my throat, and I put my arms around her. She'd read my mind, all my fears, all my worries.

Javi came up by my side and lightly touched my waist. "Can I join the party?"

"Fuck yes," I said and opened an arm so he could be part of our hug. We stood like that for a couple minutes, just holding each other, just breathing.

Then Arianna kissed me, her mouth feathering over mine, her tongue seeking entrance, and I let her in, our tongues dancing together, the touch reminding me how wonderful sex was. It wasn't something to fear.

Not with people who cared.

She released me, then Javi kissed my cheek, my jaw, the corner of my mouth, and I turned my head so our lips touched, then I took control of the kiss, and his moan called forth an answering need inside me.

I *wanted* to do this. I wanted to give myself to Javi. To Arianna. To the both of them.

I broke the kiss, still holding onto them. "I love you both. So much. So much it hurts." I reached out and caressed Ari's belly. "And I'm going to love your child too. Like it's my own. Because it's going to be a part of both of you."

Arianna smiled. "And maybe someday you and I will have a child too?"

I took a deep breath. "I want that. Someday."

Her smile lit up the room. "I'll hold you to it." Then she started unbuttoning her blouse. "Let's get this party started, gentlemen."

Javi smirked at her. "I'm not sure we qualify as gentlemen."

Her coy smile made me laugh. "Maybe not. You're both far too dirty-minded."

"Look who's talking," I said.

Her grin widened. "Well, I guess I have had the dirtiest fantasy so far." She peeled off her blouse, unzipped her skirt and stepped out of it as she approached, wearing only a black lacy bra and panties.

She stopped in front of me and walked her fingers from my chest down to the belt of my slacks, little flares of desire springing up in their wake, my cock perking up as her fingers neared. "So, tell us, Daniel, what's *your* fantasy?"

My mouth went dry. I could have anything I wanted—if my body would let me. "I want to make love to you both at the same time."

Her lips curved into a smile that made a million promises. "And how exactly would you like things to play out?"

"Maybe how we did with Javi before—except with me on the bottom and you facing me."

Javi touched my shoulder. "You're sure? We don't have to. We don't *ever* have to."

I cupped the base of his skull and drew him close, kissing him fiercely. "I want to. I want to give myself to both of you at the same time."

Reaching up, Javier slid his hand along my shoulder to the back of my neck. He was testing me, I knew it, and I didn't flinch when he caressed the skin there, when he dug his fingers into my hair, when he tightened his grip, turning it from exploratory to possessive.

"I'm ready, Javi."

His thumb moved idly at the junction of my neck and jaw. "And if you're not, that's okay," he murmured, his gaze dipping to my lips before coming back to my eyes. "Just say so, at any point. It will *not* be a problem."

I breathed in and out slowly. I did want this. I did. But something in me calmed at his words.

Ari touched my belt again, then put her hand on Javi's belt as well. "The two of you are still wearing too many clothes!" she said, like we were two naughty children.

We all started laughing, and in a frenzy of kisses and caresses, we got each other naked, the three of us piling onto the bed, me on my back, Ari on my lap, and Javi by my side, kissing and stroking both of us when we weren't doing the same to him.

He leaned over and started sucking my cock, and his hot mouth enveloping me was nothing short of heaven. Ari had risen up on her knees to give him access, and he surprised her by shifting to dive between her legs as well.

Having her quivering in my arms while I watched Javi lap at her pussy made me happy in a way I'd never expected. The three of us were a unit. A triad. Our own little universe. And we got to make our own rules.

We got to define what love meant to us. What commitment was for us.

What was normal—for us.

Javi alternated between the two of us until we were both gasping. Then he got off the bed and retrieved the lube and condoms from the nightstand. He handed one to Ari, and she rolled it down my stiff cock, making sure to smooth it over me very carefully, no doubt touching me far more than was necessary. Not that I minded one bit.

When Javi uncapped the lube, I bent my knees to give him access to my hole. He slicked up several fingers, then started running them up and down the crack of my ass, finding and circling my pucker.

Quivers started in my belly, and I took a deep breath, both Ari and Javi watching me so intently, my face grew hot.

Ari must have realized how I was feeling because she kissed me, blocking Javi from my view. Rising up, she glided her slick pussy along my shaft, both of us moaning from the contact, and I started to relax. I looked around Ari's shoulder, my gaze meeting Javi's.

He started to probe me, just with the tip of a finger, his eyes still on me, and I nodded. Ari was a good distraction, her full tits right in my face, and I latched on to one of her nipples, sucking on it until she gasped, then I tugged on it with my teeth and she cried out, her nails digging into my shoulders.

Javi slid a finger inside me, and I stiffened. He stopped moving it. "You okay?" he asked.

I released Ari's nipple. "Yeah. Just need a sec to get used to it."

He gently started to move the finger in and out, and the sensation was far more pleasant than I'd expected. And then he rubbed over my prostate, and I groaned. Fuck, that felt good.

Just like sometimes with Coach.

I froze and my eyes sprang open, meeting Arianna's gaze. There must have been something alarming in my expression, because she said, "Javi, stop."

He stilled and started to withdraw his finger. "Wait," I said, taking a deep breath, then slowly letting it out.

This is Javi. This is Arianna.

This is us. *Not him.*

"I'm okay," I said, my voice as rusty as an old door hinge. When Javi didn't move, I said, "Really, I am. Just needed a second."

"Okay." He started again, thrusting his finger in and out until I moaned and latched onto Ari's nipple again, tweaking the other with my fingers.

She was so goddamn sexy. Javi was too, with that look of complete concentration on his face, all that focus on me.

He rubbed his finger over my prostate again, and I kept my eyes open this time, reminding myself where I was, who I was with. Keeping my focus on the here and now.

"I'm going to add a second finger," Javi said, as serious as a surgeon, or someone defusing a bomb, and I started chuckling.

"What's so funny?" Ari asked.

"He sounds"—I couldn't stop giggling the more I thought about it—"he sounds like he's trying to cut the right wire, you know?"

Ari started laughing and Javi did too. "I do, don't I?" he said.

I reached out and touched his forearm, my hand sliding down it until our fingers entwined on the mattress. "You're the best, Javi."

"Damn right I am," he said, giving me a cocky grin as I felt the added pressure of a second finger. He was careful, giving me time to adjust, and soon he was sliding them in and out, each glide over my prostate like a jolt of electricity.

I wanted him inside me. I wanted to feel him loving me that way, wanted to turn myself over to him, wanted to give him my trust.

Wanted to replace every bad memory of Coach with a good one of Javi.

I couldn't erase my past, but I could build a new future, one filled with love and joy instead of abuse and pain.

I could be someone else. I didn't have to be a victim anymore. I didn't have to be ashamed anymore. This was the message Greta had been giving me. And only now was it finally sinking in.

"I really love you both," I said, looking at each of them. "You've been so patient with me. And you never gave up on me."

Ari leaned forward and kissed me. "Always."

Javi peeked at me around her hip, then planted a kiss on my thigh.

"Always." He gave me a wide grin and wiggled his fingers inside me. "Ready for a third?"

I blew out and nodded. "Yeah."

The pressure increased, and I felt an intense burn that was painful, but also pleasurable. I breathed through it, Ari stroking my cheek and sliding her wet pussy along my shaft again, reaching between her legs to rub my crown against her clit before teasing me with her entrance.

"You okay, *hermano*?" Javi asked.

I smiled up at Ari. "You bet I am. Our girl is the best entertainment."

He chuckled and nipped at her hip, and she swatted at him. Then she turned back to me, continuing her teasing of me, letting me slip inside her a bit, then raising her hips so that I couldn't sink inside her. I placed my hands on her hips and pulled down, making her take me.

We both groaned, and Javi said, "Fuck. I have the best view ever." His hard cock pressed into my thigh, and I rubbed my leg against it.

Ari swiveled her hips and rose up, then came back down. "Ready for Javi? I'm sure he's dying to get in on this."

I took another breath, held it for a second, then blew out, nodding as I did. "I'm ready." I made eye contact with Javi. "I want you inside me. Now."

"You don't have to tell me twice." He grinned and withdrew his fingers, then I felt the blunt tip of his broad cockhead pressing against my hole. "Let me know if you need to stop, okay?"

I sucked in a breath and held it. Ari stroked my belly. "Breathe, *mi amor*. The more tense you are, the harder it will be."

I nodded, holding her eyes, focusing on the clenching of her pussy around my cock, then Javi pushed forward, the pain intensifying. "No!" I shouted, the word blurting out before I even formed the conscious thought.

They both froze, and Javi stepped back, coming to a stop by my side. Ari leaned forward and stroked my arms, my belly, her eyes locked on mine. "Breathe, Daniel, breathe. Slowly, in and out." She demonstrated for me, and that's when I realized I was hyperventilating.

Fuck. I closed my eyes and turned my face into the pillow. Why couldn't I just get over this?

"*Cariño*," Ari said, her small hand turning my face to hers. I looked up at her, and she smiled. "You did really good. Next time—"

"No. There isn't going to be a next time when it comes to this." Javi blanched, and I grabbed his wrist. "I mean that *this* is going to be our first time. Today. Now. We're doing this. I'm getting through this."

He shook his head. "Look. We already pushed your boundaries really hard today." With his free hand, he stroked Ari's breast, and she clenched around my dick, making me groan. "Let's just play with Ari and try again another day."

I tightened my fingers around his wrist. "I don't want to wait and keep building this up to be this insurmountable thing."

"And I want you to enjoy it." His dark eyes held mine, the love in them clear.

"I will. Because it's you." The words weren't just pretty bullshit; they were true. And something inside me settled. "It's *you*, Javi. You." I looked up at Ari. "And you."

"Okay," he said. I let him go, and he got back into position, teasing my hole with the head of his cock until I started rubbing against it myself. "Ready?"

"Yeah. Let's do this," I said, and Ari rose up as Javi pushed in, the burn still there, but she swiveled around my shaft as she descended, her pussy gripping me tight, and the mix of sensations was so overwhelming, all I could do was ride it out, focusing on my breathing—in, out, in, out—my eyes catching Ari's, then Javi peered around her shoulder. He'd stopped moving, and I realized his balls were pressed against my ass.

He was in. All the way in. And I wasn't ready to jump up. Or hit him. I was fine.

Javi looked at me, a question in his eyes. "You tell me when it's okay to move. *If* it's okay," he said.

The burn was fading. I felt full, very full, but the sensation of Ari riding my cock, along with her little pants and whimpers, was distracting me from thinking too hard about what else was happening.

And having her making love to me at the same time was one more reminder that this time was something entirely different than anything I'd ever experienced.

I nodded at Javi. "I'm ready for more." He pulled back, then rocked forward gently, his cock dragging across my prostate, and groaned. "Fuck," I said, the only word I could form.

"Keep going?" Javi asked, his voice low, gravelly, straining as if he were holding up the weight of the world.

"Yeah. Do that again."

He rocked in and out, and Ari slid up and down my shaft, and I thought I was going to lose my mind. It felt great. Amazing.

And it was pure pleasure.

"Faster," I said. "Both of you."

Ari rose above me, her fine, full tits bouncing, and Javi nipped at her neck and tweaked one of her nipples, making her cry out as they both started moving faster.

Maybe I should have felt trapped, caged, with them both surrounding me the way they did, but instead I felt safe. Loved. Cherished.

Complete.

A deep moan wrenched out of me. "Daniel?" Javi asked.

"I'm fine. More than fine." I reached out, finding his wrist where he was holding onto Ari's hip. "Just fuck me, okay?"

He looked down at me, his pupils blown, his cheeks flushed, and his hips snapped forward, the invasion too much and not enough at the same time. I clutched his wrist, and he sped up and bit down on Ari's shoulder, making her gasp and clench around me as she shuddered through her climax.

The sight of her going over, the way she bore down on my shaft so tight, and Javi's groan as he pistoned into me—it was all too much, pleasure spiraling inside me up through my cock, and I came with a shout.

Javi's strokes grew shorter, harder, his breath coming in harsh gasps, then he shuddered against Ari's back.

Laughing, he planted a kiss on her neck as he withdrew from me. He stepped over to the side and leaned down and kissed my lips, lingering for a second before pulling back.

"We fucking did it," I said, looking from him to her, my chest feeling so light, it was like I hadn't realized a weight had been sitting on me.

"Yeah, we did," Javi said, his eyes sparkling.

Ari's gaze flickered between us both. "You two couldn't have done it without me, you know." Her tone was light, teasing, but she was right. She started to rise off me, but I pulled her forward, into a kiss, her hair falling around us in a curtain.

I cupped her cheeks. "I never, ever should have left you."

Tears welled in her eyes. "If you hadn't, we wouldn't be here today."

It was true. The pain we'd all gone through during this last year just made what we had now all the sweeter.

All the more precious.

And I was never letting it go again.

Chapter 15

DANIEL

"Hurry up, Ari. We're going to be late," I called to her through the bathroom door as I peered into the full-length mirror, trying to adjust my tie. It was our last night at the vineyard and we were throwing a final dinner party for ECC and its clients. Overall, the retreat had been a huge success, especially on a personal note.

Coming to stand behind me, Javi chuckled. "Let me help you with that."

I leaned into his broad chest and observed us in the mirror, loving how we looked together. He wore a black suit with a crisp, white shirt and a vest with white piping and white buttons that crossed over on a diagonal in front. His tie was striped black and silver. And he looked fucking incredible. His arms went around me and straightened my tie. He patted it down. "There you go. All better."

I turned my head and pressed a soft kiss to his full lips. "Mmm…" I moaned. "I love your mouth. You have the sexiest lips."

"I thought *I* did," Ari said, stepping out of the bathroom.

I spun around and took her in. God, she was beautiful. The fatigue that had been plaguing her since our arrival seemed to be gone. She was radiant, her eyes clear, her smile bright and sincere. She wore a long-sleeved blue dress made of some shimmery material that hugged every amazing curve. My cock hardened. "Jesus, Ari."

"*Eres deslumbrante*," Javi said, taking her hand and pulling her in for a kiss. She certainly was stunning. They both were.

"You two will be the most gorgeous couple in the room," I said, meaning it. No one, not even the actors, would look more red-carpet ready than Javi and Arianna.

Ari's smile fell. "I hate that."

"What? Being called gorgeous?" I asked, trying to tease her out of my misstep. This was going to be hard on all of us.

"You *know* what, Mr. Smartypants."

I put my hand on her hip and tugged her in for a kiss. "I do know. And yeah, it will be hard not being able to kiss you in public, so you'd better take care of that now."

She smiled and cupped my cheek. "I love you."

I grinned back. "I know." I kissed her, long and deep, and when we ended the kiss, all three of us were panting and glassy eyed with lust.

Javi adjusted his hard-on. "Fucker," he hissed at me.

Ari laughed and threaded her arms through ours. "Come on. We need to get down there."

While we waited for the elevator, I said, "Greta told me one of the couples had left early, citing irreconcilable differences. Want to guess who?"

"It's not Chad and Monica. I saw them about an hour ago," Javi said.

Ari leaned her head on my shoulder. "I hope it's not Branson and Malia. I really wanted them to work out."

"Nope," I said. "They're still here."

"That only leaves three couples," Javi said. "I'm going to say it's Joel and Rebecca Levin."

"Bingo." I put my hand at the back of his neck, and after checking that the hall was empty, I gave him a quick kiss. When his cheeks went a sweet pink, I kissed him again.

"Why did you think it was them, Javi?" Ari asked when we parted.

His eyes burned with the same desire I was feeling. Jesus. I wasn't sure I'd last an entire evening without touching either of them. He visibly shook himself and slowly shifted his gaze to Ari. She grinned. "Well?"

"Uh… um… well… they're both agents, in the same business. They're both the same age."

She squinted at him. "So?"

"They're in direct competition. That can't be good for a marriage."

"Huh. I never thought of it that way. I just thought it was great that they had so much in common."

"Too much, I guess," I said.

"So everyone else is okay?" Ari asked.

"As well as can be expected. I don't think this retreat was a miracle cure for everyone, but it looks like the couples that stayed want to continue working on their marriages."

"That's so beautiful." Ari smiled, all starry-eyed. "I'm really glad we got to do this retreat."

"Fuck, so am I." Javi's eyes shone. "I don't think we'd be together otherwise."

I gently squeezed his neck again. "I'd like to think we'd have worked our way there eventually."

"Yeah." Ari snorted. "Maybe when we were ninety."

We all laughed. The elevator arrived and we climbed in. "I've come up with a theory about who leaked the location of the original retreat," I said.

"You have?" Javi asked. He was leaning against the elevator wall, looking like sex on legs. I gripped the railing that went around the elevator to keep myself from falling to my knees in front of him.

"No!" Ari said. "Don't tell me it was Jay, and the record label did it as a publicity stunt? No wonder Raven was so pissed when they first got here."

Javi and I stared at her, him looking as stunned as I felt. "Where the hell did all that come from?"

She shot us both a very wicked grin. "I have a vivid imagination." And now I wanted to fall to my knees in front of *her*.

Javi smirked. "No shit."

"Okay," she said. "So, if it's not Jay, maybe Darren? He and Ji-woo are like night and day."

I had to agree with that. Ji-woo was a sensitive, insightful producer. Darren was a brash, in-your-face director. Everything about them personally and professionally was in diametric opposition. "Not Darren. Or Ji-woo for that matter. My vote is on Chad." I watched curiously as Javi seemed to brace himself against the elevator wall.

"No way!" Ari exploded. Her lips turned down, and she pressed a hand to her chest. "That poor guy loves Monica so much."

"Think she loves him though?" Javi asked. "She was going after any man who'd give her the time of day."

"Which was just about any man." Ari shook her head. "But why do you think it was Chad?"

I rubbed my jaw. "At the Tough Mudder, he said he was glad they'd be able to get divorced now that the cat was out of the bag about their relationship issues. That pretty much cemented it for me."

Ari tilted her head and pressed a manicured fingertip to her beautiful red lips. "He was lying. That man would rather cut off his own *rabo* than get a divorce."

Javi and I both winced. Phantom pain wilted my erection. "I wouldn't go that far," I said. "Anyway, I'm going to tell Greta, and I think we should confront Chad about it tonight."

"I'll be right beside you." The weight of Javi's words took me by surprise.

I crossed the elevator and pressed my body against his, loving every hard inch, especially the eight inches that rubbed against my erection. "That spot has your name on it."

He bit his lip and twisted his hips, making his cock slide alongside mine. We both groaned. "That spot?"

"Fuck yeah."

"Boys." Ari snapped her fingers. "Boys! What about me?"

I took a step away from Javi and pulled her into my arms. I rubbed my hand down her spine to her round ass cheek, and filled my palm with it. She moaned and pushed her ass into my hand.

Javi snorted. "Slut," he said, his tone teasing, affectionate.

"Jealous?" Her smile was so carnal, I almost came in my pants.

Javi grabbed her face and planted a passionate kiss on her mouth. "Never change, *princesa*. You're perfect exactly the way you are."

The elevator dinged, and we jumped apart like children caught playing doctor. I was certain our guilty expressions would give us away when the doors opened. Fortunately, no one was standing immediately outside. Music was playing in the dining room. We straightened our clothing, then headed in to join the others. The Monteros, the ECC staff, and the remaining couples were mingling together, most everyone with glasses of wine in their hands.

The Monteros had done a lovely job renovating the winery, and the dining room was no exception. It was fitted out with long, flowing tablecloths, white with deep red place mats. White dishes, crystal wine glasses, and shiny silver-plated cutlery marked each seat. The carpet was a marbled gray, the walls a lighter gray, artfully decorated with original paintings of Sonoma County.

"Wow." Ari spun in circles, taking in the chandeliers and wall-mounted light fixtures. "This room is gorgeous."

Sofia, apparently having overheard, came up beside Ari. "Thank you. We hope people will consider it for their weddings and fancy affairs."

"No doubt they will. I've never seen anything like it."

Sofia kissed her cheek. "I will tell Manuel you approve."

Ari beamed at her aunt. "I can't thank you enough for helping us out."

"That's what family is for. Besides, I think this will help the vineyard too." She clucked her tongue and called Brad over. She handed us wine glasses from the tray he carried. "Enjoy your drinks. Dinner will be served in fifteen minutes."

When she was gone, Brad winked at Ari. "She seriously downplayed that. Greta has already confirmed three more retreats, and that's just for this quarter."

"Brad, oh my God. That's wonderful!"

"The steady business will be a relief for everyone." He looked over my shoulder and spoke under his breath. "The boss is here. I'd better get to my rounds."

I looked behind me and spotted Manuel headed our way.

"Tío!" Ari greeted him. "I love what you've done with this room."

His face flushed. "It was all Sofía and Luciana."

I grinned. He wasn't getting off the hook so easily. "I have it on good authority that you selected every one of these paintings."

He scowled at me. "They're on consignment."

"All from local artists whom you personally contacted to make the offer."

"Tío, that's very generous of you."

"And that one"—I pointed to a painting in a place of honor above a white-trimmed fireplace—"you picked out yourself." It was of a small cafe, filled with happy people drinking and eating. But a closer look revealed that the patrons consisted of some very modern romantic groupings. There were couples of men and women, women and women, men and men. And if you looked very carefully, there were even two triads.

I knew exactly when Javi noticed. He gasped. "That's… oh wow." As though on autopilot, he approached the painting. We all followed. Ari read the artist's signature. "Tío, did Sofía's brother paint this?"

He tossed his hands in the air. "What of it?"

"It's brilliant." Javi's eyes couldn't seem to get big enough to take it all in. When he turned to Manuel, his eyes were suspiciously bright. "You meant it, what you said to me."

Manuel nodded. "I did." His voice dropped. Hardened. "All of it, including what I said about your families not accepting it, unfortunately. But know that you…" He paused and his gaze took us all in. "All of you will always have a seat at my table."

"Oh, Tío. That means so much to me, to all of us." Ari threw herself into Manuel's arms. The poor man barely had time to catch her.

Smiling, he held her to him. "*Te amo, mi querida sobrina.*"

"And I love you too, my most beloved uncle."

After a final gentle squeeze, Manuel released her and said gruffly, "I need to go help Sofía with the dinner service." He shuffled out in a hurry.

"Can you believe this?" Javi was still staring at the painting.

Ari rubbed his back. "It's beautiful."

"Honestly, when we had that talk a few days ago, I thought he was just blowing smoke up my ass so I'd fuck up and spill the beans about the three of us. Turns out he was telling me the truth. He really is an ally." He sounded choked when he added, "I want to be brave like that too."

I shoulder-bumped him. It was the only public touch we could allow ourselves. "You're plenty brave, Javi."

He shook his head. "No, I'm not. But in time, I will be. I promise you both that."

Our conversation was interrupted when Greta came up beside me. She slung an arm around my shoulders and squeezed as she gazed upon the painting. "Manuel and Sofia Montero are an inspiration."

"We were just saying something very similar." I smiled at her.

She winked suggestively. "I'll bet."

"Hey," I said. "We think we've figured out who leaked the location of the Santa Catalina retreat."

Greta dropped her arm from around my shoulders. Her eyebrows arched. "Oh?"

"Chad said some things while we were at the Tough Mudder course, and the more we thought about it, the more we concluded that it had to be him. He has the means, the motive, and the opportunity. We want to confront him tonight after dinner."

Javi and Ari murmured their support.

"Do tell. What do you think his motive was?"

"Monica seems pretty free with her affections. I'm not saying she cheated, but if he's the possessive type, her behavior would certainly have caused issues. Her contract prevented them from divorcing within six months of the release of her movie, so by going public via the leak, that restriction was removed, and the field was wide open for Chad to ask for a divorce."

"You seem to have tied this up into a nice pretty bow." Greta opened her arms. "Unfortunately, you're wrong. Chad didn't do it."

Javi edged closer to me. "How can you be so sure?"

"Because I know who did."

He frowned. "Who? This leak cost TI a lot of money, time, and effort. Not to mention that the three of us had to come here to support the change in location, leaving our business in Miami unattended by at least one of us. That's never happened before."

Greta's expression softened, as did her voice. She peered at him as she often peered at me during our sessions, her expression knowing. I'd come to think she had a special power that allowed her to see inside my soul. To examine my motives and expose my lies. Honest to God, the woman could read minds.

"And aren't you really glad that it *did* happen this time?" Her gaze lingered on his face for a moment, then moved to mine, then Ari's. "Aren't you all really glad?"

"Yes," we all said at once.

"Good."

"So, aren't you going to tell us who it was?" Ari asked.

"It was Monica."

Ari's brow furrowed. "Monica?"

"What was her motive?" Javi asked.

"I won't get into details, because it was revealed to me during a session. But, since the impact to TI was so great, I felt you had a right to know, and she agreed to let me give you the Cliff Notes. Basically, this was a cry for help."

"I knew it!" Ari beamed.

"Monica was intimidated by the age difference between her and Chad. Over time, she came to doubt his love for her when in reality, it was her own love for herself that was in doubt. She didn't think she could compete with women Chad's age for his affections."

Ari huffed. "Only a blind woman wouldn't see how much he loves her."

"Ari." I widened my eyes at her.

"What?"

"All those years you knew Javier and loved Javier, not once did you think he loved you back."

Her eyes welled. "Damn hormones," she griped.

Javi hugged her and we all laughed.

"More good news," Greta said. "Monica has also agreed to pay TI for all the costs over and above our original agreement that were a direct consequence of the change in location."

"Man, that's a relief." Javi pretended to wipe sweat off his brow. "I've been crunching the numbers and no matter what I did, we were coming out in the red. Very red."

Just then, Manuel and Sofía entered the dining room, followed by Luciana and Brad, all holding large trays with covered dinner plates on them. "Friends, please take your seats," Manuel said.

Everyone picked a chair, and I ended up next to Greta. Javi and Arianna were seated directly in front of me, but across the table. I might not be able to touch them, but I could watch them. Seeing them together, so happy, so comfortable, fed my soul. I'd known since college that Javi was in love with Ari. I'd also known he'd never tell her. Otherwise, I wouldn't have gone after her. I'd never have taken her from him like that. I'd have been happy to see them find each other. Have the family they both deserved.

What we had now was infinitely better, even though I was still scared shitless about being even partly responsible for a baby, a child, another human being. I wasn't sure that was going to change anytime soon, if ever.

Greta laid a light hand on my arm. "You look happy."

"Happier than I have a right to be." I couldn't take my eyes off them.

"And the baby? Are you happy about that?"

I swallowed as I considered how to answer. "I-I am. Both of them have always wanted a baby. A family. Now they'll have one."

"And you?"

I nodded. "Me too. I'm a part of this. For better or worse."

"I'm so glad, Daniel. And you're wrong. You have every right to be happy. More right than most."

"Javi says I need to tell my parents what happened."

"Do you agree with him?"

I'd thought about it a lot over the years. I'd wanted to share my pain with someone, with my parents. With my sister Rachel. "I miss them."

"You haven't seen them since you left for college?"

I shook my head. "I couldn't. It was too hard. The guilt…" I clamped my jaw shut.

"Now you understand that you have nothing to feel guilty about, right?"

A small smile broke out over my face. It transformed into a grin as I looked upon this woman who had changed my life. "I'm trying."

"I know." She patted my hand. "I don't usually offer this, but your case, well, let's just say, this isn't the usual patient-therapist relationship. If you want me with you when you break the news to your family, I'm happy to fly out to Miami and support you. In fact, I think it would be a good idea. I could help your family understand why you made the choices you did."

I crossed my arms. "You're saying they might not take it well."

"I'm sure your behavior hurt them, Daniel. We want them to understand that it wasn't about them. It was about you. About protecting yourself. About surviving what had happened."

Yes, she definitely had better words for explaining my issues than I did. "I'd really appreciate having you there, Greta."

"Then I will be."

I owed her so much. She'd helped me find the loves of my life. Now I hoped she could help me get back the family I missed.

ARIANNA

I pulled the car into my driveway behind Javi's and Daniel's cars. Relief had my shoulders sagging. Knowing that they'd both be at home, waiting for me, was the only thing that had gotten me through today. I'd had to go alone because neither one wanted the other to be left out. They'd wanted to hear about my doctor's appointment together, and we'd all agreed that the office was not the place for that conversation. At least not yet.

The doctor told me that during the next appointment, we should be able to hear the baby's heartbeat. I wanted both my men there with me to share that experience. We had to find a way to make that happen.

I turned the engine off and sat for a moment in the ensuing silence. I touched my belly, laying my palm against it. "Hey, little peanut. Let's go tell your daddies all about you."

I picked up my purse and headed inside. As soon as I opened the door that led from the garage to the kitchen, Javi and Daniel were there with eager yet wary expressions. "So?" Daniel asked. "Everything okay?"

Laughing, I closed the door behind me and set my purse on the table. "Let me come in first."

He rubbed a hand along his neck. "Of course. Fuck, I'm sorry."

"Hey, it's okay. This is new for all of us."

Javi took my hand, and we went to sit in the living room. I'd kept all the same furniture I'd had before when Daniel was living here. I wondered how Javi felt about it. I'd have to ask him later.

"So…" Javi began.

I smiled. "You two are both so cute."

"Ari."

"Yes, Daniel?" I batted my eyelashes at him.

"Spit it out."

"Fine." I grinned. "According to the doctor, I'm five weeks and six days pregnant."

Daniel frowned. "What?" His gaze darted between me and Javi. "Your birthday was four weeks ago, not almost six."

I chuckled. "They always add two weeks because they count from the first day of your period. Anyway, this baby is due on June 24th."

Javi looked at me, his eyes worried. "And everything's okay? With you and the baby?"

"Yes. So far. We should be able to hear the baby's heartbeat at my next appointment, which will be on December 7th." My bottom lip turned out.

"Hey now." Daniel rubbed his face in my neck, pressing little kisses along my throat. "Why the pout?"

I wanted to grab him and hold him against me forever. Instead, I sniffed. "I want both of you there for that. I want us all to hear our baby's heartbeat for the first time together."

He smiled sadly. "I want that to, but how?"

"Doctors have to maintain doctor-patient confidentiality, right?"

Javi said.

"Right."

"So, we find a doctor who's open-minded. Easy-peasy."

"Easy-peasy?" Daniel snapped his fingers. "Just like that?"

"Leave it to me," Javi said. "I have a lot of connections in the LGBT community."

"Thank you, Javi." I leaned against him and rubbed my belly. God, I was the luckiest woman in the world. I had everything I'd always wanted: a baby, a man who loved me… well, two men who loved me. Sure, none of this was happening according to my plan, but it was happening, and I wouldn't change anything. My eyes watered. Damn hormones. "I never thought I could have both of you."

Daniel put his hand on my belly. His touch was tentative, and it made me quiver. I knew how hard this was for him. "I never thought I could have both of you either." He leaned over me and kissed Javier, then he kissed me.

I watched in alarmed fascination as Daniel slid to his knees in front of me. He tugged my shirt up to expose my belly and kissed it. When he looked up, tears rimmed his lashes. "I never thought I could have this. A baby." The wonder and astonishment on his face was more beautiful than the grandest work of art.

Javi stroked the side of his face and Daniel leaned into his palm. "We need to decide what we're going to do." Javi's voice shook with the strength of his emotion. "I can't spend another night without you with us." While Javi had been spending the nights with me, Daniel had been leaving late in the evenings to go to his own house.

"Daniel needs to move in. You too, Javi."

Daniel pressed another gentle kiss to my belly before lowering my shirt and sitting down beside me. He took my hand and held it to his heart. "I'd love to, babe. But we can't both live here with you."

"I need you here. I need you beside me at night." I was begging, and I hated being a whiny bitch. Didn't matter though; I'd beg Daniel until I was blue in the face. There was no way in hell I was letting him fade away again.

Daniel looked at Javi. "You need to marry her."

"No. I already told you I wouldn't do that to you."

"Javi." Daniel sighed. "It's the only way. Look, I'm not going anywhere."

I gripped his hand harder. "Promise?"

"Yes, I promise. I want things to be smooth with your families. This baby needs its grandparents, a family. If you two marry, then there's no issue with the baby being illegitimate."

"What about you, *hermano*?"

"I'll live here with both of you—"

I started to clap. "Yay—"

"—but," he continued. "I have to make it look like I'm still living in my house."

My expression fell. "Why?"

He rubbed his face with his palms. "I'm not ready to be out yet. There's going to be public opposition to us, from your families for sure, but also from other people who figure out what's going on. I'm not saying I'll stay in the closet forever, but right now, I just... I can't deal with it on top of everything else."

I was being selfish again, only thinking of myself and my happiness. Daniel's problems were real, and even if it seemed like he was healed, he wasn't, not fully. And he was right; Javi's family and mine were not going to be as accepting as the Monteros. When we did decide to come out, it wouldn't be easy for any of us. "Okay then, we'll take this at your pace."

He nodded. "I'm going to tell my family what happened."

My eyebrows rose. "You are?"

"Mmm-hmm. Greta will go with me, and she's going to refer me to a local therapist." He smiled sadly. "I'm really still a mess. You both sure you want to deal with all this?"

Javier made a grunting sound in his throat. "You are a fucking work of art. In progress, granted. But a beautiful, rough around the edges, work of fucking art."

Daniel smiled his first real smile of the day. "I don't know what I did to deserve both of you."

"You survived," I said. "That's what you did."

He nodded. "I survived."

JAVIER

In the week and a half since Ari's doctor appointment and our discussion with Daniel about our living arrangements, I'd come to a decision. I didn't want this loose, informal plan. I wanted some kind of tangible commitment between the three of us. We needed it.

And there was still the little matter of Ari and me marrying. Daniel was pushing us to do it, yet I worried that he'd feel left out when we did.

He'd been staying over at the house more nights than not, and he'd even moved in some of his clothes and toiletries. Still, he often left early in the morning to go home and shower and get ready for work. And I couldn't help thinking it was because he felt not quite part of us.

Well, I was going to do my damnedest to make sure he didn't feel that way.

I'd been to at least a dozen jewelry stores before I found what I wanted—a set of gorgeous his and hers wedding bands, and a beautiful engagement ring. I had an additional band made for Daniel, a band that matched mine.

His and my rings—brushed inlay platinum bands—complemented the pave diamond eternity ring in platinum that I'd picked for Arianna. I'd also bought her a two-carat diamond solitaire for her engagement ring. And yeah, it had cost a small fortune. But that didn't matter. When I'd seen it, I'd wanted her to have it.

The last thing I needed for tonight I'd snuck from Ari's jewelry box.

I'd made the three of us reservations at the Palmeiras Beach Club on Grove Isle, not telling either of them where we were going. I'd used the arrival of the hefty check from Monica Dashwood to cover TI's expenses from relocating the ECC retreat as an excuse for the three of us to celebrate. The only hint I'd given them as to our destination was to dress up.

Daniel arrived at eight PM as requested, and he looked hot as fuck in a charcoal gray sharkskin suit with a burgundy tie. I was in a medium blue slim-fit suit with no tie, and Ari had chosen a form-fitting sleeveless burgundy dress that ended a few inches above her knees and looked almost demure from the front, but was sexy as hell from behind with its open back that scooped all the way down to her ass and crisscrossing straps at the top and at her waist. Those straps made me think about tying her up sometime… soon.

"So where are we going?" Daniel asked, his eyes eating up Ari like mine were.

"You'll find out soon enough." My heart racing, I led them out to my Audi, Ari taking the front seat and Daniel getting in the back behind her. He toyed with her hair as I drove, then planted a kiss on her bare shoulder.

"That dress makes me want to tie you down somewhere and fuck you senseless," he murmured in her ear, just loud enough for me to catch and stealing my thoughts entirely. Then he leaned over to me and said, "You too, Javi. You look good enough to eat."

The image of Daniel on his knees, me feeding him my cock, had me hard in an instant. "Down boy," I said out loud, glancing at my crotch, and the two of them cackled like hyenas. I joined in, my nerves calming a bit.

But when I took the turn onto the bridge to Grove Isle, they both gave me questioning looks. "When you said, 'dress up,' you meant it," Ari murmured, her eyes on the glittering high rises of the beach club on the manmade island just off the shore from Coconut Grove.

"Javi," Daniel growled. "What *kind* of dinner is this?"

My cheeks grew hot, and Mr. Happy calmed down. "It's a celebration dinner."

"Uh-huh." He couldn't have injected more doubt into that comment if he'd tried.

Ari twisted around to look at him. "Is something bothering you?"

"Are you in on this?" he asked her.

"In on what?"

"On… whatever he has planned."

We drove through the gate and onto the Palmeiras Beach Club grounds, and I pulled up at the valet stand outside the hotel.

"No," Ari said. "But let's not ruin his surprise."

I could have kissed her for that. I handed the keys to the valet while Daniel helped Ari out of the car. Then she took both of our arms, and the three of us walked inside to the restaurant. It was a balmy night, and I'd reserved us a table outside on the patio so we could be on the water.

The rings seemed to weigh a ton in my jacket pocket, and I fiddled with the boxes, my stomach doing flip-flops as Ari studied the menu and Daniel studied me.

He hadn't said a word, but a muscle ticked in his jaw, and his blue eyes bored holes into me. I tried to focus on the wine list, then the menu, but I was barely registering the words. Daniel hadn't touched the menu. He was leaning forward in his seat, one hand on the table, the other on the armrest, as if he expected to get up at any moment.

Ari closed her menu and put a hand over Daniel's where it pressed against the tabletop. A light breeze kicked up, ruffling our hair and rustling the fronds of the palm trees near our table. "Are you going to quit grinding your teeth and enjoy our evening out?" she asked him.

"You really had no hand in this?" he said to her. She shook her head. "So he doesn't know?" Daniel asked. Again, she shook her head.

"Know what?" I asked.

He stabbed the table with his index finger. "*This* is where I proposed to her."

My cheeks burned. "Well, then, I'm not very fucking original, am I?"

He held my gaze. "Why the hell am *I* here?" he said, keeping his voice low. "This is about the two of you. Not me."

I set my menu down. "This is about the *three* of us." I glanced around, and seeing that the waiter was nowhere in sight and no one was paying us any attention, I pulled the three boxes from my pocket, along with the ring I'd taken from Ari's jewelry box.

Her wedding ring from Daniel.

I lined them up on the table, my fingers shaking a bit as I avoided Daniel's glare.

"What the fuck, Javi?" he hissed.

"I was going to do this after dinner, but apparently I'd better do it right now before you fucking bolt." I held up the wedding band he'd originally given Ari. "You're going to give this to her again tonight. And she'll wear it on her right hand." I pointed to the boxes containing his and my wedding bands. "And these are for you and me." I opened the box containing his. "I want you to wear yours now." I raised my gaze to his. "Because you need a reminder that you're integral to this. You *belong* to us, Daniel. You're not some spare part, some fling we invited into our lives. You're here to stay."

That muscle ticked again in his jaw, and he rubbed his chin, swallowing visibly. "You really mean it." His voice was soft.

"Yeah, *hermano*, I do."

A corner of his mouth curved up. He looked at Ari and picked up the ring he'd given her years ago. "You really want to wear this again?"

She smiled at him and touched his cheek. "Always, *mi amor*. I never wanted to take it off." She held out her right hand, and he slid the ring onto her finger. She stared down at it, her eyes shining with impending tears. Then she looked up at Daniel. "When I say my vows to Javi before God and everyone, I'll be saying them to both of you."

"'Til death do us part, Arianna," Daniel said. "That's still true for me."

"It's true for me too." Then she focused on me. "And now you'll be part of it as well, like you always should have been."

I nudged the box containing his ring toward Daniel, and he took it out of the box and placed it on the ring finger of his left hand. I loved seeing it there.

"It matches mine," I said.

He gave me that half-smile again, then turned to Ari. "He's a pushy bastard when he wants to be."

She smiled at me. "Yes, he is."

I opened the box with her engagement ring and showed it to her, enjoying her soft gasp, then I got down on one knee. "Arianna Rodriguez, I've loved you forever, probably since the moment we met when we were ten years old." Tears spilled down her cheeks, and she wiped them away. "Will you do me the great honor of sharing my life"—I looked at Daniel—"of sharing our lives?"

She nodded, then broke into a dazzling grin. "Of course I will. Yes, yes, yes. A million times yes!"

I slid the ring onto her finger, the solitaire glittering in the light.

Daniel whistled. "What a rock, Javi."

Arianna laughed and looked from the ring to me. "You really didn't have to try to impress me."

I grinned. "I know. But I wanted to spoil the mother of my child." I leaned forward and kissed her belly, then I rose and kissed her lips.

A few couples around us started clapping, and Daniel joined in the applause.

I glanced around, my face feeling like it was on fire. I hadn't meant to make this so public—I'd intended for us to walk to the fire pit outside after we'd eaten and then propose to them there. I'd expected Daniel to be as mortified as I was, but he seemed okay.

In fact, he finally sat back in his chair, and then he put an arm around Ari, completely not giving a fuck at the curious glances we were getting, people obviously doing the math and coming up with "Does not compute."

But I was far better at math than anyone else I knew.

And I knew that 1+1+1 equaled forever.

CONTINUE THE ADVENTURE!

Hello, Vanessa here! Want to be part of our VIP Readers list and get all the behind-the-scenes scoop about what *really* happens at Total Indulgence? Want to be part of our ARC team? Sign up at www.totalindulgencetours.com.

If Facebook is more your style, join our Total Indulgence VIP Readers' Lounge!

www.facebook.com/groups/
totalindulgencevipreaderslounge

We hope you enjoyed traveling to Sonoma with Daniel, Arianna, and Javier. Whew! Who knew accountants could be so much fun? I'm still a little amazed at everything they got up to!

If you loved our little romp, please give us a thumbs-up review. We're not on Yelp yet, but we are on Amazon and Goodreads!

Next up on Total Indulgence's schedule: a trip to Switzerland with me! I'm really looking forward to this adventure, especially since I kind of know one of the guys who's going to be there. He's hot as hell… and probably won't give me the time of day. But I'm a girl who likes challenges. And oh, what's this? A picture of our VERY hunky ski guide? Looks like I definitely won't be alone! Want to see what fun I get up to? Be sure to sign up for our VIP Readers List so you get the alert when this pre-order goes live!

ABOUT DANA DELAMAR

Dana Delamar is the author of erotic romance, LGBTQ romance, and the "Blood and Honor" romantic suspense series, which is set in Italy among the Calabrian Mafia. Her first book, *Revenge*, received 4 stars from *RT Book Reviews*, was a Top Pick at The Romance Reviews, and was a double-finalist for Best First Book and Best Romantic Suspense in the 2013 Booksellers Best Awards.

Her second book, *Retribution*, received 4 stars from *RT Book Reviews* and was a semi-finalist in the Kindle Book Review's 2013 Best Indie Book Awards. Her book *Malavita* was a quarter-finalist in the 2014 Amazon Breakthrough Novel Awards, and her book *Redemption* was a finalist in the 2014 Maggie Awards and a semi-finalist in the Kindle Book Review's 2014 Best Kindle Book Awards.

Dana is also an editor with over thirty years of editing experience in both fiction and nonfiction and has worked with everyone from newbie writers to experienced pros. The books she's edited have won numerous awards and critical acclaim, including two Top Picks from *RT Book Reviews*.

www.danadelamar.com

ABOUT KRISTINE CAYNE

Kristine Cayne is the author of erotic romance, LGBTQ romance, and romantic suspense. Her books have won numerous awards and acclaim. Her first book, *Deadly Obsession*, was an *RT Book Reviews* Top Pick and won Best Romance in the 2012 eFestival of Words Best of the Independent eBook Awards. Her second book, *Deadly Addiction*, won two awards at the 2014 eFestival of Words and 1st place in the INDIE Awards, Romantic Suspense Category (a division of Chanticleer Book Reviews Blue Ribbon Writing Contests).

Her book *Under His Command* won Best BDSM Romance at the 2012 Sizzling Awards and was a finalist in the 2013 eFestival of Words and 2013 RONE (Reward of Novel Excellence) Awards, and her book *Everything Bared* was a finalist in the Erotic category of the I Heart Indie awards.

www.kristinecayne.com

ALSO BY DANA DELAMAR AND KRISTINE CAYNE

BY DANA DELAMAR

Blood and Honor: A Mafia Romance Series

Malavita (Prequel)
Revenge (Book One)
Retribution (Book Two)
Redemption (Book Three)
Reckoning (Book Four)

BY KRISTINE CAYNE

Six-Alarm Sexy Series: A Firefighter Erotic Romance Series

Aftershocks (Prequel)
Under His Command (Book One)
Everything Bared (Book Two)
Handle with Care (Book Three)
Lover on Top (Book Four)
Baby, Be Mine (Book Five)
Stripped Down (Book Six – coming soon)

Seattle Fire Series
(Six-Alarm Sexy Spin-off)

In His Arms (Book One – coming 2019)

Men of Boyzville: A Gay Romance Series
(Six-Alarm Sexy Spin-off)

Going All In (Book One)
Wrangling the Cowboy (Book Two – coming soon)

Deadly Vices: A Romantic Suspense Series

Deadly Obsession (Book One)
Deadly Addiction (Book Two)
Deadly Betrayal (Book Three)

Other Works

Guns 'N' Tulips
Un-Valentine's Day
Origins: Men of M.E.R. in *Shadows in the Mist*

Made in the USA
Columbia, SC
16 March 2019